PRAISE FOR TI

"The Rivener offers a profound, immersive experience resonating with wisdom and truth. With endearing characters and a formidable villain, it's a soulful, thrilling narrative akin to The Sandman and The Matrix."
A Page of Words and Wishes

"Littered with feeling and philosophy, violence, and mythology. This had me gripped from start to finish."
Christopher Badcock, Those You Killed

"Absolutely brilliant. An epic mix of Gaiman's Sandman and everything I wanted but never got from King's Dark Tower."
Misfit Bookshelf

"One of the most unique stories I've read in a long while. Fast paced, wild, and addictive with clear callbacks to many inspirations while retaining his own fresh voice."
Mr. Paul M. Moore

"Godsey pulls you in from the first page and doesn't let go. You emerge completely invested in the world and its characters and are left questioning the nature of reality."
Book Naked

"An ambitious genre-defying opus, The Rivener masterfully blends elements to create an expansive world. An epic tale of retribution, redemption, and discovery, fueled by a unique protagonist's extraordinary journey where flawed humanity battles immortal indifference."
The Bookbeard Review

"This does not read like a debut novel. Godsey is a wordsmith. The Rivener impresses with expert world-building and vibrant characters, echoing masters like Cormac McCarthy and Hunter S. Thompson."
Beyond Horror

"Thrilling and fast-paced, with richly realized characters reminiscent of Gaiman and King. The Rivener offers a distinctive, immersive plot, outstanding dialogue, and hints at a sequel. An ideal choice for fans of vivid, visual storytelling."
Unearthly Reads

"The Rivener has given me a new lease on the sci-fi fantasy genre. Never have I been so engaged in a book. Tied with Blake Crouch's Dark Matter for my year's best read!"
Oh How The Pages Have Turned

"Like American Gods and R Rated Percy Jackson on a wild acid trip. At times scary and mind-bending, and always full of wonder."
Probably Reading Right Now

THE RIVENER

A NOVEL OF DARK FANTASY SUSPENSE AND MIND-BENDING ADVENTURE BY

GARRETT GODSEY

NIGHTGATE
BOOKS

ISBN: 979-8-9881128-1-5

CONTENTS

SOUNDS OF THE RIVENER

The Lost Dream Playlist

This QR code and link will take you to The Lost Dream Playlist. It began as personal focus music to help my writing process. Eventually, it became an unofficial soundtrack. It's dark, meditative, and a bit trippy. Enjoy.
https://tinyurl.com/therivener-lostdream

A WARNING

This may be a work of fiction, but it is also a story that is true to its themes and characters. You will travel with them to lands both fantastic and dark. And in those places, there be monsters.

Thus, a warning:

Along with epic and psychedelic adventures, there are scenes of graphic violence, disturbing horror, mentions of self-harm and suicide, foul language, sexual violence, drug and addiction references, as well as abuse, neglect, and death involving children.

Ultimately, this tale is about people finding strength and magic within themselves and the world, despite its persistent darkness. It's about people who use their scars as fuel to do good things. It's a story about redemption, healing, and sometimes simply dealing.

Thank you, Dear Reader. On with the show.

For Zoe and Layla.
I'd come get you, wherever you were.

PART ONE
A WILD WORLD

"For, you see, so many out-of-the-way things had happened lately, that Alice had begun to think that very few things indeed were really impossible."

— LEWIS CARROLL, ALICE IN
WONDERLAND

1

KID

The paper soldier was bent close to broke, but the young man figured it'd get the job done. After coaxing the dog-leg cigarette to something resembling straight, he stuck it in his mouth and lit it with a match from a blank white pack. Letting out the first drag, he ran a hand over dark hair buzzed short enough to reveal a street-tanned scalp peppered with scars.

A breeze cooled the sweat at the nape of his neck as he tilted his head to catch the sun's warmth. It felt good to trade concrete cell for blue sky. His true name was Michael Thames. But he didn't know that. Not yet. He just went by Kid.

Hari, his long-time corner pal and giver of crooked ciggies, stood next to him. An ancient Panasonic boombox perched on his shopping cart of earthly belongings played *Wild World* by Cat Stevens. Hari hummed the lyrics and studied Kid through two circles of mirrored purple sunglass.

Crow's feet, set deep in skin the color of burnt umber, wrinkled as Hari asked, "It sure is though, ain't it?"

Kid shifted his backpack and took another drag. "What's that?"

"A wild world, baby babe. Like ol' Cat's song."

Kid chuckled as he watched the crawling traffic and exhaled smoke from the side of his mouth to avoid blowing it at a passerby. "Guess so, yeah. Get's pretty weird sometimes."

"Not weird, Kid, no way, that word's dirty. I'm talking *wild*." Hari waved his hand to indicate the world before them as if it were only a curtain. "The unpredictable, yet synchronous chaos-force of the cosmos, man. *Real* magic." He fancied himself a sidewalk philosopher and was always spouting off something new.

Kid laughed and egged his friend on. "Real magic, huh?"

"Yeah, boy. Lotta folk got that star stuff in 'em. Now that Ol' Cat Stevens—that fella was a *real* Dreamer, man. With a capital D." Hari released a puff of smoke in a wavering oblong ring and stuck his finger through it to punctuate his statement. After the ring dissipated, he asked, "Where ya been at? Tell me straight."

"Not gonna let me finish my cig?" Kid replied as he continued watching the congested road. Polk Street was a honking mess and served as the western boundary of the grittiest part of downtown San Francisco, the deep Tenderloin district—closer to Market than Nob Hill. The neighborhood was identifiable by some of the city's sorely limited public housing, store windows covered with plywood, dingy dive bars, and open-air drug deals of which he was no longer a part. That game had no winners, and he'd left it two years prior.

"Fightin' again," Hari said. It wasn't a question.

It wasn't hard to figure out. Kid's clothes were wrinkled to hell from being stuffed in a plastic bag for almost a month, and even after that long in county jail, a healing bruise still marked his face. He glanced at the wounds on the knuckles of the hand that held the smoke. Those were still fresh.

"Tell you somethin'?" Hari pried again.

Kid looked up from his hand to wait for an answer. High cheekbones framed hazel eyes with gold flecks that glinted in the afternoon light. Hari often said he was too serious for his twenty years, that he should be chasing girls and studying, not prowling around with hard crews. Same as now, Kid rarely responded to the appeals.

Hari took the watchful silence as permission to continue. "I'm no preacher, but here it is. The fuzz ain't gonna keep giving you thirty-day honeymoons, man. No way. 'Specially not with Judge Drake bout to give up the ghost. Known you from a pup, so he lets you skate, but the next one on the bench sure won't. You'd best switch it up."

"I'm looking to."

"What? Colorado? Pfft. You been talking about that for years. Greyhound bus ain't that pricey. You coulda gone, but you *still* here. Same-oh, same-oh." Hari scoffed, then added, "You a floatin' ass mofo."

After Kid's cigarette burned to a nub, he flicked it in an arc to the middle of the street, where it bounced off the window of a passing car with a splash of red embers. The clock-puncher turned from his phone to glare. Kid winked. Hari sighed.

"Boy, listen here. After a while, and a while's *bout* up, you ain't someone to save no more. Get me? People stop seeing potential, and you just somethin' to cut out. Something to sever."

"Sever? Didn't know you knew words like that."

"Shit, you know I read. Got vocabulary like a dictionary. Make your head spin. For real, though. Ain't gonna be long, and it won't be thirty days in the can. It'll be a nickel in the *slam*."

Kid sighed, not wanting to dig any further into his screw-ups and lack of direction in life from an old hippy. "Let's talk later, Hari."

"Yo, get straight. For real. Just tell me what you want."

"What do I *want*?"

"Yeah."

"I want some soup."

"Man, soup?"

"Yeah. *Soup*, man. I don't need shit. Just something to eat besides jailhouse chow. You got me?"

Hari finally gave up, releasing a huff of air. "Aight, aight. Yeah, I got you."

Kid adjusted his backpack. "Gotta run. Linh's gonna be worried."

"Worried? More like pissed."

"Yeah."

"Watch that ol' gal. She hides it good, but she's mean."

Kid gave Hari a wave-salute goodbye, then turned to walk the few blocks to Linh's pho restaurant as he thought about what his friend said.

What did he, or any of them, expect?

What even *could* he do? He was a classic "lost in the

cracks" juvie case. Once you're under the floorboards, that's where you stay.

Get it together, Kid.

Over the years, he'd heard a thousand versions of the same thing from a never-ending barrage of caseworkers, probation officers, fosters, nuns, and state-supplied shrinks. Some were cool, some monstrous, and most just *whatever*.

It was always the same.

What do you want?

Don't want nothing. Just leave me be.

You ain't someone to save no more.

You're something to sever.

2

LINH

The first time Kid went to the hole-in-the-wall soup shop down in Little Saigon, it didn't seem like the owner, Linh Phuong, would let him in. You drop the drawbridge for one street kid, then what? Next thing you know, you're like the old McDonald's on Haight and Stanyan. Gone now, but for a while was pretty much a halfway home for the lost and wandering. Somehow though, she'd decided to give him a chance, and over time they became friends.

He walked around the familiar alley and sidled up to the restaurant's back door. The kitchen hand, Tom, was outside having a smoke break. His badly receding hairline made a rounded M shape about five fingers up from the highest forehead wrinkle; he always called it the "Money Line" with a stupid grin.

"Linh around?" Kid asked.

"You know she don't leave." Tom nodded his head towards the door. "Prepping for dinner rush. But you better watch it, Skidrow. She's looking for you."

Kid rolled his eyes at the lame nickname. "Suck it, Tom."

"Yeah, bet you'd like that," he replied as Kid moved past him.

The guy could be a jerk, but he wasn't a bully. Not the worst kind, anyway. Besides, you didn't let people know they were bugging you. It was a weakness. Even small ones add up. You keep that stuff close. Besides, Kid always felt bad for the guy. He'd noticed the dynamic between him and Linh.

Every time she entered a room, his eyes would track her across it and watch the door long after she left. It was obvious he wanted to be more than friends. But, the way she looked at him, or didn't rather, it was clear he never would be. Kid figured Tom called him names because he was pissed off about the situation and would take it out on the nearest bystander—especially if that bystander took up some of her attention.

Behind Tom, the steel door to the kitchen hung open. It sported a wooden crossbar ready for a military siege. Kid peeked in and knocked on the metal. Familiar smells filled his nostrils, twelve-hour bone broth, grilled onion, fresh lime, mint, and chili peppers. His stomach growled.

After a few seconds, his pupils dilated enough for Linh to come into focus. She was how he often found her, standing at the butcher block, knife ready to chop a pile of vegetables— but instead of chopping, just staring at a vase of yellow daisies. He called into the kitchen to break her from her trance without making her jump.

"Hey, how's my favorite lunch lady?"

Linh turned swiftly enough for her long black ponytail to swing behind her. She lifted her chef's cleaver like a question mark and stomped toward him. Her white tank top exposed sinewy kitchen-strong arms crisscrossed with scars. One time, he'd asked what they were from. She'd told him, *cooking.*

"What happened to 'I'll be by in a couple days.'?" Linh asked.

"I said *at least* that. Got held up."

Her mouth dropped open. "*Unbelievable.* Kid, you vanished for a month."

"Ah, no I didn't."

She clicked her tongue. "Close enough. Twenty-six days."

"Keeping count? Come on, I'm never gone long. Like an alley dog, you know?"

Linh stepped forward and pushed his chest with the flat top of the cleaver.

"You strut around like some punk flicking cigarettes in a music video. It's baloney. You could at least let *me* know where you were." Her brows knit.

"Hey, I don't need the mom routine. I'm fine."

"I know I'm not..." She winced, swallowed, and said, "Listen, I *know* what you do. You disappear like that, and it scares me. You know why."

He stepped back. "What do you know about it?"

"More than you think. I didn't always make soup. Kid... Listen to me. Once those people get a hold of you, once they're on top of you? That's it. That's where they'll always be. You'll never get out."

"Linh, I'm *already* out. This is what out looks like. Gonna stay that way too."

Linh watched him, unimpressed.

Kid sighed, "Listen... It's good money, alright? And I'm

careful. For real. I just lost track of time." Kid adjusted the strap of his bag again.

"Lost track? For a month? You are a bullshit artist to the end. You were in *jail*. I can smell it on you. Look at those clothes and your face. What was it for this time? It looks like fighting. Bit off more than you could chew? Yeah? Break in somewhere?"

Kid sniffed his hoody and wrinkled his nose despite trying not to. She was right. He smelled worse than an old sock. But he didn't respond to the accusations. It was bait and would only entrap him into further reprimand. He waited for her to speak again, and after a bit, she did.

Linh sighed, "Don't make me feel bad for giving a damn, okay? Just *please*, next time, call me. They do give you a call, that's not just in movies. I'd get you wherever you were. Do you know that? I would. Tom always says I never leave, but I'd come to get *you*. Just... At least call and let me know you're not dead, okay? Just drop a line, Kid. That's all I'm asking."

"Drop a line?"

"Yeah, that's what we used to say." The corner of her mouth twitched as she realized she'd given him an opening and knew her verbal high ground was lost.

"Alright, I'll *drop a line*." Kid said with a grin and air quotations.

Linh rolled her eyes, "Shut up, stupid."

Relieved to see the dark cloud break, Kid said, "Alright, you dressed me down and threatened me with a deadly weapon. I got the message. Next time I'll call."

"Next time?" She raised the cleaver again. "There shouldn't be a next time!"

Kid held up a defensive hand—lot of good it'd do against the woman's kitchen-axe. "Easy, easy! You know what I mean. Are we good now?"

She dropped the cleaver and huffed, "Ugh. Fine. Not like anyone could stop you from doing what you want anyway. No matter how idiotic. Maybe the dummy's the one who tries." She waved him away with the knife. "Go. Be useful."

He did as asked, making quick work of some pots, pans, and an ancient banged-up noodle strainer the size of a car tire, then sat on a five-gallon bucket in the corner of the kitchen. Kid waited, letting his thoughts wander as his head swam in the savory kitchen aroma.

He would never tell anybody or even write it down to be found, but he liked to think that if he'd known his mom, she would be tough and sweet and a good cook like Linh. He figured that's what real moms did. She was one of the good ones. Mysterious though. There was only one time she'd let a clue slip after a busy day and a bottle of wine. Kid learned that the vase of yellow daisies she kept on the counter, refreshed with new blossoms weekly, wasn't just for decoration. The flowers were a small shrine to a baby daughter she'd lost. Her daughter was called Bian.

After the accidental reveal, Linh excused herself, blamed too much drink, and went to bed. She never mentioned her daughter again, and Kid didn't ask. He was thankful she returned the favor and never asked about his nonexistent family. Some things are better left unsaid.

Maybe that was why she wouldn't let him say no to a meal anytime he came by, regardless of if he had any money. *Maybe* that was why he decided to trust her as well.

There was an unspoken camaraderie. Just a couple of lost people. It was a relief that it didn't require any out-loud analysis. The connection was just there. He needed some sort of mother, and she needed some sort of son.

So, it came as no surprise that she worried about him.

If she ever left the restaurant, Kid would worry about her too.

The fact was, despite her worry Kid liked what he did. He liked it a lot. Running packages around the city for an outfit called The White Lotus.

Usually, the gigs were simple pick-ups and drops. But, occasionally, he got lucky and had to climb, sneak around, break in, run away, or even fight. Was it stupid? Yeah, definitely. But mainly, it was exciting.

Linh was right, though. The drops could be risky, and the real danger came if you missed one. It was well known that if you screwed up, you weren't fired. You weren't suspended to think about what you'd done. You just disappeared.

Despite the risks, he made enough money to survive, stay above the drama, and exist in the world the way he wanted. There's something to say for that.

The crunch of plastic brought his wandering mind back to the kitchen as Linh squeezed a lid onto a cardboard container. She was careful to make a good seal, and fastened it with some masking tape, then dropped it into the bag, which fogged with steam as Kid put it in his backpack.

She surprised him by placing a hand on his face, extra warm from holding the soup. He wasn't expecting physical touch and rarely received it—aside from violent situations and altercations with authority. He almost flinched away, but the peaceful resolution of Linh's golden brown eyes kept him steady.

"Kid. Look at me." She held his face still. "Don't wait so long next time."

His face blushed hot. "Yeah... Fine, okay."

Then she smiled and turned around to continue her work in the kitchen. As he stepped outside, Kid stuffed some cash in the pocket of her hanging jacket. She wouldn't take his money anymore, and he'd stopped trying to argue with her about it a long time ago.

3

NEST

Excited to eat, Kid walked fast enough to make his calves burn. He was heading to a seven-story building in the heart of the Tenderloin, masked in fraternal decay with the rest of the pocket neighborhood. Much of the 'Loin was gentrified with overpriced whiskey bars and hipster ramen shops. But, this particular street was the last vestige of the old T.L., a refuge for recent immigrants, government-subsidized housing, addicts, and other societal fringe. Around there, no one would complain if some punk climbed up a fire escape.

Kid double-checked the soup container in his bag—it was safely stowed and sealed. That sorted, he tightened his backpack straps and looked up at the lowest platform, which hung about twelve feet off the ground. He ran at the brick wall, jumped and kicked off for an extra few feet of vertical, then grabbed the cast iron edge. He performed a swinging pull-up and cleared the railing in a seemingly effortless series of motions.

As he climbed the creaking iron ladders leading to the roof, Kid kept an eye on the street below, ready to duck against the wall. But nobody was around, and he reached the top without interruption. He vaulted over the lip of the yellowed stone façade, expertly missing the tin-can tripwire alarm he'd set. Then Kid stopped, took in a big breath, and smiled. He was home.

On the far end of the building stood a hexagonal atrium. It was the size of a tiny home, tall and skinny, perfectly San Franciscan. Two stories of windows wrapped the entire perimeter in a circle of grimy frosted glass, the old kind with the pitted surface that refracts the light and shapes behind it like rippled water.

Kid stepped in through a makeshift plywood door and pinned it open with a cinder block to let a breeze flow through. A lofted platform made of wooden pallets and blocks held folded-up blankets and clothes inside plastic bins, along with another couple of bins for dry food, water, supplies, and a few sagging bookcases.

The shelves held all kinds of books—London and Faulkner, King and Barker, Verne and Tolkien, each beat to hell with dog-eared pages and filled with scribbles. He'd never owned a new book and wouldn't know how to treat one. Alongside those were piles of magazines—mostly Rolling Stone, Scientific American, and Popular Mechanic: science, sound, and stories, the good stuff.

Funny thing about system kids most people don't realize —it's not like the screws at Fresno Reform hand out smartphones and PlayStations, yet time must be occupied. The easiest way to kill the clock with the smallest chance for drama is to read. Orphanages, boys' homes, detention centers —they almost always have books. Sometimes chess. Occasionally handball. And of course, bullies and ass-draggin' block fights. But those experiences teach things too. It's surprising to most folks how well-rounded the education of a lost boy can be.

After laying his bag down, Kid peeled off his nasty clothes, tossed them in the to-be-washed bin, and kicked it toward the open door to air out. All he still wore was a rawhide necklace from which hung a simple silver ring, engraved *M+S*. It was all he knew of his origin. An M and an S. He didn't even know what the letters stood for. They were most likely his parents' initials—but like his life's common thread, even that was uncertain.

He walked across the tiny living space to a corner where he'd built a gravity shower, the kind surfers use at the beach. Nothing complicated, just a big water tank suspended above a flat concrete area where he'd cut drainage. After the flip of a spigot, he stepped into a stream of cold, clean water with a refreshed sigh. Careful to conserve, he made it quick, lathering up, scrubbing down, and rinsing off in less than three minutes. Happy he no longer smelled like an old dog, Kid toweled off then put on clean underwear and black jeans, leaving the rest of himself undressed to finish drying in the summer air.

A hammock hung a few feet off the floor, and after retrieving the soup container, he hopped into it with a practiced swing. He peeled off the plastic lid and started shoveling it into his mouth with chopsticks as he gazed out the windows. The view stretched for miles in a hundred-and-eighty-degree panoramic view. A real estate agent would have a heart attack if they knew what they were missing.

Through the open door and thin single pane glass, the sounds of the city wafted up from street-level—birds, wind, and the murmur of traffic far below, punctuated by the oddly rhythmic beeps of car horns. The incoming breeze stirred a hanging mobile he made from discarded projector lenses and hunks of colored glass. They tinkled against each other as they swayed.

From the hammock, Kid could see the cornice of the building. A pair of falcons, peregrines, made their nest there for years. He could hear one of them calling out in a classic raptor screech, swooping somewhere high above, waiting for a pigeon to dive-bomb. The sound was comforting, as always. Kid liked to think of the two birds, who he'd named Cloud and Zoe, as his friends. They raised chicks each year, two in each batch. They were working on a third now, safely inside their eggs, beautifully mottled red and brown like blood agate.

Watching the parents raise the chicks from hatchlings to fledglings was fascinating, teaching them a bit by showing but mostly just waiting for them to learn independently. How terrifying that must be to leave the comfort of the nest and launch into the air, nothing but a deadly drop below you, jumping anyway. No confidence, no skill. Just pure naivety and hope. Then against all odds, succeeding. Flying, gliding, and swooping around on your own as you watched your mother and father do. Mothers and fathers teaching you things. What a concept.

Kid turned away from their nest to look off into the city as he finished the soup, slurping up even the densely seasoned broth at the bottom of the container. Judging by the sun, he figured it was about three or four in the afternoon. His mind began to wander into the fuzz that can only come from the combination of a fresh shower, a nice breeze, warm sunshine, and a full belly. The last thing he heard before falling asleep was a car alarm bleating in the distance. It reminded him of the thumping electronic music coming from the front doors of dance clubs at night, the ones he was often curious to enter but rarely did. Oontz oontz, beep beep, oontz oontz.

He dreamt of being a falcon, flying high above the city, swooping up and down and around, hunting in the blue light just before sunrise. Past the city's edge, he glided over a coniferous forest of yellow pine, Douglas fir, and juniper. It extended to the horizon, fading out in a gradient of foggy green. In its center towered a great shining spire. It called to him—mesmerizing, pulsing with a deep earthen heartbeat, bathing him and the land in a rhythmic sapphire-blue dawn.

4
DROP

S taccato vibrations buzzed from the burner in his pocket. Kid grunted, extended into an excellent toe-curler of a stretch, then swung down from the hammock, landing quietly on bare feet. After digging the phone out of his pocket, he tapped the text from his only contact, 'B.' The message read:

B1725

He padded across the cool cement to one of the bookshelves and dug around for the cipher key. Hidden behind one of the stacks was Treasure Island. Kid pulled it out, flipped to page seventeen, then converted the last two letters of the twenty-fifth word and tapped out a reply.

K1404

B replied. *Land.*

It was the correct cipher key used to authenticate communicating parties within a reasonable doubt. Kid tapped back: *Send.*

Sac+Pagoda. 7 pm. White glove.

Nice. On it.

Just say confirmed.

My bad. Confirmed.

...

Confirmed.

Received.

"Hell yeah!" Kid hooted as he flipped the book up, spinning it into the air before catching it and chucking it back to the empty spot on the shelf. "Guess what! We're getting paid!" He hollered at the birds as he hopped on one bare foot while fighting a sock onto the other. "Might even grab some snacks from the pet store if you're good! Watch my stuff while I'm gone!" Zoe squawked and flapped her wings, hovering momentarily before settling back down.

"White glove" meant that he needed to take extra precautions and that this would be an in-person pickup and drop. And *that* meant some serious cash—the same as twenty regular jobs. With money like that, he might have to make good on all of his Colorado talk. According to Hari, people were starting to smell his bullshit. Sleepiness from his afternoon nap was a long-gone memory, and his skin tingled with adrenaline. At nearly six, it was time to work.

Kid finished dressing, adding black combat boots, a faded yellow Buzzcocks t-shirt, and his favorite ratty grey hoody. Then he knelt in front of his stash spot under the palettes to gather a few tools of the trade.

As always, the item at the top of the stash spot was the box that originally held the silver ring that now hung constantly around his neck. It had been tucked into the milk crate where his infant body lay the night he was dropped at

Fire Station 3 on Post and Ellis. The box was made of cedar, still aromatic after many years. He held it to his face and took in the scent with a deep breath. On the back, a bronze plate engraved with an elegant script read:

Cognosa's Fine Things—Circum Agora, Middlemost

Over the years, Kid searched many times for a place called Middlemost. There were a few streets and neighborhoods in the United Kingdom and on the American east coast, but none connected to a 'Circum Agora' and no inhabitants or stores called by any variation of 'Cognosa's Fine Things.' He didn't stop at Google either, going so far as to dig into the San Francisco Public Library's historical archives. Nothing at all. Nada. He still thought about it occasionally but stopped searching—giving in to and embracing his inherited anonymity.

After sliding the cedar ring box to the side and giving it a loving pat, he grabbed a crowbar and a few extra twenty dollar bills, along with a well-used lock-pick set and some chunks of porcelain from a busted spark plug (AKA 'ninja rocks' for quickly and quietly breaking glass). The picks, crowbar, and porcelain shards were illegal to carry around since they constituted burglary tools, especially as a combo. Regardless of the danger from authorities, he might need them all this evening, so they went in his backpack. Besides, it's only illegal if you get caught, right?

With his gear packed away and slung over his shoulder, he

climbed down the fire escape, going down each floor as quietly as possible until he reached the bottom. He scanned the area to make sure nobody on street level was looking up in his direction. No one was. As usual, they were paying attention to what was in front of them, not anything above them. He swung down, dropped to the pavement, and headed north to Chinatown.

The light dimmed as the sun dropped behind the hill he crested. Street-level took on the bluish color of dusk, and nearby the sound of wooden chairs clackety-clacked as a restaurant prepared to close. Buses trundled up the steep hill from downtown, taking people in their twenties and thirties home after a day at the office. They were jammed into the bus like a full pack of cigarettes, almost everyone staring at their phones, casting a pale glow on their faces.

Get it together, Kid.

For what? To join those zombies?

He scoffed and rounded a corner to a pedestrian-only pathway between blocks. Near the center of the block was the pickup point. Ben was sitting at a knee-height concrete bench, watching some high-schoolers play volleyball through a tall chain-link fence. He wore a dark grey suit, no tie, and a top shirt button undone. His left eyelid hung lower than the right —making him look perpetually skeptical.

Kid had been working with Ben for about a year, and they didn't tell him much. But based on his observations, the guy was a mid-level lieutenant type, probably keeping track of several runners who, by design, Kid never saw.

He sat down and dropped his bag on the ground between them, then leaned over and pulled out his journal, leaving the bag open. He spent the next few minutes doing his authentic best to capture the motion and form of the volleyball players in quick gestures with a black ballpoint pen. Over a year, they'd exchanged only one word outside their cryptic text messages. Kid said, "Hey," and received no response. So when Ben said more than one word, it was a surprise.

He spoke quietly without turning his head as if he might be talking on the phone into earbuds, "You're on this one by luck, Kid. I lost my best runner this morning—hell of a lot better than your scroungy ass."

"Lost him? Like, dead?"

"Don't ask stupid questions."

"Should this be a partner run?"

"The fuck for?"

"I like making a little money, but doesn't mean I wanna get nixed."

"It'll be fine, trust me."

Kid's eyebrow twitched as he thought, *When people say 'trust me,' it's usually the number-one reason to do the opposite...*

Before Kid could suggest otherwise, Ben said, "Untuck your panties. You're perfect for this—a nobody that nobody knows. Understand? This is your chance. Don't fuck it up." Then he dropped the package in Kid's bag. It was about the size of a loaf of bread and weighed a few pounds, judging by the dense *thunk* sound it made. Then, with knees popping, Ben stood and walked away. On top of the box inside sat a small slip of paper. It read:

52 Old Chinatown Lane. Apt 315

5
ALICE

Several stories above Kid's alleyway rendezvous stood a girl called Alice Unknown. At eighteen, she should have been finishing high school and prepping for college. Instead, she was a soldier. Too young to drink but old enough to understand killing and dream of escape.

According to the traditions of her upbringing, at the age of seven, she'd selected her name from a favorite book—one weaving tales of hidden wonderlands, strange potions, talking cats, and murderous royalty. Then, at fifteen, Alice added *Unknown.*

She did so because, first of all, it sounded cool. If you're going to choose your own call sign, you may as well pick something that could go on an album cover. Second, she was taught that names have power. The exact pronunciation of her power would be something she owned alone. And third, it was a way to take ownership of the fact that she was adopted and never given a name.

According to The Young School, she never had any papers

or verifiable history, which was usually fine—she preferred not to think much about lineage. But more often than not, it was an unavoidable question asked by lips and eyes everywhere. Based on the Bay Area's immigration statistics, she suspected a mix of some white European descendants along with Chinese, Filipino, Japanese, and maybe even Vietnamese, Thai, Korean, or Cambodian. The list was long— pretty much any and all were possible on America's west coast. Perhaps if she'd grown up in a typical civilian community, she could at least claim Hapa. But even that was out of reach for someone raised in the shadows. Around any normie, she was just a weirdo.

Between her array of freckles, almost-almond eyes (made cat-like by black liner), and chin-length hair (currently dyed platinum silver), she knew she looked like a wannabe rave kid. But she didn't care; she liked it. The rest of "what" and "where-you-*really*-from-though" didn't matter either, not really. Because she knew that what counted was what a person could *do*—and that, like many things, a smart girl kept to herself.

To kill time as she watched the clandestine handoff, Alice took in her favorite hobby. Cornerstore scratcher tickets. She finished scraping the foil off another with a baby blue pinky nail. It was a dud—just like the last three. Not even enough cash won to buy more. She crumpled and tossed the losing tickets to the side and scowled at the wind as if the blame for losing was on its airy shoulders. Alice tried to flick the silver hair out of her face, but her bangs were currently at that annoying length that refused to stay behind an ear or hang gracefully.

From her vantage point, she could see down to street level and watch the handoff through a reflection in a store window. She recognized Ben, who she knew as part of the White Lotus syndicate. Lotus and The School were occasionally-cooperative rivals within a larger collective organized around leveraging the secret power of The Dream.

Sitting next to Ben, taking the package, was some boy about her age—maybe two or three years older. Alice couldn't make out every detail from this distance. But she could tell he was in good shape, if a little too skinny, like a runner or maybe a featherweight fighter. Scars marked his buzzcut hair, and his lips were positively *fluffy*. Not just some boy—a *cute* boy. Her mouth turned up in a mischievous smile.

I suppose if I have to steal, I'll steal from you, she thought.

As Alice watched, Ben stood up and walked away. The boy spent another few minutes drawing in a journal, then closed it and put it inside his backpack, using the same movement to adjust the package inside.

Then something strange happened.

As he touched the box, the air around him shifted like it was taking a subtle breath. A minute aberration that would never be perceptible to someone without Alice's specialized senses.

Well, that was interesting. What was that?

Okay... No muggings of cute boys.

Not yet, at least. Wait, watch, and learn.

She followed him along the rooftops and listened through a single earbud to hold music from the Berkeley Student Radio Station, 105.5. It played a retro-sounding synth track she recognized as River of Darkness by The Midnight. Alice nodded slowly to it as her lithe, athletic legs carried her walking, trotting, and jumping between eaves. The radio station offered tickets once a week at a few different times. They would announce the raffle, and you had to call in during the appointed time. If they picked your number, you won two tickets to whatever show they discussed that week. You couldn't find that kind of thing online. It made it worth downloading the app to listen to the station. Radio was old-school.

How could a girl fool around with raffle tickets and still manage a little espionage? Because she was the best, that's why. She wouldn't say it out loud; that lacked class—and more importantly, stating your power for all to hear lessened its potency. And because she was better than any of Mother's children, the matriarch underestimated her; they all did.

At this distance from The Young School, the ancient woman's psychic hold weakened. Alice could feel some of her autonomy returning, running through her veins like warm gold. She could taste it, and she wanted more. If she could get her hands on the item the boy now carried, then maybe, just maybe, autonomy would no longer be a dream fading in and out from the cloud of Mara's domination. It would be a new reality.

The audio recording squawked, "You are caaaaller nummm-ber—FIVE— stay on the line!" Five was read in a robotic tone, indicating that it was injected into the prerecorded sentence.

This week, the tickets were to The Red Queen, a psychedelic dance-rock band out of Long Beach. She had checked them out online earlier, and they looked phenomenal. The lead singer had an androgynous alien mystic thing going on, somehow managing to personify both the cosmic masculinity of Lenny Kravitz and the seductive femininity of Prince, or the artist formally known as. In the image she'd seen, his shirt was only buttoned once near the bottom, showing off his skinny rocker abs and his curly black chest hair. He looked like a real artist. Beautiful. Almost angelic. They were going to play at The Sand in East Oakland tomorrow night. According to the reviews she read online, it was a converted warehouse that managed to be cozy and expansive simultaneously—perfect for dancing and being close to the band.

She hoped to win the tickets. God, she really, *really* hoped. Alice lost count of how many times she had tried and failed. And every time she failed, she considered putting the weight of her finger on the table, loading the dice. It was certainly within her skill set. All it would take was a quick visit to the radio station, then a touch and a few words, and they would give her anything she wanted. Berkeley wasn't far; she could manage it between check-ins to The School in a few hours, much like she was currently handling an attempted jailbreak on a summer afternoon.

But, no—gaming the system wouldn't do. For one, moving people hurt them. Mother didn't care about that, but Alice did. And she wasn't a cheat. Maybe a little sneaky at times— but hey, that's not *cheating*—that's battle tactics.

Besides, more than winning, the goal was to delve into the concept of randomness. It fascinated her. Was it real? As far as Alice could tell, no matter the odds, a thing happens or doesn't. Until it does, it never has. Once it has, it always did.

Our universe is either a collection of random events colliding with each other constantly, or it's a clockwork of absolutely *nothing* random. Which was it? Chaos or mechanism? Fate or fallout? She chose, or hoped rather, for the former. Otherwise, what was the point of all this pain and struggle? What would be the purpose of The Dream? And if there was such a thing as fate, was it she it favored?

Her cheap way into the machinations of destiny? Lottery tickets and raffles. She knew it was stupid, especially alongside everything else in her life. What would she even do if she won? Her lifestyle didn't allow for stuff like going to shows. But she was going to change that, finally. If her information was good, and it always was, the boy now carried a totem—one of the most powerful ever found. With it, Alice would get the leverage she needed to finally escape.

Alice stopped along with the boy at the entrance to a narrow alleyway. She smirked as she watched him look around and mistakenly think he was alone before doing an acrobatic kick-jump off a brick wall and pulling up to the apartment building's fire escape. She continued watching him over the edge of the rooftop border wall and noticed even more scars on the back of his head. What was he, some kind of parking garage cage fighter or just a persistent bike-crasher? Either way, it was intriguing—which is better than cute or cool. Her grin widened to a smile.

And to top it all off? He was clearly not just some civie. There was no way, not with that psionic air distortion around him earlier. Did he have the talent? If he was a traveler of The Dream, he wasn't one she had ever heard of. Alice had only just learned of his existence, yet he was already making her ask many more questions than she was used to. It made her supremely irritated but also deeply curious. No, there would be no early-onset-robberies of ruffian street kids. She had considered that earlier, but now a new path was cut and her course corrected. Alice Unknown would follow and see down which hole the white rabbit ran.

Typical for a San Francisco summer, rain clouds collected above, bringing a damp chill with the wind. Alice pulled her jean jacket tighter. She loved the smell of coming rain. It was the scent of change. As she watched the boy climb the fire escape and disappear into a roof stairwell, the recorded music and repeating message continued playing from her earbud. Suddenly, the hold music cut, and the line went silent. She sucked in a breath and examined her phone, worried that she dropped the call somehow while multitasking between raffles and spy games.

"Hello!" The voice squawked in her ear, "Number Five! Are you there?"

Her mouth hung open.

"Hello?" The voice repeated.

"Hi!" She put the other earbud in so she could listen better, almost dropped the phone, then brushed the hair from her face to behind her ear, from where it immediately fell back down. "I mean, yes! Yes! I'm here!"

"Hey, Number Five..." The voice sounded young, college-age. He was putting on a deeper radio voice that wasn't really working. Still cute, though. A radio job must be fun. He said, "Yeah, so... I hate to break it to you..."

Alice waited in ecstatic silence—she knew the game from listening to other winning callers. At last, the DJ continued,

"You won! Two tickets to Red Queen at The Sand tomorrow night! Be there or be squaaaare! How does it feeeeeel?"

She always hoped she wouldn't be one of those girls who squealed when she got excited, but you don't know until you're in a squealing type of moment. Her grin spread wide, and she shrieked, "I feel One-oh-five-five Aliiiiiive!!!"

6

CHINATOWN

Kid tromped down the flight of wooden stairs leading from the roof. A track of aged green carpet ran down the center, nearly worn through in the middle where the foot traffic was heaviest. The walls seemed like they had been white at some point, but now they were an inauthentic yellow from decades of city air, human oils, and cigarette smoke. Unidentifiable cooking aromas and muffled snippets of conversation drifted into the stairwell as Kid made his way down. He reached the third floor without passing anybody, and just as he was about to leave the stairwell, he noticed movement out of the corner of his eye.

A mangey-brown cat with white feet. It was sitting on the landing, watching him with intent golden eyes—one leg hanging out to the side nonchalantly. He couldn't help but feel an unplaceable sense of deja vu. Then Kid scoffed and turned back to the stairwell door.

He popped out and walked down the hall, then stopped in front of 315, painted in black on a bronze frame. The door was well worn, with kick marks at the bottom from people opening it with their feet. It was already open—just a crack.

The hair started to stand on his neck.

A second knock opened the door another few inches, revealing a small living room with orange and brown shag carpet. He couldn't hear anyone but called into the apartment anyway.

"Hello?" Kid waited for an answer. When none came, he called again, "Anybody in here? Delivery for three fifteen."

One of the stone-solid rules of white glove drops was *never* leave a package without a contact present. They were supposed to be there and would have the same short code from the text messages. They had always been there before. If it was a bust, he'd have to protect the package, contact Ben, and figure out what to do next. Not ideal. Would they blame him? They weren't the type to let a bad drop ride easy. Ben said not to fuck it up. Kid did not want to test the lazy-eyed lieutenant's definition of fucked.

He called into the apartment again.

The acoustics of his voice bounced around inside so that it just *felt* empty.

"Yo!" Kid barked, voice cracking from the sudden loud use. The reply was silence, pungent and sticky. "Alright, coming in. No guns, okay? This isn't Florida."

He stepped inside the apartment, hunched low, ready to duck and cover his head. Once inside, he waited past the entryway, getting a feel for the space. Unbeaten and un-shot, his shoulders shifted down and away from his ears as he relaxed and took a look around. Long tapestries of Chinese characters adorned the walls, yellowed with old smoke. A well-worn recliner, a stack of books on a side table, and an ashtray piled high with cigarette butts. Against the wall, an aquarium, its filter and pump whirring and sucking, a dozen brightly colored fish swam in their little world, blissfully unaware of Kid's anxiety. The golden light of the setting sun filtered through the glass of closed French doors leading to the fire escape.

Kid turned away from the doors to look into the kitchen, where he noticed a dark patch on the otherwise yellowed linoleum floor. It was the black of orthopedic shoes with velcro straps, the kind that old folks wear. Attached to that, wrinkled beige socks and blue-veined ankles disappeared behind a wood panel wall.

It seemed abstract for a strange second; then he realized it was a foot.

Not moving.

His breath caught, and he wanted to run. But you can't just bail, not on a white-glove drop. Moves like that turn bad boys into bay anchorage. Don't lose the package, that's the main thing. If you can't make a drop, you better have a damn good reason. Need evidence of effort. That's what this called for. Check on the old guy. Call an ambulance, maybe. Take a picture, just in case. *Look, hey guys, see? I tried to deliver.* Plausible deniability, there it was. That's what Kid needed. Deniability.

He walked around the couch to the kitchen's entryway, careful not to touch anything. A pool of blood surrounded the man on the floor. It was fresh, still shimmering like a liquid instead of that opaque matte-plastic look of after it dries. The old man wore a wool cardigan Swiss-cheesed with stab wounds. There were at least ten holes in the guy. Burned and blackened fabric curled away from each one. His neck and face were contorted in a frozen look of fear and pain. The veins were dark violet, swollen, and stretched like they'd been smoked from the inside.

Kid tried and failed to swallow past the dry cotton that invaded his mouth. At least he didn't have to feel bad for not calling an ambulance. The old dude was super dead.

Time to go, Kid thought. *Hurry up and bounce. This is some shady shit.*

He reached for his phone to snap a pic when he heard the front door close. Spinning around on a squeaking boot heel, Kid stopped short.

Where there used to be an open door, an exit, a way out, now there were two pools of mirror shadows stealing the warmth from the room. The black wasn't just deep. It was hungry. It smiled.

"Heya," said the girl with dark mirror eyes, juxtaposed against her popping a wad of pink chewing gum. "Checking on Granpa-Dampa? What a sweetie."

"The sweetest." Echoed a boy, who, until that moment, Kid was unaware existed. He stood behind and to the left, blocking the French double doors leading to the fire escape. They'd snuck in behind him, deadly quiet.

The boy's hair was trimmed short in a buzzcut, and the girl sported a stylish bob of razor-straight black hair. They were almost identical, aside from their slight vs. stocky build. Twins. Creepily young ones. Maybe fifteen years old at most.

The girl said, "We were here when he passed. So sad." She made a brief pouting face and took a step closer. "Do you want to know what he said?" She popped her gum and answered herself, "He asked me to find a box for him. Funny, right? Know anything about that?"

The girl opened her hands in a welcoming gesture as she again stepped forward, now just two steps away. "How about it?" Her mouth smiled, but her eyes did not. "Do you have anything like that in that bag of yours?"

Kid noticed her fingers. They looked like she had dipped them in red paint, the paint drying on her fingernails. Ten holes in the man's cardigan. Ten red fingers. *What the hell? How did she?* The realization of the surreal murder weapon switched his brain into the high gear of fight or flight.

It was time to go. But his exits were blocked.

Wait. Look without looking. See without turning.

Over the boy's shoulder. The French doors to the fire escape.

They're open—just a crack.

Were they open before? Kid didn't think so.

When did that happen? Didn't matter.

Open now. Good.

Then, Kid saw the street cat, brown with white feet, same damn cat, sitting outside on the iron railing, watching everything, amber eyes glinting in the diminishing light. It tilted its head as if listening to something far away and hopped down, out of sight.

"Well?" The girl asked.

Kid replied, "Sorry, just thinking. I'm not supposed to leave it, but you two are family? I think I can make an exception."

Haircut didn't respond. She just watched.

He kept talking, "Sorry about your grandad... Must have been a heart attack. To think you can go just like that." He snapped his fingers. "Spooky. Puts things in perspective, you know?"

Kid did his best to hide how freaked out he was. If she sensed his fear, she'd eat him. He knew it, could feel it in his bones. Growing up in the system, on the street, you get a nose for it. Real danger has a smell, and it smelled like this. Like rotting honeysuckle.

He continued, seeming to make a decision, "Yeah, alright. If you're family, I'll leave it with you. Honestly, that'd be great. Probably saving my job—my boss is a real tight-ass."

She studied him for what felt like a long time, tilted her head slightly, then said, "Works for me," and held out her hand.

"Hang on a sec, just let me get it."

Voice calm, hands steady. Fear will get you killed.

7
RUNNER

"You don't have to sign for it or anything, not like I'm UPS," Kid said as he brought his bag to the front and reached inside. He had one shot. It needed to be smooth and fast.

Instead of the box, Kid grabbed the crowbar and whipped it out—swinging it in a spinning underhand pitch at the dead-eyed boy by the fire escape doors. The steel struck his chin with a crack of bone, and he tumbled to the side into the fish tank. Everything came crashing and splashing down, flooding the living room with water and sound.

Kid had begun sprinting toward the French doors the millisecond the crowbar left his hand, and he was fast. But the girl was fast too. She snarled behind him, and what felt like five burning hooks stabbed into his left shoulder, attempting, but failing, to stop him.

He dashed through the open doors, jumped to the skinny railing, then leaped across the gap between buildings like an Olympic hurdler doped up on the fear of death. He cleared the chasm, landing on the adjacent fire escape with a jarring clang.

Boots smacked iron as he took the ladder rungs two at a time, climbing toward the roof. Two floors below, the dead man's door ripped off its hinges with splintering wood and shattering glass. Kid reached the top, swinging onto the roof and skidding on gravel. His shoulder burned like hell.

No time to breathe.

Run.

The rooftop was covered in hanging clothes, left out to dry in the sun. They whipped past his face like Buddhist prayer flags on a mountain pass, trailing a whiff of laundry detergent. A dozen paces behind him, he heard the sound of fabric ripping, accompanied by pursuing footsteps in a percussive beat.

As he escaped the last line of drying clothes, the building's edge appeared abruptly before him, and he slid to a stop. Quickly, Kid scanned the wall of the building across the gap, and he spotted a black drain pipe leading to street level.

Could the drainpipe hold his weight?

Could he even make the gap?

Didn't matter.

No time left.

In a deep part of him, he knew if they caught him, he would die.

Jump, fool.

He took a few steps back, then sprinted and flung his body into the air. At the apex of his leap, he felt weightless, and for a fleeting moment, time seemed to crawl—details becoming surreal and vivid. The bay wind brushed his cheeks and hair, cold from the dampness of his sweat. The sounds of honking horns and an ambulance in the distance. Firecrackers, the kind you throw on the ground with a pop.

Pop pa-pop.

Children laughing, basketballs hitting concrete.

Then gravity, reality, and time regained their hold on him, and his fall began. Kid brought his feet and hands in front of him, allowing them to absorb his lateral momentum upon hitting the wall, then centered his hands and feet to pinch the drainpipe like a human vice clamp.

Sliding down at speed just shy of free-fall, the old metal stripped away troughs in the flesh of his palms. He ignored the pain in his shoulder, which was now a searing white heat spreading up his neck and down his left flank. As the ground sped toward him, he pushed out and away from the wall to give himself some room. Kid hit the ground in a roll, ending in a crouched position on the damp alley floor.

He heard a whistle from the rooftop, followed by its companion whistle at street level. Understanding that was his pursuer, Kid turned away from the source of the whistle and attempted to run but slipped in the alley muck. As he stumbled, his right shoulder dropped a few inches, and something whizzed through its previous location. It buried itself with a piercing *THWUNK* into the side of a graffiti-covered dumpster a few feet in front of him. It was his crowbar. He knew that because one side was yellow, just like his. But it was embedded in the side of a dumpster? A human did that? That's not possible. Is it?

Kid scrambled down the alley, pulling a stack of crates into the path behind him, then bolted out into the street, crossing it without looking. A grey Honda slammed on its brakes and laid on the horn. Inside was a woman in a yellow and blue Golden State Warriors hat, yelling and giving him the finger. He sprinted across the street and through Saint Mary's Square.

As he ran, he swung his bag around to the front, zipped it up, then flung it back. Miraculously, the package was still inside despite the bag being left open from when he threw the crowbar out. Not sure if anything was lost, he'd find time to look later, if there would be a later. He needed to get the package back to Ben, let him know what went down, and get out of this crazy deal. If he could get the package back unharmed, he figured he'd be in the clear or as close as he was likely to get after this circus. Bringing it back would come later. The first step was losing these homicidal nut jobs and staying alive long enough to worry about it.

Kid vaulted over a cardboard box balanced on a park bench, sending playing cards in all directions. The group of men around it exploded into shouts of Cantonese and agitated hand gestures. A glance over his shoulder revealed the prodigy-of-crowbar-throwing still in hot pursuit, a couple dozen yards back. He didn't see the twin sister anywhere, couldn't imagine she had even made it out of the building yet.

The park's edge came up fast, followed by a street full of moving cars, trucks, and a city bus. The final bottleneck to get out of the park was a set of stairs that descended straight down and then jagged to a hard right at ninety degrees. He ran down the straight part, then, to try and skip the turn in the stairs, attempted to vault over the railing to the street. He realized in mid-vault that his left arm was not following instructions anymore. Instead of being the crucial pivot point he needed, it hung uselessly at his side like a dead fish.

In the flight of his spectacularly failed vault, his foot caught the railing and set him into a spin. Six vertical feet later, he hit the sidewalk in a jarring collision of body, bone, and concrete. Most of the impact went to his left shoulder and head as it bounced from the pavement. Lightning bolts of pain shot up his neck and down his spine. His vision flooded with stars as he worked to get back up, first on one knee, then standing. Desperately, he looked out into the traffic flow for an exit; his face pulled into a tight grimace of pain and fatigue.

He saw his chance. Moving up the street at about twenty miles an hour was an 80s model Toyota truck, colored rust-red, with a makeshift wooden box attached to the bed—big enough to make the contraption look like it would tip over at the slightest turn in the road. Layers of colorful graffiti covered the side, the most legible of which said 'Panty Dropper' in a thick curly blue script. The box was partly filled with flattened and stacked cardboard collected from the streets and local businesses. He could hear Mexican Polka music coming from the truck, heavy bass and horns, *bomp* bomp, *bomp* bomp, and the deep growl of a hundred internal combustion engines running beside it in a murmuring herd.

Before he could look back and check for his pursuer, he heard the telltale sound of shoes smacking concrete just a few feet behind him. No time to lose. He sprinted out into traffic like a hunted rabbit bursting from the brush. Cars honked, and people yelled, but the guy driving the old jury-rigged Toyota didn't notice him over his blaring stereo. Kid intersected the truck's path, coming in just behind it as it rolled by. He grabbed the side of the box, nearly pulling his good shoulder out of the socket, and rolled over the rear gate onto the stacks of cardboard inside. Home free.

Or not.

Two pale hands grabbed the gate, cracking the wood. Between them, a pale face contorted into a grimace of intense focus. The jagged gash in his chin was bleeding all over the place. That smell again. Molting flowers. Death.

Kid was in the truck feet-forward, so his face was now only inches from the dark-eyed boy. He tried to reach and punch him, but his useless left arm reduced the attack to a painful flop. His vision spun, and the world stuttered, falling behind him on its side, threatening to fade out.

No, nononononono. Not yet. Not *yet.*

Rather than passing out, which was the last graceful thing his body and brain wanted in the world, Kid summoned the last of his strength as Darkeyes began to make real progress pulling himself into the truck.

With the force of will that can only come from adrenaline reserves and a basic animal need for survival, Kid reached out with his good hand to grab the back of the freak's shaved head. Gripping his clammy skull with all his remaining strength and digging his fingernails into his scalp for added purchase, Kid pulled their heads together to meet with a sick crack.

The header made Darkeyes flinch with a grunt, but he remained firmly attached. Kid realized the bastard couldn't hang on *and* defend himself and took full advantage of the fact. He smashed his forehead into nose bone again. This time much harder since he'd closed the distance—a whip crack *SPLACK* of hard bone on cartilage.

Then, again. And again. And *again*.

Over and over until he felt the nasal structure collapse.

Warm blood gushed—spattering the truck gate and both their faces.

Darkeyes finally released his grip on the truck gate, and Kid heard his body hit the street. Shoes smacked against the pavement in a repetitive staccato spin like a baseball card in the spokes of a bike wheel, followed by screeching tires, smashing glass, and a cacophony of blaring horns. Finally, almost gratefully, Kid's vision washed with crimson starbursts, and he collapsed into darkness.

8

MARA

A mile from where Kid lay unconscious in the back of a box truck, a vast stone penthouse perched atop an Art Deco skyscraper. Within its chambers, Mara Tiamazedeh smiled as she ran her fingers down her lover's arm. The smell of carnal sweat hung in the air, so sweet when fresh. She savored it, knowing that after an eon, it would likely be her last opportunity for such indulgences. The flames from the candle stands covered their two bodies in warm light. The room was large, and without windows, dark by design, far corners shadowed like black velvet.

Her companion asked, "How'd you get into all of this? I mean, you're kinda young, aren't you? No offense. I've lived in this city a while now and spent time with some *very* well-off divorcés and lonely wives. I'm talking *loaded*. People that make the rich look poor. And I still never knew there were actual castles on top of some of the buildings. I always thought they were just for decoration. Are you, like, an internet billionaire or something?"

His real name was Bernard, and with his friends—Bernie. But that name's no good for business. Just terrible all around. He'd decided his parents were sadists. His life-coach Janelle had suggested 'Sven.' It was more mysterious, she said, sexy, smoky. It could fit a boy toy or a Viking, maybe both. Nobody needed to know he was from a small town in Minnesota and never finished high school.

"Oh? Tell me. Why might you think age has anything to do with it?" Mara replied, still sleepy from sex.

Man, Bernie thought, *you got some dragon's breath, girl.*

Halitosis or something. He could tell she tried to cover it with sweet-smelling stuff, but the odor remained. Like spraying down a compost bin with lavender Febreeze. The potpourri helped, but you could catch a strong whiff of nasty underneath. But her funky mouth was far from the worst thing he'd had to deal with for this kind of money. If he could handle red wings and bawling post-menopausal housewives begging to run away with him to Mexico, he could handle bad breath. Bernie considered himself a professional and kept his game face on.

"If you're not born into it?" He replied, "Everything. Taking over the world takes time, right?"

"Time is a fantasy, arrived at by those with enough imagination to dream of death." Mara ran her fingers over his hair and thought, *what must it be like to imagine a future, as only one can when it is their first time through the gate?* Her first time was far too long ago to recall clearly—like trying to remember the fleeting summer interests of a child.

"Okay, so you're, like, a philosophy chick. Are you one of

those kids who skipped high school and went straight to Harvard or whatever?"

"Something like that."

"Don't take it the wrong way. It's interesting, but—"

"Don't worry. I've heard it all before. I look younger than I feel. What's that they say? An old soul." Mara smiled and changed the subject. "What would you do if you could live two hundred years?" Her eyes twinkled. "Or a thousand?"

Bernie replied, "A thousand years? Man..." He laid back on the bed and clasped his hands behind his head to provide a headrest, one of his favorite moves—he knew girls liked the opportunity to admire his physique. He worked hard for it, so why not? Mara obliged and ran her hands along his chest and stomach. "I don't know... Nobody else can live that long, right?"

"No, not many."

"Alright, so pretty much anybody I knew in the beginning would be dead. Then anybody else I would get to know would die too. Guess I'd just be watching people die all the time! Doesn't sound all that great, to be honest. Are there spaceships? Like, nice ones? Is the world some kinda Mad Max wasteland? Am I rich?"

"To all of the above and more, the answer is always... *Maybe*. There are no guarantees, love."

People calling him 'love.' Making *this* kind of money for a couple hours of work in castles on top of skyscrapers. So cool. Not something you'd hear about back in Pohawky, Minnesota. So glad he left, forget what his high school friends had said. You'll never make it, Bernie. Stay here where it's safe. What are you gonna do, huh? Be a movie star? Everyone out there's fruits and loops. That what you are, Bernie? A Fruitloop?

"Well, I guess I'd make sure to get rich. Being poor for a thousand years doesn't sound fun. I'd probably take up some of the stuff I always think about. I want to learn to play guitar."

"Guitar?"

"Yeah, get really good. You know Esteban?"

"Who?"

"He's this guy I saw on TV who sells lessons. Kinda looks like Antonio Banderas in that movie where he's got a gun in his guitar case. Desperado, I think."

"You don't need more than a lifetime for that."

"Okay, okay, so, then I'd travel. Explore, you know? It could be cool, no rush, learn a bunch of languages and meet girls. Just have fun, I guess."

"Just have fun? For a thousand years?" Mara asked in a mocking tone.

"Well, I get to stay young, right?"

"Of course."

"Then yeah, sounds dumb, but everyone's dead! Might as well have some fun!" Bernie laughed and ran a hand through his blonde hair, another one of his signature moves. He wondered if the bb-cream skin toner he used needed a touch-up. "Why, what would you do?"

"*Children*. I would have *many* children. If the strong don't propagate, then what's the point? How does one build reciprocity with the infinite maker?"

"Er... yeah. *Totally*." Bernie chuckled. "Over my head again,

Harvard. You got kids now? Kinda young, but I don't see why n—"

"No. These bodies aren't capable. Something goes sour when... Never mind."

"Huh? What's all that?"

"Shhh... It's not important."

Mara sighed and laid her head on his chest. The dried sweat made the skin-on-skin contact sticky, so she laid on her hair, positioned with a sweep of her head. She thought the dark brown looked good against his pale skin. One would think everyone had good tans in California, but not in San Francisco. As she reclined, she noted the afterglow of the love they made was leaving.

Many ask, *What would you do with an infinite life?* Some answer, *Reach for the stars. Build an empire, steer the course of humanity.* But what happens when you have already accomplished those things? Or attempted them and found them a waste of time? What happens when you are finished, as close as one can get, and realize that the stars are still out of reach? Out of reach even for those who do not die? What do you do when you learn that humanity is ultimately a lost cause, a rebellious herd, unresponsive to carrot or stick, destined to run riot from a cliff top?

She had become irritated and tired. It was time for a proper climax.

Mara murmured, "Tell me, love, you're ready for round two."

Bernie chuckled, "Oh, I don't know. I think I need a few more minutes."

"But you're so young and still just a one-shot pony?"

"Young? That's funny coming from you. And I think it's one 'trick' pony. Believe me, I have *lots* of tricks."

"Show me then. Until you're ready, we will play."

"You bet. What do you like?"

"I want you to take me, slap me, choke me. I don't want to be in charge right now. As you choke me, do *not* stop unless I tap your leg. Promise me you won't stop unless I tap you. I can take it."

"Oh, you like it rough? I can do that."

"It's important that I do not have to *make* you do it. You must take my air with your own free will. Do you understand? *Promise me.*"

"What?"

"Promise you won't stop unless—"

"Unless you tap. Got it. Lay back."

Bernie, with the stage name Sven, pushed Mara back with his hand on her chest above her breasts until she lay in the pile of rumpled sheets and pillows. He began to massage her sex with one hand and tighten his hand around her throat with the other. It was far from his first time doing something like this, and it was a popular request. He loved the eye contact—waiting for the moment she would give in. It was such a rush, the best part by far. The control. He wondered what it might be like to be on the receiving end. He had never found out but would like to. Why did he always have to be the dominant one? Kind of a bummer. Maybe she'd do it. She seemed like the mistress type, especially with this castle dungeon thing going on. He'd have to ask later; she seemed like she might be a repeat client. She was *totally* into him. He let her throat go to give her a slap across the mouth, watched her eyes dilate in pleasure, and then returned his hand to her throat, tighter now.

"How we doin', sweet thing?" He asked.

Mara ignored his idiot pet name and replied with a moan, mouthing the word, *More*. Bernie obliged and tightened his grip. She writhed in the passion that leads to climax. Her face turned red, tiny splotches of petechiae blooming on her cheeks. Bernie started to worry, and he read that petechiae was a bad sign. But some clients took things further than this. One rich Korean girl up on Nob Hill told him, *That's what makeup's for,* as she covered her neck in concealer. *Nothing like taking a fuck bruise to work with you*, she'd said. So, he figured a little choking was no big deal. The lady wanted it and paid for it, and he was a pro, after all.

Again, Mara mouthed, *More, don't stop*. But now her eyes were turning red with busted capillaries. It was time to chill. He relaxed his grip to give her some air. She immediately leaned up and slapped him, shockingly hard for such a petite person, nearly knocking him off the bed. His head rung, and his lip bled, spattering two drops of red onto her tanned breasts.

"Don't stop until I tell you to stop!" Mara let out a slow controlled breath to stifle her anger. "Do as I say, and I'll pay you double. *BUT.* If you fail again, I will fucking end you. Now. Try again. *Be* better." To punctuate the command, she pulled his head back by his hair, licked the blood from his lip, released him with a jerk, and laid back down.

Mouth stinging and head ringing, Bernie renewed his grip on her throat—both hands now, with stoked anger. Bitch slapped the shit out of him. He'd have a fat lip. Messing up his face was bad for business. Alright then, she'd asked for it. He'd give it to her good. She'd beg him to stop this time.

With both of his hands busy around her neck, Mara took over the job of massaging rhythmically between her thighs. After a few minutes, they returned to that knife's edge moment. The edge of consciousness and climax, of light and dark, of give, of take, of rip away. At last, she came—body-shaking, tears flowing down her cheeks to wet the pillows. Bernie wondered if he should let go now, but she hadn't tapped his leg. He wasn't going to mess this job up—he just bought a new car, a baller M3, and parking in San Francisco was expensive as shit. Bernie needed the money and held on. Mara's climax plateaued then receded, and her thighs ceased shivering as she faded to unconsciousness.

Bernie's face flushed from the excitement. What a rush.

Her face was pale and still. Finally, he let go.

Give her a sec, she'll be back. A second came and went.

Nothing. He grabbed her shoulders and shook.

She didn't wake, so he rattled her harder, bouncing her against the pillow. His look of excitement quickly mutated into a frozen mask of fear.

"Fuck! Hey! Wake up, you weird bitch!" Terrified, he turned to the door and yelled, "Hey! Guard guy!" His call echoed then dissipated in the shadow-filled room. "Somebody!"

Nobody came.

He shook Mara's body again and again, hoping for a response. Slapped her. Nothing. Hit her again, harder. Again, nothing. He screamed in her face and shook her hard enough to chip her teeth. Nothing. Her lips and face stayed as pale and still as a doll. The tears dried on her face, leaving little salty streaks.

At last, he gave up.

He stared at his hands, terrified.

Bernie sat that way for a long time.

Finally, with a sniffle, he snapped back to reality. His eyes darted around the room. It seemed like they were still alone. Why wouldn't they be? What an odd thing to think. But he couldn't shake the feeling of someone watching.

His entire body trembling, hands most of all, he decided to put on his clothes and get out of there. She didn't know his real name. *Oh, BernieBernieBernie, what the fuck, man...* If he could leave without anyone seeing, maybe... maybe...

As he tried to put on the second leg of his pants, hopping precariously on one foot, he tripped and fell to the concrete floor with a smack. Grunting from the fall, he finished putting on his pants from his position lying down. He got up onto all fours and found his shirt under the bed, shrugging it on as quickly as possible. It was inside out. Fuck it who cares.

Bernie struggled to get one shoe on. With no socks, it was hard going. As he was putting on the second shoe, a door opened. One he hadn't seen before, hidden in the shadows of the cavernous room. He shuffled to standing, trying to accomplish the impossible task of blocking the view of the large bed with his comparatively small body.

The person who opened the door stepped into the dim candlelight. It was a younger girl, maybe twenty at most. A sister? She looked remarkably similar to the girl lying in the bed, albeit a few years junior. She was barefoot, covered only in a black silk nightgown that stopped where thigh began.

"Oh..." The girl whispered as she rubbed the sleep from her eyes with a closed fist. "What happened here?"

Something in the back of Bernie's brain recognized the smell again. Her breath. Flowers and death. But so slight as to be unnoticeable by the conscious mind.

"Nothing!" He looked at the bed and then back to the girl. "I mean... It was an accident, I swear! We were just playing around, and—oh god..."

"And it went too far?"

He sniffled. "It was an accident!"

"But why... Why did you kill me, Bernie?" The girl with sleepy eyes asked.

"No! I didn't! She asked me to, and I tried to stop! She wouldn't let me! She wouldn't let me stop! Wait! How do you know my name? How do you—" Bernie's eyes widened. "Wait, what? Kill *you*? You? What the—? I didn't kill anybody! How do you know my name? Ahhh, *gaaawd* what's going on, man?" Bernie bawled, tears streaming down his face, snot quivering on a busted lip, mouth turned down in a comically curved frown like a drama mask.

The girl pulled Bernie's head down, and the sobbing man sniffled against her chest.

"I didn't mean to, honest. You have to—"

"Hush now, it's okay. You're not in trouble. I believe you. Shhh."

"You do?" Bernie snort-hiccuped and looked at her hopefully.

"Of course. I *asked* you to keep going. It was beautiful. Thank you, Bernie Bear. You've given me a wonderful gift," the girl cooed in his ear as she stroked his blonde hair.

"But—but, I don't understand,"

"And you never will. Now you have to sleep too. She needs company."

The new vessel which housed Mara's transferred essence lifted Bernie's head from her chest and held it between her hands. She gazed into his eyes and smiled, kissing him on the tip of his sniffling nose.

She whispered, "Oh, Bernie Bear... End your dream. *Now*."

At her command, Bernie twitched, and his eyes rolled back in his head. He gagged on air, his tongue, and on the snot and nasal refuse his crying released. Veins bulged in his neck and face, the capillaries bursting in his eyes, flushing the white to a bright red. Blood dripped from his tear ducts, joining the stream from his nose, creating a tricolored semi-viscous flow. A final cough left a fine spattering of crimson on Mara's face. Her nostrils flared at its scent like a horse tasting the air.

She guided him to the bed next to her old vessel as his body went slack. They would sleep together, companions for eternity. She couldn't remember the name of her previous container, which now lay pale. Had she ever known it? No, she thought not. She knew its animus was now severed, lost in the place beyond The Dream.

She sighed. Even as she watched the two cooling bodies, the sweet rush following the blissful climax of death and return was already receding. It didn't last long at all anymore. Mara was a death junkie with sky-high tolerance and knew it. But luckily, she could afford the habit.

The first time Mara died, she succumbed to suffocation by sand, surrounded by nothing but the stars and a night wind to cool her ravaged body. She arrived at that seemingly final moment by surviving the raiders five days prior.

A young Mara had smeared herself with the blood of her mother and sisters and hid under their torn bodies. After the men left, she crawled for two days to the next village. Sadly, it was burned to the ground as well. The next town and her last hope were across a desert, a day's journey on foot, and through the canyons of Wadi Mujib. If she could make it there, crawling across the ground, she might find water and possibly survive. So, Mara pushed on. For three more days, she crawled, hiding from the scorching sun during the day and screaming in pain as she persisted across the dirt and stones at night. But eventually, her shattered pelvis, battered organs, and eviscerated body refused to continue.

Upon death, as all do, she passed through the in-between place. The river where all drops of life must flow, to eventually find their way again to the great sea, to then be undone, diluted, and redistributed into the aether—finally raining back down on the lands in the hearts of the new.

However, her essence did not complete the journey.

The starlit dune was not her end.

Mara was an anomaly. Something inside her, something that she still did not understand, prevented her from moving on. Luck. Genetic mutation. Psychological affinity. Pure, righteous anger. Impossible to say. But as far as she knew, she was the first, or at least the first to do anything grand about it. The first to travel through The Dream and return. The first to move across the permeable boundaries between minds to a new life in a non-infant vessel while retaining her memories.

She took her first replacement vessel from an

unsuspecting nomad girl at the arrival of her first moon. From the moment she overtook the girl, her birthing blood turned black, dried up, and never returned. It was the same for every vessel she took in the many millennia to follow. Mara could not create life, but also she could not die.

Since then, she learned that time and existence are simple twining circles—rings from which she could escape, and others too, if so designed. However, after a thousand lives, she concluded that life was not worth saving. The raiders never left. They simply changed clothes and tools. Humanity was not a gift; it was a mad dog. Now more than ever, in need of a grand culling.

She missed the old days when the sun was a god, the moon his sister. It turned out that Helios was nothing more than a distant explosion. One, to swallow the world in a cleansing blaze.

That fire needed to come sooner. Once the lost totem was back in her hand, she would make it so. She would finish the job she'd started at the fall of Zeboim. No more pin-holes scattered across the paper between worlds—a soul lost here, a child missing there. It wasn't enough. It was time to tear The Dream apart. In its tattered remains, humanity would sleep, never to awaken.

9
DREAM

A beach of golden sand, fine as talcum powder. Gently rolling hills falling headlong into dunes. Tall grasses dancing in the wind. Each tassel performing an undulating bow—all in musical synchronization, like the procession of a million attendants to a queen. The star-filled sky was too close as if attached to the bottom of low-hanging clouds. Many of the pin-lights flickered and died like malfunctioning neon signs.

What is this place? Kid wondered.

The last thing he remembered was blacking out in the back of a truck. This place, though, felt like a dream. Sort of. If it was a dream, it was the most realistic and vivid he had ever experienced. It felt closer to what people fantasized about virtual reality being like at some point in the not-too-distant future. Real-seeming in every way but different.

He could smell the sea and its salt.

He could feel the sand against his toes.

Kid had tripped on magic mushrooms and acid plenty of

times, even peyote twice, and ayahuasca once—usually at Ocean Beach and Golden Gate Park, or occasionally just walking around the city with headphones and sunglasses. In fact, he liked to consider himself an experienced psychonaut. Thanks to that, he wasn't wholly knocked sideways by the sheer strangeness of what was happening. Somehow, in a way, he had unknowingly prepared for it. But still...

This was something else.

This was a whole other level.

This felt like he somehow teleported to a different planet with similar but slightly different laws of physics. There was gravity, light, texture, and sound, but each was somewhat peculiar. Something like plugging your nose and equalizing the pressure in your ears, but with your entire perception of reality.

pOp.

What the hell was going on?

He held an arm out to observe. His tan skin appeared bluish in the strange low-hung starlight. His shoulder felt like he'd pulled a muscle, but otherwise it felt fine. Running his fingers over his forearm hair tickled, and that was nothing new. It was just typical hair on an unexceptional arm. Kid looked back up to the very much *not* typical scenery.

If this was an intense hallucinatory trip, he knew from experience that it would go wrong if he let anxiety get the better of him. Bad trips are not fun. It's better to go with the flow, keep things light, and accept what is given with an open mind. Let the river lead. If you fight the current, you'll surely drown and be swept away.

Go with the flow, he thought. *Go with the flow.*

He shook his head in disbelief and decided to do the only thing he could—walk forward, take in the sights, and see what could be seen.

The ocean was a restless midnight blue, with infinite lapping and trading of spaces, reflecting the low-hanging star-freckled sky. The water rushed onto the sand taking its territory, the sand giving it away freely and flowing into the waves in rivulets. When the waves reached the end of their uphill journey, the point at which they could go no further, they retreated. As quickly as they came, they relinquished the conquered ground, leaving behind small floating fortresses of white sea foam, some of which followed, dancing back out into the water. Others stayed behind, staking their claim, momentary colony outposts in a strange world of soaked moon-glittered grains.

As he walked down the beach, Kid looked out across the waves to the horizon, which, like the stars, felt strangely close. Angry lightning flashed, revealing that it wasn't the horizon that was too near but obscured by a dark storm that stretched across the world. Lightning flashed again, illuminating clouds of midnight purple, squirming as if pregnant with a swarm of elver eels. Kid shuddered and turned away.

After some time, Kid noticed movement in the distance. Down the beach, someone huddled into the blanketing folds of an oversized green rain jacket. They paced back and forth in the wet sand, adjusting the lines on at least a dozen fishing poles held by forked sticks. The fishing lines lay in the shallows, awaiting a catch's telltale yank.

As if on a string of his own, Kid felt pulled toward the fisherman and doubled his pace, his footprints punching sand as he made his way. Perhaps the lone man could answer some questions about this place. The gap between them shrank quickly to a dozen yards.

"Hey!" Kid hollered through cupped hands, hoping to project his voice through the hostile wind coming off the ocean in cold, wet torrents.

The fisherman looked up and stood to his full height, revealing himself to be quite tall and somehow elegant with jeans tucked into black rubber boots. Thin, but not in a gangly way. His skin was brown like burnt umber, eyes as golden as a cat's. He seemed both young and ancient at the same time. Ageless.

Kid was sure he'd never seen the man before, yet he was somehow still familiar.

"It's about time," The man said, his voice deep and reverberating like an ancient church bell.

"What's that?" Kid asked as he studied him, trying to place the face. In addition to his unsettling golden eye color, the man seemed to radiate strange energy. As the distance between them closed, Kid's arms and neck hair stood up as if pulled by static electricity.

"I say, it's about time. Twenty long years, I've waited. Much has passed."

Kid forced a nervous chuckle, "Sorry, man. I don't know you."

"Sure you do. I've worn many faces and met you in many places."

"If you say so, but I still don't—"

"You're thinking now, *am I mad?*"

Kid thought it wouldn't take a mind-reader to guess that.

The man continued, "You couldn't know. This was by design. If *you'd* known, *she'd* know. But it's time to wake up. The rooster crows."

Kid's face scrunched in half-knowing. A song, tip of the tongue. Something about the unique skin color, the eyes...

"You know pieces of me, as many do. My fragments are found throughout the worlds. Within each dream. Once, I watched you from a street corner." His eyes brightened, and he held up a finger, "A moment, please, let me dance with your memory."

The man tilted his head as if listening to something far away. He blinked, apparently finding what he was looking for, then turned back to Kid, hunched his back as if impersonating an old man.

In a gravely, cigarette-scarred voice, he said, "It's a wild world, baby babe. Like the ol' Cat says." The man winked and laughed Hari's rough laugh, then coughed and added, "Where ya been at? Tell me straight."

Goosebumps covered Kid's body, and a drop of fight-or-flight adrenaline trickled down his spine. The man sounded *exactly* like Hari. Not an impersonation. It was as if his mouth was a speaker playing a recording of Kid's old friend. There was no mistaking it. He'd listened to Hari's unique gruff voice for years. Kid moved his feet to a position he could run, roll or pivot away from, unsure what would come next.

"What the fuck?" If Kid could have spoken more eloquently, perhaps he would have, but *what the fuck* was the best he could do. Beyond that, he was struck silent, watching and waiting as his hands moved to a defensive posture. As he did so, he winced from a burning pain in his shoulder. Where the girl grabbed him back at the Chinatown apartment? What did she do to him? He pushed the thought away.

Again in Hari's voice, "Simmer down, boy. We *still* friends, ain't we?"

"Stop that, for real."

The man coughed, clearing his throat, and laughed. He said, in his original deep timbre, "We *are* friends. As we always were, as we always will be, in whatever form we take, whether four-legged or street saint. Most recently, our paths crossed in Chinatown—in the home of a dead man. You see—I've opened doors for you." At this, he grinned, showing a gap between white teeth you could fit a coin through.

Kid did not speak. He didn't want to let on how scared he was. If this was a trip or a dream, it was the nearest to insanity he had ever come. Perhaps he had already passed the event horizon of mind-found and mind-lost. Regardless, he resolved to appear stoic, hide his fear as best he could, and study the strange man. His hands lowered, but only a little.

The stranger frowned, "Come now. Stretch your mind, alley dog. We haven't much time for games, but I don't want to spell it out. That's no fun. You sense it. You smell it. You feel my truth. You *know* you do." A few strands of hair blew loose from the wind. He licked his fingers and smoothed them back, tucking them under the rain jacket hood—what a strange thing to do in the middle of a conversation.

A ridiculous thought occurred to Kid. Despite the strange man's clues, it still took a while to click, probably because of how stupid it was. But, in this surreal place, it didn't seem so ridiculous. "On the fire escape, and the stairwell... your eyes... the shabby cat..."

"Tut tut, shabby? Come now, that's not nice. We both know the streets are hard on the handsome." He smiled again, the hood of his rain jacket fluttering against his cheek. The hair he smoothed blew free again. It started to rain. He stuck his tongue out to catch a drop, which, of all the things, struck Kid as the most strange. It seemed like something a child would do.

Kid said, "The balcony door. I was right. It *was* closed at first, wasn't it? I thought so. After those twins showed up, though... it was open. That was you? You opened the door for me and," Kid inhaled as his hands dropped a bit further, "you were a cat."

A man who was a cat. Walking in an alternate universe dream world. Somehow, none of it *felt wrong*. It all *felt* real. Like the hair on his arm. Somehow things that would make no sense in the ordinary world were taking hold of Kid's mind as historical truths—more like simple memory than insight or epiphany.

"Meow." The man laughed again in the strangely comforting timbre. "I'm sorry that I couldn't do more. Subtlety is still the name of the game for me at this point. But you made it! That's what counts. The acrobat alley dog, here at last."

The tall man moved to adjust the line on one of his fishing poles, scanning the darkening ocean horizon as he did so. The storm was noticeably closer. He continued, serious now, "Today was important. You were running on instinct. Knowing a person's nature is critical to working with them. So, to that end, thank you for surviving. Thank you for choosing to fight. Thank you for letting me know you better thoroughly through your actions. My friends call me Horacio." He extended a long-fingered hand. It did not look like the hand of a fisherman. It looked like the hand of an artist, a musician, or perhaps a puppeteer.

Still not convinced, Kid examined it like a dead rat. "You smell like a hustler. What even are you, man? A figment of my imagination?"

"What am I? Hmm. *That* is a question, isn't it? I'll turn it back to you. What are *you*?"

"Me? I'm real. That's what I am."

"Are you? Really real?" Horacio's golden eyes glinted, and he didn't wait for Kid to answer. "If so, then what am I? Well, I suppose... at my foundation, I am a *hedonist*." He smiled. "I exist. I *enjoy* existing. It's something I want to keep doing."

Kid didn't respond to Horacio's words or his still outstretched hand, choosing instead to watch, half expecting him to turn into vapor and blow away with the sea wind. Horacio pulled his unshaken hand back to his body as if it were wounded. Kid's lips parted, about to speak, then stopped. He wanted information and needed to find some bearings. But if he asked this odd man for it, that would be like admitting he believed. But what else was there to do? For the present moment, all he had was this strange situation—as unbelievable as it was, he may as well try and sort it out. Don't fight the current unless you want to have a bad time. Go with the flow.

Kid sighed, then spoke, "Look... I like a good trip as much as the next guy. But, what... where..." Kid grunted in frustration and cursed under his breath. "It feels like... I *must* be dreaming. I'm tripping, right? I hit my head back there.

This is all in my banged-up dome. But... It feels real. Still... not real enough. This is... Man... What the hell's going on?"

Before answering, Horacio turned his head to survey the ever-darkening sky. His eyebrows knit, marring the previously perfect skin with wrinkles. In some moments and tricks of light, he looked exactly like Hari, but then he'd shift his position, the light would change, and the striking resemblance would vanish. It was like a crystal prism had been made into a man, hiding many other likenesses behind its opal facets. His lips pursed for a moment, then parted to speak.

"You are not far from the truth of the matter. This *is* a dream. Rather one part of *The* Dream. Capital T, capital D. It is produced by consciousness, which some call soul, spirit, mind, chi, anima, etcetera, so on and so forth. Your mind is a door that opens to a place that connects all other living souls, each one presiding over its own unique portal, just like yours. All minds create this place, and all are connected to it. *This* is The Dream. The Animus Mundi. This is where you are now. This is why it seems so strange, for it *is a dream*. But it is also quite ancient, and it is quite real."

It somehow felt like he was explaining things Kid already knew. It made strange yet familiar sense. On some of his adventures with hallucinogens, he thought he felt a connection between things, someplace beyond the body. Especially with ayahuasca and peyote, those were powerful, genuinely moving journeys. It seemed that he glimpsed some level of reality that was typically hidden. Of course, at the time, he wrote it off as tripping balls because he never prescribed wholly to the metaphysical, although many people did. He read some of the books, of course—Doors to Perception, by Aldous Huxley, was one of his favorites. But that was as far as he took it. Kid always chalked it all up to entertaining quirks of the imagination. But this was so far beyond that.

So... either, A—He'd entirely lost his mind

Or, B—The golden-eyed man was telling the truth.

At least for now, Kid chose to believe, not that he had much choice.

This place was The Dream, but he was not dreaming.

Go with the flow, Kid. Go with the flow.

His hands finally dropped fully to his sides, and he winced again. The pain in his shoulder and left flank was increasing by the second. Again, Kid pushed it away and with a resigned breath, asked, "Alright, how'd *you* sneak into the mind motel?"

A micro twitch of a congratulatory smile played on Horacio's mouth. "Some come here by accident. Some can travel here by will or with special tools, like the one you've got in your knapsack."

Kid reached behind to feel for his bag and felt the bread-loaf-sized wooden box inside.

"This? The package?"

"Yes, rather, what is inside. An animus totem. This one is particularly mighty. And despite being locked, it knows your tune and has helped to bring you here."

"A totem? Like a carved spirit animal or whatever?"

"It's just a word. They are artifacts of stored animus. A physical manifestation of empathy, of connection, like gravity or electromagnetism, the powers that draw, pull, and riven.

Like any other collection of energy and matter, they come in all shapes and sizes and exhibit all manner of characteristics."

Kid couldn't help but roll his eyes, "Right... That explains it. And you have one too? A... *totem?*"

Horacio continued. "No. You see, humans travel to the dream via talent, tools, or coincidental synchronism. Others... like myself, are *made* of the dream. The Dream *dreams* you see, and *that* dream, a sliver of it, that is *me*."

And there it was. Kid lost the thread again. He was trying to keep an open mind, doing his honest best. He grimaced in strained confusion.

"You were... born here? In my head? Man..."

Horacio reached forward to place his hands on Kid's shoulders. Under normal circumstances, Kid would have shrugged the unwelcome touch away. But as before, he felt strange energy radiating from the man, keeping him glued still.

"My boy," Horacio said from inches away. "Your head is only a *doorway*, a conduit of power for this place, a temporary waypoint for a single note of universal jazz—one of billions. I am *not* in your head. *And neither are you*." He whistled a world-weary sigh as if this was not his first time having the conversation. "It is not complicated to explain. It is only difficult to accept. Perhaps I should have awoken you at a younger age when you were less... fragile. Please, try harder."

Kid shook Horacio's hands from him. "Fragile? Motherfucker, I'm not fragile."

Horacio raised an eyebrow. "No? Are you strong? Then act like it."

Kid's eye twitched as he stuffed his temper down. If the

guy didn't look so much like his good friend Hari, he would have swung at his jaw already. Instead, he took a deep breath and told himself *yet again* to keep an open mind.

"Alright, man, so... what do you want then?"

"Simple. I want us to survive. I want us to *be*."

"What, you think we won't?"

"At this pace? No. Most certainly not. Do you see the storm? That is no common weather front. That dark wall is a harbinger of the end. The scales of power lean dangerously in a direction that we can no longer pretend will rebalance on their own. If we let them tip, it all comes down."

"What comes down?"

"All of it. Everything. We are in *danger*. They are tearing apart The Dream."

"So people can't dream? Who cares?"

"It's more than that. The Dream is the connective tissue of consciousness. If it ends, we end. Already, men sleep longer than they should. On this path, the whole world will follow suit, and she will not wake. A forest cannot live without soil, air, water, and connecting mycelium. Yin and yang. Sun and moon. Interwoven."

"Sure. Whatever you say. But why am I here? *Me*. You said you were waiting? I don't get it. What the fuck for? I don't matter. Never have. I'm just a gutter punk, man."

"Just? No, no. You are much more. You are a missing piece. Or rather, a *hidden* piece. There are many fighting this, and you are being called. The battle will require every tool and volunteer we can muster. To that end, I am a collector and a connector of objects and souls with the power to balance. Disputants to the dark. You are needed. *You*."

Kid chuckled and shook his head, "Listen, I can't. This is so far past nuts. You gotta look somewhere else, okay? I can't help you. Never could, never will. But the box, that's one of your objects? A tool?"

"Yes, its contents. The totem."

"So take it, man. Lotus will try and kill me for losing it, but I don't care anymore. If it gets me out of this freak show, then so be it. I'm fast. I can run. Take the box and let me out of here. Got it? Take this voodoo thing, and let me go."

"There is no *out*. You are a piece of this."

"No! Listen, motherfucker—I don't want the bullshit you're selling!"

"That is inconsequential. *It* wants you. The Dream, the totem, fate. This is a path from which you cannot run."

Before Kid could continue his protest, Horacio's eyes moved again to the sky over the sea. The storm was a gangrenous green-black and much closer now. He frowned and said, "Dwell on it later. In the coming days, you will learn. Some things must be seen and felt, not told. For now, however, you have a need more pressing." He turned back to face Kid. "You are dying."

"The what now?"

"This place is more easily accessible to those on the blurred edge between the living and the not. I'm afraid you are much closer to the latter. You may not want to fight. But do you want to die?"

The nagging, squirming burn in his shoulder told him it was true. The toxic pain now spread over his entire body, branching from the epicenter of his shoulder like a leafless tree covered in thorns.

Do you want to die?

He'd be lying if he said he didn't think about it often. The nest was seven floors up with no guard rails. But Kid realized the answer was *no*. Not yet, anyway, not like this.

He acknowledged, "I can feel it. What did that girl do to me?"

"She poisoned you."

It was undeniable. Kid felt the dark toxin running through his body. It scared him. But he would not let this man, or any other, see that fear.

Despite Kid's effort to mask it, Horacio read the worry on his face. He continued his plea, "We don't have much time. Her contamination is traveling quickly through your body and your animus. Your dream. When it reaches the center, The Story of Kid ends. Badly."

Truth. Burning infection. Dark spreading inside him. It pulsed steadily like a clock. But one not made of gears. One of twisting, groping, gnawing things.

"Fuck," Kid spat.

Horacio watched.

Kid continued, "Alright, hustler—your face says you have a plan. Tell me what it is. Because whatever *this* is," his eye twitched in pain as he moved his shoulder, "I don't want it. Let's make a deal. You get me fixed up. Then we'll *talk* about fights. Just talk. No promises."

The tall man took a sharp breath and clapped his hands together. "That will have to do for now. Because if you die, we will lose the totem as well. We cannot have that. You will have many more questions, and I will answer them in due time. I promise you this. But now, it's time to go. Because first, to carry out the rest, you must live."

The storm loomed only a mile away as if to emphasize his words. A wall of black as tall as the stars, twisting the twilight into sickly tatters. The writhing entities inside it were more apparent than ever. The wind picked up, swirling in furious gales, carrying sand, small sticks, and other detritus. The shrapnel forced their eyes near closed, a tiny gap left open between eyelashes to see.

The Dream howled, phasing between deep earthen groans and sky-shattering cracks of lighting. Heavy rain fell like a thick velvet curtain cut from a stage, a resounding *whumph* as the first million drops reached the sand in unison, followed by the growling chorus of the raging storm.

Horacio shouted over the din, "Take this! It will help you! A token, tuned to my dream." He tipped his body into the wind, took Kid's hand, and carefully slid a wooden ring covered in scuffed red paint onto his finger. "I'm going to send you back!"

He squatted and used cupped hands to dig a trough around Kid's feet in a circle, a few inches deep and wide, which filled with rainwater, creating a moat. The surface danced with the falling raindrops as he drew another larger circle two feet behind Kid, racing to beat the rain. He dug a channel between the two circles, connecting them in the middle. The resulting symbol looked like eyeglasses. The water between the two collided, and the connected shape glowed ghostly turquoise.

"Go to Linh! She can help!"

"Linh? You know Linh?"

"Yes!" He leaned forward to avoid having to continue screaming to be heard. Rain dripped from his nose, and light danced upon his face. "The Silver Doe. You know her as Linh. We're friends, comrades of old. She knows you better than you realize!" Horacio flashed his gap-toothed grin. "When you're free of it, when the poison is gone, come find me. I trust that you will want to. I'll be waiting for you at The Sand."

Before Kid could consider what that final cryptic sentence meant, the circle of light around him grew taller. It seemed to have a personality, a life of its own. It danced around Kid in a spinning, bouncing rhythm, like a primitive tribe celebrating a wedding around a flickering bonfire. Optimism and hope around jubilant green flames. The glowing fire reached the top of his thighs, enveloping them in a strange prickling sensation, which worked its way up to his shoulders. He could no longer sense his body, seeming to consist of only a pair of floating eyes.

The fisherman yelled, "Brace yourself!"

"For what?" Kid yelled back.

"For the fall!

Horacio moved to stand directly in front of him, shoulders square to his, the midnight storm framing him from behind in its billowing darkness. He gave Kid one last look, a curt nod. "Don't forget! The Sand!"

Then, he reared back and kicked him square in the chest. Kid's body, the one he forgot existed, folded around Horacio's foot, and he sailed backward. He expected to fall to the beach, then get up and knock the fool out. Instead, he fell into nothing.

No... Something.

But not a tangible something.

The color of heat, with the scent of snow.

During the commotion, the circle in the sand behind him had grown to the size of a well, large enough for him to fall through without touching the sides. The well became a massive cavern, and he was at its center, falling into forever. Kid's gut lurched into his throat. He closed his eyes, willing himself not to vomit, stars exploding behind his eyelids. Light pulsed around him as he plummeted into the place between dreams.

After a time, upon re-discovering some mastery of himself, he opened his eyes again. He no longer had a sense of up or down, inside or out—he was swept up and rolled around with no independent power source, like a floating bit of fibrous plant matter in a turbulent river.

He struggled, but there were no handholds to be found. No ground from which to fear an impact. No walls to search for a handhold. He fell and continued to fall through a nothing filled with the half-memories of early morning, gliding by like music from a passing car. Maybe he would fall this way forever and never return home.

Is this what happens when you die?

Kid found that he was afraid. His thoughts circled to what he last said to Linh. He told her he wouldn't wait so long to return. It seemed that was a lie. He felt sure he would never leave this place. He would never be able to tell her goodbye.

PART TWO
CRACKS BETWEEN

"The wind had dropped with the sun, and in all that vast world of branches nothing stirred. Any moment, it seemed, the woodland gods, who are to be worshipped in silence and loneliness, might stretch their mighty and terrific outlines among the trees."

— ALGERNON BLACKWOOD, THE WENDIGO

10

POISON

Kid entered the waking world on all fours, ejecting vomit onto a black iron street gutter with punctuated spasms—each contraction wrenching his torso painfully. A few more dry heaves, and at last, nothing remained but the burn of stomach acid filling his mouth and dripping from his nostrils. He fell to the side in a heap, staring at a spinning night sky, its edges glowing with the orange off-light of the city. A few of the brightest stars were visible through the urban light pollution. They swirled and winked at him drunkenly.

After a time, his awareness grew to include the frigid sidewalk against his back. The cold prevented his body from breaking out in new sweat. He was thankful. He decided to lay there a moment and watch the world spin.

Eventually, it slowed. Stars and streetlights swung across his field of vision, then finally decelerated their orbiting journey to become vibrating spotlights, bright and painful to look at, but at least they stayed put. Kid rolled his head to the side, providing yet another familiar bolt of pain.

From that sideways, ground-level viewpoint, he took in his surroundings. The sidewalk dug into his cheekbone as he swiveled his head. Through a one-eye-squint, he read the street signs Bayshore and Waterloo. A half-block away, a glowing backlit plastic sign. San Francisco Recycling Center, green letters on dingy white. He knew the place well enough.

Apparently, the truck driver discovered him when he dropped off the cardboard load for recycling. He reacted in the way that would disrupt his workday the least, dropping Kid off on the sidewalk to fend for himself. Judging by the position of the moon and the lack of pedestrians, it was around two or three in the morning. Kid cursed silently to himself; he'd been knocked out for hours. Horacio's voice was still in his head.

The Dream. Quite ancient. Quite real.

He looked down at his splayed fingers. On his right index finger was a wooden ring covered in scuffed red paint. How? How did he still have the—

"Gaaaaw-damn, you got *whooped,* huh?"

Kid turned to see a burly middle-aged man teetering a few feet away. He wore a pair of white New Balance sneakers at least five sizes too big and had at least three times as much curly black hair on his face as on the top of his head.

"Made a mess too," The man said, using a half-empty pint of brown liquor to point at the puke in the gutter.

"Just give me a hand, will you?" Kid reached toward the welcome passerby and scooted his feet under himself to better prepare to move to a standing position.

The furry-faced man sat his booze down carefully on the

sidewalk, guarding it a moment to ensure it wouldn't tip. He stepped over to Kid and planted his feet wide. A thick-fingered hand, shiny with callus, grasped Kid's and pulled him up with surprising force, causing them to fall into each other. They very nearly tipped over backward together in a comic heap.

Kid pushed off the human lean-to and did his best to look steady, his weight balancing dangerously on his heels. The world still spun. Although, it turned more slowly now, lazily, like a carousel of plastic horses lit by flickering carnival light.

"Been there a time or two, tell you hu-what," said the man from the corner of his mouth while bending over to reclaim his bottle from the sidewalk. "This yours?" He pointed to Kid's bag, a foot from where he picked up his bottle.

It lay next to a pile of crumpled papers and other street trash by a splintered wooden light pole. Lucky thing the recycling truck driver didn't take it as the price for his ride. Or anyone else, for that matter. They would have had a good haul with the cash inside, plus an artifact that gave people the power to enter hidden dream worlds. Pure luck that it was still there. Things near the street in San Francisco didn't stay un-stolen for long.

It all sounded unbelievable, but it didn't *feel* unbelievable. Besides, there it was—the new ring on his finger—the Ring from Somewhere. Kid wondered if it had powers or whatever, like in comics, or if it was just to prove to Kid that there was a lot more to the world than he previously thought.

He looked up from his hand and spat some excess bile on the ground. A bit stuck in his nose still stung, and he couldn't seem to get rid of it. "Yeah, man, that's mine. Thanks." Stepping towards his bag resulted in new swimming buzzes of pain with each footfall. He slowly bent over and grabbed his bag, standing up and slinging it over his shoulder. Kid stifled a grunt, forcing a new grimace of pain into a facial tic.

The man studied Kid's face as his body swayed. "Hey fella, you gonna be alright?"

"Yeah. Nothin' but a thang." Kid said with a forced smile.

The man chuckled and replied, "That's right. No thang but a chicken wang." He smiled and patted Kid on the shoulder with his big calloused hand.

Kid winced from the pain the pat caused. "Alright, my man, I think it's time to land this bird."

He grunted and let Kid on his way.

With ragged-breathed effort, he made it four blocks to a busier street. Just four blocks, and he felt ready to pass out again. There was no way he could walk to Linh's like this.

Linh. She knows you better than you realize.

He straightened himself up and did his best to look like the presentable type of person who stands swaying at a corner in the dead of night, then stepped off the curb to hail a cab. There weren't many left anymore that didn't require an app, and apps took credit cards, which Kid didn't have. Thirty minutes passed before one finally appeared and had the heart or desperation to pull over.

The cabbie lowered the automatic window and called out, "You look like hell, youngblood. But I'm feelin' generous tonight. Ain't gonna leave you hanging, but I got standards. Prepay forty bucks, and if you blow chunks back there, I'm kicking your skinny ass to the curb and keeping the cash."

"Fair enough," Kid croaked as he handed two twenties through the window. "Larkin and Turk."

The door unlocked with a ka-thunk, and he slid into the beat-up black leather. Kid saw his face in the rearview mirror, and where it wasn't ghostly pale, it was bruised and splattered with dried blood. *This cabbie is some good Samaritan. I wouldn't pick me up. No way.*

The cabbie put the car in gear and drove without another word. Kid leaned against the door and put the window down. A bright screen in a meaty plastic housing was mounted on the back of the passenger seat. It blasted bright advertisements, assaulting his seared brain. He closed his eyes to defend them and let the cool darkness of the night air blow over his face.

The cab bounced on spongey shocks like a boat on choppy water, each bump answered by a spasm of pain. The soft glow of streetlights passed over them as they made their way through the city. Through his closed lids, each light was like an illuminated planet whisking by, coming in slow and dim, then bright and focal and brief. Each globe seemed to orbit around the chipped yellow sun of the cab. There was Mars. And Jupiter as well.

"This good?" the cabbie's voice brought his meandering mind back to attention.

"Yeah, across the street, over there by the alley."

The cab pulled over and stopped on whining brakes.

"Good luck."

"With what?"

"Whatever you're dealing with, son. Ain't my business, but I hope you're getting help. I been there. Hanging on the world with white knuckles so I don't fly off to outer space." He studied him in the rearview, then turned around. "Here, take my number. Me and some guys, we meet up every week, just to, you know, *talk*. Sometimes it's good to talk. This city's small when it needs to be."

"What are you talking about? A.A. or something? Man, I'm fine. Just had a rough night is all. Thanks for the ride." He tried the door, but it was still locked.

"We all get rough sometimes. That's human nature. Ain't smooth, get what I'm saying. Just take my number, you know, for whatever."

"Will you open the door if I do?" He reached forward with a grimace to take the business card.

The cabbie held the card for an awkward moment, warmth expressed in his soulful eyes, then unlocked the door. "Name's Jamaal. Take care, son."

Kid replied with a nod and a grunt, then stuffed the card into his jeans pocket. He slowly swung one foot out, then the other, grabbing it by the pant leg to help it along. Then, dutifully, he stepped out into the low yellow buzz under the streetlight and shut the cab door with a thunk.

He stumbled and scraped his way along the sidewalk and down the alley to the back door of Linh's place like a low-budget zombie. His bag felt like it weighed a hundred pounds, and his battered body felt half paralyzed. Lights and colors swam in his vision. He made it to the steel door, just barely. Its familiar rust and bulk felt like a welcome home hug. He pressed the door buzzer with his forehead, resting momentarily with a sigh.

After some time, how much time he wasn't sure, he kept losing track of it; he heard a shuffling behind the door, then the scrape of the cross-bolt being lifted and set to the side.

The door slid open, and he rolled from his tripod position into a rag-doll fall through the new opening, unable to hold his body up any longer.

Linh was there to catch him. She was sturdier than she looked. Kid was not surprised. She smelled like strawberry shampoo. Her hair was still a bit damp from a recent shower. The coolness felt nice on his face.

"Tom, close the door. Kid? What happened?"

"Missed a delivery. Motherfuckers got me." He pointed to his shoulder with a shaking hand.

Linh stuck a finger into one of the burned holes in his hoodie and brought it back with a pained hiss. A bit of black smoke trailed off her finger. Her face contorted from concern into child-like fear. Then, as quickly as it fell, the mask rearranged itself.

"Kid, let's get you upstairs and lie you down. Tom, help me."

Linh got out from under Kid's arm, and Tom put him over his shoulder, fireman style. Tom carried Kid into the apartment and laid him down as gently as possible on the couch. The apartment was cozy and simple—all hand-me-downs, but clean, like it was decorated from a Goodwill. The sofa sat beside the apartment's only square window that featured a grand vista of an hourly motel across the street—its name 'The Westchester' lit in magenta neon. She took a seat on the coffee table next to the couch.

After rummaging around somewhere else in the apartment, Tom appeared next to her with a large black leather bag. Linh yanked the heavy-duty zipper to open it and pulled out a pair of sturdy scissors, which she used to cut his shirt. It did not seem to be her first time acting as a combat medic.

"Hey," Kid complained, "wait... this is vintage..."

"Hush, or I'll make you wear a Christmas sweater."

He whimpered at the destruction of his original Buzzcocks shirt, but another wave of pain distracted him from further protest. Linh laid the sliced pieces of the shirt away from his body. The sweat and blood-stained strips of yellow fabric radiated out from his torso like dirty cotton sun rays. The smell of toasted tobacco wafted into the room as Tom lit a cigarette by an open window. A car alarm bleated in the distance. The ceiling light was uncovered and painfully bright, revealing too many graphic details of the carnage in the living room. Purple-black spider veins spread from the charred flesh of Kid's shoulder, emanating from four puss-filled puncture wounds the size of small fingertips. The rest of his skin was a clammy blue-grey, decorated with a thousand trembling beads of sweat. Along with dark bruises on his ribs, he had the beginnings of two black eyes, and his torn hands were covered in grime and blood. Kid looked like shit.

Linh asked with practiced calm, "What happened?"

"Delivering a package... nothing new," Kid replied through a pain-clenched jaw. "But... the old man... he was already dead when I got there. These freaks, maybe junkies... I don't know... tried to get me and my bag, but I got away. One of them hit my shoulder with something. I don't know what, but it messed me up bad. Then it's blurry. Hard to remember when I was awake and when I was out of it. There's a lot that doesn't make sense. No sense at all. Straight fucking bananas. Crazy dreams. Crazy. Then I woke up on the sidewalk down in

Bayview and got a cab here. I'm sorry, I didn't know where else to go. Didn't want trouble at the hospital."

"Junkies?"

"Yeah, or PCP, bath salts, some new shit or something, I dunno. Their eyes were all pupil. They looked strung out, but they didn't move like bobbleheads. And they were young. Didn't talk like it, though. They killed that old man. I know they did. Black holes in his chest, just like my arm. Would have killed me too. Could smell it on 'em. Like a sick ward. Ever smell that? Someone dying? Like the bottom of a trash can. Rotten and sweet at the same time. Dark eyes. Dark heart. Dark..." Kid was becoming incoherent.

Linh took his face in her hand and turned him gently to force eye contact. "Kid, you're not telling me everything. What about the dreams?" She took her hand away to rummage through her bag.

"Don't know, Linh. Doesn't make any sense. None of it does. I'm trying my best to keep it together, you know? But I think... afraid... maybe I'm going crazy." Kid coughed, grimaced, and clutched his shoulder. After a moment, the wave of pain subsided somewhat, and he relaxed.

"You're not crazy. Tell me what happened."

"It's fading away, hard to keep a hold of..."

"Try."

"...a tall man. Dude looked like Hari. Just like him. But, young and sculpted, and like... magical. Golden eyes, like a cat. Said he *was* a cat. A cat!" Kid chuckled, bloodshot eyes rolling deliriously as he continued, "A big storm, big big big, like a pit of black snakes. Gonna eatcha up. Something's in the package —a *totem*. Find Linh. She knows. He gave me a ring. How do I have this, Linh? If it was a dream—if I'm not crazy—then how do I have this ring?"

He moved to show her. Linh held his hand and ran her thumb over the wooden ring's chipped red paint.

"Horacio," She whispered with a frown.

"That's what he said! *Hor-ayshi-oooh*. Am I imagining this too? Ah, man... I'm losing it, losing it—" Kid shifted excitedly, grimacing from the pain the movement caused. "Losing it bad, bad—losing it bad..." His fevered eyes rolled as he babbled.

"Kid. Settle down and stay still. Listen. It would probably be better if you were crazy. If you were dreaming or if this was all just one of your silly sunglass trips. But it's not. You're *here* now. You were *there* then. If you will believe someone, believe me, okay? This is real. Dangerously so. Now, I need you to tell me more. Focus, okay? I need you to focus. What about the package? You mentioned a totem."

His eyes swam but found her. "It's in my bag, never opened it, never. Tell Ben I never opened it. I don't know what's... Horacio said that it took me to The Dream." Kid giggled, and his eyes again rolled to white as he returned to soft babbling, "Capital T capital D. Whatever *that* means. Capital *D,* man. Stands for *dicked*, that's what."

Linh reached for his backpack, and Kid's eyes shot open, showing red splotches of burst capillaries. He shouted, "Don't open it! You do, I'm done. They'll sink me." He groaned, "Probably already... Ben's gonna... ugh fffuu..."

"Tom? Get ready. We're blown. If they're not already here, they will be soon."

Previously a quiet cigarette-smoking wallflower, Tom's

demeanor shifted abruptly, becoming tense and militant. His heavy footsteps receded down the hall as he left to prepare. Outside, it started raining. Droplets ran down the window.

Linh laid her hand on Kid's chest. "Worry about Ben later. First, you need to survive this." He tried to focus on her, but his eyes swam worse than ever, doing sickly figure-eights as his head lolled. She pushed him gently, forcing him to lie down completely. "I got you. I'm here."

Kid whispered, voice ragged and tired, "That's what you said... you said..." His eyes rolled, fluttered, then closed. "Said you'd come get me if I called...said..." A last trailing mumble, "You'd come find me..."

She rested her hand along the side of his face. "Told you."

11
WATCHER

After Alice Unknown watched the cute street boy escape the Chinatown apartment, she knew Delilah had infected him with a blight. He favored his left side, and she noticed the burn holes in his shoulder. Poor guy. His final hours would be awful. How he was surviving *hours* instead of seconds was a complete mystery. Regardless, nobody lasts forever.

In addition to the nasty things a blight did, it left what was known as a shard in the victim. And with the right know-how, they were as trackable as any GPS beacon. Thus, the twins followed the boy, and she followed them in turn. The two hunters were blissfully unaware she was watching them case a tiny apartment above a run-down Vietnamese restaurant.

Hidden inside was the boy, and she would meet him soon. On the one hand, she felt bad for not robbing him before he tried to make the drop in Chinatown. If she had, he would likely never have met the twins and would have been spared this agony. But it wasn't the right time. Instead, she waited and watched, listening to what most would call intuition. Alice knew better than to use that misnomer, however.

As a graduate of The Young School, she knew unequivocally that The Dream was woven from the interlaced strands connecting all things. In addition to that knowledge, Alice was a special kind of traveler—one with the talent to feel the slightest fluctuations in those connecting fibers.

When the boy touched the package containing the totem, she felt and saw the fabric between things move—like a planet's orbit causing a tiny wobble of its central star. So, she didn't intervene. Not then, at least.

Alice's patience was rewarded with quite the show.

Three events so far. Two could be coincidences. But three? That was something else entirely. Fate? Orchestration? Synchronism? Who knows, but not a coincidence.

First, the roof-jumping street kid gave the slip to the twins in suped-up stolen bodies. Escaping them should have been difficult for a pro, much less some tramp—especially one hobbled by a blight.

Second, despite nearly nine hours of infection, he was still alive, even if just barely. Most would have collapsed in a few paces if not on the spot.

The third event was the most interesting. Despite being wholly uneducated and untrained in its ways, he walked The Dream. She felt it, clear as day. His traveling animus had shone like a lighthouse in the distance.

While tracking the twins and waiting for the boy to

return, Alice spent several hours considering how that might be. Perhaps he was naturally attuned. Rare but far from impossible; she grew up in a school full of such people. Most were cherry-picked at a young age, but logically, there were plenty roaming about with no clue they were capable of being a traveler of The Dream. It was possible that his ability woke under the duress of survival. At the very least, she figured that was true. But she also understood that could not be all there was to it. The situation was evolving beyond simplicity and happenstance.

The third possibility was that the totem helped him travel to The Dream. That made sense. And that meant he connected with it. Unlocked it. At least partially. But the chances of a key and totem appearing in the exact location simultaneously seemed impossible. It *seemed* completely random. She chuckled to herself. There is no such thing as random. It's either off or on. Yes or no. Zero or one. Someone had flipped a switch. She felt it. Someone pulled a breaker, and now the current was running. Things were getting interesting.

After the boy escaped the twins and things started looking dicey, Alice sent her phone on a ride to nowhere in the back seat of a Jeep Wrangler. What she planned next would take her far into the dark grey, and she didn't need anyone tracking her.

Fortunately, she'd picked up an ancient iPod at a thrift store to still listen to music in situations like this. Someone filled the thing to the brim with all sorts of music nearly twenty years ago, so it was like a time capsule. She loved it. After thumbing through the playlists, she finally found a song that felt right for the moment. It was a funky dance track with lyrics that made you nod your head. LCD Soundsystem, a song called *North American Scum*.

She tapped play and practiced footwork along with the driving music, shell-top Adidas shifting and sliding on the rooftop gravel. Raindrops spattered her forehead and cheeks as she watched, waited, and danced.

12

GLASS

Linh rummaged through her bag and pulled out two necklaces, both with misshapen bronze coins hanging in their middle. They were ancient, from a long-gone Byzantine. She received them from a mentor in what seemed to be another life. The coins absorbed an impressive amount of twin ley energy in their long lifetime, which she could sense as they rested in her palm. They would help her navigate Kid's blight-tainted dream, into which she would shortly venture.

Almost anything can be a totem and serve nearly any purpose, ranging from the powerful to the preposterous. In this case, twin brothers owned the coins, accompanying them throughout their lives. As they rested against their breasts, the coins saw the trials of youth, love, battle, and death. They were drawn to one another and could be used to locate an animus lost within The Dream. This particular totem's key, Linh knew, was the love that connected siblings. For the coins to do their job, both new wearers needed to care for one another similarly. That emotional connection served as a magnet and anchor.

She looped one coin around Kid's neck, laying it next to his other necklace, a simple silver wedding band engraved M+S. Seeing the silver ring again brought back a flood of bitter memory.

Michael Thames & Saría Landros. Kid's parents... Twenty-ish years ago, they escaped Mara's hold. What could allow them to do such a thing? Wrestle free from the iron grip of an ancient? The answer was love. The kind parents have for their first child.

Sadly, their freedom was short-lived. Only one year after their departure, they were caught and forced to return. Mother, father, and sweet baby boy were tortured and studied because of what they were and had managed to accomplish. Saría did not survive the ordeal. But, somehow, Michael escaped with his son.

The guilt and shame of destroying the Thames family nearly drove Linh mad. It didn't matter that Mara made it happen. The darkness in her heart remained. Only the realization that she carried her own child brought her back from the brink.

With that knowledge, she also abandoned her life at The Young School. Like Michael, she ran. The ancient queen's soldiers came after her, but tracking a skilled navigator is not easy.

After her own year of harrowing, continuously narrowing escapes, Linh made the difficult decision to leave her daughter in an orphanage. No name, no history, no connections or family. She reasoned that it would be safer. Bian's armor would be her anonymity.

Years later, when the chase finally slowed, and it felt safe enough to do so, Linh searched for her little girl. To her despair, it was in vain. Even with her significant powers, she could not find even the smallest of threads.

That same year, again in the depths of depression and close to ending things for herself, Horacio appeared at her doorstep with a tale and a task.

He said that for what was done, she owed a life debt.

Horacio said it was time to pay.

With her whole heart, Linh agreed.

It turned out that Michael was forced to make the same difficult choice she had. He knew that if agents of The Young School found his child, he would be indoctrinated, put to death, or sold. It was a fate he refused to allow. No matter the cost.

With that vow, Michael gave his boy to Horacio, who tucked him away in the American social services system. Dangerous and rife with abuse, but anonymous. A name can hold power. But for Kid and Linh's lost daughter, the lack of one would ensure some semblance of safety.

Thus, on that day at her doorstep, Horacio charged Linh with watching over Michael's son from a careful distance.

It will be painful to watch him grow, thinking he's alone.

But it's necessary. Important for what comes next.

You will want to save him. But you must not.

This is the only way.

Keep him secret until it's time.

Because if he knows, they know.

And we cannot allow that. Not yet.

Do you understand?

She did. Over the years, Linh often wanted to step in, but she controlled the urge. However, Horacio never said she had to stop Kid from drawing near on his own accord.

So, when the boy arrived at her restaurant, by pure chance, if you believe in such things, she welcomed him. And as that careful emotional distance inevitably and fatefully closed over the years, a child saved her for the second time in her life—at least in part. He illuminated the relentless darkness of losing her child and destroying others. Kid gave her a second chance to be some semblance of a mother.

Now, it was time to pay him back.

She would find his spirit lost in the malignancy of his nightmare. Or she would die trying. That was her truth.

Linh sighed, ending the long breath with her shoulders back, head up, resolute. She looped the old coin over her neck and let it lay near her heart. Next, she pulled a small glass tube from the bag. Tinkling could be heard as it moved against other bits of glass. The liquid inside was translucent blue, like sea ice.

Kid's eyes were closed. Linh said his name, but he did not respond. His jaw clenched tightly in pain. His eyes moved restlessly behind his lids. The rain grew heavy and flung itself against the window with the patter of a crazed symphony.

Still holding the glass vile in one hand, Linh called down the hallway, "Tom?"

"It's time then?" He replied. Tom's hands were wrapped in boxer's tape, and his wiry arms now seemed martial and capable.

"Yes. But you know how rusty I am. I'm using a sopor, so I'll be in deep. If things go poorly, you know what to do."

"Linh... With a blight... even if you were sharp as you used to be, those things... they're no cake-walk. You sure this is what you want to do?"

She raised a warning eyebrow. "What do you mean, Tom?"

"I mean, it's not like he's yours. Never was. No one asked, just showed up. I'd understand if you didn't—"

"What? What do you think you understand? No, that's enough of that. I'm doing this. That's final. Will you be my nightguard or not?"

Tom's worried face shifted to a small reassuring smile. "Yeah, yeah. Of course. I'll keep an eye out just like I always have. You'll be in and out just like you've always done. It's been a while, but talent doesn't die, and I'm not as geriatric as I look. Skidrow's gonna owe me a pack of smokes, though. The nice ones. Davidoff."

Linh studied Tom's face. In their odd upbringing together, there were few people to trust. The physical and emotional conditioning of The Young School meant that maintaining a real friendship behind the façade was nearly impossible. But they managed it. They made a good team back then. She walked The Dream. He guarded her sleep. This night would be no different, although now they were much older, faces lined with age.

"He hates when you call him that, you know. Anyway, I'll hold him to it." She popped the cork off the vial between pointer finger and thumb. "Hit the lights."

She held the glass tube to her nose and took several deep breaths to pull the powerful drug into her nasal cavity and lungs. Linh recapped the vial and set it down on the wooden floor. Her cheeks flushed scarlet as she lay down on the coffee table, her legs dangling. She felt like she was falling back into the table as if it were a bed of cumulonimbus clouds. As she watched Kid's face, his eyes continued to dance under curl-lashed lids below a forehead covered in trembling beads of sweat.

Linh reached across and held his hand.

It was there—his thread, dangerously thin and taut.

He had time, but not much.

Bringing her right hand to her breast, she beat her chest three times near her heart, directly on top of the ancient coin.

One. Two. Three. Slow and strong.

The beats echoed through her mind like a door knocked at the entrance to a church, each beat reverberating larger and louder than the last, bouncing against the stone and disappearing into the timber rafters with the cooing doves.

After the third beat, her pupils dilated to their maximum size, and the bright yellow ceiling light grew like an exploding sun. She shut her eyes against the too-bright light and relaxed her hand against her chest, the other lightly grasping Kid's. The woman, whose name these days was no longer The Silver Doe but Linh Phuong, fell into The Dream.

Tom flipped the overhead light off, leaving only a short dim lamp. It cast long shadows over the side-by-side bodies of Linh and Kid, her's calm, his trembling. Tom sat beside Linh and carefully brushed a loose bit of hair back into place, leaving his hand to frame her face.

He spoke softly, "Be careful in there, will you?"

As his hand rested on her head, he looked out the window

at the rainy night. It was late and early at the same time. 3:14. The Devil's Hour. An ominous time if one took up in lucky and unlucky numbers, which Tom did, or if one took up in the supernatural, which Tom did as well.

He preferred the term extraordinary over supernatural. Extraordinary implied that it was within nature but not well understood and outside the bounds of everyday experience, while supernatural indicated that it was outside of nature. He knew well enough that many surprising and unbelievable things existed in the natural world.

As the neon light across the street painted the rain red, Tom could not shake the feeling that there were no coincidences, that there *was* such a thing as fate. She was a vindictive bitch, uninterested in tales of retribution, the needs of mortal men, those who live but one life, love, and if they're lucky, are loved back, then die.

13
TWINS

Through the eyes of his stolen vessel, Poe McAvoy watched the apartment across the street. From the third-floor window of their cheap hotel in the Tenderloin, he could see light flickering through a small square window. Without turning, he asked his sister, "Think the old Doe's out yet?"

Delilah McAvoy, whose animus was currently in control of the hijacked body of the adolescent Wan Ting Jiang with the stylish bob haircut, did not answer. She was listening to her blight shard. It took several hours to root into the boy's dream, but it was now pulsing a clear signal that they had followed.

Rather than immediately storming the entrance, they decided to stake out in a disgusting hotel across the street. It smelled like body odor, stale sex, and burned plastic—the telltale aroma of smoked crack or meth. The drapes seemed to suffer a necrotic wasting disease, their disintegrated remnants hanging on by browned and blackened strands. A single stained mattress, no box spring or sheets, lay in the middle of the tiny room. Imagining that parasites were waiting at the edge of the bed for an opportunity to take a ride, she kept her distance. She wrinkled her nose again. The *fucking* smell.

It brought back terrible memories of a tainted youth; one Mara saved her from—the life of pretty little girls, surviving alone, tucked away in the recesses of a rotating list of ratty San Leandro apartments. Pretty little boys often shared the same fate, though less publicized. Poe was an unwilling rent boy too, but if the fact continued to bother him into adulthood, he kept it hidden.

Delilah willed herself not to breathe. The fact that it was a hijacked nose and not her own did not help matters. The connection to the psyche was there. She refused to sit down or touch anything. As usual, Poe seemed unperturbed and leaned casually against the wall. With the hotel room lights off, their bodies were concealed in shadows, only subtle contours edge-lit by red neon from the sign for the hotel above their room. Then the rain came on, droplets refracting crimson light as they ran down the window.

Their view allowed them to watch the restaurant's entrance, the apartment's single window, and the alleyway alongside the building. Delilah considered finding a way through the window, but the building's face was sheer, and she had no equipment to rappel from the roof. In any case, she and Poe had a different strategy. The twins could not afford another mistake. They would wait until the odds were in their favor.

After Poe chased the boy, she hadn't bothered to keep up. Although she was surprised her blight didn't kill him, she was confident in her tracking shard. The mishap turned out to be good fortune. Not only did her shard lead them here, but it also appeared two long-escaped animus agents were harboring him. She didn't know what they called themselves now, but once upon a time, the middle-aged female traveler's codename was the Silver Doe, and her lifelong nightguard, The Tiger. She thought they were cheesy handles, but whatever. After an illustrious career as agents of The Young School, they went missing. Delilah was just a teenager at the time. Barely graduated herself. But even now, after twenty years, Delilah remembered the havoc The Doe's betrayal caused. What luck, here they were, alive and well, running a hole-in-the-wall pho joint less than a mile from the school's Northern California headquarters.

They planned to let her go into the boy's dream. While she was asleep, she would be weak. The twins would take out her nightguard, then recover the totem as their mission from Mara demanded.

But for her, for fun, she would also end their lives.

That she would do for herself, after all, self-care is essential.

At last, she replied to her brother, "No, they're still up. Watch the light. They'll dim it when she goes under."

"Sure we can't just jump them now? They look ready for a retirement home."

"Blowhard. You couldn't handle them both."

Poe acknowledged, "No, probably not. This body's about trashed."

He touched the badly broken nose on the face of his frame, Li Qiang Jiang of the short black buzzcut. One of two bodies of

Chinese orphans they'd stolen by hijacking their minds through the connecting pathways of The Dream. Trafficked across the Pacific, they had no idea that this would be their purpose—to be disposable vehicles for the exploits of The Young School.

He could only breathe through his mouth without annoying gurgling-whistle noises. To add to matters, his elbow was shattered from throwing the crowbar and falling from the truck. When he moved it, pieces of bone ground in the elbow.

All in all, though, his frame still had some mileage left. There was now, and the now was good. Recovering the totem *and* two truants would be a big deal. Gold stars all around. Might even earn some time off he was desperately craving.

"Stop fidgeting," Delilah said, the tone of big sister clear, even if older by only ten minutes.

Poe gave his sister a nah-nah smirk, dropped his hand, and slid it into his pocket.

The twins waited and watched, their dilated black eyes reflecting the night like still puddles. The rain came on more heavily. After some time, with an exasperated huff, Delilah opened the window a few inches to let in some desperately needed fresh air, then stepped back to the side.

Poe glanced at his sister, "You know you don't *need* to smell anything you don't wanna. You always were terrible at sense channeling. I never knew why you were Mara's favorite."

"We each have our talents."

The truth was that she wasn't Mara's favorite. No matter how badly she wanted to be. No matter how hard she worked.

No matter how much she sacrificed. There was The Doe, and then after a brief time in the sun, there was Alice. Fancy bitches who'd never put the real work in, not like she had. *Nobody* put it in like she had. But now they'd know. All of them. No more shadow, no more doubt.

She would extinguish The Doe for good and take the totem home. That would prove her worth with finality and even push Alice, the upstart, down below her. She stood a bit straighter, a smile playing at the corner of her mouth. She looked at her brother. Suppose she would need to bring the idiot along. He was useful. He could be *her* tiger. Or dog, more like. She swore he looked like one watching for the mailman, his jaw hanging, mouth breathing.

"What?" Poe asked, catching her stare.

"Love you." Delilah applied her sweetest smile.

His eyebrows raised briefly, then he relaxed and smiled, "You too, sis."

As they watched, just as their minds began to wander from the length of the stakeout, the apartment light dimmed to a subdued yellow.

Poe straightened, "Alright, shins in."

"Shins in?"

"Yeah, like a cannonball. 'Let's go, *shins in.*' Know what I mean?"

She stared at him like an insect.

He grinned. "You're no fun."

Delilah found it interesting that a person's mannerisms and facial expressions transferred through to a frame, so much so that after a bit of experience, it didn't matter who they were riding. They were recognizable. Of course, mannerisms could be camouflaged for better subterfuge, but that wasn't Poe's talent. He was a pretty bruiser, and that was about it. Amazing how different twins can be. The fact simultaneously amused and disgusted her.

"You're an idiot," she said.

The twins waited ten more minutes, then left the hotel room, down the ratty, stained stairwell, and continued past the bored night clerk. The whispy-haired potato of a man eyed the young siblings leaving the hourly hotel together for only a moment before returning, unphased, to his glowing phone. They barely blipped his radar; he'd seen just about *everything* before.

14
BLIGHT

The area into which Linh suddenly dropped was so pitch black she could not tell if her eyes were open or closed. The fall was abrupt, like someone changing the TV channel, one reality crashing into the next without subtlety. This was how it was with a sopor. Going into The Dream naturally was better, akin to one song fading into the next. Linh would have preferred that, fading instead of falling. She used to step in and out with a gentle breath. But those were the old days.

She lifted the ancient necklace over her head and extended her arm, holding the dangling coin like a lantern as it glowed faint white-blue. Turning slowly in a circle, she watched the light dim, brighten, and dim again. It was telling her which direction to go. Unfortunately, beyond way-finding, it illuminated nothing in the darkness but her hand and a bit of the closest cool, damp air.

Walking carefully forward, Linh whistled a light melancholy tune, a song from her childhood. She wasn't sure what inspired it. Linh hadn't so much as hummed the old lullaby in twenty years. But for some reason, for now, it felt right. The melody echoed softly and swam through the air like the ghost of a child dancing between trees.

She placed one foot in front of the next, exploring the ground before shifting her weight. The whistled tune helped her morale and assisted her way-finding, her proximity to a wall discernible by the character of the echo. Using this technique, she found the closest barrier of rough wet stone. It seemed she was inside a cave or perhaps a natural cellar. Running one hand along the wall and the other waving in front of her to prevent a painful collision, Linh made her way forward.

Caution was crucial as this was no typical partition of The Dream. Everyone has their little microcosm, their dream within the greater Dream. It's where they venture when they sleep, where the subconscious and deep memories reside. The dreamscape commonly known to all. But one could dive far deeper than that, and with Kid's dream tainted by blight, the peril would be intensified by orders of magnitude. It was a broken maze in which a person could become permanently lost.

But if anyone could find Kid's lost spirit, it would be Linh.

If she didn't, he would not be graced with simple death. He would remain comatose; his spirit lost within itself. Eventually, his physical body would die, but his animus would remain. It would drift in the places between dreams and, thanks to the blight, would endure a never-ending cycle of his most tortured memories. It would be a true and vicious hell.

The cave shuddered with a resounding thud, tearing her

away from her thoughts. It was like a bomb impacting somewhere nearby. She coughed on dust as it shook loose from the stone ceiling and rained to the floor.

Her veteran experience made her all too aware that the tremor was the mark of something happening in the waking world, shaking her sleeping vessel.

They had been found.

Time was shorter than ever.

15
BOY

For the second time in less than eight hours, Kid awoke in a very different place than where he'd lost consciousness. However, on this second occasion, he was unaware that his new surroundings were strange. Due to the psychic taint Delilah infected him with, Kid did not know that he should be in Linh's apartment. He was only aware of the current *there*, the present *when*.

In his cancerous dream, deep in the recesses of his mind, Kid lay on the remnants of an old queen-size bed in a typical low-income suburban tract house. A ceiling fan spun listlessly, with fuzzy dust collected on the leading edges of its drooping blades. Everything in the home was covered in a layer of yellow grime as if it had been abandoned for years. The house's layout was such that he could see the front door from his spot on the bed. Oddly, it was open. Sun shone on a patchy yellowed lawn.

Kid's hand moved to his chest to pat his keepsake ring for

reassurance. But three things were strange. Two of which he was aware.

First, there was an extra necklace—from it hung a coin so old that whatever had been printed on it was indiscernible.

Second, his left hand was stained black, like it was dipped in ink.

And third—unbeknownst to him and outside his awareness in this twisted place, his body had taken the form of his past. The stained hand that grasped the necklace for reassurance was that of a skinny, malnourished twelve-year-old boy.

Before dwelling on the strange coin or the dark stain, Kid realized he could *smell* the yellow dust covering everything. He could feel particles enter his nose and mouth as he breathed. It tasted acrid and spoiled, obviously toxic.

With sudden urgency, he jumped from the bed and stumbled outside. Once in the sun, he took in a thankful gasp of fresh air and studied the area through squinted eyes.

Not for the better, his surroundings were immediately apparent. It was the neighborhood of the last foster home he'd survived before choosing to run and make a living on the street. But it didn't feel like a memory. To Kid, this place in his past was real and, at the moment, all he could know.

Kid was lost and straying farther with each child-sized step.

A mailman walked by, wearing short blue shorts, hairy tanned legs with muscled calves, and long wool socks under sensible brown shoes. He flipped up the sunshade attachment of his glasses. "If it ain't *the kid*. Can't say I'm an expert, but pretty sure you're 'sposed to be in school."

"I was sick—"

"Then why are you outside? You shouldn't be outside."

"Patricia said it'd do me good," Kid lied.

The mailman raised an eyebrow. "She probably just wanted you out of her hair."

"I guess," Kid agreed, eyes moving to the concrete sidewalk.

"Alright, well, get on home before you start trouble." He adjusted his satchel, flipped the sunshade down, and walked on.

Like most adult interactions, the short conversation ignited Kid's fight or flight response. He clenched and unclenched small fists, willing his heart to slow down. Through secondhand Wrangler jeans with faded knees, he reached down to scratch his thighs where cigarette burns were in various states of healing—some fresh and still stinging, some scabbed over, and dozens of small puckered scars.

The light in the sky was fading, the dusking purple filtering through the line of trees beyond the power plant at the end of the block. The buzzing electric transformers cast long steampunk shadows down the length of the street. They seemed to grow and grasp at him. A violent bang echoed in the distance, scaring the black crows from the trees in screeching droves.

Kid turned away from the frightened birds and back to the task at hand. His foster, Daryl Hodgekiss, would be home soon. If the school had called, he and Patricia would know that he cut class today. Daryl would call her Patty Cakes, then slap her gigantic rear while winking at Kid through his Coke-bottle bifocal lenses, pushing them back up his nose with his thick red finger, red like his tree trunk neck and flaking rosacea cheeks. His short-sleeved western-style work shirt would be stained yellow at the armpits. In the breast pocket would be a half-empty soft pack of Pall Malls. As always, his bulk would overcome Kid, and when it did, it would reek of stale smoke, halitosis, and gasoline. He'd take a big pull of his cigarette to stoke the ember red, and it would melt a small circle into his thigh.

Kssssssssss...

The sound of skin burning.

The sound that's spelled like a kiss.

If you cry, you die, shitheel.

What even are you?

Hard to be mean to an alley mutt. But let's give it a try.

Hold your hat. Here comes another.

A deep drag of the half-burned Pall Mall. Yellow bottom teeth showing as he inhales smoke deep into his lungs. The cherry long and red-hot like a Christmas light.

Kssssssssssss...

I see you thinking about it. Don't even.

You cry, you die. Remember that.

Keep it with you. I'm making you strong, boy.

Knee-on-chest compression. Stifled whimpers.

Hot pink wounds. Tomorrow, yellow scabs.

Let me see your eyes.

You cry, you die.

Ksssssssssssssss...

Instead of going to that house, Kid could run to the woods as he often did. There was a special place where they couldn't find him for at least a little while. A place where he listened to the birds and replied to their songs with his own. There, he built a makeshift fort on the side of a ravine down by a stream, where the sunlight shone through the leaves to project dappled patterns on the forest floor. But Daryl or Patricia would eventually find him—like always. If not them, then the well-meaning gas station clerk, the mailman, or Old Lady Gifford down the street, one of the few other people living in the nearly empty neighborhood. They thought it was a good Samaritan act to send him *home*. But that's not what it was. It was hell.

But Kid knew this game. It wasn't his first lousy foster, just the worst of the bunch. You just had to hide. But where do you hide when there's nowhere to go? You hide inside yourself. You build a little fort buried deep in the woods of your mind. Once you figured out how, it was easy. A little room deep inside to lock everything away. You can handle anything if you just put it in the room.

Maybe if he kept practicing, Kid could learn to hide forever. Then he would forget about this town with its empty thin-walled tract houses, yellow grass, buzzing power plant, cigarette burns, and cat food dinners. He would be free to go and do as he pleased. But first, he would survive. *That's* the name of the game. You hide where you can, and you survive.

Kid released a resigned breath and crossed the street to enter the house where darkness lived. As soon as he entered the foyer, Patricia stepped around the corner from the living room to confront him. She had been waiting. Her hands rested on the bulging shelves of flesh under her stained nightgown, which she wore constantly, even to the supermarket.

Her lip curled like a dog's. "Look who's home. Where've you been?"

He tried to discern if she knew he didn't go to school. He wondered if it would even matter if she did know. Would it be worse if he lied? Should he take the punishment now or later? Daryl wasn't home yet. She wasn't as bad as him, *usually*. Kid considered these things with darting eyes—the calculus of the cornered.

"You answer me *now*. Where Have You Been?" Her eyes gleamed with a cruel light. She seemed as excited as she was angry. The gleam told Kid that there would be no correct answer.

Kid summed up his courage and replied, "Didn't go."

"And you don't even try to hide it. Hmmph. Not even ashamed. Just like I tried telling Papa, that scab of a boy won't amount to a thing. Trouble and trash. Trash and trouble, hand in hand. If it weren't for our grace and our patience." She hocked up a loogie and swallowed it back down. "That does it. You're going to timeout. Take them off."

Kid's brow twisted. "Not that—"

"Off."

"I'll go, I'll go, just let me keep—"

Her hand shot out, grabbing a handful of his shirt, and she shook him violently.

"Off! Off! OFF!" Spittle hung from quivering lips the color of bruises.

Then, just like that, Kid went to his hiding place, the place inside his mind. His face softened to slack, gaze pinned to the distance, somewhere beyond the wood-paneled walls, somewhere in the forest beyond the power plant, in a dilapidated fort, camouflaged with moss and mud.

His clothes lay in a small, sad pile at his feet. Patricia kicked them to the side to land in a box of stinking cat litter. She grabbed him by the neck and pushed him forward. Somewhere, far away, it hurt. Somewhere, far away, he was ashamed—all seventy hungry pounds of him.

"What'd you do to your arm? Why's it all black? Have you been playing in the dirt?" She wrinkled her nose, pushed him forward by his small neck, too skinny for his age, and continued shoving him down the hallway like a cow in a corral.

They passed the living room, with its lover's pair of La-Z-Boy recliners sitting in front of a gigantic seventy-inch TV, the most expensive item in the house. Advertisements projected blaring color and sound, something about an exceptionally absorbent towel on a two-for-one special if purchased immediately. The salesman's teeth were too white—sharp bits of exposed bone.

"Move it." She pushed him harder, causing him to trip and fall to his knees. "Up!" A foot to his bare, already bruised ribs. "UP!" Another foot to his testicles, which were exposed by the fall. Pain exploded, deep and black in his brain, bringing him back to the moment. Then a twisting yank to his hair pulled him back up to standing. Somewhere in Kid's mind, he reminded himself to shave his head so that could never happen again.

As they marched, they passed a long glass china cabinet. Inside were dozens of small porcelain elephants. Each hand-painted sculpture should have been dusted a few times per year, then set back in the case. But these hadn't been wiped in a very long time. They watched with painted smiles from beneath a sheen of toxic bone-yellow grime.

They arrived at the basement doorway, off the side of the kitchen. Patricia grabbed a key, hidden within her glacial bosom, and unlocked the door's thick padlock. She shoved him in, trying to get him to trip and fall down the stairs as he had in the past. But he didn't fall. He'd learned to catch himself in a trot midway down, bare feet on splintered wood. By the time he reached the bottom, the wedge of light behind him disappeared, followed by the *click-ka-chunk* of the lock echoing in the basement dark.

Kid walked across the packed dirt floor to a familiar light that played in the otherwise pitch-black basement. It was the tiny flickering flame of the water heater pilot light, partly obscured by its metal cover. It had been his comforting friend over a hundred times by then, often several hungry days at a stretch. It gave him light and, through a small leak in its side, enough water to survive dark days.

He sat before it, cross-legged and naked, imagining he was a caveman crouched by a campfire. Instead of cobwebbed floor joists in the darkness above, he imagined stars. Orion. The Little Dipper. And Aquila, the eagle which bore the lightning bolt of Zeus. Kid imagined the moon and basked his upturned face in ghostly white light. He imagined being surrounded by a forest of golden-leaved aspen trees, protecting him, watching him with charcoal eyes.

Kid wondered what ancient people thought of the moon. What did they think of the stars before they were named? And about dreams? During a time when people thought of mind and body and the world as connected and unified, a time when all three simply were and would be.

In his mind's ear, a melody whistled in the distance. It was sweet and slow, almost sad. The song seemed to weave between the imaginary trees like a timid wind. Over the night-glinted snow, the tune sifted through the distance to land at his heart. It lifted the boy's lost spirit, and he felt less alone.

As he watched the tiny fire, black mold grew on the basement floor and walls. It stopped at the edge of the light as if allergic. But eventually, it found its grasping way into the long shadow cast by his body, squirming toward his exposed back.

16

CRACK

After fumbling her way through the darkness of the cave for what felt like far too long, Linh glimpsed a soft light in the distance. A brisk wind whistled through the entrance, rustling her hair. She stepped out into the light, revealing a narrow red rock canyon. The sky was open, cold, and blue. The narrow pathway between the stone opened to both the right and left. Which way should she go? Where was Kid hidden?

Directly ahead, a small gnarled pine tree grew from a crevice in the stone, twisting to find the sun. Under different circumstances, she might carefully remove it to create a natural Bonsai. Linh hung the necklace from a branch and waited.

For a long moment, it did nothing. Then the coin began to sway as if in a gentle wind. Before long, the sway grew to a swing and eventually, the swing pushed hard and stayed to the right, stirring the air and defying gravity. She removed the necklace from the branch and returned it to her neck, patting it softly like the head of a helpful child. She turned and walked in the direction of the coin's swing.

The sun began setting just as she came upon a stream cutting through the canyon, which she followed until the narrow passageway opened to a temperate forest of deciduous and coniferous trees. Sun-dappled leaves lay on the ground, crackling as she passed. The coin gently pulled her along, letting her know she was heading in the right direction.

She came upon a small hand-built fort perched on the side of a washed-out ravine. After moving closer to inspect it, she crouched beside it, reasonably sure it would not hold her adult weight. Inside, she found evidence of youth—tattered comic books, interesting sticks whittled into spears and an assortment of red and brown river stones she recognized as blood agate. It was Kid. She could sense him. Almost smell him via the empathy-laden artifacts. She held one of the river stones to the coin, which vibrated in a low hum against her chest. She smiled. He was close.

Continuing in the same direction through the forest, following the hum of the necklace, Linh found a trail and followed it for a few miles. At last, it led her out of the woods, where she emerged onto a concrete sidewalk in a suburb of dilapidated tract houses. The place was yellowed and abandoned, as if investors had purchased the land and built the place up but never sold most of the homes before declaring bankruptcy and moving on. It reminded her of the news coverage on similarly abandoned suburbs following the 2008 financial crisis.

The closest home stood a short distance away, with television light flickering through the windows. Upon seeing the grimy house, the necklace ceased to glow. Whatever inherent power it carried, whatever the last spark from the ages, seemed to be gone now.

But it did its job. Kid was closer than ever.

In the house with palpitating light.

His signal was faint, like a mewling animal trapped under rubble. But discernibly *there*. There was something else she could sense. Something cold, dark, and dangerous.

SHAKOOOM

Again, the world shook as if bombed in the distance.

Who was at the apartment in The Real? The people who infected Kid? Someone sent by Mara and The Young School? Or another faction entirely? It didn't matter, not really. She knew this day would come eventually, and it didn't change what she needed to do now. Linh hoped Tom could keep them safe—just a little longer. No, it wasn't about hope. It was knowledge. She *knew* he could. He would. He was her nightguard.

She whispered, "Hang on, Kid, I'm almost there."

Linh walked along the sidewalk to the house, ducked under the eye line of the flickering living room window, and wound her way around to the side, following a worn dirt path that ended at a faded wooden gate. She opened it and snuck through, continuing in a hunched trot to the back door. Through a bay window, she could see a messy kitchen and the ominous TV glow jumping down a wood-paneled hallway, lighting the area like a weak strobe.

Linh tried the backdoor, found it unlocked, and let out a quiet, grateful breath. To reduce noise, she removed her shoes and hid them behind the adobe pot of a long-dead tomato plant, then stepped inside, cautious of squeaking floorboards. Linh paused to listen. A phlegmy cackle echoed down the hallway, confirming her suspicion that whatever lived in the house was there. She sensed darkness like hungry, sentient oil spilling from under shivering static.

Where are you, Kid?

Give me a breath, a sound, anything. Rustle the tree, will you?

Then she saw it. A pulsing swathe of black mold, the telltale sign of an animus blight. It covered a door under a set of stairs—likely leading to a cellar or pantry. Once inside the mind, the blight found and fed on any negative emotion, like maggots gorging on decay. The deeper the pain, the better— old shame, guarded phobias, suppressed desires. Eventually, it would evolve into a matured demon of the psyche, known among travelers as a heart's bane.

Linh brightened. The heavy padlock that held the door closed was attached with only a handful of Philips head screws—it was meant to keep things in, not out. If she could find a screwdriver, she could remove the lock without needing a key. Fading sunlight crept in through the bay window, sickly yellow upon the crusty dishes and overflowing trashcan covered in buzzing flies.

Suddenly, she heard the front door open.

"Patty Cake, Patty Cake," chuckled a gravelly voice.

Heavy footsteps moved down the hallway.

The woman replied, "Baker's *man*. Come on, Honey Bunch, take a load off."

The low voice again, "Where is the little shit?"

"I put him in timeout. Can you believe he skipped school again?"

"Oh, I can believe it."

"Could you take care of it? My show's about to come on."

"Housewives of wherever? I don't know how you watch that stuff."

"Don't judge." The phlegmy giggle. "So could you? Please, baby?"

"Yeah, yeah. In a minute. Let me catch a breath and a beer. He's not going anywhere. Maybe leave him down there for a couple of days. It's the weekend."

"Afraid if we don't plump him up a little, the school's going to notice."

"Yeah. Probably right. Okay. We'll do him quick, then. Did you pick me up some smokes? I only got a half pack left."

"Of course, baby. Got you a new carton in the fridge."

"Good deal."

Footsteps thumped down the hallway, coming toward the kitchen. Linh searched for a place to hide and saw the stairwell leading up. Not a great hiding spot, but she had no other choice and stepped up to the first landing, pressing herself as flat as possible against the wall.

Daryl Hodgekiss stopped in front of the fridge and opened it. Linh could see his flank and shoulder, the striped Western-style shirt pressed against his skin with sweat. It had turned semi-transparent, showing the mat of hair and white tank top beneath. He shuffled around, and Linh heard a crinkling sound, then the metallic strike of a lighter, followed by the foul burning smell of cheap tobacco. Then the *snick* of a cracked beer, followed by a long guzzle and belch. A chair creaked as he sat down.

From around the corner of the stairwell, Linh saw the

kitchen table and the man's thick forearms. He methodically laid out eight cigarettes, one at a time, and lined them up, carefully making the row straight and square. Next, he laid down a metal Zippo lighter. It was decorated with the face of a grinning enamel pig, surrounded by the words *Get lit at Porky's*. Daryl stood and plodded over to a narrow drawer, rummaging inside until he found a two-foot piece of rope. He coiled the rope and laid it next to the Zippo and cigarettes. Then he unbuckled his leather belt, pulled it out of his pants with a practiced FFFWIP, and laid it next to the rest.

He grunted in satisfaction at the organized display of torture tools, chugged the rest of his beer, then crushed the can and threw it onto the overflowing trash. It tumbled to the floor in a crash of aluminum, temporarily frightening the buzzing flies into an agitated cloud. The big, red man stood, pulled another beer from the fridge, and ambled back down the hallway to the living room.

Linh realized she had been holding her breath the entire time and released it in a careful woosh, grateful to pull new air into her lungs. What were these people getting ready to do to Kid? Is this what he dealt with growing up? No wonder he never talked about it. Suddenly her upbringing in the punishing environment of The School didn't seem uniquely terrible.

With trauma this dark and deep, the blight would proliferate.

She needed to act fast.

To save Kid, would she have to battle the thing? If so, could she win? She had never heard of anyone surviving a fully grown heart's bane. The tactics taught in The Young

School were to isolate and neutralize, usually by destroying the host. Clearly, that was not an option. Luckily, this one was still young—just beginning to form. Maybe she could handle it. Maybe. But if she didn't hurry, the infection would proliferate. It would continue feeding on Kid's trauma, and the creature would mutate from shadow memories to monstrosity.

She pushed her thoughts away as she searched for something to remove the lock from the door. In the corner of the kitchen was the skinny half-width drawer from which the large man had taken the rope. Linh figured it was a miscellaneous junk drawer. Like every drawer of its kind around the world, it should have buttons, paper clips, tape, batteries, maybe some rubber bands, and, if she was lucky, a screwdriver.

Linh padded across the linoleum floor and opened the drawer. Sure enough, there it was, peeking out from under the debris—the black and yellow handle of a Stanley screwdriver. She removed the items burying it as silently as she could.

Upon closer inspection, it turned out to be a flathead, not Philips—but it was the right size to work if she jammed it in tight. While the TV laugh track echoed down the hall, Linh held the screwdriver like a knife and listened for movement. She heard no such sound and crept to the locked basement door.

Pressing the screwdriver's flat tip into one of the cross-sections of the screw, she began to draw it out of the wood. One screw out, a few more to go.

Her heart leaped as the next screw made a distressingly loud squeak.

She paused and waited, listening again for movement.

Sweat dripped from the tip of her nose.

Nothing... The hallway stayed quiet.

Porcelain elephants watched her work with drunken grins.

Linh continued one tiny turn after another, carefully timed to the TV noise.

Finally, only one screw remained, holding the locking hinge to the wall. Once she removed it, the mechanism would hold fast to the door when she opened it. But as she turned, the screw stripped, her hand slipped, and she gouged a bloody gash into her finger. She cursed silently, and her cheeks flushed red.

Refocused on the task, she pressed as much into the fastening metal as possible, giving it the extra bite it needed to turn in its worn housing. Blood ran down her hand and dripped onto the floor. Unnoticed by Linh, hungry black mold absorbed it and throbbed with a primal satisfaction.

Sweat beads glistened on her brow as she continued to work. Finally, the last screw freed itself and fell into her hand. Linh opened the door, creaking on old hinges, the lock hanging to the side. A long sweeping rectangle of light revealed something like a heap of black laundry, at least a few feet tall. As the light lay upon the dark shape, it squirmed, releasing a smoking stench like burned hair. The shadow sloughed away, falling to the packed dirt floor, scurrying away in parts and pieces like rodents. What remained was a naked, seated child. This place of nightmare memories had changed him into a young boy, yet Linh recognized him immediately. It was Kid.

Then there was a voice behind her.

It stunk of smoke, beer, gasoline, and sour milk.

"Aren't you a cutie? Must be one of the next-door girls."

With a start, Linh noticed that her hands and body were changed into those of a small girl. The creature put its word onto her and changed the vision of herself in this place—as it did to Kid, forcing him into the form of vulnerable youth. Her heart lodged in her throat, a beating lump of fear marking her as a child.

But there was a part of her still, one trained for such things. She knew that this was not yet out of her control.

Not yet.

She *chose* to be her adult self again, with the strength and experience inherent there. She chose *hard*. Willed it to be. The power pushing against her psyche was fierce, like trying to sprint through waist-deep water, dark and fetid.

After great effort, she emerged. She was free.

She was Linh Phuong, once known as The Silver Doe, and she was fierce.

Daryl Hodgekiss howled in primal rage as he mutated and expanded. His shirt burst, popping pearl snaps off to ricochet against walls. Pants ripped as well, loins hanging like dead fruit. The creature's skin turned the black-blue-green of a long rotting corpse with a putrid smell to match. The blight, which had now become a heart's bane, grinned with bleeding eyes and rows of thin teeth like rusted orange scalpels.

Linh's training jumped back into her like the crack of a bullwhip, and she ducked low just as the beast's tree trunk of a forearm came sailing at her head. Its arm crashed into the wall, leaving a massive hole. The house shook with the impact, and dust motes drifted from the ceiling.

Strange, even in this place, the hole revealed a black void.

There should have been insulation, wiring, and framing two-by-fours. Instead, it was as if the darkness of deep space was hidden only by thin, counterfeit-wood paneling. Mirroring the opening, the sky outside went dark—the dream world now shrouded in a moonless night.

Linh rushed to standing and drove the screwdriver into the soft spot below the thing's armpit. Through the vicious tear, where there should have been gouts of blood, there were instead rays of darkness. As they spilled out, they created thick shadows wherever they landed.

The creature made of anti-light and pain howled again, the sound shaking the windows. Again, it swung at Linh. Its fingers tore through her shirt but just missed her skin. As its arm went wide, momentum carried its body to the side, revealing another weak point.

Linh wasted no time and hopped close, stabbing its neck above the collarbone where the carotid artery would be— assuming it had such a thing. A new black beam ejected into the small kitchen, and the beast fell to its knees. Running on instinct, Linh kicked the edges of the hole in the wall.

As it wailed and attempted to stand, Linh used its momentum to sling it in a Judo throw into the hole to nowhere. The beast Daryl Hodgekiss toppled into the nothing place as if jettisoned from a spaceship airlock. Loose cigarettes floating in zero gravity marked its passing.

In response to the loss of its pair, the other heart's bane tore down the hall. It crashed through the china cabinet, porcelain elephants shattering, their eyes wide with fear. It screamed in something that sounded like a combination of anger and profound familial loss.

It moved impossibly fast for its size, leaving Linh no time to get out of its path. It met her in a stampede, grabbed her by the throat, and lifted her high off the floor. Black stars exploded in her vision as the blood supply was cut off from her brain.

"What did you do? What did you DO?" Patricia Hodgekiss screamed into Linh's face and spittle slapped against her cheek. "Where's Honey Bunch?" It looked around with wild yellow eyes, "Honey Buuuuunch!" It screamed again—the sound shattered the kitchen windows and rained glass shards onto the dirty linoleum floor.

Linh fought for breath, and her feet kicked uselessly.

Behind the thing, the wood-paneled gateway gaped its starless black maw, even larger now after the passing destruction of Daryl Hodgekiss. Linh wasn't sure where the black hole led—but if she could lose both heart's banes there... Maybe, just maybe, she and Kid would survive.

She struggled to stab the creature, but her arms were too short. The beast was much bigger than Daryl—now over seven feet tall. Its nightgown ruptured at the seams revealing purpled flesh, which Linh continued to stab, but could not reach anything vital. Its jaundiced eyes did not register the wounds any more than insect bites.

Linh's vision darkened and swam.

She lost her grip, and the makeshift weapon dropped to the floor.

Then, through failing vision she saw Kid standing by the

basement door—skinny, naked, and terrorized as he watched the situation unfold. Small or not, he was the only hope now. Linh pleaded behind gasping silence.

The boy picked up the screwdriver, looked at it, then at the cadaverous blimp of Patricia Hodgekiss, then at Linh choking to death, then back to the tiny weapon.

The creature screamed, grotesque purple veins bulging in its neck and face. "We're not done yet! Not by a long shot! You're going to pay for what you've done! Get back downstairs!"

The boy whispered a reply, "I don't want to… I don't like the dark…"

"No backtalk!"

Young Kid found the courage and yelled, "I don't wanna be down there no more!"

"You shut your mouth!"

"No!"

Gripping the screwdriver in his fist, he rushed forward and stabbed the creature in the soft spot of tendons and veins behind the knee. It screamed, releasing the pressure from Linh's neck for a fortunate moment. She took the opportunity and kicked off the wall with all the waning energy she had left —pushing the Patricia Hodgekiss *thing* and herself through the hole in the wall. Its hands slipped from her neck as they tumbled into the black nothing.

At the last moment, Linh grabbed the splintered edges of the wood paneling and held on. But the thing hung from her ankle, attempting to drag Linh into the darkness with her great cancerous weight.

Kid dove forward and grabbed Linh's wrist.

He wished desperately he had the strength to pull her back in.

But she continued to slip, bit by bit.

The wood splintered and threatened to give way.

From the darkness pulling her asunder, Linh yelled, "You are not alone! You have a name! Do you hear me?"

With a final grimace and torn fingernails, Linh fell.

The bloated shrieking creature clasped to her heel like a lamprey.

She called him, "Michael Kid Thames! This is your true name! Wake up!"

Then Linh disappeared into the dark abyss, sinking rapidly like a stone.

At her last willful command, combined with the utterance of his up-to-then-unknown name, Kid rocketed up and through the layers of The Dream, landing back in his material body with the force of a meteor.

17
WOLVES

Kid sat up, ramrod straight and heaving in oxygen like a Tarantino post-overdose in a dimly lit living room. As weak as the light was, it felt sun-bright and burned his eyes. He cursed as his hand shot up to protect them. Peering through a crack between fingers, fuzzy shapes began to appear. Linh on the coffee table, pale body lax, sweat-soaked hair stuck to her forehead. Her arm hung to the side like the cross-arm of a construction crane, held horizontally by the mechanical lock of her elbow. Tom waited at the head of the stairwell. With his boxer-tape-wrapped hands, he looked like a mini-boss from a video game.

Memories flooded in, like an info-spike to the back of his brain. Just moments ago, he was a naked child watching his surrogate mother and best friend—best friend? Yes, best friend—fall into a black hole of *nothing* with a bloated carnival show of his ex-foster hanging on her leg. Before that, he stumbled through a blackout haze and dreamscape with a rotting arm after running from the Chinatown apartment of a dead man. Now, he lay on a couch in Linh's apartment. Had it been only a day? It felt like a second life, come and gone.

Kid's armpits and waistline were sticky with dried sweat, and his damp jeans clung to his legs. His nuts throbbed like they'd been kicked, and his face felt like he'd head-butted a brick wall. *But*—glorious 'but'—he could feel his arm and side again. The terrible numbing electric pain was gone. Although now, to his fascination, it was covered in what looked like a tattoo of black geometric fractal patterns. They ran from his fingertips to his breastbone and seemed to sway as he watched them like tall grass in the wind. He splayed and flexed his fingers, grabbing the air in front of him, testing its reliability to *just fucking stay air.*

THUD.

The room shook. Plaster dust fell from the ceiling. Rain beat against the glass. The air smelled like spent firecrackers.

Linh.

The fresh memory of her face as she fell into the darkness with that monstrosity hanging on to her leg.

Michael. Kid. Thames.

Wake up.

He rolled off the couch to land on his knees with a grunt between the sofa and coffee table. He reached over to touch Linh's face and arms. They were cold. Kid grabbed her shoulders and shook her. "Linh!" No response. He pressed his ear to her chest to listen for a heartbeat. Silence. Terrible static silence.

"Linh! Goddamnit! Wake up!"

Tears streamed down his face as he sobbed. He shook her again, her head lolling back and forth.

"Knock it off already." Tom called over his shoulder from the stairwell, "That's her vessel you're treating like a rental. Linh's gone, Skidrow. She faded out while you took a cat nap."

"Cat nap? Eat shit, Tom. Do you have any idea what we just went through? What I just saw? There were monsters. And I swear to fucking god, they were real."

"Yeah, I know all about it, greenhorn. And who brought them here? We should've kicked that golden-eyed cocksucker down the road when he came with you. But Linh, she's been killing herself with guilt, always has, ever since she lost Bian. Horacio took advantage of that grief. He knew damn well the state she was in."

"When he came with me? What are you talking about?"

Tom wasn't listening and continued without answering Kid's question. "We had a pretty good life. It wasn't perfect, but we were close. It was decent. About as good as a fool like me could've asked for. Now what? She's gone. It's all gone. Because of you and that cat-ass sonofabitch."

CRACK.

The sound from below, which could have been mistaken for thunder the first time, came again—this time accompanied by the sounds of splitting wood and groaning steel.

"That door brace is about to go. Wolves been beating at it for a while now. I'll give you one chance, not because I like you, 'cause I don't. Because Linh did. Leave. Run off to wherever it is you always do. It doesn't matter." The muscles in Tom's neck and shoulders twitched as he clenched and unclenched his cloth-wrapped fists. He stared blankly down the stairwell.

"Back up, man. What do you mean she's *gone*? She's right there." Kid pointed at Linh's body. "Right there! We were dreaming. Like, five minutes ago!"

"Skid-fucking-row. Are you still dumb enough to think that was *just* a dream? What'll it take to convince you? For once in your life, shut your idiot mouth and open your mind's eye. She's gone."

"But... She can't be *gone*. How can she be gone?"

Finally, Tom turned to Kid. "What did you see? In the end."

"She was fighting against these... things. They were my old foster parents, but... mutated. During the fight, a wall broke. But behind the wall wasn't like insulation and wires and stuff. It was just dark, like there was nothing, like outer space. But no stars, nothing. They fought and fell in, together, her and the monsters.... They all went in there."

Tom nodded, "That darkness you talk about, behind the cracked shell of your poison dream—most likely, that's The Void. Her essence is *there* now. In the *not*. What happens when you take the batteries out of a flashlight and throw them in a river?" Tom's lip curled over his wide straight teeth. "It's our animus, our source, that travels The Dream. Linh's is lost now. You watched her fall into the black, and you didn't do a goddamn thing. Now her light's gone. You should be there too."

Kid's face spasmed, showing teeth, and he held back hot tears, "Tom, man, I tried... I really tried... but I was too small. Just a kid. I'm fucking sorry, alright! Tom, let's go back! We can get her. Let's go! Tom! We can go together!"

CRACK.

More splintering wood and wrenching metal.

A picture fell from the wall, its glass shattering on impact. The shards lay across the floor in a pattern that felt meaningful somehow, like tea leaves at the bottom of a mug —a design of chaos and irreversible damage.

"Nobody comes back from that. From the black behind The Dream. And you're infected with something nasty I've never seen. The answer is *no*. Get out of here. You've done enough. I'll deal with this." Finally, Tom locked eyes with Kid. There was murder there. "I'm only going to tell you one time. Leave. Don't turn around. Don't come back. Stay the fuck out of my way." Tom turned back to the stairwell.

Kid watched his trembling back a moment longer, then turned to Linh. Pale. Cold. Slack. He moved to brush her sweaty hair from her brow but stopped short and pulled his hand back, feeling that he didn't deserve to touch her. She was special and, somehow, clean. He was... not.

Tom was right. This was his fault. Leaving before causing any more damage was a good idea. It was a mistake ever coming here, sticking around, allowing himself to grow close. To think he had a family. He was dangerous. Malignant. Cancerous. He always had been. Where he went, he brought pain, or it quickly blossomed.

Rising like a rag doll pulled by strings, Kid searched for his belongings. The sliced remains of his yellow Buzzcocks shirt lay on the floor. He cursed his immaturity at the expensive purchase. It had cost as much as two white-glove drops.

The kind that'll get your best friend killed.

After pulling his hoody on, he picked up his backpack and

unzipped it to check for the box. It was there. Piece of shit box. He looked back at Tom, who stood resolute with closed fists.

"What about you?" Kid asked.

"What about me?"

"Those guys play for keeps."

"So do I."

———

Tom ran down the stairs leaving Kid behind. Once at the bottom, he waited for the next attack.

CRACK

Then, as quietly as possible, he lifted the crossbar off the door frame and hefted it over his shoulder, readying it like a massive baseball bat. Standing to the side, Tom waited. When the next battering ram came, the unbarred door slammed open and banged against the concrete wall of the stairwell, followed by a small rolling dumpster being pushed by Poe in the hijacked teen body of Li Qiang. The dumpster clanged up a few stairs and stopped, jamming askew.

Tom swung the crossbeam at the head of Poe's stolen frame, but the rolling dumpster complicated the attack, and Poe dodged the worst of the blow by dropping low. From his ground position, he kicked at Tom's knee, which rose in time to block the attack with a hardened shin. Tom's raised foot drove back to the ground to counterbalance as he dropped the crossbeam and kicked. His boot thwacked against Poe's blocking forearm, and Poe rose quickly in the space between attacks, using the upward motion to launch an uppercut, followed by an elbow, then a forward knee, all of which were blocked deftly.

Poe retreated backward into the alley. Already soaked, the pouring rain splashed against his saturated clothing and ran down his body. "Looking a little slow, el Tigre," he said, maintaining eye contact as he adjusted his footing on the wet pavement.

"Fast enough."

"Anybody still call you that? Tiger? Probably have a new name now, huh? What is it? Kitchen Rick?"

Tom ignored him as he circled, looking for an opening. "Which of Mara's lackeys are you?"

"Bet you'd like to know. How is the ol' Doe?"

Tom twitched a micro-expression of grief, never much of a poker player.

"Guessing not so good? Bummer. Haven't seen the pair of you kicking ass since I was a freshman. It would have been fun to go at it."

Tom lunged, using his talent to channel animus into physical prowess. He launched a flurry of punches and kicks, blurred by their extraordinary speed, each knocking a spray of rain droplets into the night air, tinged by pink neon. Many strikes were blocked, but Poe favored his side with the broken arm. Tom's attacks landed hard and fast on that weak side, knocking Poe farther and farther back until he pressed against the opposite alleyway wall. Soon, Tom landed blow after clean blow against his face and ribs, yet Poe's frame continued to smile through a wash of blood and broken teeth.

"What's so funny?" Tom yelled as he punched a hole into the brick wall, fragments of red clay misting the air.

138

Poe chuckled, coughed bright red lung blood, and glanced to the side. "Too easy, Tiger."

Before Tom could react, he was knocked out cold, falling to the ground like a bag of sand. The sneak attack came from Delilah swinging his discarded crossbeam. While he lay unconscious, she jump-stomped on his hands several times, breaking the bones thoroughly. The sound echoed in the alley like smashed chopsticks.

"Think I got them all?" She said to her brother.

Poe grimaced, "Fuckin' hell. Sounded like it."

"No more kung-fu shit from you, kitty-boy."

Delilah giggled, zip-tied his hands, and dragged Tom through the alley muck.

18

WAKE UP

The box was heavy inside the bag, as heavy as it had ever been. Kid held it against his chest as he sat on the window sill. One leg hung into the rain, the other still in the living room, foot on the wooden floor. Linh's sad body remained lax, her construction crane arm extended to the side. If not for the contextual horror show, she could be sleeping. Her beauty juxtaposed sharply against the grotesque positioning of her body. Tom would take care of her and give her a proper goodbye when the fight was done.

Kid turned his tired neck to look out the window and its single-story drop. Against the brick wall outside lay a discarded sectional couch. It looked cushy enough. It was far too convenient. Almost as if fate wanted him to run. Hide. Survive. Stay hidden this time, don't hurt anybody else. Who is Michael Thames? Doesn't really matter. Who cares. If you run and hide, nobody needs to know your name. Your name can be anything you want. You can change it every day.

He looked back one last time and sighed. He wanted to

stay, watch her, just be with her. What did the Jewish folks call it? Sitting shiva. But he didn't deserve that. She was silent and cold because of him.

With no more consideration, he swung his other leg out and dropped to the soggy couch below. He landed with a spring-breaking clang and a grunt, but the couch did its job—protecting his body from the fall. Then, instead of immediately standing, he just lay in the funky, soaked fabric. It smelled like a wet dog—an alley mutt. Just like him.

Staring up at the pink neon sign, with rain pelting his face, he clutched the bag to his bare chest, exposed from the unzipped hoodie. He wished he could hide from this, but there was nowhere left to go. One of those things that stays with you—a broken bone that, even after healing, aches when a storm is coming. No matter how many places you run or how many times you change your name, there it is, waiting.

Kid sat up, shook the rain from his head, and watched the water run down his hands. The trickling drops magnified the strange black markings before falling to the concrete—geometric illustrations proving what his friend had done for him.

Why did Linh die?

So you could cry in the rain like a little bitch?

There are things you shouldn't run from. People you stand by through the end. Doesn't matter if it hurts. It's not about you. Never was.

You're not much, but you're better than this.

Maybe you can run from yourself, your pain, and your past.

But you don't run from this. You don't run from Linh.

The woman deserves everything you got.

She said you have a name.

Michael Kid Thames.

Wake up.

He growled and awakened with a new purpose, jumped to his feet, ran toward the alleyway, and stopped short at the corner to peek around. The Creep Twins were facing away from him as they maneuvered Tom's unconscious body.

Shit. That's not good.

What now?

I don't know.

Something.

Do SOMETHING.

He stepped around the corner and sprinted at the exposed back of the young girl with the dark bob haircut. On any other day, he would feel guilty about attacking a fifteen-year-old girl. That day was not today. The distance closed quickly, and he jumped.

In mid-air, he brought a hand back to deliver a flying punch, the kind he would have launched at a dogpile yard fight back in juvie. A total sucker punch, but this was no time for fighting fair.

Kid aimed for the base of her neck where spine meets skull. If he got lucky, a hit like that would knock her out for a long time, maybe worse. Then the battle would be one-on-one, and he might have a chance. He'd managed the dark-eyed boy once; maybe he could handle him again.

For a brief moment, it seemed like the Hail Mary strike might actually connect. Then the girl turned, looking just as she had in the Chinatown living room—a cool haircut framing bored, dead eyes.

In a brief but seemingly stretching instant, her shape doubled and mirrored like the image produced by a damaged VHS tape. One millisecond she was in front of him. The next, she was directly behind. She yanked him out of the air with supernatural strength and locked him in a rear choke hold.

She pulled the bag from his back and whispered, close enough for her breath to move the tiny hairs on his ear. It smelled of death, sick and sweet. No longer a subconscious observation but a real and present stench like rotting meat with a couple squirts of cheap grocery store perfume. "Nice try, street stain. No more running. Now we get to play."

The boy watched, his eyebrow raised in what seemed like disbelief. His face was too mangled to tell for sure. Kid had never seen someone that badly beaten still standing.

"Man of the hour. Got some balls on you, I'll give you that," he said, the words sounding more like 'maaanadahuur' through his broken mouth.

The dead-eyed girl reprimanded him, "Shut up, Poe. You're embarrassing." Then she turned her attention back to Kid. "I swear, if you keep doing all the work for us, we'll have to put you on payroll. Are you looking for a job, that it?"

Kid coughed and attempted to speak.

"What's that?" She relaxed her stranglehold to let him talk.

He rasped, "What the hell are you people? Fucking zombie ninjas? Just take it. Take the box. Leave us alone. No more trouble, okay? You've done enough. You don't have to kill Tom too."

"You think this is enough?" The girl asked. "Not by a long

shot. See, you've annoyed me. And for that, you have to pay. My irritation has a price. You understand?"

"Whatever you did to me, that black shit, it killed my friend, okay? She never did anything to anybody. Isn't that enough for you? You murdered my best friend. Kill me too. I don't care. Just take the box, and at least leave Tom alone."

"You think I killed your friend? No, you did that. I only wanted the box. You could have given it to me back in Chinatown. I was honestly considering letting you live. You were a nobody. But you're somebody now. *Now*, you're the guy who pissed me off. *Now* you're the guy who ran. Then you went to *her*. And she never did anything to anybody? Please. You have no idea. Trust me—she deserves this and more." The girl yanked his neck, pulling his ear close to her mouth again. Through rotting flowers, she spoke, "*You* killed her."

She renewed the strength of the hold until Kid started choking, his feet scrabbling against wet asphalt.

The boy stepped forward, "Come on, Delilah, that's enough,"

"Shut up, Poe! It's over when I say so."

Poe groaned impatiently as if they were simply running late for dinner. "Come on. This is a waste of time. Doe's gone, and this old fart's not bothering anyone again. Let's get out of here." He started walking.

Delilah screamed at his back, "No! I'm not done!"

The rain slowed to a drizzle—dripping from the fire escapes and eaves, hitting trash bags, cardboard, and corrugated sheet metal. The result was a humid percussion symphony. The wet asphalt reflected pink neon light.

Then, a new voice entered from above. "I say you're done too. Now the vote's three to one, if you count Chokey."

Delilah tracked the area to find the speaker as she shuffled back, pulling Kid by the neck, his booted feet searching for a hold that wasn't there.

Shoes smacked the pavement, and the new voice gained a face.

Delilah spun, dragging a gasping Kid along.

"Alice? What the fuck? What are you doing here? This isn't your trip."

"When you mess up this bad, somebody has to pick up the slack before the opportune moment evaporates."

Delilah's nostrils flared with anger. "We have it under control, geek."

"Clearly not. This is what they call a dumpster fire. Appropriate for this backdrop, don't you think?"

"No! I have the box now. Everything's fine. We even found two truants. Old ones you wouldn't know about. You were still in diapers when they ran. Mother will be pleased."

"You *found* them, did you? That's a lie. I've been watching you for two straight days. This is a string of dumb luck. It doesn't take a genius to see that."

Where Delilah's eyes once shone with sadism, now they were wide with desperation. She only had one fear: looking weak in front of Mother. "Come on... Don't be such a nitpicky bitch. We're just about to finish up. Go fuck off like you usually do."

Alice scoffed, "Yeah, sure. I let you take it and spin things like you're some tactical mastermind. Then maybe there's a promotion to captain, and I have to take your idiotic orders.

No, thanks." Alice moved a couple of steps closer. Poe watched from his position well away from the action, favoring his right side and breathing heavily.

Delilah ignored the question and continued her thinly veiled plea, "This is unnecessary. It's done now. Just go." Kid coughed under Delilah's forearm. She twisted his head to shut him up.

"Okay, *fiiine*." Alice smiled and flipped some wet hair out of her face. "You get riled up too easy, you know that?"

Delilah's shoulders moved back, and her eyes narrowed. Alice never let anyone else win, especially not her. She asked, not wanting to hear the answer, "Alice, what are you really doing here?"

19
THIRSTY

"Sometimes, the truth can be fun," Alice replied, the neon light reflecting from the edge of her face and platinum hair. "First off, you did screw up, as usual. And you are an awful person, as always. But here's the situation in simple terms your smooth brain can understand—I'm taking the totem and leaving The School."

Delilah's eyes widened in surprise, and she repositioned her feet—readying to maneuver in a fight, pulling a choking Kid along as her shield.

Alice continued, "No more School. No more *Mother*." She took a breath and let it out, relieved to be saying these things aloud. "No more uprooting the souls of lost children for counterfeit gods who should have died a long time ago." She gritted her teeth to contain the emotion. "My heart is scarred enough for a lifetime, Delilah. I'm finished. *Out*. Get it?" She reached out. "Now, give me the bag and I'll let you both leave without pain."

Kid watched the scene unfold, sneaking wheezing breaths

through a pencil-size hole in his windpipe. Delilah noticed and tightened her hold. Kid gagged.

"Why are you telling me this?" Delilah asked, her eyes as dark as midnight water mirrors.

"You would have found out back at school anyway," Alice replied. "I'd rather tell you now and watch your face scrunch up."

Delilah's face ticked as she stifled the prophesied expression. "Do you realize what you're throwing away? You don't, do you? You've been given everything. *Given*. Never had to pay for any of it." She growled, "Spoiled little bitch as always. The answer is *no*! No! Get fucked, Alice." Delilah glared at her as she told her brother, "*Poe,* get her."

Her twin attempted to walk but stumbled to his knees and coughed bright lung blood onto the wet alley. "Sorry, sis. My frame's beat to shit."

"Whatever," Delilah hissed. "You two always had a thing." She continued dragging Kid, who was losing consciousness. "Try and take it then! Let's see what you can do before I twist his neck."

"What makes you think I care about this dork?"

"Because you're soft, Alice. Always have been. I *know* you —the egg-head with no stomach. You've always had skill and smarts, hiding your weakness behind them. But the world is full of pussies with potential who never live up to it. You can't hack it. You never could. That's why you're going to try and run. You're not worried about your conscience. You're just not good enough." Delilah laughed. "It's just like you to shit on what Mother's done for us. You've always had it all, so you wouldn't know what it's like." She scoffed and added,

"Whatever. Doesn't matter. Do you really think you can escape? Go ahead. Run. I give you a week, tops, and you'll be cold on a slab, just like that dumb bitch inside."

Alice shrugged, "It's true... I'm not like you. Or Mara. But you're forgetting about the second thing."

"And what's that?"

"You talk too much. *Vanderhook Nephilim.*"

With the intonation of the last syllable, Delilah's head jerked back, and a trickle of blood ran from her nose to drip off her chin. As her eyes rolled, she released Kid and everything else, falling as fast as gravity would take her. The blood and her body hit the pavement simultaneously.

Alice turned from Delilah's empty frame to Poe. "You understand, don't you?"

"Come on, Al," Poe replied. "You know I do. Wish I could join you. But Mara's still got me tied up tight. How'd you get out from under her anyway?"

"I'm a work in progress."

"Ain't we all."

"I hope you don't get in too much trouble."

His smashed face broke into a grin. "Trouble's nothing new. Besides, not as bad as you're gonna get it. Mom'll be super-pissed. Although... I bet, if some amends are made, she'd still take back her golden child." Poe studied her. He looked proud. "You always make those gate bombs look easy. I never could do it."

"Yeah, well, you're the pretty one. I'm the smart one."

"When did you plant them?"

She smiled. "A lady never tells her secrets."

The corner of Poe's mouth twitched. "Course not."

"Let me know when you want to go on the lamb with the cool kids."

Poe replied, "Well, let me know when you want to share your tricks. Otherwise, that shit's never happening."

"Alright," She replied. "Are you ready? I'll try not to make this one hurt."

He took a breath and let it out. "Yeah, let's get this done."

Alice spoke, "Ominous Gusto."

As with Delilah, she had snuck into and manipulated Poe's dream at some time in the recent past. The technique was known as a gate bomb. Its activation allowed her to force shut the connection between Poe's animus and the vessel he commandeered. As with Delilah, its utterance dropped his frame to the ground, where it lay empty, pale, and finally, truly dead.

Alice stretched her hand to Kid. "Hey, are you okay?"

He stood, slung the bag over his shoulder, and studied the stranger.

"What in the absolute *fuck* is going on?"

"Jeez, how about *thank you*."

"You gonna kill me with a spell too?"

"No, I don't have any problems with you. Besides, they're not dead. Well, those frames are, but that wasn't me. I just kicked them out. And it's not a *spell*."

"Their frames? Kicked them out? *What*?"

"*They*—Poe and Delilah. Animus agents, like me. They stole those kids' bodies like two hot cars. We call the stolen ones frames. They got them by breaking in through the pathways of The Dream. I can't save the original animi—we don't know where they go when displaced. Well, we have ideas, but nothing certain. So, sadly, that's that. But I sent Delilah and Poe home."

Kid grimaced at the new jargon. "Dude, whatever."

"Listen, jerk—you should be thankful. You'd be dead if it weren't for me."

"Don't bullshit me. I see what's going on. At best, I'm collateral."

"Oh, you do, do you? That's what you think?"

"It's pretty obvious."

"No, not *oBvIoUs*. I've been watching you since you picked the box up in Chinatown. You're not just some street kid. Nobody survives Delilah's blight, well, nobody *before*—but you did. Then you somehow managed to use a locked totem to walk The Dream without any training whatsoever. I felt you in there. I bet you saw a strange ocean, didn't you? And stars that were too close?"

Kid twitched in acknowledgment. "And you just happened to be friends with those two wack-jobs."

"Friends? Ha, no. They're more like family since I didn't get to pick them. Know what I mean?"

Unwilling to admit that he did not know what she meant, Kid watched her and chose not to respond.

Alice continued, "Listen, this is important, and you fit into it in a big way. I don't know exactly how yet, but I'm going to figure it out. Until then, you're not leaving my sight. This situation puts you on my *team*. So, you'd better get used to it because we have work to do. You don't have to like me, but don't make me make you." Her eyes flashed dark. "You won't like it if I make you."

Again, Kid chose not to reply to this demanding girl.

Sometimes if you ignore the dramatic ones, they'll calm down. He turned away as he rubbed his shoulder, noting again that it no longer burned, and thought of Linh. Walking the dream... A strange ocean... Stars that are too close... Lost animi... Before he could further debate with the platinum-haired raver chick, he heard a painful whimper.

"Tom!" Kid called and trotted over to him.

He leaned against the wall, head hung low from his injuries. Blood had stopped flowing from the back of his head, but the stains were spread across his shoulders. He held his mangled zip-tied hands to his chest.

Kid grimaced at the sight. "Shit, man..."

"I'm fine. Get these off me," Tom grunted as he motioned to the plastic ties. He was pale from the concussion, one eye dilated more than the other, his hands like twisted hooks. He had to be in agony. The fact that he was even conscious was amazing.

"How are you standing? What are you all? Mutants?" Kid asked.

Tom sneered. "Is that what you learned in your comic books?"

Kid sighed in relief—Tom was talking shit again, which meant he'd likely survive. He pulled a small key-chain pocket knife out of his bag to cut the ties. Tom suppressed another groan as the assistance moved his hands.

"Come on," Kid said, "let's get out of here before they come back."

Alice said, "It'll be a while before they surface after a gate bomb. An animus takes at least a few hours to make it back upstream. Plus, I don't hear sirens. So, we're safe for a little while. I could use a glass of water."

Kid scoffed, "Are you serious? Water? Right now?"

"I'm quite serious. My *spells,*" She wiggled her fingers as if casting one, "drain me badly. I prefer a double-double burger, strawberry shake, and animal fries, but I'll settle for some hydration. You owe me that, at least."

"Owe? I don't owe you shit. I'm no fool. You're here for *you*, not me. What's owed is an explanation. Everyone knows what's going on but me. So, for the love of God, catch me up. This is fucking insane."

Alice appraised Kid and made some hidden decision. "That's fair," She said. "We'll trade. Besides," she nodded at the upstairs apartment, "don't you want to save your friend?"

Kid and Tom both looked at her with sudden wide-eyed attention.

Alice continued, "I can feel her, but just barely. Judging by the sad puppy looks on both your faces, you think she's dead. But she's not, at least not yet."

"Why didn't you say that in the first place? We're just standing around? What's wrong with you? And how do you know—screw it, never mind—more dream-shit. Come on!" Kid ran to the door, looking back only once to ensure Alice and Tom followed. He shimmied past the crashed dumpster and sprinted up the stairs.

The living room was exactly as they'd left it. Low light glowed from the lamp on the floor, casting long shadows. Linh stretched out in a macabre coffee table crucifix. Kid slid on his knees beside her and moved the sweat-stuck hair from her forehead with a careful hand.

20

THREAD

Alice stepped into the dim yellow living room—the only light came from a small lamp resting on the floor. Kid watched her enter with a newfound semblance of hope. Guarded hope, but hope nonetheless. She closed her eyes and placed her hand on Linh's chest, directly above her heart. The older woman felt familiar to her somehow, even pale and still. After several deep breaths, the strange girl with silver hair spoke.

"She's not dead. I'm certain."

"What do you mean? She doesn't look alive. Her animus was lost." Tom replied.

"The Tiger. I've heard of you. And I saw you move well enough for a traveler, but you're no great empath. Maybe you can't feel it, but *I* can. There's a thread, humming with tension, attached to wherever her spirit has gone." Alice studied Linh's slack face. "She's special, isn't she?"

"Yes." Tom and Kid replied in unison, glancing at each other awkwardly.

"Who is she to you?"

Tom spoke first, "She's... my friend."

Kid added, "She saved me. In... *there*."

"In where?"

"In my dream."

Alice nodded, "In *The* Dream. What happened? Tell me."

As quickly as possible, Kid relayed the story so far.

She listened attentively as Tom left to ready a go-bag.

When Kid finished, Alice said, "Sometimes it's easy for me to forget that we're not all raised in this. To be thrown into the deep end must be confusing. Outside, I was unkind and I'm sorry for that." She moved her bangs behind an ear from where they fell back down. "Now, there *is* some good news. I sense a string that will lead to your friend if we keep pulling it. This isn't over. But it *will* be soon if we don't do something."

"What do you mean?" Kid asked.

"Your friend Tom is correct. Her animus is lost. From the sound of it, and if the theories are true, she's in The Void— which is not easy to accomplish. It's not like rifts open up left and right when you bump against a wall. If that were normal, The Dream would have shattered long ago. It makes me wonder if there are more holes and cracks or if this is unique. Somehow, I doubt it." She frowned. "This is disconcerting."

Kid let out a huff of air, "The Void? Rifts? Animus? I need a wiki with you people!" He growled, kicking a side table across the room to crash against the wall. "Her mind is gone? Just tell me how to get to her! Where *is* she?"

Alice glanced at the crashed table, then back to Kid with the expression of irritated patience one would take with a child. "Well... that's not easy to answer. Nobody knows for sure. As I said, it's theory. It's not a place you go and come back. I mean, some people supposedly have—bits and pieces —throughout history. It's led to many ideas about the afterlife, prophets, reincarnation, heaven and hell. So, we're reasonably sure it's where our animus—what some call spirit —goes when our body dies. But it's not supposed to *stay* there. It's where it's made new again, to be reborn in a new place, a new vessel. Or so the scholars say."

"So what, purgatory?"

"Going there accidentally, being lost there—yes, I think purgatory would be accurate."

"And she, what, fell in? In my dream? She fell into limbo through a hole in a wall inside a fever dream in *my head*." Kid ran his hand over his buzzcut hair. "This is fucking stupid."

Alice's look of tried patience was quickly waning. "No. What's *stupid* is refusing to open your mind to the intricacies of reality, even when they are put in front of your face and *patiently* described in detail. You're getting a lot more answers than most. Get me a pencil and paper. I'll show you."

Kid didn't move. She responded with a commanding head nod that said, *do it now.* He shuffled to Linh's desk, rummaged around, and returned with the requested items. Alice laid the paper on the floor, drew a circle, oblong on its side like a dish, and pointed at it.

"This is *everything*—the universe. Whether there is an

outside edge will be debated forever, but for demonstration purposes, I've drawn it with one. Got it?"

He nodded as he glanced at Tom moving around in the back of the apartment. It seemed Mr. Money-line didn't need a tutor. Kid felt irked to be the only one held after class for not understanding a lesson.

Alice drew another circle inside the dish shape and shaded it in.

"Inside the universe is The Dream."

"What's in the middle, there?" Kid asked.

Alice flashed him a look telling him to hang on. In the center of the second ellipse, she drew a vortex, puncturing the dish and narrowing it to a point that went off the edge of the paper.

"In the center is The Void. The Dream is both the path to arrive there as well as the barrier which protects everything else from falling into it. The Dream is the shell that keeps it contained. Your story implies that Linh fell through a crack in the protective barrier. The implications are disturbing."

"Okay... so The Dream is inside the universe, and The Void is a hole inside that?"

Alice doodled some more as she answered, "After grossly simplifying a universe woven of far more dimensions than we can comprehend into a 2D drawing, yes."

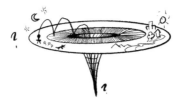

Kid massaged the bridge of his nose. "How the hell do you fall through a crack? She's lost in what, an outer space drain? Looks like a black hole. Or like an artist's rendition or whatever."

"Yeah. I've considered that. Maybe it is one or something similar. It furthers the point—you don't just walk up to it and fall through. It's not a place you go until you die and your animus is severed from your body."

Kid raised an eyebrow.

"Don't you see?" She said.

"No," Kid growled, "I don't fucking see. I'm not a, what did you call Tom? A traveler? I'm not a goddamn traveler, okay? I. Don't. Fucking. See. I'm *trying* to see. Your little picture helps, and I'm really straining here, I promise, but this shit is bananas."

"The totem, fool," Tom said as he returned, carrying a packed duffle bag in the crook of his elbow.

Alice added, "Yes, exactly—it confirms my research. The totem allowed this. Or, at minimum, it has taken advantage of an already thinned barrier."

"The thing in the box," Kid said.

"Yes. And full disclosure, if it's not obvious, or you didn't catch it back in the alley while you were kind of choking on the ground, I want it too. I need it. That's why I jumped into your fight. It was my last chance to get it. It's my ticket out of this mess."

Kid replied, "Fine. You can have it. Thing's cursed."

"You believe in curses but not alternate perspectives of reality?"

He rolled his eyes.

Alice continued, "Listen, I'd love to take it off your hands and go on my merry way, but I have an idea. And I think the two of you might like it. Try and keep up."

She stood, hands gesturing as she paced back and forth. "People have been fighting over this particular totem for a *long* time. It must harness *serious* power. A game-changer."

Tom brought Alice's requested glass of water, managing to use his injured hands like clamps. After a distracted glance of gratitude, she drank the entire thing without stopping, dripping water onto her shirt and drying her face with her jacket sleeve.

"Now," she said, "here's what I'm thinking. Clearly, it allows the user to enter or manipulate The Void somehow. That is a *big* deal. For both offense *and* defense." After setting the empty glass on the floor, she went on, "For some of these ancients like Mara, there's nothing that can stop them—they're too good at transferring and controlling the path of their animus after a vessel loss. Your average run-of-the-mill person, traveler or not, gets swept up into The Stream after a vessel death. They follow that path, The Stream, then get—we think—reconfigured in The Void, and then spat back out some new place without memories or any understanding that they were ever comprised of pieces of a previous consciousness, to begin with. But people like Mara, if you can still call them people, know how to stay out of The Stream. Or jump out of it early before ever hitting The Void. Then, they take on another vessel instead. They keep all their memories, their personality, everything. And there they are—*again* and again. Over and over."

"They're *immortal?*" Kid managed to look even more lost, face scrunched into pure disbelief.

Tom answered, "Yeah, pretty much."

Alice went on, words flying, "Immortal, or something pretty close to it. None of the ancients like to reveal their ages and are zealous about protecting their identities. But from what I've gathered, and it's quite a bit, I'm good at gathering —Mara has to be *thousands* of years old—maybe even tens-of, I have no idea, no consistent records go back that far. And I don't even know if she's the oldest." She exclaimed with her hand. "It's messed up, right? But here's the thing. If you could somehow force their animus into The Void, skip them past The Stream, past the part where they usually escape the normal machinations of death? They would be gone. Actually, *finally*, gone—as dead as any other normal person would be."

"We could finally kill Mara?" Tom was hungry at the thought.

Kid asked him, "You know about this stuff too?"

"Us and that vulture go way back."

"Yeah," Alice acknowledged, "I heard Delilah. You two went truant a long time ago. Don't tell me the story, we all have them. But yes, I believe with this tool, we could have the power to end an ancient. That explains why they all want it so badly. It's like an arms race, and this is the first A-bomb. Your friend fell into The Void without dying or traveling The Stream. At the very least, the totem helped tear through the thinned fabric between The Dream and The Void. That proves its power."

Tom shook his head and said, "That's a jumped conclusion and wouldn't prove anything even if it were true. Not really. What's it matter? They've always fought amongst each other since the dawn. It's nothing new. People get used, people die, and children disappear. The cycle continues."

"Don't make me spell it out," Alice said.

Kid brightened, "If it can send someone in, maybe it can get them *out*."

"Exactly! It's a door. Or a doormaker, anyway. Or a key to a door. I don't know exactly. But think about it. It can't be one without the other."

"You really think we can get her back?" Kid asked.

"I mean, I don't know for sure, but what other chance is there?"

His eyes narrowed. "Why don't you take it now? Why help us at all?"

"These things aren't normally active unless they're

unlocked. And trust me, it's no small task. Most sit on shelves and in vaults, completely useless because not a single person alive has a clue how to get them to work. Despite that fact, against all odds, this one seems to have partially opened just by being near you. Somehow, you're a key. I need you to finish opening it. I doubt I could do it on my own."

Alice walked to the window, looked out, listened, then, apparently satisfied with the silence outside, returned and continued, "So, from my end, if you can unlock it, that's the mushroom cloud over New Mexico. My ticket is scratched. Lotto won. I'm willing to help you and your friend along the way in exchange."

"And of course," Kid replied, "I can't ditch you either since I have no clue what the fuck I'm doing with all this dream shit. I need you just as bad."

Alice gave him a pixie wink that felt out of place with the tone of the scenery but made him blush anyway. "You're a quick study. So, that's that. I help you try and save your friend, and then you give me the unlocked totem. I go away. Everyone gets what they need."

He shrugged. "If you're serious, if you can help us get Linh back, I'll do whatever you need. As long as I don't have to hurt kids or dogs, I don't care what it is—I'm ready to fuck shit up. Just get me to her." Since their time in the apartment, his expression of confusion eroded, revealing a quiet determination.

"Same," Tom agreed. "I don't care how wild this plan is —I'm in."

Alice nodded and continued, "Alright, it's a deal. Now let's get the hell out of here. Tom, do you have somewhere to keep her safe for a while? You're pretty banged up there and probably not front-line material for a while, no offense, so you can be her guard while we run scout."

"Not my first time protecting her. She'll be safe."

"Great. Now, we need to figure this thing out. Not sure why you're tied to it, but you are. That's good, and we can work with that. But we need more. We need to be in charge of this and know how it works so we're not getting yanked around. I don't want to accidentally fall in the dark with your friend. Linh, you said?"

Kid replied, "Yeah. That's her. And you're Alice, right? Heard that back in the alley. People call me Kid."

"Okay, cool. When we see her, Kid, let's make it intentional, yeah? If we figure this thing out, we can make it on purpose. I don't make promises lightly, so I won't make one. But I think we have a decent shot at solving this."

"I feel like I'm two more questions from having an aneurysm, but I don't care. Pop my brain. Pop it twice. I gotta get Linh back. *I have to.*"

Alice studied Kid. Again, seeming to appraise and make some secret decision. He looked beyond tired, but despite the dark circles under them, his eyes shone with something new. Something she hadn't seen in the alleyway or Chinatown. What she saw was resolve.

"We'll see what we can do," she said. "For now, we need a safe place, I'm dying for a rest. Do you have somewhere we can go?"

"Yeah..." Kid hesitated. He never took anyone to his nest and never planned on doing so. But it looked like all the chips were down. It was time to make sacrifices of whatever was left. "I have a place."

Alice sighed, "Great."

Tom reached into his duffle, pulled out a burner, grunted as he almost dropped it, and handed it to Kid. "Keep me in the loop. My number's in there." Then he slung the bag over his back crossways and bent over to scoop Linh into his arms, somehow managing to do it with only a slight grimace of pain, using his mangled hands like a forklift.

"Alright, I will," Kid replied.

They were moving forward. He decided with a full heart that he would pay back the debt of her friendship, no matter what. They *would* get Linh back. No more floating without purpose. No more hiding, lying, or running. At least not away.

Toward.

Run toward.

No matter the cost.

Remembering what Linh said, Kid whispered, "I'll come get you, wherever you are." It was a mantra and a promise.

PART THREE
ALLEY DOG

"Is the Master out of his mind?" she asked me. I nodded. "And he's taking you with him?" I nodded again. "Where?" she asked. I pointed towards the centre of the earth. "Into the cellar?" exclaimed the old servant. "No," I said, "farther down than that."

— JULES VERNE, JOURNEY TO THE CENTER
OF THE EARTH

21
BOWIE

Kid walked with Alice down the quiet paths of the urban dawn. Exhaustion and contemplation filled the air instead of words. After boosting her up to the fire escape, following her to the top, and warning her of the trip wire, they made it to his home—a rooftop nest perched on a pinnacle of the city lit by the rising sun.

"Wow..." Alice spoke, almost in a whisper, "This is... *really* cool." She turned slowly, looked around the rooftop atrium, took a few steps, swung the hammock with a finger, then more slow steps took her around the rest of the makeshift monastery. She smiled and spoke to Kid over her shoulder, "I like your books. You have a cute Quasimodo-monk thing going."

Kid chuckled and replied, "The hunchback?"

"So, he does read."

"Not sure how to take that."

She turned and squinted. "You look nervous."

"I dunno, just tired."

"Are you sure this isn't the first time you've had a girl up here?" The corner of her mouth reached for a tiny grin.

"This isn't a bachelor pad, okay? Anybody finds out about this place, I'm back on the street in a heartbeat. It's a secret. Keep it that way."

Alice pantomimed zipped lips. "Fine, jeez. But please tell me you have something I can sleep in."

"Huh?"

"Something to sleep in," She repeated as if her need were obvious. "This shirt is so nasty, they'll find us by smell alone. You're funky too."

Kid rummaged around. "Uh yeah, sure, what do you want? How's this?" He pulled out a plain black t-shirt, clean and folded.

"*Boring*. I saw something peeking out down there, what was that?"

"This?" Kid untucked his David Bowie shirt. It was faded white, with "Bowie" in big red letters over a black and white screen print with Japanese characters. It took three gigs to pay for and was his prized possession. "Um, I don't know, it's old, probably not that comfortable."

"What? No way! Bowie! Old stuff is the best." Alice grabbed the shirt from his surprised hand and held it to her nose. "It even smells cool! And it's so soft. Imagine the stories this could tell."

She shrugged off her jean jacket and started taking off her t-shirt, screen-printed with two samurai raccoons eating a massive bowl of ramen. The movement revealed a fit stomach and pierced belly button—the glittering jewel matched the blue stripes on her shoes. Kid couldn't help noticing that—

like the smattering of freckles across her nose and cheeks—she had a dusting of tan specks tracing her ribs and hips, following the lines of her curves and disappearing behind a low-cut waistband.

"Turn around, perv, you're not getting a free show."

Brought back to reality, Kid glanced at Alice's raised eyebrow, then blushed red-hot and spun back to the plastic bin. He hurried to throw on fresh boxers and jeans to get rid of the wet ones he had on. This random girl would see his ass, but that would be better than trying to sleep in soaked clothes. He knew from experience that was next to impossible. A shower sounded phenomenal, but he was dog tired—some deodorant would do.

"Cute butt. Okay, you can turn back around."

He imagined saying, *thought you said no free shows,* but was still too embarrassed at his temporary lack of gaze control to deliver a clever comeback. As he pulled on the clean shirt, Alice studied the strange markings on his left side and arm.

"Fascinating. I've never seen anything like that or even read about it, which is rare. You said it appeared after Linh was lost? After you woke up?"

"Yeah... What do you think it means?" Kid held his arm in front and examined the marks. They were mesmerizing—the snaking movement under direct observation induced vertigo.

"Honestly, I have no idea. We'll find out, I suppose."

"Science experiment Kid, at your service." He pointed at the box. "What's next with this thing? How do we turn it on?"

"Again, no idea. Sorry, I don't have all the answers. But we'll figure it out. We're a good team. I can *feel* it. Can't you?"

It was Kid's turn to raise an eyebrow. "Uh... no. We just

met. And you're weird as hell. My friend is dying, remember? Try to be a little less cheerful about it."

"Ok fine, fine. But I'll grow on you, I promise. First, though, rest. God, I am so tired. I could sleep a week." Alice looked around for a soft place to rest.

"You can have the hammock." Kid surprised himself by giving up the prime sleeping spot. He already gave up his best shirt. He supposed it was a start to paying her back for saving him, even if she didn't do it for any charitable purpose. It was also payback for giving him something to work toward. The world did not seem so bleak with the new prospect of finding Linh. His instinct was to avoid hope, but now, it was all he had. Faith would be his fuel until this thing ended, one way or another.

Alice hopped into the hammock and almost fell out. She steadied herself with hands on each side. "Whoo! Are you looking for a lawsuit or what?" She swung back and forth, leg hanging out, the suspending ropes creaked in their metal sockets. She stared out the window and spoke quietly, "Oh wow, you can see everything from up here..."

The early morning light cascading in between the broken and scattered rain clouds bounced across the many windows and lit the edges of the buildings like icing. Kid started to say something but realized that Alice already fell asleep. The hammock was still swinging. Her lips parted as her breath deepened, and her hands nuzzled under her armpits to stay warm. Kid grabbed an extra blanket, a thick one with a pattern you'd see on a kilt, and threw it over her to keep away the chill. For himself, he spread out a couple more blankets on the wooden pallets and laid down, then took out Tom's burner, popped the battery in, and typed out a quick message.

How's our lady? You make it safe?

She's still sleeping. No change. You?

Kid started to type out "all good" but deleted it. Things were not all good.

Instead, *I'll check in tomorrow. Get some sleep.*

Not likely.

Kid turned the phone off, took the battery out, and made himself comfortable. He could hear the falcons rustling around, preening their feathers, preparing for the morning hunt. Traffic still hadn't picked up, which was odd for the hour. Usually, the drone of engine noise would already be drifting up from street level. But before another thought about why it was strangely quiet could enter his mind, Kid fell asleep. It was dark, dreamless, and uninterrupted.

22

CRASHED

"Fuck!" Delilah ripped the blanket off, slinging it to the floor. She yanked the IV out of her arm and jumped to the ground, cursing as the catheter she forgot to deflate yanked out. She stood on shaky bare feet that hadn't been used for two days. The nearest possible victim was a laptop. She snatched it up and flung it against the brick wall with a crash of glass and aluminum.

"*God*DAMNIT! That fucking *biiitch*." The words emphasized to their breaking points as if they could be made a literal curse to cross the span of distance and time.

Suddenly, the lights swam, and she stumbled to a trashcan, vomiting bile from an empty stomach—eventually dry heaving and falling to her side in the fetal position clutching her belly in one hand and her head in the other. She ground her teeth to stop herself from whimpering like a weak animal. Getting gate crashed was a bitch, and Alice didn't go easy on her. It was only thanks to Delilah's extensive training that she wasn't a steamed vegetable.

After a few minutes of focused willpower and practiced breathing, she pushed herself up, got to one shaky knee, and stood. The room swam again, but she braced herself against a butcher-block counter that bordered one side of the room and managed to get the nausea under control.

The space was secured by thick walls and a heavy vault door that could only be opened from the inside to protect their vulnerable sleeping bodies. Standing by the two beds in aluminum stands were automatically refilling IV drips to keep them alive for a few days without food. The mirror behind the countertop showed a pale reflection with dark circles under eyes and a mane of strawberry-blonde hair, wild from sleep. Similar to the effects of a concussion, the gate crash left one of her eyes maximally dilated—only a sliver of aqua-green iris remained visible. The white shirt and underwear she slept in were soaked in sweat, the thin cotton made translucent.

Delilah fought another wave of nausea and a head-splitting migraine. "Christ on a fucking cracker. Ugh..." Swallowing the tingling saliva and willing her stomach to quell, she shook with anger as her palms pressed against the counter. She whispered over and over to keep her mind tethered to the real world, "Gonna kill her gonna kill 'er gonnakiller."

After a few minutes, Poe also woke, his heavily tattooed body similarly covered in a sheen of sweat, typically over-styled quiff of red hair comically askew. Alice kept her word and was reasonably gentle with his crash, so he wasn't in terrible condition. He pulled his IV and catheter out as well, more gently than his sister had. It wasn't as painful as most people figured, so long as it was adequately deflated.

"Simmer down, Del."

She shouted, "Simmer down? Fuck you simmer!"

Clearing the five-foot gap between them in a leap, Delilah rained down blows as his hands protected his face. In their authentic vessels, not much damage was done. Although she was well trained, she was slight in build. Whereas at six-five and two-fifty, he could go toe-to-toe with a division-one tight end, and that was without animus augmentation. Plus, she wasn't *trying* to hurt him. At least he didn't think so—not this time.

Poe engulfed her hands with his own and sat up. "Yeah. Chill out. Breaking our gear to hell won't solve anything. Alice got the jump on us—nothing we could do. It was uncontrollable."

"Uncontrollable! *You* let her go! You fuck!"

"Come on, be fair. My frame was trashed, and you know it. I'm surprised it didn't fall apart during the fight with El Tigre. There's no way we could've known Alice would swoop in at the buzzer. Just no way at all. We did the best we could with what we had."

Poe stood up from the hospital bed and grabbed a nearby towel to dry off, running a hand through his hair and attempting to put it in order. He dialed the lamp to medium brightness, squinting at the added illumination to both their faces, then bent over to stretch his back and hamstrings. He straightened back up and said, "She's the last person anyone would've guessed to jump ship. The golden child. Can you imagine? Nobody could. That's my point. Mom's going to freak out and forget all about our mission. You know how she is."

Delilah growled in frustration, "You don't get it! I don't care about that!" She stepped back, lowering her hands. "I *care* about Alice getting the better of us. How did she plant those gate bombs? Undetected! You, I get. But me? My animus is locked down tight, and I keep it that way. She would have to know my true name. *How* did she get it? Or is there some other way?"

"Del, you know her as well as I do. If there were another way, she'd have it. If you thought your true name was hidden perfectly, most likely it wasn't, at least not from her. Even if it pisses you off, she's the best gate-crasher we've ever seen. Shit, she's good enough, she probably hit us from the front, plain as day. Do you remember her saying anything to you over the last few months that seemed out of place?"

"No, of course not!"

"She could've honed a shiv and snuck in," Poe continued softly, working to calm his sister while driving toward a solution. "Did she tell you stories or ask any questions that got you emotional? Riled up? She do anything like that?"

"No!" Delilah's defiant tone trailed off and petered out, "Maybe... I don't know." Her left eye twitched at the admission. Alice had a way of getting her worked up, and they both knew it. A memory tied to an emotion worked well as a shiv, nothing like a true name and a deep sentimental page, but it could be effective in deft hands.

Delilah toweled off and pulled her hair back into a ponytail. After stretching her neck side to side and around, she pulled some clothes out of a wardrobe. She shoved her legs into a pair of black jeans and threw on a shirt and boots, finishing up with an expensive black leather motorcycle jacket. "Doesn't matter now anyway, she can't use the same shiv twice, and now we know to watch out for her. What's her plan? She can't possibly believe she'll get away with this."

Poe replied, "She said she wanted out. Can you blame her?"

Delilah stared at him. "Is that a joke?"

Her brother shrugged.

"What? Do you want to leave? Is that it?"

"What? Nah. Just a vacay."

"To do what, idiot?"

"What else? Get drunk and chase some ass."

"Shut the fuck up. You want Dagan after you?"

"Let the old pedo try it. The last time was a long time ago. I'd waste him."

"Poe, don't say stuff like that. Ever. It's dangerous. I don't... just shut up, okay? Just shut the fuck up."

He raised an eyebrow, unable to recall the last time his sister sounded like she cared about anything. "Relax, I'm joking. Gotta admit, though, drinking a giant margarita and scoping some San Diego booty shorts sounds most excellent."

"Whatever. You're an idiot."

Poe laughed, then turned to dress similarly in jeans and a moto jacket and grabbed his phone. They'd stopped trying to *not* dress alike some time ago—it happened naturally. Best not to fight it.

"Should we let the old lady know it was a bust now?" He asked. "Might let her cool off some before we get there."

"Fuck no. How about we say nothing about our monumental screw-up and tell her Alice stole it."

Delilah tapped out a message that they were heading in

and jammed the phone into the breast pocket of her jacket. She grabbed her keys and helmet, then marched to the private elevator of her three-story SOMA penthouse. Poe would follow in his car, an old stinking shit-box he loved to death for reasons Delilah couldn't figure. From the panoramic window, the silhouette of the Bay Bridge shimmered in the dark. An art installation of animated LEDs covered the vertical cables that held the bridge aloft. Thousands of lights turned on and off in a mathematically mapped cascade like a waterfall.

23
MOTHER

A knock at the door released Mara from her thoughts. "Pardon," Dagan called into her room. "Delilah and Poe to see you." Her head guard wore a well-tailored suit, smartly hiding a low-profile bulletproof vest and Beretta M9 sidearm. Even after all the years, Mara could imagine him with leather and a saber.

Having a fondness for his rare combination of cruelty and loyalty, Mara brought Dagan through many vessels to keep him alongside her—his first transference taking place after the sack of Akkad. Dagan served Mara faithfully ever since. His current vessel was aging but capable. He paid the receding hair and dead grey tooth no mind, always preferring the authority of age and the comfort of the well-worn over the beauty and novelty of youth. In this, he and Mara agreed to disagree.

"Good news, I hope. Bring them in, Dagan," Mara commanded as her pulse quickened in her new vessel's throat.

She stood from her chair at a grand twenty-person dining table in a cavernous stone hall perforated by stained glass windows. With her breakfast of poached eggs and smoked salmon only half-finished, she slid her silver knife and fork to the side and turned toward the door.

Poe entered first, broad-shouldered and fiery. He was often foolhardy but predictable and ultimately dependable despite his whining. Delilah followed him, moving from behind Poe to his side and overtaking him to meet her gaze first like a last-minute racehorse—always so desperate to impress, so hungry for love she would never receive.

They both stopped several feet in front of Mara and knelt with one arm on their knee, mirroring each other, his left on his left, her right on her right. Was that intentional? Hard to say. It was something they had always done, ever since she took them under her wing and brought them into The Young School as dirty adolescents pulled from an East Bay whorehouse. They showed promise as travelers and were not groomed for further subjugation.

Mara padded forward on bare feet between them. As she did, she ran her fingers through their hair. She sighed and stated, "Tell me why your hands are empty." Mara rested her hands on their heads. They did their best not to flinch away and leaned in.

Even in a new vessel, they knew Mara at an instinctual level, would know her even without seeing a body similar to every other she used since knowing her. They were all different yet somehow always the same. And her aura—that never changed. Mara's psychic weight was a tangible thing, at best like a warm blanket on a cold day, at worst like a black hole filled with fire.

Poe spoke first, "It was stolen."

Delilah added, rage barely controlled, "*Alice* has the totem! She ambushed us. *Betrayed* us. I always knew—"

"Shhh." The next moment of silence landed heavily, punctuated only by the gentle sounds of kneeling figures breathing and fingers running through hair. Mara commiserated, "Don't fret. Some things are out of our control."

Delilah replied, "We didn't—"

"Never mind, lamb. What did you learn?"

"It wasn't just Alice. There was a boy and The Doe as well. Even her nightguard, all so close. They've all been in the city, under our feet, this whole time. Nearly twenty years, I remember when they abandoned us. The boy, though... At first, he seemed like a nobody, something random. An artifact."

Mara's eyes narrowed. "At first?"

"I left a blight in him, but he was resilient. He managed to escape and hide, running to The Doe. She succeeded in clearing the blight from within his dream. But not before it took her animus somewhere I can no longer hear it."

Mara pressed on. "Somewhere?"

"There's only one place she could be. The Void."

"Yes. Astute observation. And a curious turn. What else?"

"My blight echoed something I think you'll like. The boy has a name."

Poe glanced at his sister and the surprise reveal.

"Show me," Mara whispered, looking down with a maternal smile that was as sweet as it was venomous.

Delilah swallowed as sweat broke out on her forehead and neck. Mara held the heads of her two acolytes gently in her hands. Then, she jerked their faces together in front of her waist. Mara gripped their hair in her fists and twisted back, forcing their eyes to connect with hers. What they saw was a dark reflection of themselves. Their bodies seized as if hit by a jolt of electricity, eyes dilating and rolling back to white, jaws clenched tight. Poe and Delilah twitched as if in an epileptic fit. Seconds ticked off like loud minutes as Mara saw their pages, their memories. Finally, she released them, gasping for air on all fours.

"Thames." Mara rolled the name around in her mouth. It tasted sweet. "Michael and Saría's sapling. This is *quite* a surprise. Horacio is back in the game then." She smiled. "This *is* interesting. Your blight, can you hear it now? Where are they?"

Delilah shook her head. "No, Mother. I'm sorry. I need to rest. Alice broke my attunement when she crashed us."

Mara examined her hands in disgust, suddenly aware of the candle-lit shine of oil from Delilah and Poe's hair on her skin. She wiped it onto her gown, leaving dark smudges on the expensive silk. Her lip curled, and she hissed, "How long were you under? Did you not even think to bathe?"

"I'm sorry, Mother. We thought we should hurry..."

"I can smell your cunt!" Mara bellowed as she palmed Delilah's face in her hand and shoved her backward with superhuman force to slide across the floor, coming to a thudding halt against the stone wall twenty feet away. Mara strode across the hardwood floor almost soundlessly but for the subtle swishing of her gown and padding of bare feet. Her dark hair flowed behind her, shining like a tapestry of black silk. She knelt in front of her adopted daughter's crumpled form, silent, watching. Delilah's chest raised and lowered with slow, careful breaths. She was uninjured but aware that could change at any moment, terrified to incur any more of Mara's wrath.

Poe watched, head straining toward his sister. He could not move until Mara allowed him, incapacitated by her invisible psychic leash. Through the pathways of The Dream, she held dominion over all her children, mind, body, and animus.

"Even as a traitor, your sister is more useful than you will ever be."

Delilah stayed silent.

Mara sighed, "But you can still help." She pulled Delilah onto her lap, caressing her face and hair. "Do you want to make me happy?"

"Of course, Mother. That's all I want."

"But you're too weak. Don't you see?"

"I'm sorry. I'm so sorry," Delilah cried.

"Shhhh, now. I need you to be strong for me."

Delilah's eyes shimmered, pleading. "How?"

"That last bit you've been hiding. The one you hold close before you sleep. The one you mourn when you think no one is watching. Give it to me. Your last selfish strand. Once you are truly empty, I will reshape you."

The fierce, violent woman, reduced to a girl, sniffled. "Mother... Anything."

Mara continued, "You will walk alone. You'll leave your twin. I'll fill you with the current of the ages, the conduit for the power that flows out from us the moment we fall into The Stream."

"Del, no!" Poe strained, still unable to break the invisible bonds.

"Bring me that knife, child," Mara whispered to him without turning away from Delilah. He fought the command, but it was no use. His legs stood without his permission, his body walked to Mara's breakfast plate, his hand took the knife, his feet brought him back, and grimacing, shaking, and sweating, he held it out for her as asked. She stared at the silver blade, silently commanding Poe to do the impossible. He fell to his knees and scuffled forward.

Mara pointed to Delilah's eye and said to him, "Here."

He whimpered as he leveled the knife in front of his sister's face.

Their mother spoke, "He holds you back. Sever your last thread connecting you to the weaknesses of the Materia."

"Make me better," Delilah begged. "*Please*, please, make me better." Tears rolled from unblinking eyes down her cheeks and absorbed into her hair, which appeared auburn in the dim light.

"I want the totem, the boy, *and* your sister. Find them. Bring them back."

"Yes, anything."

"You will lose your heart but gain my love."

"Yes... yes... please..."

Mara cooed, "Sleep now, lamb. Wake a wolf who sees."

She glanced at the silver knife, then at Poe, and commanded, "Take it."

The blade dug into Delilah's eye socket like a spade in bleeding soil. Twin screams echoed off the stone walls, eventually dying to whimpers. Poe cried and called out to his unresponsive sister. Mara smiled sweetly. It was turning out to be an interesting day, after all.

24
RIFT

With Poe and Delilah dismissed, Mara sat back at the dining table and finished her breakfast. As she licked the blood from the knife, she thought about her previous vessel, which was odd. She didn't usually consider them. Perhaps it was a sign of the times. Her new vessel would last two to three similar years before she traded it in. It was a pretty one, as all were before it. Its face showing not a single wrinkle or blemish. In death, as in life, it was perfect as a doll, discarded at the appropriate moment. How many had she taken? She never bothered to count. Even a tally would have frayed long ago in the many thousands.

Mara loathed even a whiff of the decline that comes with age. It came as no surprise that the human race disgusted her so. The irony that her animus was far older than any of the stinking animals currently on the planet was not lost on her. Mara chewed and swallowed the last bit of egg, then wiped her mouth and lay down the napkin.

She called out, "Dagan?"

"Yes, Mother?" He answered, stepping into view.

"Come with me. I have something to show you."

She walked through a timber-arched hallway adorned with more stained glass. Dagan walked just behind like a well-heeled dog. They passed through the hallway, then turned down another before entering an elevator.

Dagan said, "Is all well in The School? My apologies, but it has been some time since I've made an appearance."

"It's something beautiful. You'll see." Mara pressed the button for the deepest basement level.

After a long journey downward, the freight car opened. The pair exited and walked wordlessly, ending at yet another brushed steel doorway, adorned only with a keypad on which Mara quickly tapped in a code. They entered an office filled with warm lamps, several sitting areas of stuffed black leather chairs, walls lined with dark wood shelves filled with books, and an expansive raw-edge desk.

Still barefoot, Mara walked to a panoramic window and looked out on a vast underground institution. Dozens of students wore identical outfits like gym sweats. Light grey with a green stripe around the left bicep, decorated with symbols denoting class level, accomplishments, and rank. The tutors dressed similarly in black smocks and red armbands. Aside from the militaristic style of clothing, it all looked like something out of a conceptual digest for progressive Scandinavian living—all open plans, light-colored woods, well-groomed plants, and warm light. It was a place that would produce the highest test scores and most well-rounded pupils in the world, albeit in a deep subbasement and under constant guard.

Some children were too young for formal classes and instead played tag, climbed jungle gyms, and skipped hopscotch. Older students grouped around teachers in Socratic discussions or trained in acrobatics, martial arts, and wrestling. Many sat crosslegged and silent in states of deep mediation as they practiced various techniques to travel to, from, and within The Dream.

Mara spoke, "Tell me what you see, Dagan."

After studying briefly, he answered, "Many students are missing." Dagan was agitated. "What happened? I wasn't informed. I will find—"

She shushed him and replied, "Not missing. They're sleeping."

"But why?"

"First, just one. That was nearly two weeks past. Then there were two. Then four. Eight. Now sixteen. This group has lost almost a third to deep comas. The number will double again soon."

"I assume you looked inside them. What did you see?"

"All their vessels are empty—their animi are gone. If things continue at this pace, The Young School and all but the most talented humans in the city will be silent in a few days."

"As in Zeboim…" Dagan turned to Mara. "So, it's another rift, then?"

Mara watched the students and teachers below as she replied, "Yes."

"But we lost the entire city, and this will be much larger. How do we stop it?"

"We don't. We speed it up and use the momentum to end the world's dream."

He swallowed and waited for her to continue.

"Zeboim was an accident, indeed. But we learned—after all, many great discoveries begin as accidents. The Wisemen thought it a plague." Mara coughed a sarcastic laugh. "Thought it an act of the God or gods. I suppose they were right in a way, but they've always been confused about who these divine characters truly are. We found that if vessels are over-harvested, if too many animi are lost, the imbalance creates fractures. Since then, our goal has been vessel management and the sale of longevity. Thus we worked to harvest sustainably."

She clasped her hands behind her back. "But I saw potential then, Dagan. An opportunity to do something noble for this world. An act which will be deeply sacrificial, but also profoundly good. That ember of an idea has grown into a blaze within me."

"Mother," Dagan said, "I'm not sure I understand."

"We have watched a thousand empires rise and fall, have we not? They cycle pointlessly in mortal hands, no better than generations of maggots in compost. You see, *we* can move vessels when our bodies begin to die." Mara pressed her hands to the glass. "Sadly, humanity cannot do the same. Their vessels expire, and with them, any modicum of wisdom gained in life like a candle flicker. This is their weakness."

She put her hands on his shoulders and looked into his eyes. "I don't need to kiss you to convince you. You have seen the truth, same as I. Mankind is rotting. Has been for millennia. The decay has spread into the soil and the air. To survive, they must change. Yet, they cannot. They are not capable—mere children. And like children, most things must be done for them. As I am their mother, I will do this thing. First chrysalis. Then metamorphosis."

Turning back to the window, she continued, "This time, unlike Zeboim, there are more animi, so many more. This will be unconfined and ravenous. Those few who survive and resist the pull to the dark sleep will be worthy of the new world."

Dagan asked, "But, Mother... How?"

"Thanks to our work over the last era, we have already displaced enough raw animus to tear a sizable rift. You can see the proof of that in the children sleeping. Even the talented are falling in now. I assure you, the weak are falling in droves outside The Young School. But to accomplish what we must, the rift needs to be bigger still. For that to happen in reasonably short order, we need the lost totem and, if possible, a spiritborne youth."

"Spiritborne? But the child was lost."

"The Thames boy has been found."

"The child of Michael and Saría?"

"Yes, the same. One and only. He has the totem, and he is also its key. A coincidence, I think not. The only child known to be born of a man and a dream, a being made of both worlds, possessing a weapon to sever them all. He is as close to pure animus as we will find, and unlike a vaporous being like Saría, or the other pure spirits in The Dream, his animal half will make him tangible and useful."

Mara reached to caress Dagan's face. "This is destiny, my eldest love. With the boy, the totem, and the rift, we will have everything we need to build something new. Something better. Something pure."

"What if we don't make it past the horizon?"

"Isn't that always the risk in great pursuits?"

"Indeed."

"Killing and dying is mercy made fit for a mother."

Dagan watched the students but said nothing.

"Are you afraid?" Mara asked.

Without hesitation, he shook his head. "No. I'll follow you anywhere, even to the black, if that is where we are going." He turned to her. "How then? Alice is on the run with the boy—surely that changes things."

"I'll take care of my daughter. Simple teenage rebellion, it's nothing."

"Alright, and you sent Delilah, but she is... unstable. Do you believe she will succeed in bringing them all back? Why not send more? Send me?"

"Her real job is not to bring them back."

Again, he waited patiently for Mara to continue.

"You see, long ago, when we painted our bodies with the blood of our foes—before we learned to tame horses—we ran barefoot. We hunted sprawling herds of big game without injury. Do you know how we did this?"

Dagan shook his head.

"By chasing them. The ignorant animals would run under the belief that they were escaping. Then, they would race headlong exactly where we wanted. We would choose a cliff. And that is where they would fall to their deaths. Our reward was collected at the blood-soaked base."

Mara smiled as she watched the students through the tinted glass pane.

"We don't move. We are the jagged stone."

25
QUASI

In the rooftop sanctuary, Alice still slept, and Kid lay with his hands clasped behind his head. It seemed like years since he felt this rested and wanted to savor it. He did so for another half hour, feeling the warmth of the late afternoon sun hanging in the sky, the cool bay breeze, and the calming silence.

After a while, he stood reluctantly and went to a small hanging mirror, taking off his shirt to examine his face and body. Double black eyes, abraded palms, and bruised ribs. Nothing worse, surprisingly. His biggest complaint now, if you could even call it that, was a sore back and legs. It felt more like he went through an intense workout than the nightmare game show ass-kicking that had transpired. Kid shook his head in disbelief and put his shirt back on.

The strange girl sleeping in his hammock proved the impossible. Her mouth hung open, just as it had when she fell asleep hours before. A bit of drool shone on her lip as she snored softly. She saved their lives and gave them hope. Having apparently switched sides, she wanted to help further.

Why?

She thought he could activate the totem for some vague reason.

He still didn't know what the thing even was.

Regardless, despite any suspicions he might have, the number one priority was helping Linh. That meant there was only one way to go until new pieces were on the board. At some point in the night, he made a promise and would not break it. He would not run from this.

Alice snorted in her sleep and scratched her nose.

Kid admitted she was charming in a goofy, annoying, smart-ass way. But he also knew that was one of the best ways to get somebody's guard down.

It didn't seem like she would wake easily in the next few minutes, so Kid took the opportunity to bathe in the gravity shower. The rain topped up the water level, so there was no need to rush. Kid watched the water run down his body and turn murky brown before snaking down the drain.

The geometric markings went from his fingertips up his arm and covered his left pec—stopping at the sternum like one of those Yakuza tats. He flexed his arm. It didn't feel like it had yesterday—as if it was rotting off and filled with acid. It felt fine. *Better* than fine. His arm felt great, like a coiled spring buzzing with electricity.

After he toweled off and put fresh clothes on, he grabbed a few things to eat. It wasn't much but would do. Cheese and crackers, peanut butter, jelly, hummus and pita bread, trail mix, and a couple bottles of water. He looked up to the still-sleeping Alice, reached out, and shook the hammock.

"Hmm? Hey!" She tilted her head, sensed the drool on her lip, and quickly wiped it away with the back of her hand.

"Hungry?" Kid asked.

"God, yes. I'm starving. Watch that hand. I bite." She swung a leg over and flipped out of the hammock at comical speed but managed to land on her feet and hands. She stood and looked at the hammock with her head tilted. "These look safer on Insta."

Kid laughed, "You have social media?"

"No," she huffed, "We're not allowed. But I stalk civies all the time."

"Civies?"

"Civilians. Normies. Reggos."

"Right. Yeah, I do the same. Pretend what it'd be like. College and quarterbacks, parties, and girlfriends. Road trips to Vegas."

"Vegas? Ew."

"Or wherever. Yosemite. Tahoe. Yadda-yadda, blah-blah. I always thought snowboarding looked cool."

"I suppose you seem like the boarder type. But it's a bit sad, isn't it? Always on the outside looking in."

Kid's mouth twitched with suppressed emotion after realizing he had revealed too much. "Guess so. Anyway, here." He motioned to the spread of food. "Grab something. We need to talk. I got questions."

Alice nodded. "I'm sure you do." She took some pita bread, made a pocket, filled it with peanut butter and jelly, then stuffed half of it in her mouth. Talking around the mouthful, she exclaimed, "Mmmff! So good! Thank you." She smiled, showing a gross mouth full of food. They both laughed hearty belly laughs. It felt good after everything. With some difficulty, she managed to swallow without choking. "Okay, go for it. Ask away."

"Why are you helping me? Really. Why do you think I can unlock this thing? You seem like some super soldier. Are you sure you can't do it? Something's sketchy about this."

She chewed another bite and thought for a moment. "Oh, we passed sketchy a long time ago. You jumped into The Dream with that totem, not even trying. Our calibration for normal is pretty out of whack, but still, that's not even close. Like I said last night, those things are four-dimensional Rubik's cubes. Thousands must be gathering dust, waiting for the right person and circumstance."

"There are more? What do the rest do?" Kid asked.

"All sorts of things. There are keys, beacons, compasses, power-ups and power-downs, weapons, and items of defense, and many others that are mysterious and unknowable."

"So what, like magic?"

"You can call it what you want—whatever keeps your brain from melting. But here's the deal, using the word 'magic' means you don't get it yet. This stuff is as real as this rooftop, The Dream, and everything else. Nothing is magic, and everything is. This thing we call the universe, the world, reality?" She emphasized the word with air quotes. "It is maximum-freaky. Hang out with me and you'll see what I'm talking about."

"I'll try to turn my brain off for a while. Seems like it's getting in the way."

"You're not wrong. Adult minds get tripped up easily. That fact is why the younger the mind, the easier the jump. You noticed Poe and Delilah's frames?"

"Frames?"

"That's what we call stolen bodies, to differentiate from an authentic vessel like yours or mine."

"To take the humanity out of the task."

Alice sighed, "Yeah..."

"I see. And yes, I noticed they were young the first time they tried to kill me. Like middle school assassins. Why do they stink?"

"You caught that?"

"How could you miss it? Stunk like death. That's how I knew to run."

"In a way, it is death, but most people can't sense that. You've got talent."

"Like a sixth sense?"

"Sixth, seventh, eighth. The world has many facets hidden beyond the apparent edges of liminal space. But that's a different topic. Let's get back to the totem. It reacted to you without you even touching it. What are the chances of that totem ending up so close to someone with an innate synchronization? Beyond rare. So rare it can't be random. Can't be."

"What, like fate? Destiny?"

Alice grinned, "Totally."

"Or we're puppets on strings."

As they talked, they finished the entire spread of food, even the crumbs—which they picked up with tongue-wetted fingers.

Kid asked, "Back to my first question, what's the next step? Got any ideas to turn this thing on? I might be your Huckleberry, but you're my guide."

"Well, we can't go to just anyone. I don't know who all is on Mara's payroll or within her influence. And it's not just her —she's up there, but one of many generals, not the queen. The larger organization is called the White Lotus Society, and they have their greasy tentacles in everything."

"White Lotus? That's who I was originally transporting the package for."

Alice winked at Kid, "I know."

"Figures," he chuckled. "So, they were stealing it from themselves?"

"Honestly, that's not even surprising. Create an international conglomerate of evil, and you will have some in-fighting. It could work to our advantage, but it sure doesn't make things any less complicated. They might even be working together, using the drop and theft to make somebody else think it's lost. There are a lot of moving pieces and possibilities."

Alice let out a sigh, making a raspberry sound. "I can't use normal channels to learn about this thing. The research I've been doing so far has been on the very down low, and there's just not a lot to go on. We need an expert who won't rat us out. Every idea I have is probably a trap."

"Which means you don't have any ideas."

She scowled. "I have ideas. They just suck. What about you, outlaw?"

"We could do what I normally do when I don't know what to do."

"What's that?"

"Nothing."

"Nothing?"

"Yeah, check it out. I was reading about this guy Archimedes and the subconscious mind. You'll like this—seems to fit the theme here. He's banging his head against a wall about this math problem for forever, can't figure it out. Trying to figure out how to calculate the volume and mass of an object," Kid stopped orating to ask, "Have you heard this one?"

Alice was enjoying Kid's professor side. "Nope. Go on."

"Okay, he's frustrated, trying everything, getting nowhere. Finally, he just gives up and decides to take a bath and relax. He fills the tub, strips down, and slides in the water with a sigh."

"How do you know he sighed?"

"Fair point, I've never had a bath."

"Never?" She raised an eyebrow.

"Don't look at me like that. I'm a shower guy." Kid nodded in the direction of his hand-built body-washing rig. "They seem nice, though. Who wouldn't sigh when sinking into hot, bubbly water?"

Alice shrugged.

Kid continued, "So, he's in the water, definitely sighing. Just happy to relax for a bit before going back to work on the problem. He's blowing bubbles and wiggling his toes when suddenly, he has it. The water went up when he got in the tub. He figured it out! You can measure the volume and mass of an object by the amount of water it displaces. He jumps out and runs through the streets, yelling, 'Eureka! Eureka! I've got it!', old bare butt bouncing for the world."

"That's something I can't unsee."

"Shhh—"

Alice flashed real anger at being shushed, which Kid didn't notice.

"See, he just had to relax for a minute and let his back-brain chew on the problem. He was thinking without thinking. Seeing without seeing. As soon as he chilled out, the answer was there. If you want fate to take its turn, you gotta unclench your butt cheeks."

She laughed, evaporating her brief flash of anger, and replied to the monologue, "Okay, let's unclench our cheeks."

Kid and Alice sat with the window open, listening to the sounds of the city. The falcons were somewhere unseen but not unheard, their calls occasionally echoing in the air. Alice wished she had her phone, there were a few contacts she thought might be solid, but she threw it away after winning the tickets to avoid tracking.

Remembering her iPod, Alice took it out and handed an earbud to Kid. He raised an eyebrow but then got the hint and put it in his left ear as she put the other in her right. They lay down on the blanket-draped pallet, and she set the device to shuffle. It played *Kazakstan*, by Brian Eno, from the album Music for Installations. It was a thoughtful, dark, and appropriately dream-like meditation of a track. They listened through the whole twenty-minute song while watching the stained glass mobile swing gently in the breeze.

Towards the end, Kid felt his breathing slow, and his eyes started to close, falling into that fuzzy place between wake and dream where thoughts wander. He half-dreamt of several things but eventually settled on the golden-eyed Horacio, the strange fisherman from the beach by the tempestuous Dream Sea.

Don't forget, the amber-eyed man said, just before kicking Kid in the chest with a rain boot. But he did forget. Because of the tumult of the last two days, details were fuzzy. But there it was, waiting for him to relax.

When you're free of it, when the poison is gone, come find me. I trust that you will want to. I'll be waiting for you at The Sand.

It didn't make any sense before. But now it felt meaningful.

Kid came to full attention and sat up.

"What?" Alice asked.

He spun on crossed legs to face her and told her a more detailed version of his experience in The Dream. "He said he'd wait for me at The Sand once I got rid of the poison. That mean anything to you?"

She immediately thought of the tickets and sat up like a bolt. "Yes!"

Alice told him about winning the radio raffle two days before. They were to see The Red Queen at The Sand in East Oakland. It seemed like random luck. But it was clearly not. Kid thought of the many fishing lines Horacio had in the shallows of the Dream Sea and realized they were likely not metaphorical.

"The show. It's tonight," Alice said, nearly dumbfounded. Then, with eyes wide and sudden excitement, she squealed, "This is it!" She pulled Kid to standing, jumping, and dragging him in a bobbing circle. "Yes! Oh my gosh, this is what I'm talking about. Lightning strikes! There is no such thing as random. We are in it! The flow! Fate! Destiny!"

The exuberance was contagious, and Kid picked her up as they spun in a bouncing dance. After a moment, he realized what he had done and sat her back down. Her face was now only a hand's length away from his. The distance at which you can identify the individual strands of color in an iris—the yellows and oranges that make brown. The patches of fine peach fuzz where the ear stops and cheek starts—the rise and fall of the throat just above the clavicle.

Their cheeks flushed scarlet, eyes quickly darted away, and they scrambled for something to busy themselves. Kid fumbled around and began cleaning up the packaging trash from their meal. Alice bent quickly to help, causing their heads to bonk.

"Ouch!" She squeaked. "Sorry!"

"Ah, no, my bad, seriously, no worries," Kid rambled.

Alice straightened back up and looked around, desperately trying to find a good reason to put some distance between them. She said, "Hey, does that shower really work?"

"What?" Kid looked up and over, confused, then grateful for the distraction. "Yeah, like surfers use. You just pump and go."

"Quasimodo MacGyver up here in his cute little clock tower. Mind if I use it?"

"Knock yourself out. There's soap and stuff. Just make sure

all the water goes down that janky drain I made. Otherwise, it'll end up smelling nasty and draws flies."

"Gross," Alice replied. "Thanks."

As she disappeared behind the plywood wall to shower, Kid sat down and exhaled, grateful for the moment to recollect himself. He glanced at his backpack on the floor and pulled it closer to check out the bread-loaf-sized box. It was a potent reminder of what was at stake in the world away from the rooftop. Giggling and flirting? Ridiculous. Get it together, Kid. His best friend was dying, and on top of that, what would he do about Ben and The Lotus? Kid hadn't messaged or reported anything. Their package was missing. Their associate was dead. They'd be looking for him. If they found him...

No problem. Just don't get caught.

Now about this box.

He pulled it out of the bag and laid it across his lap. It consisted of plain cardboard and no markings other than some scuffs it received from its questionable courier. He figured this would put him in the transporter hall of fame. The package was banged up, but he didn't lose it. That's where the rubber meets the road. Not losing it, that's the thing. But once he opened the box, the sanctity of the envoy would be officially broken.

Was this the point of no return? Or did he pass that threshold some time back? Was it the moment he discovered the dead body in Chinatown? Or when he chose to run from the twins? Maybe it was when his child-self attempted to save Linh from the darkness of his dream. Perhaps it was the decision to walk down the alleyway and fight instead of running away. Possibly it was now, this second. Maybe it was the day he was born.

Before fully committing, he ran his hands across the smooth cardboard one last time. Using his pocket knife, he sliced the packing tape on the side and flipped open the short end. Dark wood showed through the opening, a box within a box. It fit perfectly and slid out slowly from the resulting vacuum, strangely satisfying as it finally popped out with a puff of air.

It looked old, like some Indiana Jones, Ark of the Covenant old. It even smelled ancient, like a forest floor. There was another scent, though, just below that... oil and metal... like a torn-down engine block. Kid ran his hands across the contours of the images carved into every surface. Centered on each side was a carving of a tall oblong disk, like a portal. From that centered disk, mirrored images of animal herds and people ran in opposite directions. The images continued flowing around the box until they met head-on at an identical disk on the opposite side. On one side of the disk, the characters appeared alive and happy, as if they were dancing or playing. On the other side, they were all skeletons, spirits, and monstrous things.

The box had no visible seams, latches, or anything that would lead someone to believe it could be opened. When Kid shook it, which seemed dangerously chaotic, it made no sound. It appeared to be an ornately carved block of dense wood, almost stone-like, and that was it—a fancy doorstop.

"Ghosts and monsters? That's not scary at all," Alice said. So focused on the box, Kid didn't hear her finish showering or approach. She crouched next to him. "Are you having any luck?" Her wet hair dripped onto the wooden pallet forming dark splotches. One droplet hung stubbornly to the end of a platinum lock.

"Nope. It's a puzzle box. Or nothing but a block of wood."

"Can I see?" She moved all her hair to one side in a graceful motion. Her hand dipped as she accepted it. "Woof— it's heavier than it looks."

Kid's eyes met Alice's. "Think it's dangerous? I mean, to us, right now?"

"What, like, radioactive? I don't know, but it doesn't feel like it. At least not at the moment. It seems inert." Alice ran her hands across the surface. She discovered nothing new and returned the box to Kid with a frown.

They packed light, just one bag with a few burners and the box, which Kid returned to its cardboard container. He didn't like to go without tools but anything else and they might not make it past the doorman at The Sand. The sun was quickly setting, painting the sky in streaks of blood-orange. The air was strangely devoid of the typical traffic noise. Kid wondered if there was a Giant's game on.

Alice stuffed her hands in her jean jacket pockets and asked, "We should avoid an e-trail. No credit cards or bus passes. How do you want to get over there?"

"You're the spy."

"Even spies get stuck."

He nodded, she was right. It needed to be offline and cash. They could hop the turnstiles and sneak on the Bart train, but there would still be cameras and too many people. Kid remembered the card given to him by the cabbie. What was his name?

It came to him, and he said, "Jamaal."

"Who's Jamaal?"

"Taxi driver."

"They still have those?"

"A few. Gave me his card last night."

Another apparent coincidence—fishing lines in a sea.

With everything ready to go, Kid closed the bag and slung it over his shoulder. "I don't know if any of my old burners are comped, so I'll make the call a few blocks away. If the nest gets blown, we won't have anywhere to go except to Tom, and I'd rather keep his place off the radar until we know more about how to help Linh."

"The Nest?"

Kid squinted. "Guess I said that out loud. It's what I call this place. Because of the falcons."

"Actually, only the female is a falcon. The male is a tiercel."

"Right!" Kid said, clearly impressed. "You know about birds?"

"No, no, not much. I just heard the tiercel thing in a nature documentary. But I have another fun fact for you. The name peregrine is tied to the word peregrination."

Kid stared as if to say, *Yeah, and?*

"Peregrination means to journey. It comes from the Latin peregrinus, which means foreigner. As an adjective, it can be used to describe someone or something of the wandering sort. A pilgrim or traveler. And funnily enough, that's what they call us, you know."

"Pilgrims? Like the old colonial dudes?"

Alice giggled, "No, not that word. Travelers. Us. Those who dance between dreams. You're one of us now, if only just barely." Alice managed to smile in a way that was half embarrassed blushing, and half proud academic.

"Sounds pretty cool when you say it that way," Kid said.

She shrugged. "I like words."

"Nerd."

"Takes one to know one." Again, she found herself grinning. It would be irritating if it weren't so welcome. In her line of work, she didn't get to make friends. It wouldn't take a mind reader to realize Alice was incredibly lonely, as was Kid, each in their own way.

"So, did you raise them?" She asked. "I saw the incubator over there." Alice glanced over to the wood and glass contraption. It did not look functional.

"No, they're wild. But, I thought about bringing up some pigeons."

"That'd make you a proper roof-dude."

Kid couldn't stifle a smirk. "Yeah."

"So, why not?"

"Found out they eat them. Plus, aside from their family, falcons prefer solitude."

"Seems like they're okay with you, though," She said.

"Yeah." Kid beamed with unhidden self-satisfaction. "We're cool."

"How long have you all been here?"

"Few years for me. They live up to twenty in the wild and were here already when I found the place. So, who knows? I've seen them raise two broods so far. Working on their third batch of eggs now."

"Really? What do they look like?"

"The eggs? They're pretty. Red and tan, spotted like a river rock."

"I wish I could see them."

"Yeah, me too. I only know what they look like because I googled it. You can't get too close. They tolerate me being nearby, but they're still wild. I named them, though."

"Yeah?"

"Cloud and Zoe." Kid smiled.

Alice smiled back and replied, "Those are perfect names."

Talking about the birds brought authentic happiness to the surface. But as soon as Kid became aware of it, his smile faltered. He thought of Linh, the oppressing gravity of the situation, and sudden shame for letting himself get distracted. Smiling, small talk... flirting? Get it together. You ain't somethin' to save. You're something to sever.

"Come on, let's stop screwing around," Kid said as he walked away.

Alice's smile deflated as she nodded and followed.

26

BRIDGE

On the way down the fire escape to street level, Kid again noticed how few people or cars were around and wondered what event might pull people away from the streets. Maybe a baseball game or possibly the big music festival, Outside Lands. He couldn't remember when exactly that was. Burning Man sometimes cleared the city out like this, but that wasn't happening for a few more months. It didn't seem critical, and he pushed the thought away.

Kid had to call the cab, but knowing that Ben, The Creep Twins, and whoever else was hunting them, they needed to get off the street. The pair walked a half-mile to a laundromat called La Jefecita and ducked inside. Before leaving to make the call, Kid left the totem with Alice and told her that if he didn't come back shortly, to go on. She nodded solemnly.

Once a few blocks away, Kid pulled out Tom's phone and checked in. There were no updates. Linh was still barely alive, and Tom sounded haggard, like he hadn't slept. Next, Kid pulled out the business card. It read '*Jamaal Jackson - On Call Personal Transport, Serving the entire Bay Area.*' He punched in the number and waited. After six rings, the call connected.

"You got Jamaal." White noise and wind could be heard on the cabbie's end. He was talking on speakerphone with the window down as he drove.

"Hey," Kid said. "You gave me your card last night. The *non*-puker you made forty bucks on."

"Course, I don't give my card out to everyone. Feeling better?"

"Like a million bucks," Kid said, not at all sarcastically. He really did feel pumped, like he'd slammed an energy drink. He switched the phone to the other ear and asked, "Got time for a ride over to Oakland?"

"Sure thing. Ain't a fare to be found today, son. Hunting all day and not a soul."

"Yeah, messed up, right? Where is everyone?"

"Got me. Must be something. Where you at?"

Kid walked up a side street and stopped under a shade tree. It was planted in a small square of dirt littered with cigarette butts and used hypodermic needles with bright orange caps. A lone hipster on a cafe racer brapped-brapped by, trailing pungent two-stroke exhaust.

He answered, "La Jefecita Laundry in the TL, down by Jones and Eddy."

"Aight. See you in a few, heading from The Inner Sunset."

He thanked Jamaal, ended the call, popped the battery out, and threw it in the trash. Then Kid trotted back to the laundromat, slowed at the entrance, and walked in. Alice was dancing in a corner, listening to music through her headphones. Maybe Kid should have been annoyed at the nerve she had to dance in a situation like this. But instead, he just watched. White Adidas shell-tops with baby blue stripes moved rhythmically across the black and white checked linoleum with little squeaks as one combo transitioned into the next. Her eyes were closed. Thin lines of sparkling blue eyeshadow matched the stripes of her sneakers. When did she have time to put on makeup? Girls were mysterious like that. She danced as if nothing else was happening in the world, no losses of friends or reality, no fights for survival, no supernatural battles between good and evil.

Nearby, a young Hispanic mom with big eyelashes was washing her family's clothes. She smiled at Kid, apparently aware of something he was not. The mom's attention was enough to snap Kid out of his daydream. He strode over to Alice and pulled the earbud out of her ear. "Is this your phone? Jesus. They're gonna find us. Come on." He grabbed her hand to pull her towards the door.

She didn't resist and instead allowed the distance to close. Once near, she whispered, "Relax, Kid. It's okay." Alice smiled and pulled the old-school iPod from the inside pocket of her jean jacket. Kid jerked a glance over to the Laundry-Mom— she was no longer paying attention to them and was watching TV as she folded clothes. He turned back to Alice and relaxed.

She said, "I threw my phone away last night. I'm a professional, remember? Like, bonafide secret agent status. Don't worry so much."

"Sorry." He said, grimacing in embarrassment. "My brain still isn't used to remembering iPods exist. Freaked me out a little."

"A little?"

"A lot."

"Over me?"

"It was self-preservation."

"Are you sure about that?" The corner of her mouth reached for a grin. "Besides, if you can't find time to dance in moments between, then what's the point?"

Kid didn't want to get into it and ignored the hook. "Can I see it?"

Alice rolled her eyes and handed him the retro device with a cracked color screen.

"What were you listening to?"

"LCD Soundsystem."

"Old school."

"Yeah. I wish I were from back then."

"They had good music, that's for sure. Where'd you find this?"

"A thrift store, same as anything else worth my money. I love vintage stuff."

Kid said, "Yeah, me too. I have a bunch of books that—"

Cutting their conversation short, the Laundry-Mom exclaimed, "Oh my..."

A local news channel broadcasted a report of a building in the city that caught fire in the early morning and was recently put out. Kid and Alice immediately recognized the smoldering remains in the background behind the blue-suited reporter and the red digital ticker tape reading: *Breaking News, Fire in the Tenderloin.*

A column of smoke obscures the sky due to a major fire that broke out in the early morning hours today in The Tenderloin neighborhood of San Francisco. The cause has not yet been determined, but officials say it could be linked to many fire hazards common in restaurants and older buildings.

The blaze that engulfed the two-story building was successfully put under control by the city's courageous firefighters. The neighboring buildings were saved and suffered only minor damage. As of this broadcast, two bodies have been recovered from the scene, as of yet unidentified, due to extensive fire damage. Back to you, Jackie.

Thank you, Aaron. Our hearts go out to those lost souls and their families. And our thanks go to the brave men and women who fought the fire and helped protect our city.

"Did Lotus do that?" Kid asked, to which Alice replied with a somber nod. The scene transitioned to another anchorwoman behind a big desk, accompanied by a floating image of someone on life support equipment in the intensive care unit of a local hospital.

Now, in other news: an alarming number of people in the city have fallen into inexplicable comas. Over the last few days, cases have risen dramatically. Today, we've brought sleep health expert Dr. Dahlia Holden, Professor of Neuroscience and Psychology at the University of California, Berkeley, to help explain what's happening. "Dr. Holden, thank you for coming."

"I'd like to say my pleasure, but I don't believe that's the case."

"Indeed. Thank you, doctor. What can you tell us about this?

Is it viral? Something in our water or food? Should we be worried?"

"Well, Jackie, what I can say is—"

Alice scoffed. "If only Jackie-with-the-weather knew how right she was."

Kid asked, "What do you mean?"

"This does seem viral, in a sense. You've noticed how quiet everything is, right?"

"Yeah, for sure. Must be a big event or a game."

"Unfortunately, no. I don't think that's it."

"What, then?"

"Do you notice any similarities between these people and Linh?"

The connection was logical but so out of touch with Kid's previous concept of reality that he hadn't considered it. Horacio even mentioned too many people sleeping, but, like many of the vaporous details of his walk in The Dream, he forgot that til now. The people on the news were all in comas, barely alive, like their lights had been turned off.

"Fuck. Linh's not the only one then."

"No." Alice frowned. "It doesn't look like it."

"So, what does this mean?" Kid asked.

"I don't know, but it's not good. My hypothesis? There are more holes in The Dream than the one Linh's animus fell through. If that's true, then this is much bigger than us. Her situation is the first visible crack in a fundamentally damaged structure."

Kid chewed on the new information before responding. "Well, for now, we don't know enough to do anything about it. Maybe our path to Linh will help us understand what's going on."

Alice nodded and said no more as they continued watching the news. The video reel showed entire hospital wards of sleeping people. There were hundreds, if not thousands. Likely many more unaccounted for, still asleep in their homes and apartments.

After a bit, Jamaal's paint-chipped taxi pulled up on whining brakes. They walked outside and slid onto the vinyl bench seat. The miniature TV still played over-bright commercials but was less intrusive in the light of day. The remains of a recent fast food meal littered the front passenger seat, filling the car with the aroma of deep-fried something. It was oddly reassuring. Kid had a newfound appreciation for the mundanely real.

Jamaal nodded to Alice in greeting and asked, "Where we heading?" He was in his late forties or early fifties, wearing a grey knitted Warriors beanie. Curly black hair covered his arms, and a small photo of his wife and two children was stuck to the dash in a green paperclip holder—all details Kid missed on his previous, and very blurry, early morning ride.

Alice responded, "We're going to The Sand in East Oakland. Do you know where that's at?"

"I know where everything's at, shorty. I'm one of the classics. Hang tight."

Jamaal put the cab in gear, pulled out, and drove a couple of blocks past the side street where Kid had gone to make the phone calls.

"Shit," Kid hissed as he pulled Alice down into the back seat.

A blacked-out Audi A7 Sportback with diplomatic plates was parked next to a tree in the small square of dirt. It was Ben, looking the same as always with his lazy eye and nondescript grey suit.

He held Kid's disassembled burner in one hand as he spoke into a different phone in the other. They watched him from as low a position as possible until he passed out of sight. After putting a few more blocks between them, Alice and Kid slid back up.

"Whoa," Alice said. "That was fast."

He chewed his lip. "For real. Don't know how they had the number on that fresh burner unless they watched me buy it. That's freaky. What else do they know that we think they don't? Fuck."

"And *that's* why I'm still in business," Jamaal laughed as he jumped into the conversation. "Uber's a no-go when you wanna get funky."

It was easy to forget a cabbie could hear everything you said. Alice asked, "And you're still giving us a ride?"

"Girl, I could tell your boy was sketch last night. But hey, my kids gotta eat. 'Sides, y'all got something about you. Dimension, you could say. I can feel these kinda things, you know. Lemme tell you something. I had a dream. A wild one. Wanna hear about it?"

Jamaal didn't wait for positive affirmation. Like most cabbies, he was used to talking when he felt like it. "In the dream, I walk out my place, early in the morning, before the sun come up—like I always do, babies still sleeping. I walk out to warm up the cab, and what'dya know? This beat-to-hell street cat's sitting on the hood of my ride. Big golden eyes.

This cat says to me, *Hey Jamaal, don't leave the kid hanging. Get him home."*

The cabbie mock-shivered to make the point. "Trippin, right? Woke up tingling all over, like my body was a foot fall asleep. Didn't know what it meant at first. But, hey, youngblood, I'll give you one guess when that dream was." Jamaal made eye contact with Kid in the rearview mirror, waiting for an answer.

"A cat, huh? Guessing the day before you picked me up."

"Winner, winner, chicken dinner."

Alice shifted in her seat, she wasn't expecting anything other than a simple cab ride, but she knew that not all with the innate talent to travel The Dream were on an official roster. Many believe that every man, woman, and child has the ability. They think it's in our DNA, part of all of us, hardwired in our brains, down to a cellular level like breathing. But in most people, the ability is unrealized.

"Who are you exactly?" She asked.

"Just Jamaal, sweetheart. I get people where they need to get, that's all. And when I can, I get some a little further. Don't tell central I'm smuggling bayside." He smiled, showing big beautiful teeth.

Something about him settled Alice's nerves. She could feel an authentic kindness, a kinship. She could feel it, like she could feel a lot of things. Some nodes in the Animus Mundi were adjacent or similarly toned, harmonically inclined.

"Thanks, Jamz," Alice said, giving him a nickname without permission.

He seemed to like it as his dark skin blushed as much as it

could around his smile, and he did a happy tippity-tap on the steering wheel with his fingers and kept driving.

As they made their way across the Bay Bridge, the gigantic dock-loading cranes of the Port of Oakland passed by to their right. They looked like mechanized dinosaurs grazing on the fruits of a thousand multicolored shipping containers, red, blue, orange, and brown. They all noticed the number of cars on the road increasing as they headed east. It seemed that whatever was causing people to go into comas hadn't crossed the bay. At least not yet.

27
CRIB

W atching the face of her sleeping baby daughter, Linh was content. Happy even. For the first time in all the years since they parted. Since she gave her away. Since she abandoned her. But it was okay; now she had her back. Linh knew that everything she had seen and done meant to lead to this moment.

She arrived, finally.

Little Bian was sleeping sweetly in her blonde wood crib. Mother and daughter illuminated by a powerful ethereal spotlight. Outside that lit circle, the opaque shadow held guard like a frozen tidal wave.

Fragments of floating memories toyed with her. Fighting a beast in Kid's tainted dream, the heart's bane, which had become the mutated creature Patricia Hodgekiss. Time was different in The Void, dilation multiplied by dilation. She fought the thing for many days before things went dark. Or was it months? What happened before all that? And after?

Impossible to determine. Gauze memories the same color as her now white hair.

How long?

If she were capable of counting, she'd know.

Nearly three relative years thus far.

But it didn't matter.

If she lost her mind, there was nowhere else she'd rather be.

Here with her Bian.

The baby stared silently.

Intelligently.

The irises of her infant eyes were hypnotic pools of black ink. Linh felt herself gently drift like riding a cloud into a wave of sea foam, the all-encompassing dark silk shroud of a persistent opium dream. Barbs hid under tender puffs of cotton, sharp and rusted. Those that pierce and tear and don't let go. She forgot what came before, forgot about battle, forgot about the world, forgot about Kid.

The only things that existed in her universe were the baby, the crib, and the prison wall of shadow surrounding her tiny circle of light. If she had the sense to do so, she would call for help and beg Kid to hurry. But she had no such sense, and instead, Linh watched the child, eyes locked, unblinking, as her life passed through fingers like chalk dust.

28

CLEAN

After her "surgery," Delilah slept for several hours in one of the blank white rooms in The School's medical ward. When she woke, she found a traumatized Poe, told him to stop being such a pussy and that her eye didn't hurt. Then she shared the intel to which she had gained access. The blight Delilah left in Kid allowed her to see everything he had seen since their fateful collision in Chinatown, at least in The Real. When she tried to access his time in The Dream, it was a blank space awash in static and swirling colors.

From what she *had* seen, Linh's nightguard escaped in a beat-up Ford Crown Victoria, which they would find quickly enough, and Alice was having a gay old time, flirting and fucking around. Spoiled bitch. Delilah would get back to the transference room in her penthouse, clean up, and tune back in to her blight shard to see where the little shits were now. Then she'd find them. Then she'd make them hurt.

Delilah rode her Ducati back to SOMA and barely made it

without crashing. Her depth perception was jacked due to the missing eye, and new power coursed through her head like an electric wire. The lobby guard noticed her now hellish face, but part of his job was never to ask questions, no matter what the tenants got up to—especially those on the upper levels. After a too-bright elevator ride, she entered her home and immediately undressed, kicking her clothes and boots to the side of the foyer.

She walked naked to her minibar and made a stiff bourbon Manhattan, gulped it down, made another just as stiff, and sipped that one as she went to the toilet and took a desperately needed three-day shit that came out like a charcoal briquette. Delilah showered, long and steaming hot, scrubbing her skin furiously until it was rubbed raw and stung under the scalding water. She welcomed the pain and took it in like medicine.

After stepping out of the shower, toweling off, and blow-drying her hair, she cleaned her teeth and gums with gleaming steel dental tools. She cleaned and cleaned and cleaned, quickly and roughly, until her mouth was full of blood.

Clean, clean. Clean as a bean.

After spitting a glob to the red-spattered sink, Delilah grimaced at herself in the mirror. Crimson teeth and a ghoulish empty socket stared back. The supernatural wound needed no bandage or treatment. It was as if the eye had been burned out years ago rather than cut out so recently. What remained was a darkened, puckered pocket.

"I was beautiful," Delilah said. And she had been, strikingly so.

Not anymore.

"Who are you?" She asked the thing in the mirror.

A person? Perhaps. For a time.

Delilah spat the next question at the mirror, "Now?"

No one. I am Mother. I am her will.

But, before? Once... When I was a girl...

Shut up. I was pain. Just pain.

No longer. Not now.

"Not anymore."

The last piece of that girl is gone.

The one Mother saved from the vicious grey, from what happens to pretty girls there—surviving damp concrete apartments stinking from the sweat of old men and splotched with black mold. Tarred lungs, empty hearts, callused hands. The grey walls changed, but the girl remained. Shards. Collected in the gut like razor-blade kidney stones.

My last shard, the last strand, the last sham of esteem.

Delilah's remaining eye roved about, studying what was left.

Reliance on the past. A crutch.

Since then, many frames. But no matter how many faces she stole and destroyed, the little girl remained—lost, jagged, and angry.

Delilah whispered at her reflection in the mirror, barely audible, "Now, at last, the girl is gone. She's free."

Finally, now, she was clean.

Clean, clean,

"Clean as a bean."

Delilah stared at herself for a long time. Then, she cried. Hard and heavy with chest-wracking sobs. Something pent-up released while looking at her destroyed face. She sobbed and gripped the sides of the sink as if she could somehow squeeze her anguish out of herself and into the porcelain if she could just press hard enough.

I shoulda told 'er

Beauty see

She's in the eye of the beholder

She let out a howl, the sound of the last bit of her humanity leaving her body. Her cries morphed from a low chuckle to a hoarse laugh, then into a hysteric cackle echoing around the big marble bathroom. Finally, she quieted down to a singsong hum. Delilah rinsed her mouth and wiped everything down until it was spotless.

Clean, clean, clean as a bean.

She found that when she closed her good eye, the missing one *came on*. It was like turning on an infrared scope. Delilah could see the connective energy of the world in ghostly outlines. She wondered how she might ever fall asleep again if this was what she would see when her eye closed.

But once on the transference table—hooked back up to the IV drip of nutrients, sopor, and catheter—she found that she could fall asleep quite easily. And not just that, she had new abilities, new control over where and how she could go. She was no longer limited to a single destination determined by a mnemonic page and a true name. She could see connected nodes of The Dream like a glowing web, stretching beyond the horizon.

Delilah also sensed that she could now jump bodies like a bird between trees, switching frames at will—a power usually reserved for the most powerful ancients.

Tuning into The Dream, she listened for what remained of her blight living inside Kid. After a short time, she heard its call from a cab crossing the Bay Bridge toward Oakland. Quietly, unnoticed, she dug for the information she needed. Scrape a little here, burrow a little there. *There* it is, almost got it. Just a bit more, scratch and squirm, pull and pry, *almooooosssst* got it. *There*.

The Sand.

I'll see you there, my new friend.

We will dance.

She smiled and tongued her raw gums.

How long the night goes remains to be seen,
Ready for another, if you know what I mean.
Give a pound to the polly girl and give her a twirl.
Clean, clean, clean as a bean.

29
PUSH

Making short work of the 880 coming off the Bay Bridge, Jamaal's cab dropped into the exit just past the Colosseum Bart Station, passing homeless encampments under every overpass. Rows of tents —both manufactured and makeshift, dozens of bicycles in various states of assembly, all surrounded by piles of trash and stacks of worldly belongings. The rest of the area consisted of one and two-story commercial buildings, liquor stores, pawn shops, laundromats, and thrift stores.

The club came into view as they pulled around the last corner and passed over a mosaic crosswalk. The building was adorned with a mural of flowers, butterflies, and Saguaro cacti —covering it from sidewalk to roofline. No signage gave it a name, but drum and bass reverberating through the night air marked its presence.

Jamaal let them out at the curb and refused Kid's cash, even after the third insistence, saying it made them even for overcharging the other night. After thanks and goodbyes,

Jamaal slid the shifter to drive and pulled away without another word. It seemed he had simply been a strange and beautiful person whirling into and then out of their lives without much explanation, like a meandering, up to then unnamed, quantum particle.

Kid watched him drive away, then said, as much to Alice as the dissipating exhaust, "So, you're telling me life has always been like this and I just didn't notice?"

She replied, "One hundred percent. What's surprising is almost nobody sees it, or notices it rather. Seeing and *realizing* you're seeing are not the same. The universe is a strange place."

They walked to join the back of the entrance line, which was the only indication that the building was a venue and not an abandoned warehouse. It was maybe fifty people deep and growing longer by the minute. After the silence of the city, it was comforting to see crowds of people.

In front of them stood a trio of club kids decorated like tropical birds. One in a shirt patterned like a Rubik's cube, another in a yellow tracksuit, and the last sporting blue eyeliner running from eye corner to hairline. They bounced from one foot to another, excited, ready to dance.

Rubik lit a cigarette and passed it between them, sending its white vapor into the contrasting night air. Kid realized he had no desire for nicotine and wondered absent-mindedly if Patricia Hodgekiss had somehow absorbed his addiction and taken it with her into The Void. The association caused him to think of Linh again after only about a ten-minute break from constant anxiety. His heart ached at the thought of her. He hoped this was the right move. If not, they were wasting time going to fool around at a dance club of all places.

After making their way through the line, they stood near the entrance. A bored gum-chewing ticket-taker held a hand out. Her hair was dyed mint green with one side braided in tight corn rows, giving her a post-apocalyptic punk vibe.

"Tickets?" She blew and popped a bubble that matched her hair.

Alice stepped forward. "I won some!"

"Oh yeah? You this week's radio girl?"

"Yes!" Alice yelled the radio station's slogan, "One-oh-five-five Aliiiive!"

Gum Girl raised an eyebrow. "Take it easy, homeschool."

Alice blushed and jammed her hands in her jacket pockets.

It was the first time Kid saw his outlandish new associate look uncomfortable, the first time she accidentally dropped her intellectual bravado and too-casual-for-the-situation attitude. He felt bad Alice was embarrassed, but it was endearing to see past the front. Somehow, it made her real.

"Here." Gum Girl grabbed two paper tickets from her back pocket, tore off the tops, and handed the stubs to Alice. She then pointed over her shoulder with her thumb to the bouncer standing at the door a few yards behind. "Get in there, you kooks. And loosen up, will ya? Looks like your dog died."

Alice unbunched her shoulders and pulled her hands out of her pockets. Smiling, she replied, "Thanks."

The bouncer was a hulking cliché. Black leather vest, no shirt underneath, and a razor-shaved head covered in tattoos accompanied at least three hundred pounds of marbled biker beef slab.

"Bag."

"Staying with friends," Kid replied, trying to sound nonchalant. "Just my overnight, man."

"Gotta check it. *Man*." The bouncer held out a massive hand with rings and tattoos on every finger.

Kid handed his bag over, and the bouncer opened it.

"That's a lotta phones, chief." He raised his brow, which wrinkled his forehead all the way up into his shining dome. He had one of those fatty necks that fold into big rolls like taquitos.

"I just fix them to make money. All good."

'Tell it to the judge. I don't give a shit. What's this?" He pawed the cardboard box with his sausage fingers.

"Just a package. A gift for a friend. The one we're staying with." Kid felt beads of sweat break out on his neck. *Fuck. Why didn't I rehearse this?*

"It's a package or a gift?"

"A gift."

"Sure this time?"

"Yeah 'course."

"Don't sound so sure. Open it."

"Ah, come on, big guy, it's no prob—"

"Big guy? Shut the fuck up." If the bouncer hadn't been serious before, he was now. "Open the box or kick rocks."

Kid obeyed, reaching into the bag to pull the cardboard box off the totem. What could it hurt? Not like he'd know what it was, aside from a fancy doorstop. But the box wouldn't budge. The vacuum seal hung on, and Kid's nervous fingers kept slipping. The bouncer's face was turning redder by the second.

Some club kid heckled behind them, "Yo! What's the holdup? The show's starting!" He looked like the kind of guy who'd complain in any line—be it grocery, DMV, or dance club. But he was right. The bass from inside had increased in tempo and intensity. They heard cheers, and the crowd behind Alice and Kid was getting agitated. They were causing a scene.

Alice looked at Kid, then glanced at the intruding heckler. Kid caught the hint and turned to distract him.

She stepped in and reached out to touch the bouncer's arm. "Hey, we're sorry about all this. What's your name?"

The bouncer began to pull away, turning an even angrier shade of red, then was stopped by what seemed to be an invisible force field. He looked down, surprised to see that the force came from a slender hand with blue nail polish. When he saw her hand, his body relaxed. He looked up at Alice's face. "My name? Name's Vincent. Vinny."

"Vinny. That's nice. Vinny, what?"

"Vinny, what," He repeated Alice's phrase sleepily.

"What's your last name, Vinny?"

"Oh well, that's Marotta. Name's Vincent Marotta. Middle name's Donatello, after my grandpa on Ma's side. They come over from Italy... back in... well, I guess I don't know when. Long time ago, though. That's what Ma said." Vinny spoke to Alice as if in a dream.

The bouncer's attention started to wander to Kid and the heckler, but Alice brought it back by squeezing his arm and whispering, "Vincent Donatello Marotta. Look at me."

He panned back to her and smiled like he'd sipped hot cocoa.

Alice said, "Vinny. The bag is fine. You think we seem alright."

He stared at her, dumbfounded. Then his eyes opened wide in realization. His pupils dilated, accompanied by a soft intake of breath. He looked down at the bag, then back to the platinum-haired girl before him.

"Yeah, yeah. This bag's fine. You guys seem alright." Vinny zipped the bag and handed it to Alice, oblivious to the existence of Kid. "Here you go. Have fun. And hey, come find me later, okay?" Vinny smiled, his cheeks and chest flushed, breathing heavier than he should have been for a guy just standing there. "You're cool. Let me buy you a drink and get you in VIP."

"That sounds nice," she replied.

"Hey, I never got your name."

"No. You didn't. Have a good night, Vinny." Alice grabbed the backpack in one hand and Kid in the other, then walked through the purple-lit doorway connecting to a hallway leading into the club. Kid followed her like a scolded pup on a short leash. Amazed, he looked back and forth between her and the bouncer, who, moments before, was certainly not their friend.

Vinny watched them go, squinting darkly at Kid, then back to Alice, where his scowl blossomed again to the goofy hot cocoa smile. The expression somehow didn't look out of place on the burly biker. Maybe it was his natural state when he wasn't working the door and acting like a hard case. His smile faded only after Alice passed around the corner and out of sight. He shook his head as if trying to rid it of a repeating clip of a song.

The hallway glowed in fluorescent paintings and graffiti tags, lit intermittently by purple blacklight flickering above. Kid shouted over the increasing volume as they drew closer to the main event space.

"Alice, that was *awesome*. What are you, a Jedi?"

She didn't turn to acknowledge the question, just shoved Kid's bag back to him. Her shoulders hunched forward as she stomped rather than walked. The space between them grew.

He called after her, "Hey! What's your problem?"

Alice halted abruptly, and Kid stopped short just before running into her. She turned on her heel and shouted into his face, "Awesome? What was your plan, hotshot? Just wing it? I thought you were supposed to be some savvy street player."

"I'm not exactly a front door kinda guy. Seems more your speed. You had the tickets. If it were up to me, we would have snuck in behind some roadies like the Scooby-Doo gang."

"Scooby—" Alice's nostrils flared. "Ugh! Is this a joke to you?"

"A joke? Fuck off! That's *my* friend I'm going after. You're the one who keeps finding time to dance and giggle and screw around. Besides, you have superpowers, and you're pissed about it?"

"You wouldn't get it!"

"Try me. I'm getting pretty open-minded lately."

"It was an empathy push. It hurts!"

Kid looked her over. "What do you mean? You don't seem hurt."

"Not me, brainiac. *Him*. It hurt *him*. "

"He seems fine too! Shit, I think he likes you!"

"Use your head! How will we ever make it through this if you don't think? If we can't even make it past a bouncer, we're screwed! It's not just *your* friend. My life is on the line here too!"

Kid squinted at Alice's mood swings and little insults, thought of a rebuttal, but swallowed it and said, "Yeah, I know. I get that. Your help's appreciated, for real. But maybe I'm not top of the class, okay? Help me out here."

Alice's posture did not soften. "It hurts him because it changed him. I rewired him. Destiny? He had one, and I changed it. No matter how small the ripple, the universe likes to balance out and doesn't warn you how or when. Maybe that guy will be fine and shake it off. Or maybe he'll obsess over my words and lose his mind scribbling them over and over on a cell wall. Have a good night. Have a good night. Have a good night. Have a good fucking night!"

Her words choked with emotion, "Maybe he'll become obsessed and chase me down to profess his inexplicable love. Maybe he'll be too distracted by my voice in his head and walk in front of a bus. There's no way to tell! I *changed* things. I changed him. I stole his fate. Don't you get that? I went inside him, and I changed him. And just to get past a bouncer? Ugh!"

Additional concertgoers found their way into the hallway behind them, distracted by the spat only momentarily, returning to their chatter as they passed. Without another word, Alice turned to follow, leaving Kid behind.

30
WHISKEY

"Can I get ya?" Asked a bartender with ice-blue eyes caked in mascara. Kid thought she looked like a husky. Pretty but a little unsettling. He searched the area, hoping for some help figuring out what to order. He knew he wanted a drink but didn't spend much time in bars.

After too long, he responded, "Whiskey and Coke."

"What kind?"

"The kind with alcohol in it."

The bartender raised an over-plucked eyebrow. "Where's your stamp?"

Kid looked down at the back of his hand. "Guess the door guy forgot ours."

She studied him. "Ours? Who's with you?"

"What's with all the questions?" Kid glanced around for Alice but didn't see her. Despite the commotion in the line out front, it wasn't the main act yet, after all—just an opener. Still, the crowd was excited enough to leave the bar mostly empty. All that remained were two girls chatting and some roided-out guy in a flat-brim Red Sox cap who kept twitching. He pumped his head to the music, with one foot perched on his stool, the other splayed out in front of him, using the bar as a chair back. Red Sox caught Kid's sight line and gave a what's-up nod before turning back to watch the dancing crowd.

Kid shrugged. "Dunno. She's around here somewhere."

"I'm going to have to see your ID."

He sighed theatrically, fished the card out of his wallet, and handed it over. "Here." It was a fake, but a good one with his real photo on it. No reason for it not to pass. It even had the 3D hologram bit. Should do under the dim bar light.

The bartender took it, fingers covered in those fuzzy blue-black stick 'n poke tattoos, little triangles and dots, and things. She blew a raspberry through maroon-painted lips. "Twenty-six, huh? Right. When's your birthday, baby-face?"

"Come on *lady*, it's December eighth. I'm Sagittarius, like Nicki Minaj. Can I get a Jameson and Coke? *Pretty* please? It's been a long couple days."

"*Lady*? I'm barely older than you!"

"Okay then, stop sweating me, and I won't ask how many years you got."

She harrumphed, slapped the Jamie and Coke together, and slid it across the bar. Purple stage lights danced over her face.

The glass sloshed as Kid caught it and asked, "What's your name?"

"Jess." After a second, she added, "You're a smart-ass."

"So I've heard." He mocked her squint. "You're a hard-ass."

"So I've heard." Jess shifted her weight from one hip to the other, a move she seemed to have done before. "Trouble in paradise?"

"What d'you mean?"

"Your *date*. You don't look too plural right now."

"Oh, well, It's not like that. We're just friends."

"Uh-huh."

"I mean, she is pissed, though."

"Figured. I've seen that shoulder slump from this side of the bar before. I'll give you a pro tip from another estrogen farmer—*just friends* don't usually get that mad."

Kid didn't know what to make of that and sipped his drink.

Jess asked, "So, Robert then? Or should I call you Bob?" She was referring to the name on the fake ID.

"Do I look like a Bob?"

"Bobby?"

"I go by Kid. Unless I'm in front of a judge." He reached out a hand for her to shake, which she obliged. Hers was cold from making drinks. "How about a whiskey and Coke to match mine? On me."

"Why not?" Jess replied as she turned to mix one. She reached her glass over the bar and gave him a clink-cheers. "The guys coming up next, Red Queen? I saw them a while ago when they were carrying their gear in. Pretty wild looking. Like some sorta psychedelic space opera. There's even a dude with a top hat—he looks like a magician or something. Is that what you're into?"

Kid surprised himself with a laugh. "Yeah, I guess so. Been getting into some trippy shit lately." He finished his drink with a slurp and chewed on the ice cube—the coolness contrasted with the warmth spreading from his belly. He sat thinking as he watched people mill around, glancing down at the chipped red ring on his finger, a subtle reminder of the surreal task ahead.

Alright, we're here, Horacio.

The Dream Dreaming.

Puller of Strings.

What's next?

31
DANCE

Alice pushed her way into the gyrating crowd, eventually making her way to the front, just a few feet from the edge of the stage. The tropical trio of club kids were dancing in a world of their own, chewing gum, and drinking bottled water like parched desert escapees. The opening act sounded like a remixed version of some of the 80's new wave stuff, like New Order or The Smiths, but layered on top of a phasing dance beat.

She ran her fingers through her hair to move her bangs behind her ears. As usual, they immediately dropped back down, but she didn't notice. She was dancing, having a good time, grateful to be free of the negative emotions from the club entrance. As she danced, she turned slowly to scan the space. Past the crowd, she could see Kid sitting and drinking with a pretty bartender. They were laughing and smiling.

Alice felt her face flush and her hands tighten with jealousy. The emotion, specifically how it came without her permission, angered her immensely.

Good, she thought. *Have a drink. Probably your last one.*

Then she sighed, mad at herself for getting mad, and tried to push the two of them smiling and laughing from her mind. The opening act finished their set and walked off stage with scattered fanfare.

Pre-recorded intermission music kept playing, and it was good, so she kept dancing. She moved her body and let her thoughts float. Unnoticed by her, the crowd gave her room to dance—not much, but enough. Few things are more sacred than the space needed for a beautiful girl to dance.

The intermission time flew by, and without warning, the room brightened—the stage lamps suddenly turning up to the strength of spotlights. Concertgoers gasped, squinted, and shielded their faces with their hands. Accompanying the light was a deep floor-shaking synth crescendo drone—building and building until it felt like all their hearts would burst. The combination of sound and light felt like being dropped on a different planet by a military helicopter. The club kids stared into the light, tears streaming and mouths hanging open.

Finally, the lights dimmed, and a rock n' roll trio coalesced, seemingly from another dimension—guitar, drums, and vocals. The frontman looked like a cross between Lenny Kravitz and a figure skater, wearing a gleaming skin-tight pantsuit made of some iridescent material, the chest zipped down to near crotch. Tall and elegant, with skin the color of burnt ochre—body language somehow masculine and feminine at the same time. A huge afro surrounded his long sculpted face like a fuzzy halo. And painted on his forehead, a glowing white Ankh—the symbol of the old god Thot, the ruler of the moon, magic, and art—often a mediator between gods and men due to his ability to easily travel between realms.

In a deep, calm voice, he announced into the reverb-heavy microphone, "I am Horacio, and *we*," he gestured to his bandmates with a sweeping hand, "are The Red Queen." The guitarist wore a long red scarf, a double-breasted suit of crushed velvet, and pitch-black circular sunglasses, making him look like The Little Prince from The Matrix. The drummer came on stage wearing a black silk cape as a robe, then flipped it over his back to release his sinewy drumstick-wielding arms.

Horacio scanned the crowd, taking them all in. "*You*," he drew his finger across the room, "are *The Spoken*." His finger finished sweeping the room to land on his forehead, pointing to the glowing white Ankh. "Open your *middlemost* and take what is given. All of us—together—we are The Dream Dreaming. And this," he spread his arms wide, "is *agape*. True love." The word *love* echoed off the walls and rafters of the event space—*love love love love*—finally dissipating into silence. When the silence stretched to the point of feeling like it might snap, Horacio stated, "Tonight, we dance as dust."

Then he sang. To describe it so simply felt like an injustice, but of the many synonyms in the English language, none were more or less accurate. It was choral, ghostly, and religious. It reverberated throughout the venue, a kind of sound that resonates with the body's molecules, leaving the skin alight with static electricity and raised hair, spreading across nerve endings and neurons like the fractal Mandelbrot boundary of a forest fire.

Alice felt giddy and euphoric. In the crowd, everyone's

mouths were open, their cheeks wet with tears, hands splayed to the sides, palms forward as if taking in the word of God. It was a holy rock n' roll baptism for the neon age.

She recognized the sensation, and it thrilled her. What an empathy push! Like what she'd done to the bouncer, but magnified by a hundred. And Horacio was accomplishing it with no names, physical touch, addressed memories, or subliminal phrases. Just his voice and a crowd. Amazing.

Despite knowing what was happening to her, she could not shake it. She found that she didn't want to. It was heavenly. She succumbed to the euphoria and cried hot tears of joy. The heavy baseline began thumping, and the music built upon itself. As the song's leading hook dropped, the crowd seemed to implode, gyrating and dancing, and for a time, nothing else in the world existed.

As if by magic, at just the right time, the bouncer appeared beside her. *Vinny.* Everything was happening at just the right time. Just when it was supposed to—it was all so *perfect.* So *transcendently* perfect. *Synchronous.*

"Door's dead." He spoke over the pumping music, "Thought I'd come dance."

She smiled. "Hey, Vin."

He beamed at hearing her say his name. "Can't get you outa my mind." He rapped his bald head with big knuckles to make the point. "Like a song." He held out a hand, inviting her to dance.

She took it and began to carousel around him. If he was the earth, then she was the moon. It felt appropriate, he the large man hiding a kindness, her small and glowing, hiding a shadow, and The Red Queen bathing them all in a serenade of warm ultraviolet sunlight which may, quite possibly, be hazardous to their health.

A few feet away, Alice saw Kid and the bartender dancing as well, similarly under the power of Horacio's empathy push. As she watched them dance, she realized that she loved them both. She *loved* them *all*, everyone in the event space, in the world. For the life of her, Alice couldn't remember what she had been so upset about earlier, what she was afraid of, or what she wanted so badly. It all seemed silly, fleeting, and unimportant.

This, though, was important. This *feeling*. This was what it was all about. Connection. Love. Alice wanted to tell Kid all about it, what she had learned. She couldn't wait to tell him the *secret*, why this was the most important thing there was, the most essential thing there had ever been. How could everyone be so shortsighted and not notice this? Right in front of their noses the whole time!

As she spun like a Merry-Go-Round, the lights shone through her happy tears like a kaleidoscope. The Red Queen played their music, *such* good music, the sound of frost melting and dripping from hot glass, Vinny pumping his fists into the air, the grin of Christmas morning on his face, Kid and the bartender spinning and dancing, the Tropical Trio touching each other's faces, Rubik's Cube, and Eyeliner, and Track Suit. It all just made sense. Such perfect sense. It all fit together—little puzzle pieces broken just the same.

Horacio's vocal empathy push connected all of them, or rather made the already existing connections supernaturally strong and impossible to ignore.

Alice now knew, without being introduced, that the

bartender was named Jess. *Bless Jess. Clear as the day.* She had an aunt take care of her, *Aunt Regina.* She brought her up in her teens after things fell apart at home. They still shared an apartment and were like sisters. Sometimes Regina came to The Sand for a drink and some gossip—enjoying the memory of what it was like to be so young and beautiful and harbored no shame absorbing some of the attention that orbited her niece. It was like Alice could sense Regina *through* Jess because they were connected as well—memories and emotions, tactile but vaporous, like the puff from an incense stick. Cedar and myrrh.

Kid saw Alice and locked eyes. Pupils dilated like dinner plates. As the dancing moved them closer together, he reached out a hand and mouthed the words.

I'm sorry. I was a dick earlier.

Alice grasped Kid's hand in mid-air, interlocked fingers, and squeezed a heartfelt squeeze. *Me too,* she said, smiling with her eyes. It seemed as if the cosmos were created in the shade of their palms, tiny fusion reactors glowing between fingerprints.

Kid moved closer to her ear to speak over the music. "That's him, Horacio, the man from The Dream. We're here. Can you believe it? We're here. The Sand. What's next? What now? We gotta keep moving. Linh's out there! I can feel her! But holy shit, what the *fuuuuck iiiis* this?" He stretched and popped his jaw, then ran his hand over his hair. "*Aliiiiice.* I'm tripping my balls off—like I took a handful of molly... But like, not the same. *Waaaaay* different."

Alice leaned in to reply, "This is an empathy push, a big

one, from his voice. But it's clear he put things in play to get us here. We're here for a reason. I can feel it."

"Yessss, me too, I can totally feel it. So many reasons." Kid replied, smiling like an idiot.

She continued, "I don't know what's next, but this is somehow important. Maybe for now, in this little slice of time, the reason we're here is to connect with everyone, to each other, to dance, to feel something good for even just one moment. Maybe, having this affinity and understanding, it will help."

"But we gotta go... We're losing time..."

"Kid. This is one of those moments between. Dance with me."

His eyes closed as he rocked back and forth in waves of euphoria. He replied, "Alright, Alice. Don't think we got a choice anyway. Let's see where the rabbit hole *goooes*." He pumped a fist in the air as he jump-danced and yelled, "Unclench, motherfuckers! Unclench for The Red Queen! Hang on, Linh! We're coming for you!" A few nearby clubbers whistled and cheered, pumping their fists to support the strange battle cry.

They all danced, everyone with everybody, hundreds yet one. Interwoven latticework—tribal and raw, hidden from the knees down by machine-made smoke, lit by the staccato fire of dance club strobe lights. The boundaries between individuals disappeared, replaced by musical vibrations and the haunting voice of Horacio. Then, as they danced, moving in harmony, something remarkable happened.

The blend of Horacio's sonic empathy push along with Alice's innate talent allowed her and Kid's consciousness to share a space, a shared internal reality. Half their minds danced, and the other half dreamed in woven unison.

Alice watched a scene unfold in Kid's mind's eye. There, she saw a small storage room turned into a small bedroom, a small bed covered in small pillows, their aged cotton cases decorated with small yellow ducks. It was a makeshift sanctuary in the back of a Vietnamese restaurant tucked into the heart of The Tenderloin. The first place he ever felt safe. It was the first place Kid didn't feel small.

In their shared waking dream, she lay on the little bed in the little storeroom reading a little paperback novel. The door opened, and Linh stepped in. Alice held her(his?) place in the novel with a finger and looked up. Linh carried a platter with two cups. It smelled smoky and bittersweet, with hints of jasmine—Vietnamese green tea.

Somehow, it reminded Alice of childhood. She reached out with Kid's splayed fingers, grasped Linh's hand, and felt love there. She took a wisp of that essence back, across time and consciousness, to The Sand to be with them as they danced.

Kid saw something too. The pathway drawn between their hearts allowed information to travel in both directions. In Alice, he saw himself, Vinny, and Jess. He felt what she felt— the connection, the euphoria, the freedom she had at that moment. Freedom he(she?) hadn't felt for a lifetime. This was what Alice wanted and needed—the reason she was with him.

An activated totem meant freedom. And freedom meant *this*. The freedom to dance, the freedom to love, the freedom to breathe—all outside of the rules and watchful eye of Mara and The Young School. Excited and curious, Kid attempted to venture further into the heart of the dancing girl.

In her memories, he saw hallways of light pine, children of all ages exercising, learning, and training. The School. Then he saw a beautiful, dark-haired, tan-skinned woman. She smelled of both spring flowers and winter death. He called her *Mother*. She held his face in two hands and kissed him on the forehead, flooding his system with dopamine and serotonin, causing the lights to wash bright and send his nervous system fluttering. Then she spoke, something weighty, something important. It was meant for Alice, but he was listening in. To do so felt dirty, but he couldn't break away.

The woman who smelled like dead leaves said, "This blood may not be mine, heart annexed by will. And though this is not my heart, you can still break it, daughter. Do not forget your home. Do not forget your family. Have your walkabout, but come back. It was long ago, but I was once a young woman too. I know that birds must leave the nest if they wish to fly. But in the end, after it is unlocked, bring it to me. Together we will—"

Suddenly, Kid felt watched from within Alice's mind—like the sudden glare of prison yard spotlights, and he was abruptly pushed out. He snapped back to his own mind, where Alice watched him carefully as she danced. Then, apparently satisfied, she closed her eyes as the bass drove on.

32

JIMMY

As Delilah's body slept, her animus traveled the vast networked threads of The Dream. She was searching for the right frame to jump into—someone physically strong, with noise-canceling earbuds, access to a gun, and as close to The Sand as possible. It should have been impossible to pull off such a task in the short amount of time she had. But with her new powers, it was as easy as flying toward a bright flare in the distance. And she could fly so fast.

After locating Jimmy Bosko, a thirty-eight-year-old gym bro with military role-play fantasies and little man syndrome, Delilah kicked him out of his mind, then stole his body as he showered at the 24hr Fitness near Fruitvale. Once in control of his frame, she hurried to get dressed, then jogged outside to the Bart station commuter parking lot and took the Glock 36 subcompact pistol from the glovebox of his old, rusted-out Chevy Blazer. That squared, she drove to The Sand, parked at a corner behind the building, and beat Kid and Alice to the venue by mere minutes. Delilah passed a colossal bouncer and stepped inside just as the two runaway teens joined the back of the line.

When she had watched from her position at the bar, she could barely control herself as Alice walked in. Her instinct was to immediately jump the little bitch and pistol-whip her to death while terrified idiots watched. But she restrained her desire. Then when Michael 'Kid' Thames sat down just a few feet from her, cozying up to the skanky bartender, she did it again, dampening her rage. Just barely.

Then the music started, and they'd all gone nuts—everyone dancing, laughing, hugging, and crying like they were rolling their asses off at an underground rave. But she was prepared. Between her amplified strength and the headphones, she was safe from the effects of Horacio's voice. She adjusted the position and volume on the earbuds for what must have been the twentieth time—making sure they were ear-splitting loud and jammed in good and deep. They were blaring Motörhead's hardest bangers and still barely doing the job. During the transition between songs, it felt like cotton candy was blowing through her ears.

She twitched as she willed herself not to mess with her eye. Even though it wasn't missing in her new stolen frame, it still itched like a bastard. It felt like a ghost amputation, the socket aching with a relentless, biting cold.

Delilah jerked again. Even after only thirty minutes of use, the frame was noticeably degrading and becoming more difficult to keep steady. Jimmy's body was much older than what she'd usually take. Its run-time would max out at a few hours before it became useless due to synaptic degradation.

Younger frames lasted longer, but this one had what she needed. It would be alright. She wouldn't take much longer.

With everyone, including the bartender and bouncer, losing their minds dancing, Delilah reached over the unattended bar, grabbed a bottle, and poured a tumbler full of golden liquor. She drank and watched all the amped-up clubbers for a while longer. Like watching dogs do zoomies at a park, it was briefly entertaining.

She finished the drink, then fished in Jimmy's pocket for a penny and dropped it in the glass. Her old house madam always said a penny's worse than no tip. It means the service was so bad you want them to know the tip wasn't forgotten. It's small on purpose.

Pulling the Glock from her waistband and hiding it by her side, Delilah confirmed a gleaming round with a one-handed chamber check, then satisfied, stood up and moved into the crowd.

33
FERRYMAN

Kid felt his soul phasing in and out of his body as if the two were connected by only the most delicate thread. At times his attention honed in on the faces of Alice and their new best friends, Vinny and Jess. Other times it lolled around, following the trailing strobes and lasers as the four of them danced. Occasionally, it felt like his mind was hovering above the club, watching them all in third person like a floating ghost. But through it all, an unshakeable feeling of connection, capability, and potential.

So, when Horacio spoke to Kid through his mind, it did not feel out of place. Like the droning chants of Tibetan monks, a deep timber voice reverberated inside his skull.

(I'm so glad you came. I feel your worry, so you should first know that Linh Phuong still sleeps. She is safe, for now. We may take a moment, but only one—the dangerous beat will soon hammer on. There is much to do.)

(What is this? Telepathy?)

(Not exactly, Mr. Thames. That word implies the use of

unknown communication channels. But you see, these paths are known. We are all connected and have always been. One only needs a name.)

The strobing lights, driving bass, and thoughtspeak made his head spin. The voice seemed to both come from above as well as inside him, and not even ringing in his head necessarily—more like the perceived sound was a chorus created by a tiny voice inside each cell in his body.

Kid focused and thought back:

(Do I have your name too?)

(Of course. I gave you my truth the day you were born.)

(When I was born? You were there?)

(Oh, yes, each and every time.)

Alice, Vinny, Jess, and all the rest danced around Kid, unaware of his mental conversation. Who knows? Maybe they were having one of their own with the singing, otherworldly man. Kid chuckled as he moved and thought:

(So you're like, what, my Gandalf?)

Horacio grinned as he sang. *(Something like that, I suppose. Although, for now, I'm afraid I cannot travel with you for long. I'll give you only guidance, as there are other tasks I must accomplish as you similarly chase yours. The answers you need are in the City of Light—The Place at the Center of The Dream.)*

(The City of Light? That's where I'll find Linh?)

(No, but it is on your path to her. You know of the place. This will not be your first time there. The City of Light is also called Middlemost.)

(Middlemost! From the plaque on my ring box!)

(Yes, Kid. Michael and Saría's wedding band. Your parents.)

(Michael and Saría! Those are their names? Wow...)

Kid's eyes watered with aching tears. Kid smiled—a brief leap of hope.

(Are they there? In Middlemost?)

Horacio's eyes twitched in a brief expression of loss. *(Sadly, no. They are both gone. But, you knew this already, in your heart.)*

The flame of hope flickered back out to the familiar ache. Kid moved on to a more vital question. *(The other part of the label, Cognosa's Fine Things. It's there, isn't it? That's why I couldn't find it.)*

Whether it was the time Kid spent with the fantastic reality of dual worlds or Horacio's empathy push making him more open to transcendent ideas, Kid grasped what would come next.

(I need to go to Middlemost. I always knew it. The Cognosa. She'll tell me about the totem? How to save Linh?)

(Indeed.)

(And she's one of the good guys?)

(Good enough. She is invested in our mutual survival and has no love for false gods. But, you must know, this is bigger than Linh.)

(You mentioned that when we first met. You asked me to fight. I said maybe. I said we'd talk about it. We're talking, aren't we?)

Horacio smiled as he sang. *(You're a keeper of promises, it seems. By now, you've heard of the dead sleep.)*

(On the news, yeah. The city seems empty. Oakland's fine, though.)

(For now. But it spreads. A void rift created by the ancients' folly. Every moment we spend, The Dream crumbles further, and we slide toward true death.)

Kid grimaced. (*Man... What do you want? A soldier? That's not who I am. I'm a runner.*)

(*You are that and more.*)

(*No. This is out of my league. I'm doing this for Linh, and that's it.*)

(*I know she is in your heart, and you will find her. But she is a single crack in an epic fault line. You are needed, and you've proven your will to fight for those you love. You're halfway there already. Will you not fight for those outside yourself?*)

(*Sure, I don't leave people hanging if I can help it. But I'm a nobody. If this is such a big deal, you need someone else. I don't have the power to change anything.*)

(*Ah, but you do. You will see. But enough talk for now. Traveling to Middlemost requires the percussion of our united steps beating the boundary material thin. Dance like your life depends on it because, I assure you, it does.*)

Horacio nodded to communicate the psychic conversation was over and broke into an enchanting solo vocal layered on top of a stripped-down backbeat. The crowd went wild, and the flow of bodies swelled like an ocean wave.

34
ENCORE

As they danced, Kid's mind wandered between the enjoyment of the moment and the weight of dark knowledge. Suddenly, a new guy sidled close to them. He seemed familiar... Kid couldn't remember who he had or had not seen all night; his brain wasn't really working like that, but this *guy*... Something... He snapped his fingers. *Got it.* Red Sox hat. The dude from the bar. The townie who looked a little too old to be there. Red Sox smiled as his left eye twitched.

"Hey, man." Kid heard himself say, in a voice that was trying to be friendly. Something was off about the guy's energy—something about his grin. And his eyes, they were hungry. Where had he seen eyes like that before?

Red Sox nodded and smiled as he bobbed; he seemed to say, " *I'm just one of you, can't you tell? What a great show, right? Right?* But he was out of time with the music, as if listening to something different, just off-beat, something faster. With one eye squinted, Kid reached out to his shoulders to correct the tempo. The out-of-rhythm bobbing, the shark smile, the hungry glint, they were really bugging him, bringing him down—*throwing off the balance.*

Jess and Alice noticed Kid's distraction and tried to pull him back into the group. He tried to follow their pull but felt something yank him back. Looking down, he saw that one of the straps on his backpack was flopping free—it was cut.

Warning bells jangled in some distant part of his head as a hand appeared over his shoulder on the remaining strap, working to pull it off his body. Kid reached up and pulled it back on, spinning and bumping into Alice, Jess, and Vin as he did—upsetting their vibe and bringing their attention to him. The bag yanked back again.

Alice interrupted the second attempt by pushing in between them. Red Sox swung a wide sucker punch at her. She took it straight to the jaw and went sprawling. He pulled out something shiny. A gun. Aimed directly at Alice. There was murder in his eyes. That smell again, like back at the Chinatown apartment. Rotting flowers. True danger. Time seemed to slow. In a fraction of a second, Alice would be dead.

A dark rage filled Kid as he shot forward so fast that the lights passed in a blur. He knocked the gun to the ground and grabbed a handful of Red Sox's shirt, intending to provide purchase for a punch. But before he could swing, a blast of energy welled up from inside him and surged through the geometric-patterned arm that touched the guy's chest. Electric light tracers traveled through the dark lines covering his left side, culminating in a small explosion. It was anti-light, purple, and shimmering around the edges, morphing and curling like animal smoke.

The concussive force of the fist-sized blast sent the interloper flying backward through the air, arms and legs flailing. He smacked onto the concrete and slid into the crowd, which was quickly making room for the altercation, some already holding their phones out and recording.

Red Sox performed a kip up, returning to his feet in a graceful motion that belied his muscled bulk. He glanced down at the smoking flesh on his chest, then back up to Kid and snarled as he launched forward in a shadowstep, the same as Kid witnessed in the alley fight with the twins.

One second, the beefed-up stranger was standing ten feet away. The next second, light and sound faltered, and the man was replaced with a glitch-apparition, a memory of a person. But this time was different. Just as Red Sox reappeared behind Kid, his arm seemed to take on a life of its own. More muscle *command* than muscle memory. His anti-light hand knew where to go and went there of its own accord, spinning Kid as it did. Again, the hit connected with the interloper and blasted him across the dance floor.

Kid looked at his hand and arm in wide-eyed disbelief. He could feel a warm, welcoming, *dangerous* energy flowing through him, whispering to him, seducing him to do it again. Finish it. Put your hand on his head and take it all. Take his light. *Eat it* and grow, big and strong, strong enough so that nobody can ever take anything from you ever again.

Take his light

TAKE IT!

Kid found his legs moving him forward, powered by their own locomotion. He placed his shining hand on Red Sox's forehead. Watery blue eyes watched him in surprise and confusion. Kid could sense animus there. Spirit. Chi. *Soul*. He could taste it. Sweet yet savory. Salted caramel mixed with the metallic hint of warm blood.

Take it.

TAKE IT!

And he did. It was hot, silent, and comforting. Deadly and never-filling like dope from a hot spoon. So sweet. So kind. Insidious. Soul drank soul.

In a moment of confused pleasure, Kid glanced up and saw Jess. She watched him in terror, eyes wide, mouth agape. She didn't know what she was seeing, but she knew it was wrong. But seeing her fear didn't stop him. When Kid was done, the body of the would-be thief lay motionless on the sticky dance floor. Through the singed hole in his shirt, the skin was charred and bubbled, an angry combination of pink and black. But the man's face was worse. Kid left it a burnt, puckered mass like melted crayons.

Nearby, one of the other concert-goers began to spasm as if experiencing an epileptic fit, arms flailing and water splashing out of the bottle he held. It was the club kid with the shirt printed like a Rubik's cube. After a moment, the seizure ended, and Rubik's Cube stared at Kid knowingly. He glanced at the charred dead body of Red Sox, then at Alice as she stood on wobbly legs.

"Who the *fuck* are you? Michael *Thames*. Ha! Not some street punk, no, no. I see now. You're a fucking mutant. Cross-breed." She appraised his glowing geometry-marked arm. "I see why Mother wants you."

Kid stared at Rubik's Cube in disbelief; he'd been called

many things, but *mutant*? That was new. "Who the fuck am *I*? Who the fuck are *you*? How do you know my name?"

Alice interrupted. Even without the mention of Mother, she would know that foul, angry mouth and manic leer anywhere. "Delilah. How did you jump like that? So fast? You're not capable—"

Delilah, in her second stolen body of the night, answered, "You know nothing, you acid cunt." She threw the water bottle at Alice, then rolled across the floor, pulling the Glock from the dead man's hand and spinning on a knee to fire.

Vinny pushed Alice behind him with a Mack truck of an arm and charged.

Three flashes.

Strobe light freeze frames of the chaotic scene.

The shots were barely audible over the cacophony of music and shouts, *pop-pop-pop*, like firecrackers. One of the bullets pierced the secretly-kind bouncer's heart, killing him instantly. But it takes more than a bullet to stop the momentum of three-hundred pounds. Vinny's body continued forward and landed on Delilah, pinning her down. Three more flashes from the gun's muzzle, further muffled and obscured under the big man's bulk. Vinny's blood pooled like purple oil in the laser light of the show.

Jess screamed and dropped to the ground beside him. She cried and shook his shoulders, calling out his name. Her voice remained unheard, obscured by the music. Kid and Alice just stared, stunned by the strobe light horror show—glancing first to Vinny and Jess, then to Kid's hand, which seemed to oscillate in and out of the light.

The dazed crowd fully realized what was happening.

Screams erupted, and they stampeded for the door, trampling Jess, Vinny, and the interloper struggling beneath him.

With the music stopped, the only sound was mayhem. More gunfire pops and muzzle flashes as Delilah worked to escape. The shots went wild, one shattering an overhead light, showering broken glass and sparks, another punching a hole in the chest of the club kid in the yellow tracksuit. His blood spread like dark wine.

Then, there were hands on their shoulders, pulling them back.

"I believe that's our cue," Horacio said, his voice echoing inside their skulls. He was tall enough to be a head and neck above the crowd and moved like a man who was part willow tree. "Come, children, it's time to go."

Kid and Alice took one more stupefied glance back—neither Delilah's stolen vessel, Vinny, nor Jess were visible amidst the madness. They turned and followed Horacio through a steel door the guitarist and drummer held open. Muffled by the chaos, Delilah screamed in rage as they escaped.

35
BLINK

Cinder block walls, repetitive doors, and gig posters passed by in a helter-skelter blur as they ran. Alice shouted at Kid, "What was that? That power! You lied to me! Who are you? *What* are you?"

Kid's eyes shimmered with tears. "I don't know! I fucking killed that guy! I didn't mean to! I swear I didn't mean to kill anyone!"

She glanced down at his arm as they ran. The anti-light glow had mostly receded but still pulsed softly. "*You* didn't kill him. Delilah did when she stole his body, just like the twins back at the restaurant. But you did something! What was that?"

"I told you, I don't know! It just blew outa me!"

"You were... eating him. Who *are* you?"

Kid screamed, "I don't fucking know, man! I don't fucking know!"

Horacio interjected, able to speak plainly despite the noise. His words were partly in the air and partly in their heads. "He is Kid, of course. The son of Michael Thames and a spirit of The Dream, Saría Landros."

Alice exclaimed, "What? You're kidding. Spiritborne? How?"

Horacio replied, "I have pulled many strings and moved many men to have us arrive at this moment. What you've seen tonight is *potential*—the possibility of our greater survival. The next steps on that path to retribution are the totem and Linh. And as a protector of travelers and thieves, I will ferry you across the river to what lies ahead. But consider these facts then, on the other side. Our union has weakened the boundary between worlds, but already, I feel it re-crystalize. For now, we must hurry. This boat won't wait."

Alice shook her head but said no more.

The concrete hallway opened to a loading bay, revealing a box truck blocking a sizable industrial garage door. Open black containers littered the area, filled with speakers, amps, smoke machines, guitars, and other music gear.

Assuming they were trying to escape the building, Kid moved to crawl under the gap below the almost-closed garage door to get outside. But Horacio stopped him and motioned to the back of the truck.

"No, no, this way, my dears. Up, up, up you go." He spoke in a sing-song voice, which belied the stress of their current predicament.

"What, in the truck?" Asked Kid.

The drummer replied, "Get in if you want to go, bud." He still wore a top hat, which seemed extra ridiculous now. "And hurry up, will you? She's trying to get in my head. I can feel her in there squirming for an opening. She's good. I'll give her that."

"Me too," the guitarist added. "She's like black smoke. What'd Mara do to her? Amped her way up. It doesn't feel like we have long, so get a move on, chums."

Kid glanced from the truck to the trio of musicians. Under the harsh fluorescent lights, their makeup was pasty and obvious. Outside the context of the sound stage, they looked ghoulish. It felt like he was about to get trafficked. Wouldn't be the first time a nobody street kid got into a truck and disappeared.

Interrupting his suspicion, the screaming face of a stranger from outside the building appeared in the small gap below the garage door. She was around fifty years old, disheveled, and wearing soot-stained clothes. She grimaced with a few remaining yellow teeth and scrabbled to get inside. The woman shrieked like a banshee, discolored spittle flying.

Alice ran forward and kicked at her head. It was clear this was yet another new vessel Delilah stole, even more degraded than the last. This one seemed like someone entirely in the grips of a brutal psychosis. Alice shouted as the shrieking woman latched onto her foot and fought to bring her down. Delilah had no qualms burning out the vessel's muscle fibers in seconds, so with supernatural strength, she swept Alice's legs and yanked her to the ground, then started using Alice's waist, then shoulders, then throat, to pull herself into the garage. Alice swung heavy haymaker punches at either side of her face, connecting with loud cracks on each one, but they did nothing to the unhinged woman. When that didn't work, she used her thumbs to dig into the shrieking grey woman's eyes, and still, she was undaunted, making inch-by-inch headway. She would be in and on her feet in seconds.

The drummer ducked to the side and grabbed an electric guitar, a cream-colored Fender Stratocaster. He attacked Delilah with an overhand swing like he was chopping wood with an axe. The solid alder body of the guitar met her head with a sickening crunch, finally leaving her still.

Holding the blood-spattered guitar, he said, "You need to go. She's going to keep coming on this side. But she can't pull that shit in The Dream. Ain't no body-hopping on the dark side of the moon." He looked at Kid. "Yo, little man, you coming or what? The train whistle's screamin' on this ride."

Alice scrambled from under the body, stood, shook off, and jumped into the back of the box truck. She held out a hand. "Come on, Kid, let's get out of here."

He grimaced as he watched the blood pool around the rabid woman's head expand, dark and sticky looking in the fluorescent lights, then took Alice's hand and jumped in.

Horacio came in behind them and called out to his bandmates, "I trust you boys have this handled."

Sprinting footsteps approached from outside the garage, shoe rubber slapping concrete. More animalistic screams as whoever's body Delilah stole this time slammed into the steel door. The guitarist grabbed his own weapon, a metallic orange Gibson SG, and readied it over his shoulder like a baseball bat. "Go!" He shouted.

Horacio reached up and pulled down the truck door with a grey canvas strap. With a scrape of metal rollers, darkness enveloped them. Kid expected to hear more sounds of fighting after the door came down, but instead, it was suddenly and eerily silent. A silence so encompassing he could hear his ears ringing and nothing else. He could not even hear himself breathe. How was it this quiet? Why did it feel so empty?

It didn't make sense.

He realized he couldn't *feel* anything either, not the floor or walls of the box truck against his body, not even the clothing on his skin. The darkness around him felt complete and impenetrable, like someone trying to suffocate him with a black trash bag. Kid could not hear his breath, but that didn't stop him from choking. He began panic–coughing, retching, and gasping for air that was not there.

No no no no nonononono, not the dark,

I don't like the dark.

Please, please, please.

Don't leave me down there.

Just let me keep my clothes.

Please? The light?

No no no nonononononono

I don't wanna be down there no more.

Kid turned his head frantically, eyes wide, hoping to gather some pinpoint of light to see. Where was it? Where was the water heater, the pilot light? His make-believe campfire? His stars? Orion? Aquila? He choked and hyperventilated, heart racing with erratic beats.

No nononono

I don't like the dark

Please, please

Nonono

His brain burned with old fear. His lungs burned, begging for air. Finally, at the moment he thought his chest would explode, he was comforted by a familiar hand. Slender. Warm. Feminine grasping fingers squeezed his. Alice.

He heard her say something, or did he feel it?

Shhh, Kid, it's okay. *Shhh, sh, shhh.*

We're traveling through the In-Between.

We've almost passed the dark now.

The feeling of smothering plastic receded. At last, he could sense space and hear Alice's breathing, which reassured him greatly. Kid's heart slowed, and he exhaled carefully, attempting to do so as quietly as possible, trying to hide the audible and embarrassing evidence of his terror.

After gathering some of his wits, Kid spoke, "What was that? Horacio? Where are you, man? Where are we going? We gotta get out of here. Delilah's a maniac. She's gonna keep coming."

Despite the darkness, they could hear the smile in Horacio's reply.

"We've already gone."

He lifted the truck door, allowing light and frigid air to spill through the widening slit. It revealed a surreal landscape —a powder-sand shoreline peppered by giant monolithic statues of ancient deities to some lost religion and lined by a tall sheer cliff of grey stone.

Kid and Alice stepped to the corrugated steel edge and peered outside. The blue light of the night sky illuminated their faces. One after the other, they jumped out to land in wet sand, crunchy with ice.

The sky above was a shining network of strange stars, somehow closer than mid-height clouds would be, just like Kid's first venture into The Dream. Each pin-light connected to others by networks of glowing threads. Large fragments of the interconnected starry mass flickered on and off like an old street lamp. As they watched, some bits went out and did not return.

They turned to see Horacio standing in a floating square opening, the same size as the truck door, but from their outside perspective—there was no truck. The door floated above the sand as if a patch was missing from the quilt of reality.

Kid asked, "I'm not sleeping, right? How..."

"Schrödinger's Box Truck." Horacio smiled at his wit. "If you can't hear, see, or feel what's outside, is the outside truly there? And if the outside is not necessarily there, then what, necessarily, is?"

"Uh, okay, but I thought this place was only in our minds?"

"This world. That world. What is any place but another strange feat of imagination? We access The Dream through our minds, yes, but it is *always* here. And with the harmonic beat of a thousand feet, boundaries become thin. Tonight we hammered them well!"

Kid shrugged in now-practiced acceptance, then glanced around the beach landscape. "I need to check on Linh, but I guess my phone doesn't work here. You said you could sense Linh before when we were dancing, right? You said she was still asleep. Is that still true? Is she safe?"

"More or less. For now."

"More or less? What does that mean?"

"It means she is in The Void—I doubt having a very good time. But, yes, she is alive. Her animus remains intact."

"We don't know how long that's going to last. Let's go. You said Middlemost and the Cognosa. Right? Like on my ring box. Which way is that?"

Alice jumped in. "Middlemost? The Cognosa? How do you know those things?"

Horacio replied for him, "As Kid implied, we communed while we danced."

A look of mild irritation passed over her face, whether from being left out, missing the clue, or not having the idea first, was hard to say. Apparently choosing the latter, she shook her head in self-admonishment. "The Cognosa... I should have thought of her." Alice tucked her bangs behind her ears; this time, they stayed. "It's a good move. She's white hat. And Mara hates her. And it's true—the Cognosa is essentially an antique collector. If someone knows about this totem, it will be her. She's somewhere in the Circum Agora, a special part of the marketplace in Middlemost."

"Indeed," Horacio replied. Before he could add more, he tilted his head as if hearing something in the distance. "Sorry, loves, no time for more questions, not now. Delilah has become quite powerful, it seems!" By his intonation, it was hard to tell if Horacio was more worried or impressed by that fact. After showing his gap-toothed grin, he said, "I had better return, or I'll be auditioning new bandmates."

Kid peered one way down the beach, then turned and studied the other direction. "Last question before you vanish again. Which way do we go? It all looks the same." He hugged himself, beginning to shiver. "And goddamn, it's cold. If we get lost, we're gonna freeze to death."

Alice said, "Do you see that light in the distance?" She

pointed to a shining spire, almost hidden behind the horizon. If they were still in the real world, Kid might wonder if they somehow wandered close to Las Vegas and were looking at the giant blue laser shooting from the top of the Luxor pyramid—which, according to the articles he read, was visible to pilots as far away as Los Angeles.

Kid nodded. "I see. What is it?

Alice replied, "That blue light is The Stream, at the center of Middlemost."

Horacio added, "And to escape this cliff line, find the river that feeds the sea and follow it inland through a canyon. That way," he gestured down the beach, "along the shore, you can't miss it."

From the lip of the truck-door-shaped opening, Horacio looked over Kid and Alice's shoulders, scanning the horizon. Then, seemingly satisfied, he addressed them with his shining golden eyes; in the moment, they looked like liquid metal, rippled by a strong gale.

"One last thing, Mr. Thames." He reached into his unzipped leotard and removed a yellowed envelope from some hidden pocket. "This is for you—a letter from your father. I was instructed to give it to you at this juncture, should you prove yourself and make it this far. Take a moment when you find one and give it a read. Bon voyage to you both."

Without another word, Horacio of The Red Queen, the fisherman from Kid's dream, and the ferryman of the In-Between, slid the slice in the sky shut. With a jingle of metal rollers and a blink, he was gone.

36
COLD

As they walked in the biting cold, Kid opened the envelope—the seal parting easily, thanks to the solvent of time. It contained a dozen folded pages and a faded Polaroid of a smiling couple in a photo booth holding a swaddled infant. The man had light, freckled skin and intelligent eyes. Even with the smile, they seemed to drill through the photo in interrogation. In contrast, the woman's smile seemed to radiate from the print. Her tan face was framed by a wild mane of wavy black hair adorned with colored ribbons and seashells like some oceanic deity. They looked authentically happy. Kid flipped the photo over and read the back:

Us and Mike Jr. 3 months.
Golden Coin Arcade, District Twelve, M.M.
Tired, but happy.

Michael Thames and Saría Landros. Man and animi.

Lovers via The Dream. In the past hour, he went from
believing he would never know or see them to learning their
names and holding their photo. He swallowed the quickly
hardening lump in his throat and reached to his chest to touch
the necklace. With hands shaking from the cold, he read the
letter written in neat blue cursive.

My dear son Michael,

*How strange this must be. You'll have many questions, and
I cannot answer them all, but I will tell you the two most
important—about your mother and the grim task ahead.*

*First, the fun part. Your mother and I. We met in
Middlemost, in a smoky blues club with smoochy lighting.
Cheesy? Oh, yes. But she loved that sort of thing, and
because of her, so do I.*

*Now, you likely ask with heightened suspicion, "They have
blues clubs in Middlemost?" Or perhaps, more probably,
"What is Middlemost?" Well, my son. It is everything and
anything, all colliding and compressing into a jewel of
imagination (if there is, in fact, any difference between
imagined and real). It's all there, in The City of Light. This
fact is bizarre and yet entirely rational. That is the Animus
Mundi in summary—The Dream.*

*Back to your mother. Her name was Saría Landros, which
you probably now know. You've met Horacio, and while
cryptic, he's a blabbermouth. They were fond of each other.*

Kid laughed and wiped a tear from his cheek. Reading the letter was like listening to the father he would never meet sitting across from him. His way of speaking seemed to jump from the page. Clearly, he had the vocabulary of a reader, and a silly sense of humor hidden behind a severe face. Kid wiped his eyes and continued reading. Alice tried to pretend she wasn't watching.

That dusky establishment was called Baron's. Perhaps it's still around. Saría was a singer there—the best. Folks crossed worlds to listen to her voice. Unsurprisingly, I was immediately smitten, as were most men and women. It was impossible not to be. She took light with her everywhere, pulling it like one of the bright ribbons in her hair. Against all odds, despite being entirely out of my league, she took a liking to me as well. Imagine that, lanky bones, bad jokes, and all. We fell in love, our souls united, and you came soon after, woven from our interlocking strands.

Sadly, our happiness was short-lived. To my eternal shame, the battle took her some time ago, just after you were born, not long after the picture you hold was taken. The ancients wanted Saría and her spiritborne child—for what you are, what we had, and what they thought we might create again. There are multitudes of ancients, but one, in particular, is hell-bent on destroying our world. Immortal, she is ever patient, waiting for specific sets of unlikely events to synchronize, learning and evolving her tactics with each attempted execution.

I believe she is now as close as she's ever come. She learned that by using specific totems, secret techniques, and harnessing the purest power of The Dream, i.e., concentrated animus, she could rip holes in the barrier protecting our worlds from The Void.

It was Saría's spirit that this ancient kidnapped and burned for sacrificial fuel—your mother, my lover, and soulmate. As far as Horacio and I know, she was the first of the Animi ever to die... It wasn't thought possible. But it seems with enough motivation, one can even kill imagination and hope.

This ancient, the one who seeks to destroy us, the one who took your mother and stole our life, she is called Mara Tiamazadeh—The Black Rose of Babylon.

The parchment crinkled as Kid gripped it in sudden anger. It took all he had not to rip it to pieces and throw it to the sand. He drew a shaky breath through his nostrils, the air so cold it burned, then let it out slowly. Kid shut his eyes with two more careful breaths, then opened them again. He made his best attempt at relaxing and continued.

After we lost Saría, I had to hide you. Somewhere better protected than with me. Horacio has done as I asked, keeping you safe and aligning you with the totem when the time and place presented themselves. You have already made it a long way against incalculable odds. I'm proud of you, Michael.

*Next, you must venture to the place engraved on the gift
your mother and I left for you. The words will make sense
now. Past that, guidance ends. We're off the map now. I'm
sorry to force you onto such a path, or lack thereof, but this
is beyond us. More important than the desires and fears of
mortal men. If we do not end this, all will suffer the same
fate as your mother.*

*We can't allow that. With this totem unlocked and the
power living inside you, there's a chance, however slim.
You must find a way. Stop Mara.*

*And now, my last words of fatherly advice. Because of your
inevitably painful upbringing and this news I've callously
laid on your lap, you will have as profound an anger as I.
But there is poetry in that rage. Don't fight it. Learn its
embrace. Love both parts of yourself. The light and the
dark. Truth and fury. Human and animi. In that balance
is strength. To accomplish what you must, you will need it.
Take care, son, and good luck. Perhaps in some world and
time beyond these, we will see each other again.*

All my love, your father,
Michael Thames

Kid looked up from the letter to watch the unchanging
beach as they continued walking. After leaving him alone with
his thoughts, Alice placed a gentle hand on his shoulder and
asked, "May I?" He replied by wordlessly handing her the old
papers and shoving his freezing hands back in his pockets.

After reading, she let out a long breath and asked, "Do you want to talk about it?"

"Nothing to talk about," Kid said as he shivered against the brutally cold wind. "First, we figure this totem out, then rescue Linh. After that, we kill Mara and save the world. No problemo."

"I can't tell if you're serious."

"People in The Real are going into comas just like Linh's. How many are going to die?" He balled his fists. "The totem, The Void, Linh, you, me. It's all woven together. And now, this? That ol' ratchet killed my mom?" He growled, "We have to do something! But... Spiritborne? What the fuck does that mean I can do? I don't understand. I don't feel anything special."

"Well, you're here, aren't you?"

He studied her face and replied, "Yeah, so?"

"A letter has been waiting twenty years for you. You survived your life so far with your honor intact, watched your reality flip upside-down, fought shapeshifting secret agents, and battled literal monsters poisoning your soul. Now you're trudging through a freezing dreamscape, willing to sacrifice your life for strangers." Alice wiped an intruding tear from the corner of her eye, then chuckled. "You're kinda dumb sometimes, you know that?"

"Whatev—"

"No, shut up. I'm serious. I didn't think people like you existed in either of these worlds. If you're not special, I don't know what is."

Kid blushed. "Knock it off, will you?"

Alice rolled her eyes.

"We're gonna figure this out and keep going," Kid continued. "Because if we can solve it for Linh, we can untangle the rest, right? Millions of mothers, fathers, sisters, and brothers. Each of them matters to someone, just like my mom and Linh. I don't know who I am or what I have inside of me, and maybe it's just my brain going loopy from the cold, but we have to try."

"One step at a time," Alice said.

"Yeah... Frozen steps. I can't feel my hands or face anymore. Can you?"

Alice shook her head to the negative.

Another piece of the sky flickered and went dark.

Sloughing steps through icy sand.

Losing his grip on cogent thought, Kid stopped pulling his hoody tighter or keeping his hands in his pockets. Neither of them were shivering any longer—which, if they'd known anything about outdoor survival, they'd know that was a bad thing. The cold prevented any further conversation on the topic.

———

After another two hours, Alice stumbled and fell. Wobbly and disoriented, Kid helped her back up. But then, not much later, he fell too. She tried to help him stand but didn't have the strength, and the attempt caused her to collapse beside him. They were too cold and too tired to try again. They used their remaining energy to burrow into the sand, hoping it was warmer a few inches down, protected from the sweeping gales. It was—but not enough to matter.

Without thinking much of the implications, Kid lay himself on top of Alice's body and wrapped his arms around her sides to help her conserve what little heat she had left. Their intertwining bodies should have been intimate, but under the circumstances, it was simply too cold to occur to them. The last thing Kid thought before falling into an incoherent sleep was that the birthmark on her neck looked like a cute cartoon dinosaur—a brontosaurus.

PART FOUR
LOST DREAM

"*Who plays the Song of Songs upon the Hills of Dream? It is said Love is that need-player, for There is no song like his. But today I saw one, on these still garths of shadow and silence, who put a hollow reed to his lips and played a white spell of beauty. Then I knew Love and Sorrow to be one, as in the old myth of Oengus of the White Birds and The Grey Shadows.*"

— FIONA MACLEOD, WHERE THE FOREST
MURMURS

37
HURRICANE

Mara held the little girl's chin to keep her face steady. Around seven years old, she stood in a line of a dozen other children around the same age, plus or minus a few years—students of The Young School.

Under the fluorescent lighting, the secretly-ancient queen's dark eyes met and held the girl's shimmering blue. What Mara sought written in the girl's pages was a mystery to all but her. Windows to the soul, indeed.

"Mother? Please, can I stay?" The girl pleaded.

Mara replied, "We all have our purpose."

"But, I promise, I'll be good!"

"It's *because* you've been good that you are allowed to go. Be grateful, child."

Before the girl's stammer could become a cry, a nurse took her away. She would be added to the void sleep, like all the rest. Mara's loyal hound, Dagan, stood at attention as he watched her move down the line. One after another, she examined and sent them on their way. Finally, after the last child was gone, Mara sighed in disgust.

Dagan spoke, "Apologies, Mother. Stock is low."

A nurse provided a towel, and Mara wiped the oil from the children's hair and faces off her hands. She examined her nails under the fluorescent lights. They, and the toes of her still bare feet, were painted glittering crimson like a star-strewn galaxy of blood.

"The more apes there are on this rotting garden rock, the weaker they become. You saw it, Dagan. Once upon a time, we were magnificent. Sadly, no more. Decrepit, atrophied, and dim. It's as if they share a single source which is now diluted beyond measure. Regardless, the animals make up for it through tireless breeding."

Mara turned and strode down the hallway toward the elevator, which would take her to the roof of the Western Knell building. "We have enough animus. Even so, I want the totem, and I want to see the hybrid with my own eyes."

Dagan followed. "What if he manages to enter The Void?"

"Alice will make sure he doesn't."

"And if she fails?"

"Alice doesn't fail."

"If she chooses differently, then? You said she felt conflicted when you went to recollect her mind."

"Of course she's conflicted. She is a child. Alice believes she wants freedom, as all the naive young do before understanding the meaning of the word. But, choose? There is no choice. Conflicted or not, she is *my* child and will obey my command."

"Mother. I'm sorry to press, but you know as well as I that

she is willful. She came from hardy stock and was never broken like the rest."

Mara scoffed and waved her hand dismissively. "Then Delilah will perform her duty, our wayward daughter will be no more, and the crossbreed will never return."

"And if he does survive?"

"Where is your confidence today? Do you need to be realigned?"

Dagan licked his lips nervously, "No, mother. Of course not."

"It's impossible," Mara answered. "Nobody comes back from the dark. No man, ancient, nor dream dreaming. I *would* like to see a spiritborne youth with my own eyes and will be disappointed to miss that opportunity. Aside from that fact, nothing changes. Whether Horacio likes it or not, this is checkmate."

"What luck to find ourselves in these circumstances."

Mara laughed, "My sweet Dagan, I would allow no other to speak to me as you do. You truly press me this day. Be grateful that, rather than rip you open, I prefer to keep you by my side to watch man's last sunset."

Again, Dagan's nervous tongue darted out. "Yes, thank you."

"There is no such thing as luck. Even without the totem and the boy, we would inevitably succeed. A sea may be emptied via eyedropper or hurricane. It is only ever a matter of time."

38
HEARTH

"Hey, baby boy…"

A voice in the darkness.

The soft sound did not echo as if spoken in a forest carpeted by pine needles.

Again, a woman's voice, "Sweetie…"

Stronger now, scolding, "Michael Kid Thames."

His mind stirred. Thoughts murky like sea ice. Why couldn't he just rest? It would be so nice to continue this nap. So tired. Body doesn't want to move. So cold.

"Michael KID Thames. Wake UP."

His mind's eye opened to reveal fuzzy blue darkness, like a deep ocean. Alice slept beside him, face pale, breath slow. Her hair floated around her head like a halo of silver seaweed. The only light in the area radiated from her.

But the voice he heard wasn't Alice's. And it wasn't Linh's.

It was familiar, though. Who else knew his name?

"Hello?" Kid asked the dark.

But there was no response—only aquamarine silence.

"Who's there?"

"It's not time to sleep, baby. Not yet. Come on, it's time."

———

Kid awoke to the prod of a stick in his ribs and the memory of something, someone, familiar, which quickly faded. Crouched beside him was a stocky older man with a grey tobacco-stained mustache and woolen poncho. The man observed him closely, walking stick ready to poke again.

"¿Estás vivo, hijo mío?" he asked, followed by another rib jab.

Kid grunted and swatted the stick away.

"Bueno. Muy bueno. Y tu novia?"

The man, whose eyebrows were so thick they began to curtain his eyes, turned to prod Alice. Kid pushed the gnarled cane away and tried and failed to shake her awake. The man removed his poncho and handed it to Kid, who wrapped it around Alice and pulled her to a seated position. After some time and shoulder rubbing, her eyes gradually opened from a slit to halfway, and she glanced around sourly.

"Shoot. I was hoping that was a dream." Alice looked up at their caterpillar-browed savior and down at her poncho. She pulled it close and said, "Thank you."

"Por nada. Come, come. Mi nieta está cerca." He motioned for them to follow, rubbing his hands and stamping his feet against the cold.

They followed along the beach until they came to a river,

cutting a canyon through the cliff wall, feeding into the sea. How was it possible they missed it before? Or had they fallen just short of their desperately needed destination?

Kid vented his frustrations, as much for emotional relief as to keep busy and warm, "This is all really starting to piss me off."

"Starting to?" Alice replied.

"I can't count on anything to just be what it's supposed to be. Is any of this real? Am I losing my mind? Any moment I'm gonna wake up from this nightmare in a straight jacket."

"To be honest, this has all upgraded to a level of oddity even I'm not used to. But I understand how you feel. Just stay strong. Stay open-minded. We're going to get there. I know it."

"How can you know?" Kid asked.

Alice's skin returned to a healthier pink thanks to the poncho's warmth. The man walked ahead by a few paces, rubbing his arms to keep warm. "I grew up in this—The Dream, The Real, The School. This is my life. We almost died, but it doesn't even surprise me. It's fine. Well, not fine, but *known*. Like, I understand it. I know how to get around."

"Most people would say the same about being a crust punk. They see kids on the street and have no concept of how someone could survive or even enjoy living like that. But it's our life. We know how to do it—figured out the kinks. Most of 'em, anyway. It's ridiculous and dangerous, but we understand it."

"Crust punk?"

"Yeah, that's what some people call us. Probably started as a slur, but we own it now."

"But you don't run with them. You stay to yourself."

"No, not anymore. I tried, but... guess I didn't fit." Kid thought for a minute, and his guard dropped, possibly because of the cold, maybe because of Alice. "I guess I don't know who I am."

"Yes, you do."

"What do you mean?"

"You're Kid Thames."

He reached into his hoody to pull out his necklace. M+S. Michael Thames and Saría Landros.

"But what's a name? Why do they have power? There's probably at least a handful of other people with the same name out there."

"Because they gave it to you. Your parents. With love and intent. They created a moment that can't be replicated. And it's more than just the words. It's the context in which they were given. Names don't exist in a vacuum. Was your father rubbing her pregnant belly the first time it was spoken out loud? What was the inspiration? Maybe it was your grandfather's too. It's like a whole hard drive of information, all with unique time and location stamps. It's one of the most potent pages there can be."

"Why do you call them pages?"

"Instead of memories?"

"Yeah."

"I'm not sure. Words are funny. I suppose because it implies a greater story."

Kid considered that while plodding along behind their grandfatherly rescuer. He was thankful for his newfound reserve of energy and warmth, that which presumably came from his name—spoken by a spirit in the darkness of his near-death sleep. But it was wearing thin. Fast. He worried he would fall again and freeze for good, not waking up this time. But after they passed through a stretch of canyon walling the river, it opened to a gully. There stood a small log cabin with white chinking. Warm yellow light shone from square windows. A trail of white smoke drew a lazy path from its chimney to the sky.

"Aqui," said the man as he paused the tap-tapping along of his walking stick to point to the cozy house. "Mi nieta. Es cómodo allí." He put his arms around himself, pantomiming a hug. "Encontrarás calor."

He rapped on the door with his stick and waited. A woman opened the door, small in stature and heavily bundled, with long black hair spilling out from three layers of textile hood decorated with colorful interwoven geometry.

"Abuelito..." She examined Kid and Alice, brow creased. "¿Quién es?"

"Los encontré junto al mar. Estos niños son fríos."

She eased into a warm but worried smile and opened the rickety wooden door.

"Come in, please, please."

The warmth radiating from the cottage pulled them in with no further provocation. Before the door closed, the man placed his hand on Alice's shoulder, tugging at the wool, his mustache curled by his smile. "Mi poncho, porfa."

"Oh!" Alice exclaimed as she pulled it from her shoulders. "Thank you so much, really. You saved us. Thank you. Gracias."

"Nada, es nada."

As the hooded woman and the mustached man moved to the side to converse in hushed tones, Kid whispered to Alice, "They speak Spanish in The Dream?"

"They speak everything here. This place existed before language began."

After the older man left, the woman closed the door behind him and pulled a blanket over the entrance to minimize the draft. Bundled puffily like teddy bears, small children played in an adjoining room. They stopped with their blocks and carved wooden figures to observe the visitors. The woman, their mother presumably, motioned for them to continue playing, and the children obediently resumed their games. She guided the two weary travelers past the threshold and into a kitchen with hanging pots and pans, a rough-hewn four-chair dining table, and a wood-burning stove.

She opened the stove gate and added a log to the fire. "We are grateful. The world has cooled, but the forest provides warmth." She closed it and briefly warmed her hands over the cast iron before withdrawing her hoods, which bundled cozily around her neck and shoulders. "I am Nakawé. Welcome."

They introduced themselves, and Kid said, "We thought we were goners."

"Si. The ocean has grown, how do you say? Forlorn. These days, she is angry, and many have lost themselves there. It is sad."

Alice asked, "When did it begin? The cold?"

"Not long ago, Old Fire has traveled only halfway through his circle."

"Old Fire?" Kid asked.

"I see that you are not from here." Nakawé studied them curiously but not unkindly. "Old Fire is the Father Light, the most ancient in the sky. His path measures our days. What do you call him where you are from?"

Kid bluffed, "Oh right, we call it the Sun." Alice grimaced, but he didn't notice.

"And the storm?" Kid asked. "Last time I was here, a big one was on the horizon. It looked bad." Despite the added warmth of the cottage and the stove, Kid and Alice were shivering again.

Nakawé held up a finger. "Moment." She entered the adjoining room and rummaged around, returning with an armload of clothes.

"I believe mine will fit you." She handed half the stack to Alice, then the other half to Kid. "And my husband's will work for you."

They layered the clothing on, immediately comforted by the warmth of the thick materials. Alice took a deep whiff of the fabric and smiled. It smelled of sage and stove fire. After they resettled, Nakawé continued.

"The storm arrived. It is here. We are within it. It brings the cold, and most New Lights have gone dark. Now, even the Old Lights begin to flicker and die like candle flames fighting a strong wind. We are doing our best to stay warm, waiting for the bad weather to pass."

"And if it doesn't?" Asked Kid.

She frowned. "I'm afraid that we cannot fight the cold permanently. Already, shrimps and the fishes wash ashore, passed from the freeze. Soon, the sea, she will be empty, and the trees cannot fill our stove forever. But we will talk of this no longer." The children were peeking around the corner, listening. Nakawé turned to them and smiled. "The storm will pass, and we will play in the sea again. Soon, very soon." She brightened and patted her hands on her thighs. "Speaking of fishes, are you hungry? You will eat—warmth from without, warmth from within. As mi abuelita used to say."

A half-eaten pot of stew sat simmering on the cast iron stove. It smelled of shrimp, garlic, onion, and other aromatic spices. Kid and Alice's bellies rumbled, and their mouths watered. They gratefully took two bowls, and after only a moment of trying to be polite and eating slowly, they gave in to their hunger and wolfed it down, along with second helpings of a half bowl each.

After a few minutes of contented silence, leaning back in chairs, hands on bellies, Alice leaned forward and said, "Nakawé, thank you for your hospitality. But I'm afraid we have to go as soon as possible. And we hate to ask a favor on top of your generosity, but can you help us find a way to Middlemost?"

"Middlemost? So, you are of the Materia. I knew it. There is no 'sun' in this world, mis queridos." Nakawé smiled and added, "Here we call it The City of Light."

Stunned, Kid said, "So it really is a city? Like full-on?"

"You'll see," answered Alice.

"It is overflowing with life and opportunity. Although... These days, I do not know if that is still true. I have not been since the cold. It is not hard to find once you are facing the correct direction, following the river and The Stream. But you are not near, it will be many days walk. And in this cold? I would not recommend it."

"Many days?" Kid asked, exasperated. "Isn't there a faster way?"

"Yes, my brother travels there often to trade and visits us every morning. I'm sure he could be persuaded to go if he is not already planning to do so.

"So you know about our world here? The Materia?"

"Of course. Yours is the source of the lights, Old Fire, The Stream, and all the rest."

"Our dreams... they're your stars."

Alice watched Kid's face light up with wonder and smiled.

Kid sat up, excited by the final undeniable revelation that his dreams, everyone's dreams, literally created a world. And people too. Real people—like Nakawé, her grandfather, and her children. His mother. And the mothers of others. It was no longer theory and wild stories from strangers. His heart and body were currently warm thanks to their generosity. Good people. Just like Linh.

"Nakawé," Kid pleaded, "I hate to push, but is there any way we can leave now?"

"I am sorry, but no. He visits every morning to bring us supplies. And now, it is time to sleep, especially for mis niños. Tomorrow, we will speak to him about your journey. This is good?"

Kid nodded and forced a smile, flattened by worry.

They slept in piles of blankets on the kitchen floor next to the stove, their rest stymied by nightmares. In Kid's, the repeating grotesquery of a man's face melting under the shadow-heat of his hand. In Alice's, the unsuccessfully escaped subjugation of her adoptive mother's lips.

Near morning, a sound like screaming death ruptured their fragile sleep, and they jumped to their feet, pumped full of adrenaline. Upon wild-eyed inspection, the most dangerous thing they discovered was a scrawny rooster pecking at the floorboards. After a moment, it let out another blood-curdling crow.

Nakawé rushed into the room. "Sorry-sorry-sorry, Tako can't be outside these days. It is too cold." She shushed the bird and gave him a bowl of grain to eat. He seemed content with the offering and quieted down, cluck-clucking away.

"Just a rooster?" Kid asked. "Don't they normally come with lady chickens?"

Alice laughed. "Lady chickens? How do you sound so smart sometimes?"

"Whatever," Kid replied, rubbing the sleep from his closed eyes.

Nakawé answered Kid's question, "Sadly, we have had to eat them."

"How will you get more eggs?" Kid asked.

"We will see to that another day, mijo. For now, there is always work to be done, and mis hijos must grow." Nakawé's mouth tilted into a frown, then she pushed the thought away and brightened, adding with a new smile, "Otherwise, who will care for me when I am old?" She patted her thickly bundled thighs and said, "Now, you will need a breakfast."

Nakawé busied herself at the stove as Kid and Alice stretched, shaking the hard floor from their bones. She handed them two plates with a bit of fried chicken, some fried rice, and a half potato each. "I am sorry there is not more. We must balance hospitality with practicality in these times."

They attempted to refuse the food and give it to the children, but Nakawé would hear nothing of it. Her hospitality was stubborn and impossible to deny. Kid and Alice dined with guilt and gratitude.

As they ate, a thought occurred to Kid. He force-swallowed a bite to let himself speak, holding up his fork to punctuate the question, "Wait, how did we dream last night? We're already here. In The Dream."

Alice giggled, finding herself now more entertained than annoyed by his rookie questions. "You dreamt of The Real, right?"

He had and nodded to confirm.

"Yin and yang," she said.

"So, could someone from here travel there too?"

"Of course. But very few have the talent to see a dreaming animi, and even then—only vaporous hints."

Kid had thought he was fresh out of surprise and confusion. Clearly wrong, he let out a long breath. "I'm gonna stop asking questions, for real."

"Aw, don't do that. I like seeing your face scrunch up."

He rolled his eyes and took the last bite on his plate, then almost licked it clean, but controlled himself and pushed it away with a lingering eye on a bit of tasty fried potato oil.

Nakawé patted her thighs, then stood to take their dishes. "My brother will be here soon," she said. "He rarely stays long.

And I warn you, he is not a talkative man, but there is kindness under the surface. I will tend to my children. Please ready yourselves for your journey."

———

Nakawé's brother arrived as predicted, in an old blue pickup truck filled with crates. Kid was not surprised to see a Ford truck from the seventies in The Dream. At this point, why not? After speaking with his sister, he appraised Kid and Alice, then introduced himself as Ikal. After some goodbyes, thank you's, and hugs, they climbed into the dusty interior of the pickup and began their journey down the rutted dirt road. The children made a shuffling attempt to escape outside and watch them leave, but Nakawé quickly herded them back to stay warm. Ikal apologized for the lack of a working heater but offered blankets, which they piled on. Between the blankets, the clothes and scarves from Nakawé, and the body heat of three people packed onto a bench seat, the cab quickly turned cozy.

After some unsuccessful attempts at conversation with Ikal, Kid and Alice gave up and traveled for several hours in silence, watching the landscape roll by. The ridges, forests, and canyons eventually ran out into a hard-pack plain with a river cutting through it, the same river that led to the sea, its surface covered in most places by sheets of ice.

Ikal finally spoke, "The Stream."

In the distance, a spire of light shot from the ground, up and away, until finally branching out into a shining network of stars. It was like looking at an upside-down tree made of light with its root system exposed. Dark patches passed through it like shadows of beetles behind rice paper.

Kid leaned forward to get a better look, squinting at the other-worldly structure. "Before, in Linh's apartment—god, that feels like forever ago—you said people think we go to The Void when we die. That's it, isn't it? The main entrance?"

"Good guess. According to the scholars and stories, yes," Alice replied.

"Not much of a guess. If that's not a giant ghost teleporter, I don't know what is. What do they say happens after?"

She watched the beam flicker. "After our spirits travel there? They say new souls are born from the fragments of the old. We are drops of water, evaporated from a sea, reconstituted, and released from rain clouds."

"So, if we fall into the dark like Linh and The Stream stops flowing... We're all just... what? Lost?"

Ikal answered, "Nothing good, child. For now, we drive."

The city broke the horizon and grew into full view. The skyline teemed with structures and skyscrapers—ever-increasing in height toward the center until culminating at the highest point with The Stream, which burned into the permanent twilight like a quasar jet.

"I will take you to the Undermarket," Ikal said. "It is where I trade."

"And The Circum Agora?" Kid asked.

Alice replied instead of their introverted driver, "It's

towards the center, sort of a luxury shopping area. We'll need to walk."

As they neared the city, it became apparent that a reverse exodus was in progress. Thousands of blanket-swaddled people were moving toward the warmer heart of the city. There were walkers, bicycles, wagons, and ambling vehicles. Many rested in tents or around fires. Children cried, parents comforted, and those not busy with tasks stood together, watching the sky flicker. It was a crawling, starving refugee camp. Ikal's old Ford slowed to the pace of a jog as they weaved through the increasing traffic jam. Kid saw an older woman collapse and stay down despite the effort of her family. At that moment, he realized the many covered mounds he'd seen along the way were more of the dead.

Finally, they found themselves deep in the city, surrounded by all manner of buildings and people. The tightly packed structures rose high into the urban canopy, connected by bridges and catwalks like vines in a jungle. Every underpass and alcove was filled with shanty slums stacked high enough to lean dangerously. Steam drifted from gutters and vents in meandering tendrils, around each of which small groups huddled. Business logos, building signs, and car headlamps bounced flickering light from ice-covered surfaces. It all combined to form a chaotic yet beautiful neon menagerie.

As the kaleidoscope city passed by, Kid figured a person could spend a lifetime exploring just this one city, just as he had in San Francisco. But they would only see a tiny sliver of Middlemost this day. There were places to go and people to see. Sightseeing would have no bearing in this mad dash for survival. Perhaps, if he were lucky enough to come upon it, exploration might happen another time.

Ikal dropped them off at the entrance to a pedestrian-only market street lined on all sides by canopied shops of various sizes selling gear and supplies. Most butted up against buildings as if providing guard over their doorways.

"Good luck, friends," Ikal said as a goodbye. "May your journey find warmth."

39
PERFECT

The Undermarket street urchins were staring, making it obvious that Delilah needed to disguise her destroyed face before Alice and Kid showed up. There was no body-hopping in The Dream. Because there were no vessels to *hop to*—it was the place where the animi roamed. She bought a silk scarf from a street vendor and wrapped it around her head to hide her red mane with the expensive material. It would do. It was clean.

She twitched and rubbed her eye. Fucking thing was constantly itching now. It was like the side of her head couldn't fit inside of itself and kept trying to jump out. But through the supernatural sight of her scarred socket, she could see the world in ghostly outlines, witnessing its connective and identifying energy. Every being in the marketplace glowed with a unique aura, a fuzzy silhouette surrounding their body, each of a wide variety of color, shape, and rhythm, each somehow instantly recognizable and memorable to her, as if she were hardwired to an infinite spectrum-coded memory. Of course, what she was seeing were true names, all visible.

That bitch Alice wouldn't stand a chance. Not this time.

Her blight shard lost contact when the pair escaped her at The Sand and traveled into The Dream. But there was only one place they could ultimately go, so she would wait for them there. Until then, she would watch the scum ebb and flow like cockroaches on trash. She saw an old fart with a twisted headband serve bowls of some unidentifiable slop, a bedraggled mother herd her chaotic children, and peons haggling over the dwindling market supplies. The Dream was never her favorite place to visit for any length of time, but now it was an undeniable shit hole. How could a world made of spirit energy still manage to smell like anything, much less stale piss and desperation? She wrinkled her nose in disgust as she pushed the mystery away.

Another one of the children noticed her horrific appearance and leered at her. She made a nasty face back, and the runt hid behind his mother's coat. They needed that security, that bundling of fabric, that warmth to press into. She didn't need any of that anymore. Delilah knew she would never be too cold, or too hot, or alone again. She was perfect. She was clean.

Give a pound to the Polly girl and give her a twirl.

Clean, clean, clean as a bean.

Her attention shot up as she caught colorful movement of an instantly recognizable hue. *There! Ha! I can see your stink from a mile out.* Alice and Kid.

Dirty, dirty, dirty.

Delilah buried herself in the crowd but did not lose sight

of them. *Dirty. Rotten. Bastards. Weeping, whining, sores, both.* She watched them meander, faces covered, under the impression they were hidden. Oh, how she wanted to jump in their heads and tear them apart. She could do it too. The feeling was tangible. Her new ability would allow her to split their minds like eggs and drink the yolk. Her head jerked again, and she absentmindedly rubbed the eye socket.

She *could* do it. But the wait would be worth it.

Just a little longer now. Soon she could have them.

Wait, wait, wait! Wait for the gate!

Lactate! Heart-rate! UuuuuULTRaaaaaa VIO-LATE!

Delilah giggled and tongued the memory of her raw gums.

40
UNDERMARKET

Street runner and agent of the dream, they made an odd but increasingly comfortable pair. The two were no longer cold, thanks to the extra clothes they'd been given, the steam rising from vents and the warmth of their movement alongside the human herd. It was clear why so many refugees of the wilds were traveling to find similar safety in Middlemost.

The scarves Nakawé gave them also provided the benefit of hiding their faces—a wise move in the event the people who were hunting them found their way to The Dream. As Kid adjusted his scarf and thought of evading stalkers, he remembered Ben, The Lotus, and their inevitable confrontation.

"It's easy to forget that there's another world out there."

"You just called The Real *the other*," Alice replied.

"As if *this* was the main one? Exactly what I mean. Funny, right? Well, when we get back out there, er... in there? Up there? Ha, whatever. When we get back, I hope Ben is sleeping with the rest. If he's alive, he'll be on my ass. Dude's a pit bull."

"If we make it that far, we can count ourselves lucky. It'll be a good problem to have. I'll help you."

"You will? Thought you didn't make promises you couldn't keep."

"I don't. Did you think you could cuddle me back to life on a romantic beach and get away with it?"

"Ah, come on, it wasn't like that."

Even hidden behind the scarf, Alice knew he was blushing as usual.

Her eyes squinted in a smile. "You're too easy."

As they wove through narrow streets, Kid studied the other people in the crowds. Remembering Delilah jumping to four different bodies in a matter of minutes back at The Sand, he wondered about that particular hunter.

"What about Delilah?" Kid asked.

"What about her?"

"Can she follow us? In another stolen body?"

"She could never travel here before, and you can't take pure animus as a vessel. They're already un-vesseled, as it were. But she was also never able to body-hop so fast or far either. I don't know what has happened to her, but she's changed. We should certainly not let our guard down."

"What does she even look like?"

"Right, you've never seen her authentic vessel. Well, she's a redhead and about my height. Always has this sneer on her face like she's about to kick over your Lego castle."

"I wish that was all she wanted. I'm not embarrassed to admit, she freaks me the fuck out."

"Yeah... She's a vibe, alright."

"Would you be able to feel her with your power?"

"I could before, and I haven't sensed anything yet," Alice replied. "But, again, I can't say for sure. She's not the same as she used to be."

———

There seemed to be everything one would expect in any typical outdoor market: food, clothes, blankets, and daily supplies—even a few buskers performing for tips. One played a strange curved guitar, whose songs echoed across the buildings. A bit further in, a troupe of teens with cold-rosed cheeks danced synchronously to different music; it sounded like Irish bluegrass, all fast and fiddle. The place was noisy and busy, like any proper city.

"You've been here before, right? How'd you get in? Guess you didn't hitchhike in after teleporting through a box truck."

"I was always with Mara, keeping her company or running errands while she met with people."

"Evil power broker like that, bet she hangs out in those tall buildings in the middle. The glass spikes. Reminds me of the Financial District. But these are a lot taller, like in the pics of Dubai and China or wherever."

"Yeah, good guess."

"So, how *did* you get here before?"

"By dreaming. Mara has a special totem."

"All travelers can't come here?"

"No, definitely not."

"You and Mara were tight then."

"Listen, I know what you're thinking. 'I'm running around with the friend of the bleep-bleep who... you know.' Well, she and I, we aren't *tight,* okay? I'm not her buddy. More like a prize horse. Treated well, but *owned.* She would toss me in a heartbeat if I stopped being useful. I'm unsure if she knows how much I hate her, or she just doesn't care."

"Easy, I'm not accusing you. Just talking."

"Yeah, you're right. Sorry."

"Hate and fear, right? The classic shortcuts to obedience."

Kid lifted an arm and bent his torso to avoid colliding with two laughing and running children. Even in the freezing Dream, the youngest found interesting ways to pass the time. It's sad how the innocent have that talent that eventually evaporates or is stolen away.

"I'd be lying if I said that's all it was," Alice said as she continued scanning their environment for way-finding landmarks. They walked briskly but not so fast as to seem out of place. "Mara adopted me. She took me in as a toddler— before I can even remember. I was only two or three."

"Just because someone adopted you doesn't mean you owe them anything."

Alice sighed. "I know. But that's not perspective you get until you grow up."

"Learned that lesson too," Kid agreed. "So, Mara wasn't all bad?"

"No, not at first. I mean, what do you know when you're that little? I grew up in The Young School. I never knew anything else. We were taught that we were special and important. I ate the whole act—soccer mom savior with the changing face."

"Soccer mom?"

"She can be kind when she wants to. Her venom always made the honey that much sweeter." Alice scoffed, "We were raised to believe that when someone moved on to be her new vessel, they were chosen for greatness, for some nirvana. A place only the best of us could go. We would literally fight to the death for the privilege of becoming her next skin."

They walked with their hands and faces buried in the warmth of their clothes. Shoppers and traders bustled about, squabbling over minimal inventory. Kid waited for Alice to continue, and eventually, she did.

"Then a feeling developed. Maybe it's my empathy talent, I don't know, but I sensed that these girls, the chosen ones, weren't ascending. They were being thrown away, their souls lost. Left to wander in the dark somewhere. Now, with the information we've gathered over the last two days, I suspect they and countless others are lost in The Void."

"Why would she go through all that trouble? Can't she take anyone she wants? Jump in their heads if she has their true name and a couple sharp memories?"

"Sure, but that's a rough ride, and one that's almost always short-lived. Older, unsuspecting bodies are only suitable for quick missions like you saw with Poe and Delilah. Why would she do that, take some random person, if she can raise a perfect group? Trained and supple, not just capable of a transfer, but willing. Desperate even. We worshipped her. All her little children." Alice swallowed an incredulous laugh. "We call her Mother. And to *become* Mother? We were taught that it was a gift of the highest order. The best vessel is always a willing one."

"What about the boys?" Kid asked. "Or the ones who don't make the cut?"

"Well, she's been a man a few times, but not often. If they make it to graduation and she doesn't use them as soldiers, like Poe, she sells them. There are many people like her, if you can even call them that. Those who've been around for ages by doing this. Harvesting and transferring vessels every so often. There's a big market."

"What'd you call them before? Ancients? How many are there? "

"I doubt anyone knows the answer to that question."

"And now we know, even as fucked up as *that* is," Kid added, "it's pretty much just a front. Linh is collateral damage —one of millions. Mara's real goal is to use all of this animus energy to tear The Dream apart and burn everything to the ground. Immortality and the sale of it are just a means to an end."

Alice just shook her head and sighed.

After a few more turns, they passed a clanging, beeping arcade and a group of young men laughing, smoking, and drinking from a bottle of clear liquor, grimacing and coughing with each pull. Kid wondered if the arcade was the same place his mom and dad took the picture in a photo booth twenty years ago.

He spoke, as much to the air as to Alice, "It's so... normal...ish."

"What did you expect?"

"I dunno, wizards, mutants, ninjas? I mean, it is called 'The Dream,' right?"

"No, not around here."

If it weren't for the strange sky, they could have been in any open-air market in the world. Kid clicked his tongue. "Ah, I got it. It's like someone took a hundred ideas and pictures of city markets and mixed them all together. This is like the average of what people think a market should be."

Alice replied, "The way I was taught, it's the culmination of all the consciousness of the Materia Mundi, also known as 'The Real.' And I prefer the former name because both worlds are real. In any case, The Dream is a kind of mirror place created by the power of our connected minds."

"What if it's the other way around?" Kid asked.

"What do you mean?"

"What if The Dream made us?"

Alice squinted. "It's like asking what happened before The Big Bang."

"Chicken and egg."

"Exactly. Either way, though, Middlemost? It's the center. A hub on a wheel."

"Or the black hole in the center of a galaxy."

"Yeah... Maybe." Alice acknowledged. "So, this place, it's supposedly the product of all our minds. But like anything created by a committee, with that many equal votes of what or how it should be, the result is fairly predictable—within a range. It's hard to spike it one way or the other."

They ducked under a striped awning as they passed a little wood-slatted restaurant. It smelled like ramen—braised meats, nutty broth, onion, and garlic. When he glanced inside, his guess was confirmed by an older man with a twisted headband serving a bowl of the steaming stuff to a customer. His stomach growled. Breakfast had been light and many hours ago now, but others in this city were in far worse condition. He pushed the thought away as he nodded and said, "It's hard to be special."

"Exactly. Anything outlandish is overwhelmed by the majority. The fantastical stuff is in areas with a stronger consensus, places under the influence of exceptionally powerful dreamers, or in individual dreams." Alice pointed at the lights in the sky, little pinpoints of flickering blue, too close to be real stars. "In your head, it's fair game. But most people can't control what goes on there, so you end up with all the silly stuff we know and love."

"Like my recurring dream of being a door-to-door vacuum salesman."

Alice snorted, "You must have a fear of sucking."

They laughed loudly at the cheesy joke, surprising themselves and some passersby. Again, it felt good to laugh, and again Kid felt immediately guilty about it.

She continued, "But if you can control it, you can do anything."

"You mean like lucid dreaming?" Kid asked. "I've heard of that."

"That's just a glimpse of what I'm talking about. How do you think I'm able to do what I do? An empathy push? That's just nudging someone else's dream via the connection to my own."

Kid looked down at his hand and its strange geometric markings. "Seems like everyone has a trick or two. So, what's my thing? That fucked-up-melting-vampire thing."

"I'm not sure... I've never seen anything like that. Though, it seems to be of the physical school. It's not like an empathy push."

It made sense if you allowed yourself to believe. It reminded him of the Dungeons & Dragons game books with awesome illustrations. If he cleaned himself up and looked like a regular city college student, he could buy coffee, hang out, and read at the bookstores all day. *Vampiric Touch and Eldritch Blasts. Astral Projection and Dimensional Doorways.* He grinned behind his scarf. When he thought of it all through a new lens, it made it somehow more approachable—and despite the real-life danger—*cool.*

As they moved through the streets, the shops took on a more upscale look, with cleaner sidewalks, bigger windows, fewer people, and patrolling guards to keep the rabble in line. Alice let Kid know they had entered the Circum Agora, were likely getting close, and to keep an eye out for anything that might ring a bell.

"So," asked Alice, "what did it feel like? Back at The Sand? When you were... absorbing him."

"Like a bolt of lighting connected to my hand."

"Is that all?"

"Hard to say. We were pretty out of it back there, you know? Whatever Horacio did made me feel like I was rolling my balls off. But from what I can remember, it felt kinda evil, or *dark,* at least. And satisfying. Like I was releasing a bunch of pent-up energy. It made me hungry. I wanted more. Tell you the truth, it scared the shit out of me."

"Well, at least you're alive. Most wouldn't be after tangling with a blight. We can be thankful for that, but beyond gratitude, this is new territory. Let me know if you feel... anything... I guess?"

Kid looked at his marked hand, flexed it, and stuffed it back in its pocket as if hiding it would make everything better.

Then, after what felt like an endless parade of unremarkable storefronts, they saw it.

Cognosa's Fine Things

Purple neon letters arched over thick hanging curtains of red velvet. It looked more like the entrance to a carnival attraction than a store. Goosebumps prickled Kid's skin as the fantasy from the cedar box of his childhood suddenly became real.

They moved the thick curtains aside and entered, then took a moment for their eyes to adjust to the dim light. Aside from being hidden in the depths of a dreamland market, the place seemed to be an ordinary pawnshop or warehouse, and a very large one at that—filled with an expanse of stacked shelving holding a wild assortment of trinkets and boxes. However, a retail counter and disgruntled employee were not visible. But it was slightly warmer inside, and they pulled their scarves down.

After some time wading into the depths of the space, they turned around to find that their seemingly straight path had disappeared. It was replaced by yet another impenetrable wall of tchotchkes and musty wooden containers, all lit overhead by hundreds of dim orange Edison bulbs, glowing on strands that stretched into the distance.

"Nice." Kid said. "A living maze. I'm not even surprised or

freaked out, that's how much my head's unscrewed now. I think I saw this one in a movie. Next, a wall with teeth will chase us toward a deadly drop."

"Chasm," Alice added as she scanned the area, searching for anything to get her bearings but finding nothing. They could only move forward, down a long row of shelves.

"Ooh, good word. Yeah, a chasm."

Alice giggled. "We'll have to hang on the edge, and just before falling to our deaths, a single ray of hope will present itself. Maybe a rope, a secret tunnel, or a winged guardian."

"Is it a bad sign that we're getting used to all this?"

"We? This is just another day at the office for me."

Amazed, Kid asked, "Really?"

"No, I'm just being a pain," Alice replied. "Like your dad said, we're way off the map now."

Kid smiled at the mention of his father and said, "At least we're not freezing this time."

"True," she said. "Then again, it would be nice to cuddle some more."

Kid blushed, and Alice noticed again that he turned rosy so quickly it bordered on ridiculous—especially how it contradicted his permanently scowling face. It was cute and made her feel like she owned a secret key. She smiled as she ran her fingers along the shelves. "Do you think they have a Roswell alien or the Holy Grail in here somewhere?"

Kid chuckled, "Yeah, probably. I bet mummies and a real jackalope too."

She laughed. Then, they stopped at an intersection. The branching corridors of shelving stretched as far as they could see in three directions, which didn't make any sense at all.

That distance would mean miles. Surely, that wasn't the case. More likely, it was a trick of perception caused by the protections woven into the place by its caretaker and builder, the infamous Cognosa.

As they thought about which way to go, Alice grew solemn and said, "Back at the club, when we were dancing and holding hands, we shared that dream. I saw something in you, one of your memories. It seemed like a special one."

Feeling the heat in his cheeks rise, Kid replied, "Hope it was nice."

"It was."

"What'd you see?"

Alice closed her eyes to bring back the memory. "I saw... well, I think I *was* you, actually. I was in your head, feeling what you felt at that moment. I was in a storage room of some kind... It smelled like a pantry, so I guess it was the restaurant. Linh was there, and she felt so familiar... like home. There was that cute pillow with the yellow ducks."

Kid remembered. "Old cotton as soft as your best broke-in t-shirt. That was when I stayed the winter with her. She would always bring me hot tea."

They decided to maintain course and continue deeper into the vast warehouse of dusty shelves.

"Green tea," Alice said dreamily, remembering the grassy aroma. "She meant a lot to you."

"*Means* a lot to me. Present tense. Yeah... I was in pretty bad shape when she took me in."

"What do you mean?"

Kid replied, "I'd left the last foster I could stomach and was making a go of it on my own, not doing a great job, to be honest. Didn't have my nest yet, and didn't know how to survive the street. Was still learning by trial and error. Just sleeping outside wherever I could. Think I must have had pneumonia. Chest gummed up like an old gutter. I went by her shop to try and dry out and warm up a little. Not only did she give me the best bowl of pho I've ever eaten, but she also insisted that I spend the winter in her storeroom." Kid grinned. "She said 'no freebies,' though. I'd have to do the dishes and take out the trash."

"Sounds perfect," Alice said with a sad smile.

"Could you feel anything?" Kid asked. "From my memory? Or just see things?"

"I could feel."

"What did you feel?"

"Everything. All of it. It was overwhelming. But, mostly?" She thought a moment. "I felt safe. A kind of cherished security I had never felt before. The kind I imagine kids with those TV moms feel. You know, baseball games, homemade school lunches, peanut butter and jelly, and the little I love you notes."

Kid scoffed and smiled, taking a moment to treasure the thought. "P, B, and J. For sure. It was the first time for me. Well, maybe Sister Sofía back at the orphanage when I was little, but that was a mixed bag too. Linh, though, she got me from sick on the street to my place on the roof. I mean, she doesn't know about my roof spot, but she still got me there. Have the feeling she did that a lot. Got people places she didn't even know about. I could feel she was a good one from the start, different from the rest. Maybe that's why I hung around. Maybe that's why I'm chasing her down now. She's special. Kinda reminds me of you."

Surprised, Alice asked, "Oh? How so?"

"Too nice to stay out of trouble," Kid said.

It was Alice's turn to scoff; the trouble thing sounded like a cheesy line, but he continued before she could give him a hard time about it.

"I saw with your eyes too. When we were dancing."

Alice shoved her hands in her pockets; Kid noticed she did it when she was nervous. She replied, "Yeah? How was it?"

"Beautiful. Seeing all of us going wild, but through you, through your feelings. Watching us dancing and vibing, like a front-row seat to our own movie."

"Pretty trippy," Alice said, using Kid's style of slang with a grin as she picked up a random object from a shelf. It looked like one of those old bronze compasses, but the inside was filled with a dark viscous liquid like oil mixed with glitter. It seemed it might attack, so she quickly put it back.

"Sounds like you were in my head while I was in yours," Kid continued, "but we saw different memories. One from the past and one being made, right then, at that moment we all shared."

Alice studied Kid's face and asked, "Did you see anything else?"

He felt guilty about seeing the kiss and directive from Mara. *Do not forget your family... Come back. After it is unlocked, bring it to me. Together we will...*

What did knowing change? Nothing.

"No," Kid lied. "Just watched us dancing."

Alice continued to scrutinize him. "That's it? Could you

feel anything? Could you feel my emotions? The same way I felt yours?"

"I felt everything. Like you said, it was almost too much to handle. My brain, my heart, they were on fire."

"And?"

It was Kid's turn to study Alice—almost-almond eyes of nutmeg brown contrasting with silver-white hair, a strand of which was stuck on her eyelashes. It flicked when she blinked. She hid things from him, but didn't everyone from everybody? What difference did it make?

Kid thought about how it felt, through her mind, to have that freedom and then have it stolen again. You don't know how much you value a thing until it's tasted and taken away. Alice had known freedom, if only briefly. Selfishly, he didn't want to share what he saw because he thought maybe if she knew he knew, she wouldn't stay with him to get Linh. So, he obscured.

"For a moment, while we danced. We were free," He said. "Then it went away. But before that, for a second, we were happy."

They stopped walking. The box-filled aisles muffled sound and dampened echoes. It felt like they were hiding in the depths of an old library. One filled with the secrets of a thousand hidden pages.

Alice scrunched her face. "What does all that have to do with trouble?"

"Trouble? I guess, at that moment, I felt I knew you. Because I *was* you, I knew, for a fact, you'd do anything to feel free."

"And you'd do anything to feel safe."

"Why does it sound like we're comparing wounds?"

Alice shrugged and agreed, "Because we are."

"I'm not saying it's bad," Kid said, chewing his words before continuing. "But, it doesn't feel like the same thing anymore. I always had an escape plan. Fucking always. You know? But now... It's not even on my mind. Well... At least not *my* escape." Kid glanced down to kick a boot through the dust. "See, Linh, she deserves to feel safe. Like she made me feel, I mean, yeah, I could run. I could survive. Make it another day. Be *safe*." He marked the last word with air quotations. "But I've done that already. I've made it a lot of days."

Alice waited patiently as he took a moment to finish.

"But when those days are done, when you're out, what's free without the people you care about? The people who got you there. What's the point? It's all or nothing."

Kid stopped walking and turned to face her. "And now? I'm in it for all. And to tell the truth, knowing what I know, what I saw in your head, I get it. You wanna be free. But I need you, Alice. At least for a little longer, alright? We're almost there. It's taking for-goddamn-ever, but we're close."

Alice was silent, just staring at him. The dim overhead light lit her freckles like cinnamon. Dust motes floated in the air.

Flustered, Kid said, "What?"

"It was nice inside your head." She stepped closer.

"Yours too," Kid replied. Their faces drew together.

"You're right. I want to be free. You know the score, and so do I. We get this done, then we're out."

"Colorado." Kid said.

Alice tilted her head in question. "Why there?"

"Waterfalls and hot springs. They call them hippie-dips. Lots of birds, deer, and even bears. Millions of trees and wide, open spaces. Peace."

"Sounds like a dream," she whispered.

As they spoke, they closed to just inches from each other. Kid lifted a hand—its careful slowness asking permission. She gave it, and he touched her cheek. Alice's mouth parted, and her breath puffed clouds in the frigid air. Finally, their lips met.

Cheeks rosy, eyes shimmering, she asked, "What was that for?"

Kid smiled. "Might not get another chance."

"Maybe not. Do it again," she said.

And he did. This time not briefly. They pressed against each other fully—fitting together the way a man and woman's hips will, concave and convex. As they kissed, time seemed to slow, and at least for them, the world warmed. With eyes shut and lips together, they could have been anywhere. A windy rooftop. A neon alley. A snow-floored forest.

———

When at last, their lips parted, and they again took sleepy stock of their surroundings, sure enough, there it was—as if waiting all along. A door. It stood beside them, punctuating the extended shelves of containers. It was as if their kiss summoned it or woven it anew from the spell-filled air.

Kid didn't need Alice's abilities to know what would come next. He could feel it just fine on his own. The door was made

of weathered red wood, fit for a cozy home in the country—
and it perfectly matched the chipped crimson ring on his
index finger.

A token, Horacio had said, *tuned to a dream.*

Below a frosted glass window, the door was numbered
eight—a symbol matching infinity, the numeral made of black
wrought iron. Kid glanced at Alice, then lifted his hand to
knock.

41

COGNOS

After rapping his knuckles on the worn red wood, the door swung open so quickly that it was apparent someone was waiting just behind it.

"Kid! Alice! Ohhhhh!" The tiny woman with a shock of white hair squealed, "Marvelous! Just marvelous! It is *sooo* good to have babies again! We needed some babies in this stuffy old place."

Before they could question what the baby talk was about and how she knew their names, the woman bolted out of the doorway and hugged them both tightly. Her head came to about chest high.

She shrieked again and repeated, "Oh! Marvelous, marvelous, just marvelous."

When she moved from her standing position to the hug, it was possible to see ghosting trails of her, performing variations of the action that had taken place. In one translucent visage, she closed the door rather than exiting. In another, she stepped forward but saw through them, looking into the warehouse with a troubled frown. In yet another, she threw a glass out before slamming the door closed. She vibrated whenever she stood still, which seemed to be only rarely—the edges of her body taking up a thousand simultaneous possibilities.

"I just knew you would make it! Not *knew* knew, but I knew! You know? Not the most likely outcome, no, no! But the best, oh yes! Certainly! Ohhh! Just marvelous. Marvelous! Come in, come in." The Cognosa wrangled them through the doorway with vibrating multiplicative arms swathed in gauzy pink fabric. Her crow's feet and laugh lines wrinkled deeply as she smiled.

Kid and Alice stepped through the doorway behind the Cognosa, and she shut it behind them, then shoo-shooed them out of the way. She led them down a narrow hallway of what appeared to be an old-fashioned train—something you'd expect to see on a movie set from the thirties or forties, carpeted in thick red velvet, with walls of shining riveted steel.

After stepping through another arched steel doorway, the space opened up— much larger than a typical train car could possibly be. Especially odd were the walls, ceiling, and floor. Where they weren't covered by shelves, Persian rugs, and glowing chandeliers, all were made of glass. Through the transparent compartment, they could see that the train car was perched over a canyon waterfall like a bridge. Below their feet, a river rushed by, plunging into misty depths.

Above were patches of blue sky and puffy clouds, visible through a forest canopy of pine, oak, maple, and sycamore. Animals littered the wilderness in abundance. Bluebirds, cardinals, crows, American red squirrels, white-tailed deer, and many others were foraging, pecking, and nuzzling for their next meal. Along the train car walls were rows upon rows of shelved books, boxes, and artifacts. Leather-bound and elaborate, inconsequential paperback, and skulls of various species. One item was a bronze spear from some bygone era, and another was a globe, but the landmasses were unfamiliar. Perhaps it mapped a different epoch in Earth's history, or more likely, thought Kid, it was a different world altogether.

As Alice mentioned earlier, private areas of Middlemost were subject to the whims of their overseers. The more secluded a place, the more control its owner had. It seemed The Cognosa was a deft architect. Eyes twinkled, and lips pursed as she said to them, "Don't be shy. Not with me. However brief, this is your home."

The spritely woman and her two guests sat in leather armchairs. There seemed to be only one of her now, the vibrating multiplicative forms having settled down. She had a snifter of brandy at her elbow and had also given Kid and Alice small glasses of the rich liquid, their bellies now warm with the stuff. Songs of the woodland birds whistled through open panels in the glass arches overhead. It was positively cozy.

"I don't want to be rude," Kid said carefully, "but the extra-you's, what are they—um—where'd they go?"

"Oh, not rude at all. I'm surprised you took so long to ask. It shows what expanse your mind has opened to in such a short time. Or how bound you are by etiquette. At a certain age, you throw that away." She gave Kid a pixie wink. "I am animi, and I take up space in many places, many potentialities. Because of this, you see my *possibilities*. And because of the way I exist, I can envision much the same. Many branches of what *might* happen grow all around me."

The Cognosa scooted to the edge of her chair and splashed more brandy into her snifter, offered some to Kid and Alice, to which they refused, then sat back in her chair. She took a whiff and a sip, smacked her lips, then continued.

"Up until the moment you came to my door, there were many competing tributaries of *possible*. Volatile, one could say. At times, we are but ants, escaping to sea in a floating thimble. Which way will we go? Nobody knows! What you saw when you arrived was that state of chaos. Then, as we walked inside and sat down, those potentialities coalesced. In this particular moment, there is nothing to fracture away. You see, there is not a one who comes here that I have not allowed. This is *my* home, and until the day The Dream shreds, that will remain true. However, once you leave this place, possibilities will again fork away. But for now, we are here, that is all, and that is good. My essence is calm."

Kid understood and nodded. He had come a long way since the days prior, now fully comfortable with concepts of spirit creatures able to see through the unrealized potentialities of time and space. That sorted, he asked, "What else do you know? How did all of this come to be? You know about my mom? And my dad too, right? You sold them their rings, right?"

"Sold? Dear, I made them. Both were special, but your

mother was like a prism in mist. Art become life. Such was her voice and essence. Extraordinary, even for an animi. Perhaps that is how she found herself in love with a *man*." She stretched the word *man* as if it were taboo. She winked at Kid again. The Cognosa's rate of winking was increasing with her intake of brandy.

Kid continued, "And what about this plan? All this coincidence?"

"None of this is a coincidence, Mister Thames. Horacio has been working to crack this nut for a *very* long time. Then again, so has Mara. And others too. The thing with ancients and animi is this: imagine, if you will, being like them—able to wait indefinitely for an infinitely rare series of events to occur and trigger certain actions and branching strategies—a game stretching millennia. If you could do that, all those with short lifespans would see your actions as slow, random, and coincidental. A mountain does not move a river. It simply waits. In this particular potentiality, several *incredibly* unlikely events have occurred. First, you exist. Second, you have the lost totem. More on that soon. And third, we live in an era with enough animus bound to The Real for both sides of the coin, good and evil if you choose to call them that, to have the opportunity for grave impact of universal proportions."

Kid shifted nervously, causing the leather chair to creak. "So what are we then, just pieces on a board?"

"You are not pieces. You are linchpins—with the pleasure and curse of free will. Sure, you have been pushed, pulled, and prodded, but that is life. You've never been puppets, not once. You've had your agency all along, the both of you. You have made decisions and route changes along the road of life for twenty years. Those choices have brought you to this precise location—this moment. Speaking to me, holding the totem. You could leave now. But I don't think you will."

"But what does it matter if these ancients can just wait around? If we fail, they try again in a thousand years. We don't matter."

"For better or worse, that is no longer true as The Dream crumbles around our ears. Once it is gone, all of this is finished. What follows will be an era of darkness that will outlast the death of our home star. Will it all happen again somewhere else in the universe? I suppose with infinite time and space, it is a certainty. But that timeline stretches far beyond the lifespans of The Dream Dreaming or any false god. This is it for us. The midnight hour. And yet, what you do next is *still* your choice."

Neither Kid nor Alice replied, choosing instead to sit and think, listening to the birds. Their warbling music reminded Kid of the better parts of his youth.

The Cognosa slapped her thigh. "Now! Without further ado, go on then! Ask me!"

Alice and Kid looked at each other, unsure of how to proceed.

"Come, come! Ask me!" The Cognosa pushed. "What's it do?"

"What's it do?" They said in unison, not intentionally.

"At last! Haha! Well! Give it here." The eccentric woman held out her hand, into which Kid placed the box that held the totem. "It's not complicated," she said as she used a pinky nail to slice the packing tape holding the cardboard together, which she then tossed haphazardly over her shoulder. She maneuvered the dark wooden container in her small wrinkled hands. Kid and Alice leaned forward, elbows on their knees.

"You see the markings?" The Cognosa asked as she ran her fingers along the sides of the box. "One side is life, and the other side is *after* life. Flesh on one side, bone on the other. Pretty straightforward. Not *the* afterlife, of course, although there are similarities. Simply, *what comes after flat-plane consciousness*. Between the two stands a portal, a disk. For the more imaginative, it might look like a blade or a scalpel." She gave Alice yet another booze-buzzed pixie wink. "I'll tell you a secret. It is *all three*. A blade can be a tool to harm and a tool to heal. The only certain thing is potential. For this box to open, it needs to be doubly engaged. By The Real and The Dream. Conscious and Subconscious. Each with a pull perfectly equal. Inside, you will find a rivener. *That which severs and that which mends.*"

"Rivener. What does that mean?"

Alice replied for The Cognosa, "*Riven* means to cut apart. Violently."

"Cut? So, it's a magic knife." Kid grinned. "Cool."

Alice rolled her eyes. "Magic?"

"Yeah, you know, Merlin, Shazam!, abracadabra," Kid replied.

"Oh, yes," The Cognosa giggled. "Dragons and demons and wizards, oh my!"

Alice scoffed, "There is no such thing as magic."

"Says the girl who can mind-meld," Kid replied.

"It all has a scientific explanation."

"Don't think science has a hold on this one, Alice."

"Kid, just because *you* don't understand it doesn't mean it's not science."

"Hey, just because you can think you can explain it doesn't mean it's not magic. Magic is real. I've seen it."

"Oh yeah? When? When did you see magic, street boy?"

The Cognosa grinned as she watched the suddenly bickering pair. *Ah*, she thought, young love. *So volatile and fun. The only predictable thing about it was that it was unpredictable.* The real thing was much more exciting than the variations she'd seen play out in earlier visions.

"Street boy? Nice. What's your deal all the sudden? Don't worry about it, okay?"

"Sure, deflect away. Of course, you won't tell me something you haven't seen."

"I have."

Alice waited.

"When Linh came into my nightmare. I was trapped there, and she came for me."

"That's not magic. That's The Dream. I've explained that to you."

"Not that part."

"Then what?"

"When her soul, or spirit, or whatever—*her*, the piece that's *her*—she fell, no *jumped*, into The Void to save me."

Alice tried to interject, but Kid interrupted her.

"No, hang on. See, if that's not magic—throwing your heart into the black for some no-name waste of space—if that's not magic, Alice? I don't know what is. Because it sure as shit ain't science. That woman, *her soul,* that's magic. And if

I gotta use a knife to go and get her out of there? That knife better be *fucking magic* too."

Alice's eyes, previously defiant, were now intently studying her shoes. White Adidas shell-tops with baby blue stripes, how silly they seemed in this place.

"Fine," she said.

"Goody!" The Cognosa clapped her hands. "That was fun! Come, come, I want to show you something."

The little woman grabbed Kid and Alice's hands and pulled them reluctantly up to standing, then shepherded them over to the window wall of the train car. With a wave of a hand, the outdoor woodland scene vanished to reveal the city of Middlemost.

Though now, somehow, they were high in the air. They had originally entered The Cognosa's realm through a ground-level door, but now it was clear that her train car flew through the air as if on ghost tracks.

The transition was jarring, but such strange happenings were no longer big surprises. From their elevated position, they could look down and observe from a different angle what they'd seen on their journey in Ikal's truck—the sprawl of the urban lowlands flickering with the pinprick lights of barrel fires and shop lamps. A derelict outer ring of the metropolis rose drastically toward the center, culminating in gleaming skyscrapers now directly in front of them.

Thousands of windows in various shapes and sizes gleamed in a rainbow of colors, like a city of broken mirrors. And if their gaze continued upward, they could see The Stream glowing a furious blue, like an artist's rendition of a relativistic jet shooting from the center of a black hole. Kid couldn't help but wonder, for the third time, if the similarity was more than visual. Maybe this is where you went if you passed the event horizon.

"There." The Cognosa pointed to the blue spire. "That's the fifty-fifty spot. Where this meets that, beginning and the end, et cetera. And you," she looked at Kid, the pulsing blue light casting jumping shadows, "you're the Fifty-Fifty Kid."

"The Fifty-Fifty Kid?" Alice asked, eyebrow raised.

"Part animi, part human. At the edge, where souls meet the world. Kid is the key, and over there," The Cognosa pointed at The Stream, took a sip of her brandy, and smacked her lips, "that's the lock."

"I can open the box over there?" Kid asked, watching the bright beam of blue, its light dancing in the reflection of his eyes.

"You can do more than that. That's where you'll cut a hole to find your friend."

Kid nodded. "Finally. Fuck yeah. How do we get over there?"

"It's not as tricky as it looks. Especially if I show you the way." She finished her brandy with an open-mouthed swig fit for a sailor. "You know what they say, backdoor friends are best."

The Cognosa laid her glass on a drawing table covered in papers and books, then turned to a wall. With a wave of her hand, she summoned a door that grew from wood, steel, and glass. The door itself was dark iron, and the strange pixie lady grunted as she opened it by pulling a heavy lever and invited them through.

They walked down a long hallway leading from the

doorway between the realm of The Cognosa and, if the backdoor was reliable, The Stream. The hallway was dark and reflective, perfectly smooth and square as if tunneled by laser through obsidian. The light at the end of the tunnel shone blue-white at a distance of several hundred yards. The Cognosa led the way, a few steps in front of them.

Kid asked, "Won't you come with us? You seem pretty handy. Bet we could use your help."

She giggled, "High praise, Mister Thames. But no, no, I don't like to venture out of my little world. This is as far as I go, lovies. It's not safe out there for those like myself. These days, what is it you all say? We're dropping like flies." She took a breath and continued, "But I will tell you some of the things I have seen. The things I see now as we draw closer to the center. Paths are unwinding, unraveling. Perhaps my sight will be helpful. Perhaps, as is often the case, it will not. These days one must throw in her lot somewhere, and I will throw mine in with you."

Alice asked, "What can you see?"

"For you, I see only two paths. A choice. Mother or lover."

"What is that supposed to mean?"

The Cognosa replied, "Things are fuzzy. I couldn't say. Even if I could, I wouldn't. I learned long ago it's unwise to spoil fate." She then turned to Kid and continued, "And for you... I see nothing."

"That sounds bad," Kid said.

"No, the sign is simply blank. You're a wild card, the one to sneak up on that vengeful mistress Fate and give her the goose. Ooh!" At that, The Cognosa did a little mock jump and giggled. "But be careful. I see a blind spot. An eye. It is black, and it is deep, like a well. But I trust you will make it through, be careful and be true. I, and we, those of The Dream, we're rooting for you. Now, come—we are here."

They made it to the end of the tunnel—to a doorway radiating blue-white light along the edges.

"Now, give me a hug." The Cognosa opened her arms, her form shifting and vibrating. She smelled of brandy and pine needles. "Marvelous!" She cried and jumped to give them each a wet kiss on the forehead.

"Babies, be good!"

She pushed them through the door like a barmaid at closing time, shutting the door immediately. Just like with Horacio and the box truck, it was a hole in the wall of the world that shut with a wink.

42
PUDDLE

Poe pulled his 1970 Ford Torino into the alley between warehouses, slid the gear shift to neutral, set the emergency brake, turned off the hide-away headlights, and listened to the big engine burble in a low idle. In recent years, the city attempted to turn the dilapidated Bayview warehouse district into swanky condos with water views. But after learning the radioactive waste clean-up numbers were falsified, the area was left abandoned.

Thanks to the blight Delilah left in Kid, they had accessed Kid's memories back at school. They watched Tom's old Crown Vic pull away from Linh's restaurant and, once they had the plates, could use their access to city traffic cams to follow the car here. Since the two kids went into The Dream, Delilah's blight wasn't giving them information anymore, but that was okay. All roads led to The Stream, and Del would wait for them there. In the meantime, Poe's task in The Real was to eliminate Tom and take Linh's body back to The Young School.

For what exact purpose, he wasn't sure. That information was above his pay grade. Ha, as if they were paid. Kept comfortable? Yeah sure. Fancy clothes, fast cars, and penthouses. But not paid. Cash money meant freedom, and nobody got that, not from Mother. In his early twenties, starry-eyed with big ideas, he tried to collect a small personal fund. When The School found out, the punishment was harsh. Like battery jumper cables attached to nuts, except the torture took place in the mind, where it could be done as long as necessary to get the point across. The only limit in The Dream was sanity. Did he still have his? Hard to say. It takes perspective to judge something like that, and perspective was not a gift he'd been given.

The craziest part was how Mara still forced you to love her after beating you. No matter how much pain she caused, how much torture she forced you to endure, she could snuggle in close and pour her honey into your head, and suddenly, she was your shining savior all over again. Thank you, ma'am. May I have another?

You even *knew* what was happening, *how* it was happening, yet the result did not change. She knew he hated it, hated her, and hated himself. After all, Mara could access whatever floated around in his head. But even that made no difference. Poe was sure that the old witch enjoyed the fact that he despised it all and still did what he was told. It was a sadistic game she loved to play.

For the hundredth time that day, he sighed and thought, *Why am I doing this?*

Once upon a time, the answer was easy: the power, mystery, and intrigue were a huge rush. Every student was raised to believe they were something special, some secret agent working for the betterment of the world. But his naïveté ended a long time ago. Poe knew better. There was no good or bad, just people with more or less power angling to get what they wanted, one way or another, chewing up people like him and spitting them out in the process. It seemed like the only ones who didn't use their power over others were those who didn't have any.

After the seduction of false power waned, there was a time he didn't know how to be anything else. He found he just wanted to keep his sister from going further into the dark. Now, it seemed like that was a lost cause too. Mother forced him to cut his only sister's eye out, yet he was the only one who seemed to give a damn.

He loved Delilah—even if that love wasn't returned in the same way. But now? Now he felt pity. Or maybe remorse and grief. Delilah was lost. Poe wanted to stop or do something else before he was totally gone too, but he couldn't. Anytime he tried to move against Mara, his body and mind wouldn't allow it. He was conditioned—mind and body. Pavlovian to the max. Trapped.

So here the fuck he was, at this decrepit and toxic warehouse, ready to kill another man he had nothing against and kidnap the dying body of a woman who'd never done him wrong. A woman who had only tried to live her life, same as him.

He made yet another attempt to will himself to do something else. Poe tried to lift his hand to shift into reverse. Just put it in gear, back out, and get the hell out of there. The gas tank was full, and the old Torino could make it a long way.

He'd done the math many times. With twenty gallons at eleven miles per, he'd make Redding, Fresno, or almost Reno, no problem. Would that be far enough to shake her off? To break the psychic lock?

It didn't look like Poe would find out today. When his hand came up, it didn't go to the shifter. Instead, against his will, his hand went to the keys—just like with the silver knife that took his sister's eye.

After turning the car off, he pulled the keys out with a tinkle of metal on metal and stuffed them in his front jeans pocket. Then his other hand opened the door with a creak of Detroit steel.

Poe grunted in irritation and stopped fighting. Again. For now. But he would keep trying until he succeeded. If he could not win, Poe knew in a dark place in his heart that he would find a way to end himself.

He checked the clip of his Beretta M9 sidearm, chambered a round, then stood and slid the piece into his jeans. After pulling a coil of rope from the trunk and throwing it over his shoulder, he walked toward the warehouse. Poe saw his face in an oily lamp-lit puddle, thought briefly about how much he hated himself, then moved closer to scope the place out and find a decent way inside.

After picking the lock on a back door and sneaking through an office, Poe crept down a dim hallway. He held out his weapon, ready for a gunfight, but relaxed when he saw Tom passed out in his chair. The middle-aged warrior slept like a retiree at a bus stop, head tilted, mouth partly open, crooked hands resting in his lap. Poe wrinkled his nose. He was hoping for a battle that would, at minimum, make this shitshow fun.

The woman, who now called herself Linh instead of The Doe, lay nearby on a table—tucked in a blanket and with an IV in her arm. An EKG occasionally beeped, the pauses long and drawn out, measuring her almost non-existent heartbeat. High above, soft light trickled in from a dirty window.

Poe laid down some rope in a ready-to-pull noose, then sat across from Tom and watched him sleep. He twitched, apparently dreaming. Poe's hands allowed him to take his time at least, and he was grateful for that. Find happiness in the small things. But those have an ending too. Eventually, his hands grew impatient and rapped the Beretta's barrel on the steel table—metal on metal clang echoed through the warehouse.

Tom woke with a start, eyes wide and bloodshot, immediately recognizing the situation before him. "You sonofabitch! I'll—" He jumped to his feet to charge, at which point Poe yanked the rope, tightening the noose he'd put around the man's feet as he'd slept. Tom fell with a shout, then tried and failed to get up on broken hands.

Poe put his foot on his back and said, almost kindly, "That's not gonna get you anywhere. Let's relax for a minute, okay? I wanna talk."

Tom growled from the ground, "Lemme up, asshole."

"Alright. Just behave, will you?" Poe looped some more rope around Tom's wrists, tied it off, then guided him, with surprising gentleness, back into the wooden chair. "There we are."

Tom shifted, face red with embarrassment and pain. "How'd you find us?"

Seeing no reason to hide the truth, Poe replied, "Del can see in the kid's head."

"That dark mark," Tom said.

Poe nodded. "Her blight does fun stuff if the victim doesn't die."

"What do you want?"

"What do we all want?" Poe worked to restrain his hands as he spoke, making the control look like a nervous massage. "Just some freedom, forty acres and a mule, that sorta deal."

"Forty acres? That was all bullshit. Those freed men never got to keep a thing."

"That so?" Poe clicked his tongue. "Figures." His gaze panned around the room as he thought, stopping on Linh. The eventual beep of the EKG signaled him to turn back to Tom. Poe continued, "I'll be straight with you. I'm not big on how all this is turning out. Not the way I like to see things go, generally speaking." He spread his hands wide as if to take in the world. "But what can we do? Us little guys." The sudden movement seemed to excite his hands, which he did his best to suppress.

Tom watched Poe wearily. "Just *talk*, huh? What's wrong with your hands?"

Poe flexed them, sighed, and replied, "Marching to the beat of their own drum. You know how it is."

The older man grunted in easy acknowledgment. After all, he spent much of his life, his darkest times, as a reluctant bondsman—living and surviving the same way, deep within Mara's influence. It was well known among travelers brought up in The Young School that the ancient matriarch could ride your vessel and many others all at once. Not enough for a complete take-over, just a thread, but one thick enough to pull and make her puppets dance.

Poe held a hand out, and it twitched. It was becoming anxious. It had plans. "You got any idea how to get out from under it?"

"Sure. It's a cakewalk."

"Okay... and?"

"Mara's got you, right? Connected to you like a leash. Knotted up tight. Well, we all have to be connected to something. Nobody floats alone. You gotta replace her."

Poe thought momentarily and asked, "But what about you and The Doe—I mean, Linh? Both of you escaped with Mara still kicking. How'd you manage that?"

"Kicking? You're not catching what I said. You don't have to kill her. Just replace her. Now, if you want to try and retire the crone, I won't be the one to stop you. But if you only want to be free of her, you *must* replace the connection. And to do that, *first*, you must know the truth."

"What truth?"

"That she had you from the start."

"What do you mean?"

"You think she saved you?"

"That's the story."

"No. Mara groomed you. She breaks you so she can own you completely. Easily, willingly. Nobody's as easy to damn as the saved."

"I don't understand."

"Where'd she say she found you? East Bay?"

"Yeah."

"San Leandro or Oaktown?"

"San—wait, how'd you know—"

"She calls them her seed farms. *For her flowers*, she says. Mara *put* you there. As a babe. Just like she did with me and all the rest. First, she steals you. Then she breaks you. Then she supposedly saves you. Finally, she owns you."

Poe watched the barely-wavering green line of the EKG, reliving dark memories. The realization of the truth of his childhood, and his sister's, left him speechless. Finally, he shook it off and came back. "Why should I trust you?"

"Because I'm going to die."

Poe sighed, "Is it that obvious?"

Tom shrugged as he glanced at Poe's shaking hands.

"I think I always knew," Poe said. "Somewhere in me. Still, she owns me just the same. But whatever, okay, it's official now. I got the truth. What's next?"

"You either end the master or find a way to break the chain."

"Break the chain... Replace the connection. Yeah, I got that. But how?"

Tom thought for a while, wondering if he should give this man, who would kill him soon, advice on attaining freedom. Then he remembered himself in the same situation not so long ago. Tom and Linh would have never escaped if it hadn't been for Kid's father, their colleague, Michael. Despite the terrible things they'd done to his family, he had been similarly patient and forgiving.

Finally, Tom said, "The chain. It's not out here, and it's not in Mara. It's in there." Hands tied, he nodded toward Poe's chest.

Poe looked down. "In here, huh? My heart? Care Bear Stare and all that? I'm low on glitter, and philosophy's not my strong suit. How do I get in there and cut that bitch out of me?"

"That's something you have to figure out for yourself, Poe." Tom squinted, almost didn't add the last part for fear it would sound silly out loud, but it was what it was, and he wouldn't get another chance to say it. "For me... it was love."

"Love? Bro..."

"Dead serious. The one and only."

"You two were a thing?" Poe scoffed. "Never would have guessed."

"No... she didn't know..."

"Ouch. Friend-zoned?"

Tom grinned. "I'll take a lifetime of friendship with that woman any day."

"Fair enough. So, what was hers?" Poe asked. "The thing she had stronger than Mara's chain."

"Her daughter. She was her heart."

"Was?"

"She gave her up to keep her safe. Keeping her with us while we were on the run was too dangerous. Eventually, things cooled down, but it was too late. We never found her again."

"But Linh's a navigator. Best we ever had if I heard the stories right. Thought she could find anything."

"Oh, she tried. Believe me, she tried. But her girl went completely dark. Still, before all that, when Linh escaped, it was her daughter that got it done for her. Mara couldn't surpass that love. At least at a distance."

"At a distance?"

"You know what I'm talking about. When you get some space between her and you, you can start thinking for yourself again and believe that maybe you could be different. You're thinking that right now. We're having this conversation, and you're wringing your hands instead of strangling me.

At this distance, if you find something stronger, something to break that weakened chain, you can be free. But you also know damn well that when Mara gets close and touches you—every betrayal, each individual thought, and built-up hate, it's all instantly overshadowed by a sugar-sweet love. An obsession, or addiction, more like. It's completely fabricated, and you know it, yet it invades every part of you anyway. Nothing I know of trumps her touch."

Tom lifted his hands to make a point. "So, if you manage to break the chain, stay the hell away, Poe. For good. Because if you go back, you're done all over again. She's got gravity. Bitch is a black hole."

Before Poe could reply and learn more, his hands jerked—twitching and shaking worse than an old-school alcoholic first thing in the morning. He squeezed them into white-knuckled fists, holding their desire at bay a moment longer through sheer will. "Sorry to cut this short. It sounded like we were starting to build some rapport."

"Yeah, looks like time's up. Do me a favor. If you manage to get out from under it, be good to Linh, will you? Treat her right."

Poe considered it. Death bed promises. Not really his

thing. But maybe... maybe it could be. Perhaps he could be one of those guys who kept promises. He replied, "I'll do my best."

"That'll have to do."

"Maybe you'll find her... you know... on the other side."

Tom watched Linh until the EKG beeped. "We'll see," he said, then nodded, accepting his fate.

Poe stood and walked the three paces across the concrete to stand in front of Tom and finally allowed his hands to go where they wanted, securely around his sweating throat. They were hungry for it, ravenous, and jumped at the chance. The relief of not fighting the pull anymore felt as dirty as it did satisfying. The combination made him sick, and his stomach lurched. They held eye contact and seemed to share a thought —something about honor or some such bullshit.

Closing his eyes or plugging his ears would be nice, but instead, Poe listened and watched Tom choke to death. Staying present was a small duty, but it was his. After several minutes, his hands released their grip and hung at his sides, twitching. They seemed satisfied and drained with the role they fulfilled, almost postcoital.

After Poe stowed Linh away in the old Torino's cavernous trunk, he returned to the warehouse and carried Tom, the rope, and a cinderblock to a secluded area between buildings by the lapping bay water. It smelled of that trademark sea smell, which is both fresh and decaying at the same time.

He checked the surrounding area to confirm they were alone, then tied the block around Tom's midsection to ensure his body stayed close to the bay floor. Connecting to a foot, arm, or leg could lead to a sloppy job. After enough decay, it's easy to lose a boot, then a knot, and finally a body. But around the midsection, the rope would hang on to the spine and keep everything down long enough for easy access to nature's clean-up crew. There was a reason Poe never ate the famous San Francisco Dungeness crab. They'd take care of the body in a few weeks at most.

Before doing the final deed, Poe crouched and studied Tom's inert face. What was a vessel without its animus? Just a body. But still... As he had many times before, he wished these situations allowed for a proper burial. Not that Poe was religious or anything—he certainly was not. But it just seemed... seemed what? Honorable.

Despite Poe's lack of piety, he had memorized a Catholic prayer for veterans he heard at a funeral nearly a decade ago. It seemed important, religious or not, so he committed it to memory. He'd seen too many lost vessels, severed souls, sunk bodies, and shallow graves of earth and sea.

"God, by whose mercy the faithful departed find rest, look kindly on your veterans who gave their lives in the service of their country."

He rolled Tom's empty vessel into the cold green and watched it disappear below the surface. Poe stayed until the ripples were overcome by still water.

43
CELLS

Downtown was dead. There should have been pedestrians, cops, jaywalkers, cabs, trollies, junkies, screamers, dreamers, panhandlers, and yuppies on electric pay-by-the-minute scooters. Instead, it was like a post-apocalypse movie set.

All the way from deep Bayview to the Financial District, Poe counted only three people—two pedestrians and one Uber driver—each shellshocked and gawping with wide, scared eyes. Despite the desolation, he followed all the traffic rules to avoid dealing with cops if they did decide to make a surprise appearance. With his connections, it would be nothing more than an annoyance, but an annoyance nonetheless. More importantly, it would be embarrassing, so he drove carefully.

Poe stopped at a red light. Alone. He released an irritated puff of air as he held the clutch and brake, listening to the old big block motor burble—halted for no reason beyond obedience. Few things make a man feel caged within a nonsense system of rules like stopping solo at a red light. His irritation thankfully dissipated as an attractive woman crossed the pedestrian walkway. She was dressed for work, probably in law or finance, judging by the professional style of her clothes. After noticing him, she changed direction and trotted up to his window in clopping high heels. They looked expensive.

She rapped the glass with red acrylic nails matching her perfect red lips. Poe rolled it down, and she asked, "Do you know what's happening? Where is everyone?"

The woman looked scared, and Poe had the itch to comfort her somehow. He had a sneaking suspicion of what was destroying the city, but it wasn't something he would share with a civilian. Hottie or not. On any other day, he'd chat and flirt, probably get a phone number. The list of things he was good at was short, but the ability to get a cutie's digits was on it. However, this was not that day. Poe politely declined knowledge and drove on, leaving her wandering like a tourist. He figured she wasn't used to that kind of treatment and felt guilty for it as she disappeared in the rearview.

After pulling into the garage below the magnificent Western Knell building, he flashed his ID card and drove past the security guard. He parked the car in a loading bay three levels down, a depth still far above The Young School. The smell of gasoline and exhaust filled the enclosed space. After a moment, presumably waiting for Poe to arrive, Mara's hound Dagan marched through the steel doors of a commercial freight elevator.

Poe smirked. The guy marched everywhere. What a dork. Matching the uptight gait, he wore a full three-piece suit with his hair pulled back tightly enough to give him a facelift. He was the kind of guy who arranged all his possessions at right angles, whether on a desk, in an underground school for spooks, or up his ass.

Dagan wrinkled his nose. "Your auto stinks." *Auto* came out like ow-toe. It was rare, but his old European accent didn't always shake off—despite many years of practice with American English.

"All the best ones do," Poe replied.

As usual, Dagan ignored the opportunity for banter and asked, "So?"

"I've got the Doe, yeah. But shit's flipping topside. It's a ghost town up there. What's going on? You know anything about it?"

Dagan studied Poe quietly, considering. "You'll have to ask Mother." He stiff-walked to the trunk of the car. "Open it."

With a jingle of keys, Poe did as he was told.

"She's aged well..." Dagan admired Linh's motionless body before slowly running his fingers down her face and neck toward her chest. He sucked air through his teeth and grabbed a handful of breast, squeezing, groping, and pinching as he ran his tongue along his lips, darting side to side like a lizard. He muttered under his breath, "Still ripe, still ripe..."

Poe grimaced and broke in, "The hell, man. Mom's waiting."

Dagan turned and sneered, showing a glint of his dead grey tooth. He looked through Poe more than at him, with those corpse eyes, searching for weakness. Even through new frames, the eyes stayed the same. You could change a frame and the eyeballs with it, but you couldn't change the thing inside, the monster behind dirt-streaked glass.

Finally, Dagan turned back to Linh and studied her tied body. For too long. As if making a note of the scene to remember later. Finally, he dragged her out, whacking the back of her head on the car's steel, threw her over his shoulder, and walked back to the freight elevator.

Dagan gave a short whistle without looking back.

Poe cursed quietly, set his jaw, and followed obediently.

As commanded, Poe helped him bring Linh to a well-hidden area of The Young School. A place that was, in essence, a prison hospital. It was known simply as the ward. It consisted of a long hallway lined with one hundred and twenty-eight secure windowless cells. Each outfitted with beds, EKGs, IVs—everything necessary to keep a sleeping traveler healthy and breathing.

The nurses were paid well and lived on-site during their work week. On their time off, they flew in and out with blindfolds and headphones to protect the school's location. Should anyone ever ask where the place was, they wouldn't need to lie—they simply wouldn't know. The same was true for students, although if they were required to leave the premises, it was not for rest and relaxation, but to train.

Poe and Dagan, along with a broad, ruddy-faced nurse code-named Seven, placed Linh on a hospital bed. The nurse attached the EKG, then jabbed the IV needle with a rough workman-like efficiency.

The nurse left, Poe and Dagan waited, and after some time, Mara entered the room. She wore loose, high-waisted black silk pants and a matching sleeveless blouse that showed off tan arms, an elegant neck, and collar bones. Her hair was pulled back in a bun, and Mara had applied dark eyeshadow and mascara—generously, nearly to the point of soot war paint. She even wore shoes—black open-toed high heels—a rare occurrence, and Poe noted that she must be preparing for something important. Beautiful and dangerous as always, he thought, with a familiar mixture of love, hate, fear, and appreciation.

Try as he might, even with his recently acquired knowledge of what she did to him, his sister, and so many others, he could not bring himself to hate the woman. He knew it wasn't his choice, yet that changed nothing. How do you kill someone you've been wired against hating? Someone you do love in some twisted Stockholm syndrome abusive parent kind of way. Poe would have to figure that one out and fast.

Mara crossed the room and paused in front of him. "Well done, my love." She caressed his face, holding his jaw in her elegant hand.

The physical interaction amplified her mysterious power to influence animus, causing a surge of dopamine to rush through him. The room brightened, pupils dilated, and skin prickled with gooseflesh. Her praise and touch were heavenly, according to her design, the best and most potent drugs. Addicts, after all, are easy to control.

After rewarding him for a job well done, she moved to the bedside, leaned down, and whispered in Linh's ear, "My dear lost lamb, it is so good to see you again. It's Linh now, hmm? Well, you'll always be my Doe." Mara brushed the hair away from her wayward student's forehead, tucking the strays

344

behind her ears. The EKG beeped again after a long while. Mara kissed Linh's forehead, then straightened to standing; the movement of her newest frame was lithe and athletic—perhaps she'd been a dancer.

"What's the plan now?" Poe asked.

"We wait and prepare. Your sisters will be home soon, and we'll all be a happy little family again, won't we? Snug as bugs."

Poe didn't respond, just chewed on the inside of his lip, watching Linh, apparently lost in thought.

Mara flashed anger and asked again, "Won't we, dear?"

He looked up and replied, "Huh? Yes, Mother. Together again, happy as clams."

She studied his face and asked, "What is it?"

"If something is on your mind, speak up." Echoed Dagan, with violence in his voice, always quick to amplify whatever his mistress said or did.

She held up a finger to silence Dagan, then asked again, "Poe?"

"Things are bad outside. Quiet like the dead of night. As if nobody woke up this morning. You know what's going on?"

"Yes, my heart. It's a rift—as you learned from history class. Do you remember your lessons? You weren't the sharpest student, but you didn't need to be." She squeezed his bicep and smiled in an uncomfortably sexual way for one so insistent on being called mother. "I can give you a refresher."

His cheek twitched as he glanced at her lingering hand and swallowed past his disgust. Poe replied softly, "No, I remember."

"Rifts are dangerous. We need the totem now more than ever."

Poe chewed and thought.

Mara responded to his silence, "But that's not all is it?"

He replied, "Well… No. It's Del. I'm worried about her."

"How so?"

"That she's too unstable and will hurt herself." Poe modified his delivery to a version he knew Mara and Dagan would better appreciate. "I'm worried she'll fail."

"You think so?"

"Yes. If it's all the same to you, I'd like to go in and keep an eye on her. Make sure everything goes the way it should. If all's well, she won't even know I'm there. If it flops, you got backup."

Mara searched his face for a long moment before responding. She inhaled deeply, took in his scent, and replied, "Very well." She reached into her bra and fished out a small gold coin, the insignia and molding worn smooth. She handed it to him and caressed his face, sending more dopamine rushing through his synapses. "I just want you to be happy and safe. You know that, don't you?"

"Yes, Mother," Poe replied dreamily.

"Then go. It's against my better judgment, but you know I love you. Deeper than the sea. Isn't that right?" She smiled sweetly. It almost seemed authentic. "Keep a brotherly eye on things. Dagan will give you the details and update you on what's happening here. Tell Seven I'm giving you a room. She'll get you set up."

"Thought I might use my own back home."

"It's much safer here, don't you think?" Mara asked, but the question was not a question.

Poe played the game and replied, "Yeah, things are dicey outside. Thanks, Mom."

She smiled and kissed his forehead like she had kissed Linh some minutes before. She liked to use her lips to lay claim to the things she owned. Poe accepted the traversal coin graciously, still warm from her breast. Then he left to find the nurse and, for better or worse, check into one of the school's medical suites.

Cells, not suites, broski.

Poe chuckled as he walked behind Seven. You had to find the comedy in things. There's just no other way to survive.

"What's so funny?" Seven asked.

"Just something stuck in my head," Poe lied.

"Care to share?"

"Nah, wouldn't keep from my head to yours."

"Suit ya-self, handsome."

As they walked, Poe glanced in the small windows in the doors to the many other hospital rooms, *cells, buddy, these are cells*, each filled with sleeping students. Guess people weren't only passed out topside. It was happening here too. He'd heard of rifts in the academic sense, but as far as he knew, nothing so mythic had occurred for millennia.

He recognized most of the kids, except the youngest ones, who were too new to have met yet. Poe occasionally made appearances at the school—he was not an official instructor but a bit of a mascot, like the high school sports star who made it to the big leagues. He enjoyed it. Of course, Delilah hated that he did it. She couldn't distance herself fast enough from the memories of her childhood and, therefore, the children of the school. Poe was the opposite. He loved the famous big brother routine. It made him feel like he was fixing something or filling some hole. Either in himself or in the world. Helping the kids always made him feel better and more grounded, despite all the fucked up shit he'd been through and done.

The students all looked so different in these rooms. Like knowing someone strong and healthy all your life, then visiting them in an oncology wing, suddenly gaunt and wasting away, a shadow of their former self. But the kids were just sleeping, right? So it wasn't so severe as all that, but the haunting sensation couldn't be shaken.

Seven showed him to his room.

Cell, Poe, it's a cell.

His gut churned. Could he change his mind? Just turn around and walk back out, leaving his sister and Mara to their madness? Even if he didn't have Mara's goddamned psychic chain around his neck? He thought of his hands and the things they'd done. The answer was no. There was no turning back now.

Depending on how things went, he'd be under as long as a day or two. Seven set him up with an IV of nutrients and sopor to last at least that long.

"Christ, woman!" Poe barked as she jabbed his vein. She was no gentler with him than she had been with Linh. It seemed she harbored no specific vendetta.

"Oh, hush," she grumbled. "You can handle it, big boy."

After the stabbing, she left Poe to himself and closed the door behind her. He noticed she did not lock it, which he was thankful for. But he figured they could change that after he fell asleep. Small wins for now, anyway. He fought the sopor as long as he could, struggling to keep his eyes open. His mind wandered as it started to go loopy from the sopor.

Middlemost. He always thought the place sounded like someone from England named it. Suppose it was a place of many names. Must be. It was a hell of a lot older than the UK. He thought of eagles flying around palm trees as the classic rock song, *Hotel California,* played in his increasingly wandering mind. That was the fun thing with sopor, it would knock you out flat if you let it, but if you fought the knock, you could have a fun ride between wake and sleep.

He let himself adventure through a trippy half-dream in which hospital beds floated through the air like hot air balloons. On each bed stood a person, laughing, seeming to enjoy the ride. They were all ages, from small children to grannies. In the middle of the sky was a vast hole filled with big flat clown teeth. The gaping mouth laughed as it fed on everyone like a whale eating clouds of plankton.

Poe chuckled as he tripped and held the gold coin, rubbing it between thumb and crook of pointer finger, watching the hallucinatory matinee play out on the blank white ceiling. Finally, his eyes closed and stayed that way. His animus traveled to The City at The Center of Things, Middlemost, The City of Light.

44
GATE

As the backdoor The Cognosa brought them through evaporated, Kid and Alice were left standing on a grand stone plaza with The Stream at its center, blazing into the shallow sky. For three hundred yards, a path of ancient stone led to the center, polished to a high shine by the shoes and bare feet of ten thousand pilgrims. Peregrines.

Electric understanding layered on oppressive buzzing air.

Something was going to end.

What, exactly, they would find out shortly.

Their lives? The journey? Their unexpected connection?

With its impassable ring wall of giant stones and a barred iron gate, the place felt like a gladiatorial arena. All it was missing were stadium seats filled with a roaring crowd overcome by bloodlust and their wicked, hair-lipped emperor.

Kid craned his neck to follow the light beam into the shallow sky. The flickering stars in the canopy of this world reminded him of fireflies—at least the ones he'd seen in movies. He'd never seen any in Northern California. Maybe one day, he would visit somewhere that had them.

"Not that long ago," he said, "this didn't seem possible. Didn't seem real. None of it. Figured I was trippin' behind a cloud of benzos in a psych-ward. But here we are. Doin' the deed."

Alice looked genuinely worried, hands jammed in jacket pockets. Her light skin and silver hair took on a lot of the sapphire color of the shining light. She said, "Don't jinx us. We're not done yet."

Kid continued, "Yeah, I know. Don't gloat before the finish line. I'm not. Just talking. But it feels like maybe the last chance, right? So, I'm thinking, what's your plan after this? I mean, when we talked before, it wasn't really *real* yet. But now? Now, it is. We're here."

"My plan?" Her face screwed up at the thought. "Kid, it's the same as it's ever been. To be free."

"Yeah, yeah. I know. You say that. I want to be free too. Who doesn't want that? But what are you going to do with that freedom? Will you go to college or something? Travel? Wander the land going on Kung Fu adventures?"

"Honestly, I haven't thought about it. All I've thought about is out. I want out. Past that, I'm not sure. One of my teachers told me once that life is like a river. You can't see past the bends, and trying to doesn't help you where you are. Just do your best to stay dry and see where the river takes you."

"Sounds more like a rehab Yoda than a school for spooks. Also, though, that's kinda dumb."

Alice looked genuinely offended. "How so?"

"Well, you can get out of a river. Even one with rapids.

Usually, unless there's a cliff wall instead of a bank. But you just corkscrew swim. Go at an angle for the side."

"Corkscrew swim? You're an idiot."

"I'm serious. I read about it on a whitewater rafting website."

"Let me guess, Colorado research?"

Kid smirked. "Yeah."

"You were never really going to go, were you?"

Sucking air through his teeth, Kid replied, "Alright, cards out. This is something I would have *never* admitted out loud. So feel lucky and keep it a secret—I got a reputation to maintain. Cool?"

She nodded. "Sure."

"No. I was never going to go. It was my shield."

"Shield?"

"Yeah, for when people would tell me to get my shit together. Kid Thames, master of deflection, at your service."

"Did it work?"

"I liked to think so. But now, it feels different. I might actually do it if I make it out of this dumpster fire. This has all been a pretty big wake-up call, right?"

"And then some. But we're not done yet."

"Yeah, yeah. So anyway, if you get stuck going down a river with bad rapids, you should swim for the side and get out."

They were getting closer to the plaza's center now; the air was alight with static energy. "What if it's a lazy river and I have a floatie?"

"Well, I guess enjoy the ride if you're not heading for a

waterfall. But you said you don't know what's around the corner, right?"

"Right."

"And this has not been a lazy river."

"No, not so much."

Kid grinned, "So, sorority girl?"

Alice kicked the ground as they walked, "Do I look like some delta delta gamma ki or whatever?"

"You can be whoever you want to be. Even without your powers."

"I could even hide out on rooftops and give people unwelcome advice."

"Hey, just cause I have ketchup on my shirt doesn't mean I can't see it on yours. Seriously. You could do anything. Anything you want."

"No, don't think so."

"Kung fu legend then."

Alice growled, "Lay off, will you? Can't I just float for a while?"

Kid bristled. He knew he wasn't the sharpest crayon in the box, but her mood told him more loudly what he had already suspected from the beginning—she was hiding something. But it didn't change anything. Not then, not now.

His irritation moved to compassion, and he said, "Yeah, sure. Nothing wrong with floating for a while. Sometimes that's all you got. No time to course correct. Bang your last smoke and try to enjoy it. I feel you."

"Sorry, it's just... You push and push. Let's enjoy this, okay? I don't know what's next, and neither do you. Let's just *be* for a bit longer, okay?"

Kid studied her as he weighed the pros and cons of confrontation. He shifted his bag and replied, "No. Tell me what's up."

"What do you mean?"

"Ever since we kissed, it doesn't matter what comes outa my mouth, you get bent out of shape. Something's off. So, I ask again. What's up?"

"Nothing, okay?" Alice didn't look at him. "I don't want to talk about it."

"Think we're running out of time to change your mind."

"That's just it. We're running out of time. The closer we get to this thing," Alice pointed to The Stream. They were close now, only another twenty yards, "the more real it gets. I'm reminded like a river rock to the head that we can't pretend anymore."

"Pretend what?"

"That everything is okay. Yeah, we danced, we kissed. It was nice. Really nice. But that's it. It doesn't mean we get to have anything."

"So?"

"People like us, we don't get nice things, okay? We may as well stop acting like we do sooner than later."

"Alice, what are you so afraid of?"

She turned to reply, face flushed with emotion, but her attention was interrupted. "Kid! Your bag!"

"What? What is it?"

"It's glowing! Turn, turn! Let me see."

Kid did as she asked, and she pulled the box out and removed it from the cardboard. All along its sides, the carvings were glowing—the spirits, the people, the skeletons—all lit up the same ethereal blue as The Stream. She took it in both hands and pulled it in separate directions, tried to twist it like a bottle cap, shook it, clawed at it, but nothing. She growled in frustration, then held it out for Kid to try.

The second he held it in both hands, one on each side, the disc in the center of the carved relief began to shine. It was brighter than all the rest and dazzling to look at directly. It glowed brighter and brighter until, finally, a seam appeared.

Kid glanced at Alice, eyes wide, apparently waiting for her to tell him to stop. She spoke no such warning, staring in curious rapture, chapped lips parted, eyes reflecting the blue light of the box and The Stream. Kid shrugged, figured, what the hell, this is what we came here for, and pulled.

It yielded. Again that scent of old wood and gun oil.

The inside revealed a handle of a black material that absorbed light. Kid gripped it carefully and pulled out a curved blade about the same length as his hand. The whole thing was so ultra-black that no details were visible. It was as if it were not an object but a silhouette sliced from the paper of reality with a crafting razor.

"Holy shit," Kid whispered.

Alice watched, mouth agape, blue light highlighting the edges of her face.

Kid added, "Guess I should have planned a speech."

"Holy shit works. Can I touch it?"

"I don't know, seems like. Here." Kid handed the knife over, careful to turn the handle toward her. "Easy. Looks like it could cut into the quantum realm."

"Seriously. It doesn't seem any more tangible than a shadow."

She reached out and gingerly took the knife.

"Whoa, it's heavier than it looks."

"That's not hard. It looks like nothing."

"Yeah, but it's far heavier than a normal knife even. It wants to sink like it's made of lead or something heavier."

She studied the object, amazed.

"I feel like a caveman with an iPhone right now."

"Who cares. I'm ready to kick some ass."

Kid pantomimed a few karate chop motions for good measure.

"Okay, but you have to do it."

"Me? You sure?"

"Yeah, I'm sure. It's always been you. From the start."

Kid studied her face, "What's that mean?"

"Lightning strikes seem random until one hits you in the head. This is exactly where you and I are supposed to be." For the span of a few heartbeats, it seemed like her shaking hand would not do what she wanted, but whatever barrier there was, she broke through it. "Here, Kid. Take it." Her body language hinted that she feared it would explode.

They stepped onto the stone dais, now directly next to the ominous voltaic buzz of The Stream. It felt like if they stood there long enough, it would melt the fillings out of their teeth.

Kid held the umbra blade in an unsure hand.

"Just get right up in it huh? What happens if I touch it? Looks like a space laser."

"Normally, it'd burn your arm off. Some jump into it on purpose. A spiritual suicide." Alice scrunched her face. "So try not to touch it with your hand."

He released nervous air from dry lips, then held the knife

in front of him with both hands like a samurai sword. Unsure of what to expect, he braced himself for impact and moved forward inch by inch, pushing the weapon's tip into the ghostly beam. As he did, the light split around it, a shining river around knapped obsidian, accompanied by the roar of a waterfall made of a million liquid volts.

Above the rivener, in its eddy, the slice revealed a hole to midnight.

This darkness Kid had seen before.

The place behind the broken wall.

The place where Linh and the gelatinous hell-beast of Patricia Hodgekiss had disappeared. Kid opened the portal broader and taller until it was the size of a narrow doorway, like the entrance to a tented childhood clubhouse made of glowing linen.

He turned to Alice and asked, "You're leaving now, right? That's why you've been upset. Can't stay like you said you would."

She studied his eyes while considering her answer. After a few seconds, she shook her head and replied, "I'm not even supposed to let you go in there." The blue light shimmered on glistening eyes. "Mother told me to bring you back."

"But?"

"I'm not going to."

"I figured something like that. When did it change?"

"At The Sand. I thought I had enough distance... But I don't know. Either I was wrong, or Horacio's empathy push made me weak. More susceptible. In any case, she called me and reinforced her hold. I couldn't resist her then, and I can't now. I've been trying." Her lip trembled. "It's no use."

"Would you if you could?"

"I don't know... I think so. But, it's complicated."

"Yeah..."

"You don't seem surprised. You knew already?"

"Close enough," Kid replied. "I saw her in your dream."

"Why didn't you say something?"

"What would it change?" He smiled. "Enjoy the ride, right? Guess I had a lazy river of my own. So, why aren't you going to follow Mara's orders and take me back with you?"

"Because you deserve this. Even if it's dangerous. But it's curious... Her commands are more like programming than orders. She has control over me. Just like the rest of her students, her *children*. I shouldn't be able to refuse this."

"So, how come you can?"

"I think..." Alice swallowed before finishing, "Well... I don't think I was supposed to like you."

Kid grinned. "Like?"

"Ugh." She rolled her eyes.

His grin turned to a soft smile, and he replied, "Same."

Alice wiped away an intruding tear. "Really?"

He nodded. "Think it's just because we're all about to die? I heard people get horny at funerals."

They both laughed, and Alice replied, "You're stupid."

"Facts. So, what now?"

She sighed. "You do what you have to. Same to me."

"I'll figure out a way," Kid said. "I'll come for you. Wherever you are."

She shook her head. "Don't do that. If you make it out, stay out. Please?"

"I'm already out. This is what out looks like."

Alice pulled him close. Close enough to hide her eyes, the way everyone does when forced to hide inside a moment they can't camouflage. Again, Kid noticed the dinosaur-shaped birthmark on her neck and memorized it, as well as her other details. He felt that he would need them soon. The smell of lilac and sweat and cold. Her freckles and the color of her eyes, sunlight through coffee. The peach fuzz near her jawline. Cute ears with the thingy connected.

They kissed again and made it last.

———

When finally they broke their embrace, Kid handed Alice the rivener and said, "Deals a deal." Then he studied her face as if committing it to memory and pulled a piece of fuzz off the vintage Bowie t-shirt. "This was my favorite."

"I know," She replied.

He smiled. "You better take care of it."

"I will."

Then Kid turned and took a breath. His heart raced, and he tried to shake the nerves out of his hands. As he stepped into the black nowhere, he turned to get a last look at Alice, but his eyes went wide in sudden fear. He tried to yell. To warn her. But Alice couldn't hear. All sound disappeared as Kid fell into the electric crash of The Void.

PART FIVE
HUNGRY GHOSTS

"Grief reunites you with what you've lost. It's a merging; you go with the loved thing or person that's going away. You follow it as far as you can go."

— PHILIP K. DICK, FLOW MY TEARS, THE
POLICEMAN SAID

45
FLOWERS

Delilah hurtled through the air at Alice's exposed back and caught her in a full-force tackle. As she rode her to the ground, the rivener fell and clattered on the stone. They fell off the edge of the dais as flickering light cast their faces in manic shadows.

Kid and the gate were gone.

Delilah sat atop Alice's chest in a high mount and cackled, "Ha! Got you now, you dirty bitch!" Like a deranged cat rubbing against a pant leg, Delilah brushed the contours of Alice's face with her cheek. She stopped close to Alice's ear, lips grazing fine hairs. With breath like hot copper, she whispered in a sing-song voice, "Gotcha, gotcha, gotcha."

"Get off me, you wack-job!" Alice grimaced at the new Delilah, shining with madness. Her empty eye socket was puckered and pink like a hairless rat. "We're on the same team, or didn't you get the memo?"

"Oh, I know! Juicy, juicy, juuuuuuicy!" Delilah pet Alice's

face and watched her. "One is the carrot, the other is THE STICK!"

"What happened to you?"

"I got better, better, better. Better than you."

"Get off me, or I'll—"

"Or you'll what? Gate bomb me again? Why don't you try it, golden child?"

"Back off, or I'll make this one hurt permanently."

"Oh please, *huuuuurt* me. Give it to me. Hurt me, daddy." Delilah ground her crotch into Alice's sternum and moaned theatrically.

"Don't cry later when you can't eat without a nurse."

Delilah grinned her lunatic grin.

Alice spoke, "Harmonious extra."

She watched, expecting Delilah to fall like she had back in the alley. A gate bomb would boot a traveler out of a stolen vessel and should eject one from The Dream just the same. But nothing happened.

Alice managed to plant five over the years. She had only three left now. One would take. Had to.

Delilah sucked some of the blood from her inflamed gums and swallowed.

"Dangerous expo," Alice tried again.

Nothing. That lonely roving eye.

"Palladium market."

Still, nothing. Delilah's grin widened.

Alice searched for the rivener, but it lay too far away.

She had one gate bomb left. Better make it count.

Like a priest in an exorcism, Alice called out, "Delilah

Tenor McAvoy! Sister, daughter, orphan, all! Hear me! Malignant reciprocity!"

Other than their labored breathing and the electric buzz of The Stream, it was silent. Only blue light, a breeze that smelled like winter, and Delilah's gruesome face. Hard to believe she was gorgeous once.

"Seeeeee? You got nuttin' little baby buntin', nothing at all. I'm the golden child now. Mother picked ME. Me, me, me. Not you."

"Mother did this? She made you this way?"

"What, better? No, I was always better than you. Mother simply gave me a new way to see." Delilah pried Alice's eyes open. "I *seee* you." She bent down to study from an inch away as if Alice's eye were a microscope. "Yes, I do. I see *through* you."

"And still, you miss the truth closest to you."

"I see everything."

"No. You don't. This power is breaking your mind, Delilah. She's throwing you away, like all the other girls. Mara uses us and discards us when she's done. First, we're pretty and useful. Then we're trash. Her flowers for the floor."

"You're a liar! You want it for yourself. And show some respect, you spoiled brat. You can do at least that much. Never forget her name. We call her Mother."

Delilah ran her thumb from the bridge of Alice's nose up her forehead. She stopped at the hairline, stretching her face into an expression of forced surprise.

Alice struggled to pass her guard, attempting to buck and free her arms to attack, but she was pinned in tight. Delilah had always been a superior grappler.

The crazed woman whispered, so quiet it seemed only her lips moved.

Alice couldn't hear the words so much as feel them.

The sensation escalated from disgust to agony. It was like a black fungal blaze snaking its way through her nervous system.

Seething and sprouting bodies bearing rotten fruit.

Sickly sweet, noxious spume.

How is she doing this?!?

She's INFESTING me

Tearing me APART

Destroying me from the inside

God it HURTS

It BURNS

Oh god, it burns

Alice screamed.

Delilah drew in a breath as if Alice's pain had a scent.

Perhaps to her, it did.

Delilah relaxed her hold—the pain would pin Alice down well enough now and allow her to simply watch. It was like styrofoam in a fire. Melting, stinking, curling, Alice tucked into a fetal position, but only briefly. The pain forced her spine to arch, then back and forth she went like a purgatory seesaw of lit orange napalm. The red-haired maniac watched and giggled. If there were actual flame, it would dance in her fevered eye. Instead, it was the blue light of The Stream shining there.

Finally, Alice choked out, "Please! Delilah! Stop! You're killing me!"

"Yes." She rubbed her face against Alice's again, taking in her scent from up close as she whispered in her ear. "I am." After letting Alice writhe in pain for a few more seconds, Delilah continued, "The boy did his job, and you did yours. You weren't supposed to let him go inside, but that's alright. He can rot there, far away from Mother and me. As you know, I'd rather not share. Now, it's goodbye."

"No..." Alice struggled to continue speaking through gritted teeth, "Mother needs me. Mother loves me."

"Not true. She hates you and always has. It's the smell. You know how she is about that. You radiate it, ooze it, something from your bastard pores—an odor of weakness. Now, I can smell it too. It's the stink of fear."

Her nose wrinkled. "Have you ever been to a stockyard?" It was a rhetorical question. Alice was incoherent with pain. Delilah continued, "I had to drive through the Oklahoma panhandle once on a job. God, is that part of the country flat. Flatter than your sad excuse for tits, can you believe it? Well, those dumb cows, they wanted to run, or gallop, whatever the fuck cows do. But they were trapped. Shoulder to shoulder, nowhere to turn while waiting to die."

Delilah studied Alice's curled body. "That's you, Alice—a terrified idiot. I want you to hurt. I want you to cry. Then, I want you to disappear. For everything you've done, for everything you have *not* done—for everything you have never had to do."

Alice writhed in pain, and her eyes rolled back, the veins standing out on her arms, neck, and forehead. Finally, she shook out a few more words. "Think... what Mother... will do...

when she knows... it was you..." Alice forced herself to focus her vision and look at Delilah. "The one... to take me away."

"Why you? Why do you get to be pretty? You were given everything! Never earned it! You never had to pay for your power, Alice! Never! Why do you get to be clean?"

Delilah choked back a tear, then squeezed her hand in a white-knuckled fist. She willed the pain to amplify yet again. Alice responded with a shattering scream as her spine bent so severely it looked like it would snap.

At last, Delilah relaxed and allowed Alice to fall into a heap. The screaming stopped, replaced by quiet whimpers. Her skin was drawn, pale, and drenched in the sweat of fear. Alice was dying.

Delilah watched, no longer smiling. Her focus supplanted her joy. She wanted to memorize these moments, to store them away in a safe place, to replay again and again. The blue fire danced.

Then, rapid, heavy footsteps ran up behind her.

Delilah did not turn in time.

Poe crashed into her, sending her flying like a shuttlecock.

As Alice had told Kid, The Stream would cut you like a laser beam. Delilah flew through the air, intersecting the blue ray with her elbow. It removed her forearm and hand with the sound of sizzling meat. She hit the ground and rolled, then somehow stood up through the pain. Delilah looked at her blackened stump and snarled.

"Brother? How could you?" The words dripped from her mouth like acid. "You'd trade me? For her? I'm your sister! Your twin! I'm the only one who ever understood you. You'd sell that for what? A pretty girl? For pussy?"

"Del... that wasn't for her."

"Then, why?" She cried.

His eyes shone with restrained tears. "This is for you."

"What do you mean?"

"You gotta stop, Del. Maybe you'll stop if I tell you. There's something you need to know. Something you gotta already know, somewhere down deep. Just like I did when I found out, it was like hearing an old song. Not thinking about it for years and years, but then it comes on, and you know the words. It was down there. Inside."

"Poe, what are you talking about?" Her eyes betrayed her words.

"You need to know. I'm sorry, Del. The block apartments, back then, when we were little... San Leandro... You know... the... *Fuck*..." He couldn't finish the sentence. "Just kids, man."

"Shut up!"

"You think she saved us?"

"Shut the fuck up!"

"She's no mother."

Delilah's eyes widened. "No! No! NO!"

"No, Del. Not this time. That fucking cesspool? She owned it from the start."

Her face caved to an expression of betrayal, anger, and disgust. Mouth turned down in a savage frown, teeth showing like a mangey street dog backed into a corner.

"I'm sorry. But it's the truth. And we were one of thousands. Millions, maybe even, I don't fucking know. She calls them her seed farms. Can you believe that? Seeds for her flowers. The way it was back then wasn't some cruel twist of fate. It was *her*. She did that to us. To you. On *purpose*. The whole time. She bent and broke us, so we'd need her and not ask questions."

"No!" She sobbed. "You're lying!"

"You know it's true. In your heart, you do."

"No, no, NO! Mother wouldn't do that! She loves me!"

"I'm sorry, sis. She don't love nothin'. Least of all herself."

Lies. She'd hurt him for what he'd said.

Delilah focused on the aura surrounding Poe, the one only she could see, his animus, his true name. Using the power of her ruined eye, she wrenched it. Strong enough to tear it away. She'd hurt him like she'd hurt Alice. Then, he'd be quiet. Nobody else would know. If there's no one left to tell a story, was it ever real?

Maybe it was just a bad dream. Maybe she could be clean.

She twisted again. Harder.

But nothing happened.

Poe frowned. "It's like that, huh? You'd burn me too?"

"Why won't you—"

"That's not gonna work on me, Del. We're already twinned. Always have been. My pages are yours, and yours are mine." He sighed. "That seals it, then. This is for you, sis. Forgive me."

Poe rushed and scooped her up at a run. He carried her, struggling and shouting, to the flickering blue beam. It would be fast. It would be merciful. It would be clean.

"I love you, Del. I'm sorry." Tears streamed down his cheeks. "May you rest easier than you lived."

But just before he could swing her into the burning light, she managed to get one of his ears in her mouth. She tore at it, ripping a chunk off the top. Poe shouted and lost his grip. Delilah broke free and rolled to the side. She took one last vicious and wounded look back, then blinked out of The Dream.

46
KNIFE

Poe contemplated the spot where his twin had been and considered what he'd tried to do. He let out a tiny, scared sound—a mix between a groan and a growl, then swallowed it behind a clenched jaw. He wiped his tears away, angry at them for appearing without permission.

Would Delilah go back and tell Mother? He didn't think so. Not so soon, at least. Not after what he revealed. Would his sister run? Attack again? There was no way to know. She had always been volatile. Now, she was utterly deranged.

He touched what remained of his ear, sucking air through his teeth at the searing pain. Almost half of it was gone. Better dress it soon. Shit would get infected in a hurry. *Fuckin' hell.*

Alice.

She still lay where Delilah left her—unconscious but alive. Her chest rose with shallow breaths, head laying against the sharp edge of the stone dais. Poe pulled her to a more comfortable position, laid his jacket under her head for a pillow, and sat down cross-legged. He sighed a world-weary sigh and rested his chin on his palm.

What a mess. And the boy?

Kid was his name. What about him? Poe studied The Stream, where the sliced portal had been. He was in there somewhere. Wherever *there* was. The Void, according to the tales. Apparently, they were true, not just further indoctrination from The Young School. What else was true? What else should he believe that he hadn't previously?

Poe witnessed miraculous things over the last couple of days, and every time the impossible happened, Kid was there.

He wasn't sure exactly *when* he decided to go rogue and help the other team. Was it after cutting out his sister's eye? Or after trying to murder her? Was it learning, for sure, that the woman who *raised* him was the same one who'd forced him, as an innocent child, into the most unforgivable form of human slavery? Or had the switch always been on, but the circuit just needed some juice?

The why didn't matter because everything was clear now.

The juice was Kid—lightning in a trashcan.

When didn't matter, the truth was he had changed.

The *truth* was that he wanted to help. However he could.

Poe sighed. But how?

Any plan he made would be knowable to Mother as soon as she chose to look. His pages were hers, as were Alice's, Delilah's, and all her chained children. It was true that, at present, Poe didn't have any direct orders. So, for the moment, his hands were his own. But things never stayed that way for long. One thought from Mara, and he'd be her good little boy again. Her animus shard was twisted deep inside him like barbed wire through an old oak tree. It doesn't matter if you try to pull it or cut it. The occlusion stays.

Alice woke with a gasp, breaking Poe's meandering thoughts.

She shifted, whimpered, and grimaced in pain as she clutched the sides of her head. It seemed she was attempting to keep her skull together. "What..." She struggled to speak, "...what are you doing here?"

"Saving your ass looks like," Poe replied.

"Yeah... looks like... but still, why? How?"

"You know Mom. Backups on backups. She let me use a traversal coin to keep an eye on things. My guess is she wanted to spark some extra drama. She's always loved to watch her kids fight."

Alice didn't respond, focused on sitting up, then trying and failing to swallow.

"Where's Kid?" Poe asked, even though he knew. He didn't want to show his hand. Not yet.

She pointed to The Stream with a limp hand as if to say, *In there. Somewhere.*

"You got the totem?" Poe asked, even though he knew that too.

"Yeah..." She held her head in one hand as she shuffled on knees over a few feet to where the rivener lay. Alice picked up the ultra-black blade to show him. The jagged shape was reminiscent of an elongated crystal.

"That's what it was? All this for a knife?" Poe asked.

Alice shrugged, then replied with effort, "*Magic* knife."

"Right. Of course." Poe watched The Stream while resting

his chin on steepled fingers. Without turning to Alice, he said, "Go on. Get outa here. I'll keep an eye out for Kid."

Alice studied his face. "He's not coming back. Nobody does. You know that."

Poe scrutinized her in return. He'd known her since she arrived at the school, so he knew the mask she wore. Hell, he'd taught her how to make the damn thing, how to wear it, when to take it off. The answer was never. You never remove the veil.

He replied, "We don't know that. Not for sure. Kid pulled off a couple other stunts that weren't supposed to be possible. So, *maybe* he's not coming back. Slim chance, true, but if he does manage, he's valuable. Super fuckin' potent, right? I heard he's the spiritborne we passed rumors about back when I was a little greaser. You saw some of that when you were with him, didn't you? What he was."

The tiniest bit of color returned to Alice's face. Noticing how Poe referred to Kid by name, she nodded and replied, "I saw."

"Mom said she wanted the knife *and* him."

"They call it a rivener."

"Rivener?"

"Yeah, from the word riven. To rip apart."

"Well, doesn't that sound ominous? And if I didn't know better, I'd think you'd been pumping vocab for your SATs. You got big college plans I don't know about?"

She rolled her eyes.

"But as I understood it," he continued, "your mission was to bring them both back. Mom won't like a half-score."

"I couldn't. It didn't work out like that. I had to let Kid go."

Poe raised an eyebrow. Was she a friend? What could be said out loud? He chose to make a gamble and replied, "No, you didn't."

Alice searched his face for the same information for which he had searched hers.

She decided to gamble too. "No... I didn't."

"I won't tattle."

Her head tilted a fraction of an inch. "You don't have to wait here either."

How do you communicate with as few words as possible so that in the likely event your memories are scoured later, they're all vague enough for plausible deniability?

"No," Poe said, "but it's better this way. Just in case, right?"

She nodded. "And where's your sister? I was knocked out."

"Gone."

"For good?"

"I don't know."

Alice shut her eyes, too exhausted to continue talking.

Poe said, "Go on. You earned some rest. You know your way back, of course. You got your traversal coin still?"

She nodded. The old coin, just like the one Mara had given Poe, was safely stowed in the fifth pocket of her jeans. Alice put the two halves of the box back in the backpack and slung it over her shoulder but didn't do the same with the blade because she doubted she'd get it back out without Kid's abilities. She held it gingerly and walked away.

The Fifty-Fifty Kid, she thought.

You sound more like a proper outlaw every day.

She smiled at that, then turned and watched the pulsing

light. It had been fun. No, not just fun. *Good*. At times, it almost seemed like something real could grow, a different life. Blurred freeze frames like a landscape passing by the Bart train windows. Hanging out on his cool rooftop hideout, talking about birds, dancing at The Sand. Getting to understand a piece of his heart and him finding a fragment of hers. The kisses. The embrace. The way he smelled—sun-toasted laundry detergent, lemons, cilantro, and some boyish deodorant spray, probably called Phoenix or Anarchy or something just as silly. She missed his smell.

He was gone and lost in the dark.

Why? Why did she let him go?

Well, Kid wanted it. She had to, right?

They shook hands. She gave her word.

But she could have broken it. Her power could have forced him. Something good could have been done with her skill for once. Then maybe, something could be different.

No, idiot. We don't get to have things like that.

Her grief was a splintered arrow in her gut.

She broke the shaft and pushed the pain away.

47
STUTTER

For Kid, in The Void space, time passed. How much, though? Hard to say. A question with only one proper answer. It's complicated.

It folded and stretched—breaking, mending, and overlapping—then bulging and shattering again. Like modeling clay, manipulated by the clumsy fingers of children. Their absent-minded hands busy while thinking about other things. Lunch, cartoons, or why dogs fear fireworks even though they're beautiful.

Kid's consciousness quartered, mended, pulled, and scattered—frightened swallowtail birds. Disjointed memories, a pile of broken glass, arranged like tea leaves.

At some point, Kid stopped trying to assert control. Instead, he chose to go with the flow, however chaotic and nonsensical it was—taking it in like some avant-garde short film.

He smelled instant coffee. Stirred into lukewarm tap water. The kind you could get in jail if you had some money on the books or a cool cellmate. Called it keefer. Same as you called anything that'd catch you a buzz. If you downed it quick, it'd make do.

Yeah, man, that's alright.

It ain't hooch, but in county, it'll do.

Zing, batter, batter batter, zing. Yeah, boy.

The smack and pop of a handball game.

Shhwwww POP! Shhwww POP!

Hey! Over the line! Somebody else yelling over some other drama. *Yo! Put the channel back! I was watching that, motherfucker! Who you calling motherfucker, motherfucker?*

Fluorescent light cast yellow-white over a stainless steel sink and seatless toilet combo. Bulb flickering. Quivering like some other light from some other place, yellow instead of blue, but yeah, *that* flicker.

Flicker flicker *Bzzt!* Flicker *Bzzt!* Flicker *Bzz-bzz-bzzt!* Kamikaze moths suicide diving into a hot lamp, ecstatic in their final moments of glory.

Shhhkkkkrrrrt.

The sound of pulling a plastic cot skidding across cement, away from the toilet, closer to the cell door. Only a couple feet, but better than nothing. Who wants to sleep next to the toilet in a six-by-eight cell packed with three grown men?

Nobody. That's fuckin' who.

Aight, brother, you got the boat. Bunks are full. That flotilla on the ground ain't no worse than this metal bed. Trust. What you doing in here again anyway? Man, you gotta stay outa places like this. Gotta keep the air fresh, homie, know what I'm sayin'? Hold your head up like a king, and keep it fresh. Do it for your mama. Feel me? Fade out.

Faaaaade out.

Stutter.

Squeeze.

Stretch.

Tsch tsch tsch tsch.

That's the sound time makes when it breaks.

Tsch tsch tsch tsch.

The boat, the boat, the boat.

Wind against the neck, humid, sailing.

Keeping it fresh.

Fast like flying. Except straight down.

Keeping it fresh.

What's the terminal velocity of a human being?

Kid's back smacked water with a splash like a gunshot. Better than a belly flop? Sure. Just barely. Water cold like a slap across the mouth and hungry like a ghost.

Swallowing. Sinking. Retreating.

Sinking sinking s i n k i n g.

No.

Nononononono No!

Swim. SWIM!

UP.

Where's up? Toward the light.

Kid struggled with everything he had, water-laden clothes making the work double. Bit by bit, he made vertical progress. The light grew bigger and brighter with every flailing stroke.

Swim, goddamn you. *Swim.*

Lighter, brighter, almost there.

Lungs spasm, fighting to steal a deadly breath of water in the frantic hope for air.

Just a little farther.

Gasp!

Air at last—big beautiful gulps of it.

A silent sea. Water blue-black, so smooth it reflected the moonlight like a scrying mirror. Treading water now, Kid could see swirling clouds surrounding him. He read about this phenomenon but never imagined he would see it. It was the eye of the storm at the center of a hurricane.

And this storm, Kid had seen before. He knew it at a genetic level. But he had seen it from the outside looking in— from the beach with Horacio in his first venture into The Dream, in the in-between of forever-ago.

Now, he was *inside* the dark storm.

Yet, it was calm, and so was he.

To rest his muscles, he switched to floating on his back. He relaxed his arms and legs, floating and turning about in the salty water. As his breath went out, he sank. As he breathed in, the air in his lungs made him buoyant, and he floated back up. Inhale, exhale, bob a little up, bob a little down. Above his turning body, the stars and the great scar of the Milky Way twinkled like glitter strewn across black paper.

Fracturing the meditative scene, an unexpected sound echoed in the open air.

A baby crying. Not a terrified cry or a painful one.

Just hungry. Crying. Crying.

Somebody feed the baby.

Without warning, the sea solidified. As it did, it pushed

him to the surface, leaving him lying on a vast onyx mesa. The black material spread as far as he could see in all directions. Kid stood, considered the place, and spread his toes.

Warmth radiated against his chest. Not hot enough to burn, but enough to notice. He looked down and saw a rawhide necklace, the one with the silver wedding ring. *Oh yeah. That old thing?*

He took it into his palm. The engraving glowed. M+S. Michael and Saría. The heat expanded beyond his hand and arm, blooming in his chest like a candy-colored sunrise.

Hey, baby boy.

The most beautiful voice a small boy can hear, ringing inside his heart like a silver bell. It was the voice of songs sung to him long ago, reverberating through his tiny body immersed in the protective water of the womb.

Guess you go by Kid, though, don't you? Can't go calling you baby boy. Your friends'll give you a hard time. I like it. Sounds adventurous, like your dad. That's how he got me, you know. Adventure. Didn't know how hungry I was for it until I met him.

The stars' shine danced behind the salty lenses that formed on his eyes. Kid spoke out in a hopeful whisper, "Mama?"

He didn't think about why he called her Mama, not Mom or Mother. Some things just come out how they're supposed to.

Kid called again, "Mama! Is that you?"

Yes. I'm here.

Catharsis and fear. Hope and skepticism.

The yin and yang of a reunion forgotten.

"Is that really you?"

As real as I ever was. You got yourself in a jam, didn't you?

Kid wiped his nose with the back of his hand, snorted a little chortling laugh, and replied, "Yeah, guess I did."

You're not supposed to be here. Not yet, anyway.

I didn't think I'd be seeing you for a long time.

"I had to, Mama. Linh was in trouble. You know Linh?"

Linh?

Oh, The Doe. Yeah, I know Linh.

"She needs me. I don't know what I'm going to do or how I'll get back out. But she needs me, so I'm here. She's somewhere inside this place. Lost."

My silly baby boy.

You had so much time.

Your father and I did our best to give you that.

You should not have come here.

This is the place where the dead swim.

You see, none of us are supposed to be here either.

Too soon and for far too long. Multitudes.

We are not happy about it.

No, no.

See that up there?

That's no Milky Way.

That's The Rift.

The one WE ALL made.

We're going to tear down every dream in the sky.

But...

You're here now.

I didn't expect that.

That changes things.

The ghostly voice was momentarily silent, considering.

Did you feel me before? When you were cold?
You see, it's still my job to protect you.
It always has been and always will be.

As if the ancient god of the place lifted a table, the black mesa tilted up until Kid started to slide. He scrabbled for handholds, but it was too slick. The flatness morphed, curling on either side until it created a tunnel. Once vertical, he fell like a stone in an ink well.

See, THAT woman; she is NOT your mama.
Her name now is Linh...
But it wasn't always. She's the one who put me here.
She said she couldn't help it. But I don't care.
She's the one who stole you from me.
Her and ol' Inanna
Mara, The Black Rose of Babylon
Her and her harem of sycophant thieves.
So, my sweet baby boy,
I'm going to take you down deep.
Where time moves so slowly, they'll never hurt you again.
We've already slowed by fifty and ten.
Where we're going, we'll do ten and fifty again.
You'll get to live a long life before the end comes.
Don't worry.
Mama's got you.

48

BERNICE

Back in San Francisco, Bernice Simpson slept. Usually, she snored loud enough to wake the dead. Thought it might be apnea. The doctor said she could get on one of those air machines or use some of that special nose tape. But, no. That wasn't the case this time.

She slept with little to no sound and had not woken in several days. Shallow inhalations passed lips cracked like Death Valley hardpan. Each one hitched her chest as if it would be the last. Her dehydrated body and almost everyone else's in San Francisco was dying.

She had a big grey Maine Coon cat, going on sixteen years. Called him Maury after the TV show. Sweet Maury, always excited to see her after returning home from Palo Alto. It was a long commute, and he'd flop over for belly tickles as soon as the front door opened. Now, Maury was hungry for something else, picking and scratching with claws and needle teeth.

His mouth smacked like the sound he made when given

the special treat of wet cat food, the only brand of which he'd eat—Gravy Lovers by Fancy Feast.

Smack, smack, smack.

At the base of Bernice's bed lay a shredded pile of wool from her sock, soaked in various stages of drying and fresh blood. All her toes were gone except the pinky. The meat was chewed deep into the ball of her foot, and the border flesh was a malicious pink. Infected. Still, it was better that way. Better than losing the more appetizing parts of her face and neck.

Scavengers, which Maury was now, usually go for the soft stuff first. Eyes, lips, and tongue are especially high on the menu. Those were safe for now; luck be to her odd habit of sleeping with her blanket pulled over her head.

She was among the first to fall into the dark sleep and had been missing for nearly a week. Despite that fact, nobody knew. Work didn't call. Neighbors didn't complain about the trash she'd left out. Nobody at the coffee shop down the street thought anything strange. None of that happened because those folks were sleeping too.

951,627 sad souls severed from their vessels, the total climbing by the second. Their essence wandered the void, leaving their bodies in deep comas. Only a few with totems or latent abilities still walked free.

The streets were dead quiet, littered with crashed cars and bodies. It was a feast for the birds, cats, and rats. Most dogs still maintained some loyalty, but it wouldn't last. Another day or two at most, and they would join the buffet.

The city rotted as the world outside watched.

Some thought it was a cult thing. Wouldn't be the first with those San Francisco crackpots, they said. But the government knew better. The official story they pushed was a mass leak of natural gas released by geologic activity. Teams went in to assess, but they too fell into the dead sleep.

Second teams followed to help the first and thirds for the seconds. But their safety gear could not protect them. The abducting force pierced lead, steel, hermetic plastic, and amplified magnetic fields.

Finally, authorities stopped sending teams and switched focus to quarantine, public relations, and media management. The National Guard and Coast Guard built barricades choking off all entry points to the area by land, sea, or air. With its two bridges and consolidated paths southward, the peninsula was severed from the rest of the bay.

The danger zone formed a perfect circle, whose epicenter was calculated to be downtown, near the financial district. A horrified world watched via drone footage as the death radius grew outward.

49
GHOSTS

Deep in The Void, Kid Thames and the tainted spirit of Saría Landros roamed, twisting and hopping along like an indecisive tornado. The landscape was unexpectedly beautiful. Rolling green hills and broken rainclouds pierced by golden rays of the sun. The light lay jigsaw shadows across the grassy expanse. It was an empty place. But pure. An innocence sensed like a drop of fresh rainwater on the tongue.

Saría's spirit coalesced into something approaching human, like a wedding gown of decaying silk weaving through the air. She and Kid landed on the top of a green knoll to rest.

After the wind died, she said, "Time here just keeps spinning. Fifty and ten from the layer above in which Linh wilts. And she is five hundred from The Dream. I'll save you the headache and do the math. Since the day I was taken, you've spent twenty years in The Real. Here, I've wandered for ten thousand and change."

"Ten thousand years?" Kid grimaced. "That doesn't even compute, how—"

"Yes, a time of that length defies understanding. It's just a number now. As abstract as I've become. I suppose the only reason my mind hasn't completely snapped is because I was already a long-lived spirit when I arrived. Let's just say I have had a long while to think. You could say I'm the only *thinking* ghost here. The rest are just... whatever remains."

"So they're here, all the one's the ancients have taken over the years. And now, the sleepers too."

"Yes."

Kid nodded and hoped that his next question would not anger his mother. Although she seemed to care for him, she was also clearly dangerous and unpredictable. Regardless, he had to know.

"How long has Linh been here?"

"From her layer above, relative to The Real, something around a thousand days. Perhaps The Doe has taken the opportunity to comprehend what she did to me. And you. And all the rest she had a hand in bringing here."

"I believe she has. The woman you describe isn't the Linh I know. Mama, she's changed. I give you my word."

"She has, has she?"

Kid nodded. "I don't know everything, but from what I got, Linh lost her child too, a daughter. After that, she managed to escape Mara. I'm not sure how. Since then, she's spent the last twenty years hiding and grieving. Fighting the guilt of her past. The woman I know is kind. She's generous. The Linh I know sacrificed herself for me. That's why she's trapped in The Void in the first place. She saved my life and my spirit."

"Is that so?"

"It is. I'd be gone... or something worse, without her. One of Mara's soldiers, Delilah, infected me with this thing they call a blight. You know about those?"

"Of course."

"It was eating me—torturing me in the dark of my worst memories. Linh came, fought the thing, then fell into The Void through a crack in The Dream. Her act saved me but left her lost here. Mama, she's here because she saved me."

Contemplative silence hung in the air, and jigsaw shadows meandered across the hills like cattle.

"Come on! Let's all leave together!" Kid cried. "We can sort this out. I'm sure we can. I've done terrible things too. I hope you'll forgive me."

"There's nothing you could ever do to change my love. But I'm angry. I've been mad for so long. I don't know how to change..."

Her voice was that of someone who had lost most of what made them *them*. It scared Kid. Frightened him more than anything. He had heard voices like that before. Many times. Knew it like he knew himself. Voices of the lost. Addicted to escape, hatred, fear, and pain. It was the voice of entropy. It was the voice of The Hang On. Gets to be, that's all there's left. A single jagged mountain top peeking out from under an angry, seething sea.

He had to convince her. Somehow.

Kid called out to the voice of his birth mother, "Mama, you have to come back to yourself. You gotta master this anger. It's tearing you and everything else apart. The rift. The stars. The Dream."

He thought of the comas in the real world. The cold in The Dream. People falling asleep and losing their animi to The Void. It was the same result as if stolen by an ancient like Mara or body walkers like Delilah and Poe. All those souls swallowed, leaving empty vessels behind. Every time another went that way, a star in the sky of The Dream winked out. A little more of the stuff that made life possible disappeared. They were running head-first into a frozen expanse of universal heat death.

"Don't you see? You're doing the same thing to them that they did to you. There are good people out there, and we're losing them *all*. They go to sleep, and they don't wake up. It's all coming apart. If you keep on, there won't be anything left. Not awake, not dreaming. Nothing. You have to let go, Mama."

"We know about all that," Saría replied. "Believe me, we know. This is no accident. But even if I wanted to stop, I'll be the only one. The rest... They aren't *thinking* things anymore. Just dark energy now. Hungry ghosts. The storm is bigger than me. A million angry souls and more every second. All screaming for vengeance."

The spirit of his mother and all the rest had become a force. As simple as gravity or electromagnetism. Irrefutable and ancient. How do you stop something like that?

Kid did what any child would. He begged.

Saría Landros listened to his pleas as patiently as an ancient spirit can. He told her of his life and journey to find Linh, lost somewhere in The Void.

He told her about Alice.

He told her of love.

He understood that, instead of destroying him, she was protecting him from a fate like Linh's—to be lost and withering in the dark. But the balance was tenuous. A tide of rage held back by a small embankment of contradictory hope. But she *wanted* to believe. Despite ten thousand lonely years, she did. He could sense it.

"I don't see the point," she said as her light dimmed. "All this is coming down, and soon. We might as well settle in."

"Mama, I need you to listen. Listen with the love you have for me. Hear it from the love I have for you. Listen with the weight of the time we've lost. Before you're done with all this, before it's gone, I *have* to do this. I have to find Linh. I have to try and stop this thing."

Her light pulsed before responding, "You sound like your daddy."

Kid waited and sensed more coming. After a while, she spoke, "I know she brought you up, at least a part of you. Despite what she did, she was there. That matters. That counts. Better than I can say for myself..." The echoing voice halted briefly as if to breathe before continuing, "But, I'll warn you, she's good and lost. Lost like the rest of us, I suppose. Lost in her dark grief. She and the blight she brought with her are all twisted up together. Hard to say which is which now, who's feeding who. The truth is, she may not want you there. She may not want to leave."

"Doesn't matter. I have to try."

She sighed, then chuckled. "Quite the salesman. Got that from your dad too."

Kid asked, "Can you take me?"

She *tsk tsk'd* and replied, "What do you think you're going to do? Just strut in there and take her home? That creature has been feeding for almost three years."

"I don't know, but I have to try."

"I know, baby. You have the right attitude. But you're about to go up against a grown heart's bane. You won't defeat it. Not like this. You need to train."

"But I don't have time! We're already so late. Everything coming up to this moment has felt like slow motion, stopped and pulled back at every turn. I need to get in there! I'm so close!"

"If you do it now, you'll die. And so will she."

"No, I won't. I can do it." Kid let out an unwavering breath. "I have to."

50

GREY

"Just put it on, you twat," Dagan barked at the red-cheeked nurse.

Her real name was Kathy, but on duty, it was Seven. They all had numbered code names. Except for the higher-ups, but she wasn't one of them. She gave Dagan one last disparaging look, then put the necklace around her neck. A thin chain of silver, like something you could pick up at any department store for less than a hundred bucks.

Seven didn't trust anyone at The Young School farther than she could throw them, least of all Dagan. He had the eyes of a hungry man who liked to eat. She'd heard the rumors. She'd seen the way so many of the children managed to simultaneously shy away, cower, and obediently answer his commands. Growing up, one of her school friends, Susanne, she'd been like that with her stepdad. He'd had those hungry eyes too. Yep. Dagan gave her the willies. She lifted the necklace off her chest to inspect it as if it might burn her fingers.

"What's it do?" She asked.

"I need you awake. In case you haven't noticed, all the beds are full. Unless you want to end up on the floor, keep it on and tend to your duties."

Dagan was so tired of these sheep. They all had the same dead-eyed skepticism of authority. Yet, like sheep, they eventually listened and fell in line. It was the constant push and pull to get them to do what he knew they would do anyway that bothered him. Such a waste of time. It had always been this way, as long as he had been around to know it. It was unfortunate Mara never learned how to empathy push the whole world. That would solve everything. But here he was, herding idiots. He was a man of action, goddamnit, not a people manager. Even with immortality, bureaucracy, and bullshit did not take a break. Dagan's cheek twitched. He wanted to end her life, to strangle her, hear her croak as her eyes bulged.

He said, "Do you understand?"

"Yeah, jeez, I get it." Seven replied, lip curled, showing her skepticism. Everything about the man was repulsive. Especially his dead grey tooth, which could be seen on rare occasions when he grinned his reptile grin.

"Excuse me?" Dagan seemed to inflate, an aura of electric violence buzzing in his posture. He stepped into her personal space and looked down at her.

Seven shrank back, "I mean, yes. Yes, *sir*. I understand. I won't take it off, not even for a minute. Promise." She shrank further, expecting physical retribution.

None came, and Dagan said, "Good. Now go. Take these, and give them to the best of the staff and teachers. There aren't enough for everyone yet, so only the best. Not your favorite, the best. For those left out, tell them they're getting one as well. They have to wait a bit."

Seven nodded and took the pile of silver necklaces from Dagan's outstretched hand. She stood still, waiting for further instructions.

"What is it?" Dagan asked, eyeing her throat.

Seven opened her mouth to speak, then stopped.

"Goddamnit, GO!" Dagan yelled. Spittle flew from his mouth and hit her in the face.

Seven squeak-choked on a cough as she turned and trotted down the hallway. She stopped to run her keycard through the slot by the door, wiped her face as she waited for the beep-beep and swoosh, then hurried through, leaving Dagan alone.

He tugged at the shirt cuffs under his suit jacket sleeves to ensure they were peaking out at equal length. The width of a thumb. Perfect. He turned and walked in the opposite direction, the heels of his Italian calfskin shoes clicking as he went. He hummed a song to himself, a melody from the old times. It was one he and his men would sing before battle. It was going to be an exciting night. There would be death. Much of it. Over his many years, he learned to sense it and could almost smell it crossing the event horizon.

Dagan passed through the fluorescent-lit hallway toward the medical wing, which held all the sleeping students. He needed to give himself a release before the action of the evening began in earnest. Who knew, with that wrathful goddess of a woman at the helm, it might be his last night on this plane.

He chuckled at the thought. Would Mother do it? Bring it all down? He thought she might. All is well. As they say, those who fear the end do not drink champagne.

Dagan stopped at a rectangular slice of light shining from the door to Linh's room. With Seven busy and Mara occupied in the dorm level, it was untended. The keycard slot beeped as it unlocked, allowing him to step inside. He locked the door behind him and closed the inner curtain.

His breath shortened, and his mouth salivated as he watched the subtle rise of her sleeping chest in the low green light. He cracked a rare smile, revealing his dead, grey tooth.

51
FIRE

"Mother," Alice pleaded, "I don't understand. What are we doing?"

As Mara walked through the minimalist dormitory halls of the Young School, she replied, "Feeding it, my love. The Void must eat. She needs to be healthy and strong to survive what comes next."

"But, I thought we only needed the rivener for protection from the other ancients. You said they wanted to hurt us."

"That is true. I would never lie to you."

"So—"

"Protection and destruction are two sides of the same coin. One cannot be without the other. Pain and love are both irreplaceable parts of birth. Did you know many seeds will not germinate until they're burned?"

"Yes, such as Alder, Lupinus, and most notably, the Giant Sequoias. Also—"

"We are not in class today. Listen."

Alice closed her mouth.

Mara continued, "We are no different than a forest. The world needs fire. Without it, stagnancy and rot spread. We are all covered in it now, an invisible, growing malignancy."

"But the students, and everyone else, they're innocent."

"Yes, some of them. But innocence and responsibility are not mutually exclusive. Birth does not take place without pain, for both the mother as well as the child. This is the way of the universe. Soon, you'll understand. When you birth a new world."

They moved from one dorm room to the next. Each housed two students, with twin-size beds on either side and two desks in the middle. A simple beige rug adorned the center of each room. Otherwise, they were plain. The thinking was that, along with training and practice, a lack of decoration allowed the mind to disassociate more efficiently —the white wall technique. The ability to disembody at will, cultivating that talent, is necessary for a traveler. Alice had gone through a similar experience.

Most students already slept the long dream and had been transferred to the medical ward, hidden away from the rest of the school to prevent hysteria. Now any remaining witnesses who could cause issues were few and far between. It was those stragglers Mara was finishing up. She moved through the school, using the rivener Alice brought.

She used her keycard to open up another dorm room. It swished aside, and she stepped in with Alice behind her.

"Mother!" Exclaimed a little boy. He was about eight or nine years old with messy blonde hair and brown eyes. He ran to Mara and wrapped his arms around her. "Robby won't wake up! I tried and tried, but he won't wake up!

Nobody's been by for, for, well, for forever, and I'm so hungry."

"Shhh, it's okay, my love, everything is okay."

With effort, she removed the boy from his fearful embrace.

In the gap between them, she produced the rivener and shoved it into his heart. Mara smiled as she buried the knife to its hilt.

The boy gasped and looked up.

"Mother?"

He collapsed into her arms as if tranquilized by a dart gun. When she retracted the ultra-black blade from his chest, it left a neat slice, so cleanly cut it closed before spilling blood. She laid him down in the bed, positioning his arms and legs, then covered him to his chin with the blanket. If someone were just then to observe the situation, it might look like a caring parent putting a child to bed.

Despite Mara's psychic domination over her, Alice became more horrified with each passing moment. The children did not seem to experience pain with the severing of their animi. But Alice knew that not all pain was visible. Most traumas didn't make a sound or a big show. She knew the hurt of disconnection. She knew where their spirits were destined to roam—the place Kid now drifted. She thought of who she had left behind, and her heart hurt.

"Mother, please, there has to be another way! I don't want to hurt them, not like this..."

"I understand. I do. Truth be told, I've tried other tactics over the years. But they all failed—every single one. I am sure now. The only answer is a fresh start. We have to let the forest burn so new growth can occur. We need to build something unspoiled. We must return to innocence. You see, this rift and The Void? All things that begin must end. We alone can cure the world and make it pure again. Do you understand?"

"No! I didn't want to be here. I didn't want to come back. Why couldn't you just let me go? Mother, I had it, I tasted it, and for a moment, I was free. Didn't I deserve that? For all I've done for you? But now... They don't deserve this. This isn't right."

"What you want and what you need are not the same. Whether it is my triumph or curse, it makes no noticeable difference. As a mother, I must choose for you."

"But, Mother, you say you love us. Has it always been a lie?"

"No. My heart is true. But love is brief, frequent, and cheap."

"Do you really believe that?"

"It has nothing to do with belief. It is a numerical certainty. This world requires more than love. It requires sacrifice."

Mara stepped close, using an ageless hand to caress Alice's face. She tried to flinch away but could not. Her captor's eyes were honey brown and heavily shadowed, her skin flawless, and her cheeks burned pink with the excitement of her acts. She was the picture of eternal youth, a personification of infinite beginnings. The eye contact and embrace caused a familiar flood of empathy and dopamine to rush through Alice's system. The drug that was Mara's affection was all-powerful. It forced its way past her disgust, fear, and confusion—a rebellion-breaking opiate.

Alice's pupils dilated, the room brightened, cheeks and

chest flushed with warmth, and every worry washed away. The questions and fears seemed only distant bells. Each complaint replaced by the rapturous blanket of understanding via spiritual osmosis.

Mara kissed her forehead and turned. "Come, we have work to do."

52

DIN

It took some time for Saría to navigate through the infinite folds of The Void. Time which ebbed and flowed and folded. It stretched long enough for Kid to come to terms with the news that Linh took part in destroying his family. To take them from him before he had a chance to have a say in things. However, he was beginning to understand the death grip Mara had on people. Like a neighborhood dealer forcing the weak and addicted to do their dirty work.

Closer to his own experiences, he understood mistakes—understood guilt. Scars are kept, and we go on. The things we carry become sodden and heavy when it rains. Their weight reminds us of the choices we've made.

Some actions are irredeemable, but the truth is, most are in the forgivable grey. Although choosing amnesty is more challenging than holding anger, the result of the rockier path is power over one's self and the ability to channel energy into will. Whether that determination becomes a healing force or a destructive one is up to the one who wields it.

Kid knew now, power was something he did have. Something he could use as a weapon and as a shield. Unpolished and difficult to predict, it was there, waiting inside him—a spirit force built from pain, purpose, and promise.

Still, he knew that what he had paled compared to what was needed for the coming hours. To save Linh, he would battle a heart's bane. Then, in the unlikely event of survival, he would require a way to escape The Void without a rivener.

After that? If there were gods—which seemed more possible by the day—only they knew.

———

They arrived with a painful blink in an abandoned hospital. Pale light sifted through yellowed windows, and the air tasted of ash. Sadly, Saría could go no further. She explained that even with her ten thousand years, she could not stand being near the heart's bane. It released an aura like an electromagnetic field. Anytime she drew too close, it pushed her away. But not Kid. They weren't sure why.

As the omnipresent fungal bloom of the heart's bane caused Saría's essence to waver and stutter, they shared their gratitude. They had their time. Less than most, more than many. She promised it would not be their last moment together, and they parted with great effort and sadness.

Her white light dissipated, leaving Kid to search the hospital, looking into each passing room, trailing footprints in the bone-colored grit. He dared not call out, knowing that the thing which held his friend captive may be listening, watching, and hunting.

He jumped at a sudden storm of sound crashing against the hallway windows. Dozens of black crows dive-bombed the glass. The glass cracked but didn't break. Kid realized it was strengthened with wire mesh. Was this a hospital or an institution? The dark birds swarmed the place from the outside. Their death cackles and fracturing glass echoed through the empty space as each dying creature left a splatter of blood and an explosion of feathers.

"*Shhhh....*" Whispered a small, high-pitched voice.

Kid whipped around to find the source. A toddler. A little girl, maybe two years old, with hair in a small dark ponytail. But no matter which way she turned, her face remained in silhouette shadow. She brought a tiny finger to her mouth and stage-whispered again.

"*Shhhhh...* baby sleep... night-night." The last two words came out sounding like *ny-ny*. Then she giggled and turned to waddle away, surprisingly fast, like watching a fast-forward recording with many frames missing.

As she turned a corner, Kid called after her, "Hey! Wait! Come back, what's your name?" He rounded the bend, but she was gone. The only trace of her were little footprints in the dust.

Further and further into the building, he went, following the tracks and shutting the doors behind him, trying to put barriers between himself and the windows. Could the birds break all the way through? He didn't know and didn't want to find out. And the girl, was she a good thing or bad? Eerie, given the context, but she was all he had to go on.

After several turns through the dark halls, he came to a long corridor, at the end of which he caught sight of the little girl as she ran into a doorway at the end of the hall. Light spilled out from it, flickering yellow, cutting an angular beam across the floor. Each time the light blinked out, splotches of black mold pulsed with an alien heartbeat.

As the dark blotches swelled, something inside him did too. A disparate entity. Their rhythm matched. Synchronous.

Kid recognized it now like a toxic lover. It was the thing he had contracted in his nightmare. The thing he had fed the face of a man. It was still inside him, having survived by lying hidden in the coolness of his spirit's shadow.

It told him all he needed to know.

Soon, he would meet its maker.

Kid snuck to the doorway and peeked inside.

After everything he'd gone through, there she was. Only a few paces away. Tank-top and kitchen-strong arms crisscrossed with scars. Linh looked as she had the last time he saw her, except for one thing—her hair was pure white and had grown another twenty inches down to her mid-thigh.

She stood in front of a baby's crib and didn't move or make any indication of noticing Kid. Arranged around her in a neat grid were a dozen more cribs. Each held another baby swaddled in pastel gauze. Some slept, a few cried, and most were cooing, kicking, or staring at the ceiling.

Cautious, Kid studied the situation. Linh didn't move a muscle, fixed on the baby in front of her with low-lidded rapture and a blissed-out smile. He had seen that look before. It was the face of a needle man after a fix. The baby returned Linh's stare. And judging by the pink swaddle, it was a girl.

With no visible horrors close by, Kid called to her as he drew close, "Linh!" He shook her shoulders, trying and failing to get her attention. She was in a trance, stiff as a corpse, head tilted, dazed. Kid glanced around the room as if he might find help, but they were alone. Then the baby cooed and turned her head to nuzzle back to sleep.

As she did, Kid noticed a birthmark on her neck. The shape of a little cartoon dinosaur. The ones with the long neck. A brontosaurus. He stared. It took a second to place. Then it hit like a bolt of lightning.

Like so many things in The Dream, and apparently The Void too—it was incredible, yes, but mainly, it was true.

Holy shit. The birthmark. It's Alice.

She's the lost daughter? That means we're inside Linh's last memory of Alice. This must be a tainted version of the place she had to leave her. Linh is trapped here in that pain, just like I was in my nightmare.

As soon as the thought completed in his mind, the baby stirred and opened its eyes. Jet black, observing and studying —the primal arithmetic of a predator.

And was the baby bigger now than before? It was. The swaddle had grown tight, cutting off circulation and turning its face purple.

It. Not she. The heart's bane had been in the room all along. It cried, releasing an ear-piercing wail to echo off the tiled walls in a jarring cacophony. The swaddle split with the jagged sound of ripping cloth.

Kid felt his adrenaline drip like water down an electric icicle. His feet begged him to move.

"Linh! Wake up!"

He shook her again, but still no response.

"Linh! This isn't your baby! This isn't your daughter! It's not a baby at all! It's not Alice! Come on!"

Desperate, Kid slapped her across the face, leaving a bright red imprint on her pale, dusty cheek. He grimaced with immediate guilt, but they didn't have time for this. The creature was growing. Not knowing what else to do, Kid readied to hit her again.

The slap or the revelation, perhaps both, finally caused Linh to stir. Barely audible over the baby's air-raid wail, she spoke. "*Bian*... My daughter is called *Bian*. I found her. See? I finally found her." She looked down, but the swelling, purple creature was indisputably grotesque. Linh's expression transformed from bliss to confusion.

The din of cries grew as all twelve babies woke and added their screams to the chorus, building a wall of eye-watering noise.

Kid yelled, "The hell it is! That's not her!" He held her by the cheeks and spoke from only inches away, "Linh. Listen to me. Your daughter's name is Bian. Okay. Fine. But that thing is not Bian. See, I know your daughter. She works for Mara! Her name is Alice!"

Something registered. Linh whispered, "Mara?"

"Yeah. Alice and me, we're about the same age. If you'd found your girl, she wouldn't still be a baby, right? It's been almost twenty years. Bian is Alice! I know it. And I know where she is! Where she *really* is! Not this freak show. We can find her, okay? We'll do it together. But you gotta wake up!"

Her whisper crackled through a throat ragged from disuse, "With Mara? Bian... But how? How do you know?"

"The birthmark on her neck. It's like a little dinosaur. The girl I know, she has the same one. Exactly the same. Trust me. Alice is Bian. Alice is your daughter. Not this *thing*. I'd bet my life."

Linh's face changed again from confused to despondent.

"After everything I lost to keep her safe, to keep her *away* from that... *woman*. That was the whole point! The reason I left her! To keep her away. But that's where she ended up anyway? That's where she's been this whole time?"

She released a wail—the sort that only comes from a parent losing a child. Kid pulled her face against his chest, soaking up her whimpers. Then he realized that she was the only person left crying.

The gangrenous things had grown to the size of toddlers. Each stood at the edge of their crib, watching with black hive-mind eyes.

53
VELVET

Without moving his head, Kid scanned the room. The purpling skin of the creatures made them look like miniature versions of the bloated monster Patricia Hodgekiss. He knew better than to think the similarity was a coincidence.

Linh's cries muffled and whimpered and finally tapered off. She moved to lift her head, but Kid stopped her.

"Don't. They're watching, " He whispered. "Linh... Listen to me. It's okay. We'll find your daughter. She's alive. We'll find her. Found you didn't I? Right now, though, you gotta get a grip. Fast. We're in deep shit."

They reminded him of a show he'd seen about African predators. Hyenas in the dark, eyes glowing with green reflecting light, waiting in a circle around a lion's fresh kill. Looking for a chance to skitter in and snatch a piece of bloody meat with sharp teeth.

It seemed Linh had regained some measure of self-control. Without taking her head from Kid's chest, she whispered,

"Where are we? I don't... remember much. You came home hurt, that black poison, then lost in your dream. Down in that basement, a scared little boy. The cigarette burns... Oh, Kid. I'm so sorry. I didn't know... But, then, I fought that thing. I feel like I'm missing something. My body aches."

"It's okay, Linh. You saved me, my life, my soul. But, yeah, you fell into... *Here*. The Void. I tried to help, but I was too small. That monster, it came in with you. These creepy motherfuckers are it. They took a form that'd trick you best."

Linh's mouth twisted in disgust. "Banes. They find your deepest pain and mimic it. Eat it."

The little purple jackals began to climb out of their cribs. With a pattering of twenty-four toddler feet, they were on the ground, huddled together in a growing crowd, climbing on top of one another like a team of tiny circus gymnasts. A pyramid formed, the top seven feet off the floor—boundaries between individuals fused as if made of viscous modeling clay, and a unified shape emerged.

Kid and Linh backed up as far as they could, but the door behind them was locked now. When, how, did that happen? Frozen by fear, they watched the mutant evolve. Little arms and legs stuck out, this way and that, at odd disjointed angles, hands waving and grasping. Random ears, tufts of hair, and twenty-four stray eyeballs pocked the gelatinous surface. Each eye lolled about, seeking a focal point. The flesh pile recolored to greens, blacks, and yellows, like a time-lapse video of a healing bruise. It was abominable, beyond the pale of what could even be rightly called hideous. Their stomachs churned.

The Carpenteresque horror show trundled forward on fat

legs. Two of the many tiny arms grew to the size of tree trunks. Muscled like a gorilla, they were capable of smashing to kill. Its many eyes turned in unison, focusing on Kid. The room shook as it stomped forward, cribs flying left and right as it batted them out of the way. One hit the nursery observation window in the far wall, cracking the safety glass in a spiderweb.

Then the thing stopped. It observed Kid, uninterested in Linh. It took another halting step forward and stopped again, close enough to smell them as if it had nostrils. Did it? It was impossible to say what orifices hid across the thing, but its body hitched in a way that made it seem to sniff the air.

It started toward another step and stopped yet again.

It seemed unsure of what to do next. It studied and waited.

Without looking away from it, Kid whispered, "What's it doing?"

"I don't know..."

Blue light shone from Kid's left side. With effort, he tore his focus away from the creature and found the source.

It was the tattoo, emitting a pulsing glow.

The monster inflated and deflated as it did whatever its version of breathing was. The pattern matched the light emanating from Kid's mark. They were synced.

"It's focused on my arm." Kid said.

"You got that after you made it out of your nightmare?"

"Yeah, after you saved me, I woke up in your apartment, and it was there. There's been some wild stuff happening."

Linh replied, "I think it's the—"

The creature interrupted her reply.

It chose rage and hunger, launching forward to envelop Kid and Linh in its hideous mass, swinging both giant arms wide and preparing to crush them.

———

A thinking man would know that a simple punch would do less than nothing to a creature this size. But Kid wasn't thinking.

Running on instinct, street-brawl muscle memory, and power that lived and grew inside him, he dashed forward and threw a left hook at the creature's exposed rib cage. His glowing arm sizzled through the air like a blue comet, the telltale scent of burnt ozone following in its wake. The hit connected, sending ripples through the thing's eye-pocked flesh.

Before he could hop back out of range, a third appendage erupted from its side, shooting forward like a giant frog's tongue. It slammed into Kid's chest, launching him against the locked door. Before he could fall to the floor, it picked him up and heaved him across the room to land in a crash of broken cradles. As Kid struggled to rise, he felt the sharp pang of a cracked rib. The creature rushed toward him, steps thundering.

Linh grabbed a broken haft of wood, sprinted after the heart's bane, and leaped into the air to stab it in the back. It bellowed and attempted to shake her off, but she hung on. It realized that it could not reach her and, instead of continuing to try, morphed.

With cracks and pops of bone and sinew, suddenly she

wasn't hanging off its back, but off its front, directly in the path of its train-piston arms.

She let go and dropped to the ground, attempting to scramble away, but didn't make distance fast enough. The thing pulled her off the ground, dangling her in the air like a doll.

The misaligned face of Patricia Hodgekiss grew from the top of the creature like an evil mushroom. Its mouth stretched open, impossibly wide, hinging from the cervical vertebrae. The dark hole revealed concentric rings of two hundred forty tiny, sharp, bright-white baby teeth.

It howled, "Mommmmmmyyyyy?!?"

The sound was half pained-beast and half joy-filled toddler squeal, releasing a stench of putrefaction. The creature coughed out another retched sound like a cat wrestling a hairball, "HONEY, *cough*, Honey! *Hack*hack*hack,* Honey *BUNCH*!"

Its yellow Patricia eyes focused on Kid, and it reared back to swing Linh at him like a baseball bat. But before the creature could complete the motion, Kid jumped through the air and brought his shining hand down on its shoulder.

Bright light burst from the attack zone as his hand cleaved straight through, lopping the arm off. Linh fell to the ground as the creature screamed in pain. She rolled to the side and stepped back. Its many eyes lolled about in anger and confusion. The wide mouth closed and grimaced in concentration as a new arm began to grow from the stump. It started small, twisting and grasping, like a kid in a back seat reaching for a cookie. Then it was the size of a man's arm. It continued to grow as the fingers on both hands elongated to calcified talons. It would finish its next evolution and attack again any second. Kid lunged forward, dropped to a knee slide, then rose in front of the creature in a jumping uppercut.

The attack cleaved the thing in two, from groin to collarbone. Its bulk fell to either side, like freshly sliced prime rib.

The creature's last sound, a wavering pain-filled moan, "Mommmmmyyyyyy...."

The two halves quivered, then lay still and liquified, sinking into the concrete floor. Dark stains remained. The sickly scent of charcoal and spoiled meat filled the room.

A glowing scar hung in the air, weightless and shining like the glitter from a butterfly wing.

They didn't move, just staring at the wavering hole in the air. Kid's arm tingled. A familiar sensation flowed from it into his chest. Sweet and soft like velvet. The pleasure of the kill. A dark joy he hadn't felt since The Sand. It filled him with a lingering heady buzz that he shook off as Linh broke the silence.

"You're shadow marked."

Kid turned to Linh; his attention pulled away from the carnage by her statement.

"You mean spiritborne? They told me that already. This happened before. I mean, not this, exactly. But something similar with my arm. Shot a dude across a room by reflex. Then burned him to death. Well, not him, It was Delilah, she had his body. But still..." He frowned. "She was going to murder Alice. I didn't mean to kill him..."

"No, this is different. You have what made that creature inside you now. It should have killed you before, back when you were first infected. But you're not dead. That's where the spiritborne part comes in, I think. I assume you can thank the half of you that comes from your mother for your life. So, you were already half anima. And now? You're intertwined, at least in part, with what makes a heart's bane. Part light, part man, and now part shadow too."

Linh glanced at the stain in the concrete and then took a step back, unsure of what toxins it might emit. Kid followed her, not trusting the dark oily blotch either. They retreated to the far corner of the room to continue talking.

"So what is it? Like cancer, a disease, or something?"

"I don't know the answer to that question. All I can say is that you had some of the dark inside you and survived. Now... it's part of you. It seems you're stronger for it. If there are negative side effects... well... we will see."

Kid thought of the blissful sensation, the desire to keep killing back at The Sand, but said nothing. He paced around the room, never allowing his attention to meander away from the dark stain for long. It seemed to call to him. After a minute, he said, "We gotta get out of here. I'm not waiting for that thing to come back."

"It seems dead. Perhaps the only thing that can kill a heart's bane is a piece of itself."

"Yeah... maybe. Still, I'm not making any bets."

Kid continued searching for an escape but found nothing. Frustration and claustrophobia increased by the second. He threw a crib at the window, hoping to break the safety glass where the other crack already was. Maybe he could make a hole to get through. To where, though?

They couldn't keep wandering around this god-forsaken

place, nor could he sit still and do nothing. After throwing several more objects against the glass, it was clear the reinforced safety material would not break.

He crouched down and sighed.

Then, a wind picked up, strange in a closed room but no stranger than anything else that had transpired. Kid and Linh watched the wind swirl up bits of debris like a tiny playground tornado. The wind settled, and a familiar light appeared, semi-tangible and tattered like a ghost wedding dress, followed by his mother's voice.

"Poor thing," She said. "Hungry, starving, and sad. She should have gone free a long time ago."

"She?" Kid asked.

"Yes... I recognize her. Banes begin as lost animi. They finally let them out, and they look to feed. It's the only thing they know to do, trying to fill the hole inside themselves. To create such things, man can be truly cruel."

Kid thought about the creature in a new light. The eyes. He had seen it in the eyes. It had looked sad. Gut wrenchingly ugly, angry, and mean as a rabid dog, but now that his mom mentioned it, she was right.

With eyes wide, Linh recognized the voice and called out, "Saría?"

The air replied, "Doe. Or should I use your new name, Linh?"

"I never thought I'd speak to you again. I'm—"

"You're what." An accusation, not a question.

"I'm sorry. I am. I've tried to be better. To do better. And Kid... You know now? I had a hand in this—your mother, your father... I'm sorry I couldn't tell you. I'm sorry I—"

Kid interrupted her, "It's okay, Linh. It was Mara, not you. But either way, I would forgive you."

Linh let out a shaking breath, a tear rolling down her cheek. She couldn't yet form the words of gratitude, but her eyes spoke loudly enough.

Saría sighed. "Kid told me that you've been there for him. That matters. But don't ask *me* to forgive you. I don't know that I'm capable." She hesitated, then finished, "I'm here for him, and by extension, I'm here for you too."

Linh nodded, again struck silent.

"Mama," Kid asked, "how are you here?"

"The bane is dead. Whatever repelling force it emitted is gone now."

"But we're still trapped."

"Stuck is a state of mind, baby boy. You taught me that."

"How do you know each other?" Linh asked. "I'm sorry, I'm happy. It seems you've had a reunion. That's wonderful. But how?"

"Time is trippy in The Void," Kid replied. "My mom found me, then we went deeper. Spent a little time together."

"Time is good," Linh said. "You deserve more."

"It is what it is," Saría replied sadly.

Linh hesitated to ask, "How long have I been here?"

"You've been here for three years, according to my mom. How do you feel?"

"Not terrible, considering. I don't remember much. I suppose this is what it must feel like to wake from a coma."

"Join the club," Kid said.

"What do you mean?"

"People outside are asleep and can't wake up because

their animi are severed and lost here in The Void. They're falling in like you, by the hundreds of thousands, millions even. It seems like it's not going to stop. The Dream is freezing. Middlemost was falling apart."

Linh nodded. "I've heard of this, in theory. Never in practice, not in any recent millennia anyway. How long has it been in The Real?"

"The time dilation keeps confusing me," Kid replied, "but I think a day or two."

"Close enough," Saría said. "It's best not to bust your brain with it."

"Time is short, and the longer we wait, the more people fall. It's really bad. Like end of days shit."

Linh and Saría quipped in unison, "Watch your mouth."

"Sorry," Kid apologized. "Seriously, though. We gotta do something. This isn't over, not yet. Mama, we could use a hand. You know how to get out of here?"

"I didn't think there was a way. But I also didn't think there was a way to get in either, not on purpose. No soul arrived here by choice. That is, until now."

Realization dawned, and Linh asked Kid, "How did you get in here?"

"A knife. A black one, ultra-black. It was in that box from the Lotus drop. Remember? The Cognosa called it a rivener. Then at the top of Middlemost, I used it to cut through The Stream. That big blue ghost beam. Made a hole like a tent flap. Then I walked right through. You know about riveners and all that?"

Linh couldn't help but chuckle as she studied Kid. "You've been busy since last I saw you." She tilted her head.

"You look more like your father every day. He was a good man."

"Yes..." Saría agreed. "He was."

Linh frowned and continued, "To answer your question, yes. I know of these things. I was a traveler, as you're now aware. I've seen The Stream and much of the Animus Mundi. Never a rivener, though. My knowledge is limited to myth."

Saría added, "My education goes back a bit further than yours. From what I know, there were once several. Each held by the most powerful ancients. At one time, Baal controlled one, as well as Hadrian and Ravana too. Then the Asuri stole them and kept them safe. They were hidden for a time. Since this was long ago, they've all been lost or destroyed, as objects of power tend to be."

"Kid, " Linh asked, "where is the rivener now?"

He had the momentary urge to look down in shame for losing it. But the thought left as quickly as it came. Instead, he chose to hold his head up—like a king, as Hari would say.

"I gave it to Alice. We made a deal. If she helped me get here, get to you, I'd let her have it. She said she would give it to Mara to trade for her freedom. Maybe that was true in the beginning, but I don't know. Now I think it's more like a gift."

Linh responded, "Don't be too hard on her. Resisting Mara is not trivial. "

Kid nodded.

"Nonetheless," Linh continued, "a rivener in Mara's hands is horrible. Although they've almost always been in the hands of the most powerful, and they are rarely good, so not a lot has changed. But if what you say is true, if Alice is indeed Bian, if she is my daughter—"

Kid interjected, "There's no if about it. She is. I know it."

Linh nodded and continued, "Then I need to go there. I might be able to break Mara's hold. I have to bring her back to her senses. I have to try."

"I understand. We'll go together. We'll get her, I promise."

Linh smiled, "The reckless vows of youth. We will certainly need that optimism. But first, we need to escape The Void. Somehow."

Saría spoke, "I believe I can help with that."

"How?" Kid asked.

"You had what it took to get in here. You have what it takes to get out."

"But I don't have the rivener anymore."

Linh lit up, "Saría's right. You almost did it before. Did you see the mark in the air after you cut down the heart's bane?"

"Yeah, looked like a floating scratch."

Linh responded, "Exactly, you almost tore through on your own. No rivener."

Saría added, "Baby, if I give you a boost, a big one, you can do it."

"But what about you? I don't want to leave you. I only just found you. Come with us! Please come with me, I have so many questions... where were you... why did you and dad—I don't—" Against the apparent effort of his contorted face, tears brimmed on the edges of Kid's eyes.

"I'm sorry. I can't answer that right now, and I can't go with you. You've got work to do. Linh can help with some of the answers and find a man called Horacio—" Kid's eyes went wide at the mention of the man's name, to which Saría responded astutely, "if he didn't already find you. This isn't where your story ends, my love. I won't let that happen. Not like this. Not with the bit of myself I have left."

Saría paused, seemed about to add something else, but instead said, "Now get ready. Take Linh. Keep her close. Keep her safe. Like you've been doing. I'm going to give you a jump, okay? When you feel it running through you, cut your way out of here. Are you ready?"

A stubborn tear finally rolled down Kid's cheek, but only one, and that was all. He didn't have the words for this goodbye. He felt the familiar numbness of bottled loss wash over him. He nodded, then took Linh in his right arm, planted his feet, and readied his left hand, which had already begun to glow in anticipation.

His mother's voice remained resolute as she said with marked finality, "I love you, baby. Be good now."

The animus of Saría Landros grew to fill the room with blinding light until there was nothing left but white. It flowed around them like they had stepped into a snowstorm, warm with contradiction.

Kid felt the power of his mother, the last burst of her soul's flame. He closed his eyes and focused that abundant energy through himself. It flowed into his heart and down through his left arm. His hand glowed white hot. It felt like it could melt steel but with none of the dark hunger from before.

As he pushed his hand in front, his fingers connected with... something—gauze filaments of that which makes up reality. A spark of light erupted from the interaction point, and he felt the last kilojoule of his mother's love fade as he drew her power to cut the barrier between them and The Dream.

A neat slice revealed what appeared to be outer space—
the emptiest parts of it, well into the interstellar. As the
darkness grew and enveloped them, hoarfrost collected on
their skin, the moisture in their breath crystalized, and their
fingers burned with the cold. It became painfully clear why, in
a scientific sense, The Dream was freezing, and millions of lost
souls had no warmth left in their hearts.

PART SIX
EGO DEATH

"*I could see their bare, dark sides showing in several places. And everywhere and always there reigned an incredible death-silence and desolation. The immutable, awful quiet of a dying world.*"

— WILLIAM HOPE HODGSON, THE HOUSE
ON THE BORDERLAND

54
BASTARD

Poe sat crosslegged on the circular stone plaza, watching the glowing light of The Stream. It was like a campfire—just the right balance of consistency and variability to allow a person to drift into meditation.

He was thinking about how he would get out of this mess. Once upon a time, at a bar near Ocean Beach, he'd overheard a surfer chatting up a couple girls over beers and pizza. He had tried to impress them with chill surferisms and said, "Ya know, sometimes you just gotta know when to bail." At the time, Poe chuckled into his overpriced craft beer. But the words stuck with him. Surferisms to help get laid or not, they were wise words.

But how do you bail when your feet are nailed to the board? Tom said, "Love." But what the hell was that about? Sounded like some cheesy chick-flick crap. With great effort, he set aside his skepticism and forced himself to think critically about what that truly meant.

The slave connection between his animus and Mara's was

like a chain made of psychic adamantium—supernaturally and inexplicably strong. It was the same connection she used to keep all her children in love and in line. Though, most (like any well-trained domestic animal) didn't need them anymore. You go long enough under a yoke, and it becomes unnecessary—like a dog holding its leash.

Like the rest, she'd forged his when he was young and impressionable and had done many things over the years to strengthen the links further. Overcoming it would require a superior connection, like electricity jumping to a better conductor.

Tom said he had Linh. And Linh had her daughter.

Who did he love like that? Himself?

That thought made him chuckle. He loved his sister, but their relationship had always been one-sided, like loving a stone. Even though he'd seen things eventually ending badly, it didn't stop it from hurting like hell anyway. His heart panged, and he ran his fingers through his hair and sighed. Pretty sure trying to kill your twin disqualified the connection as loving.

Ever the one to make jokes at a funeral, he thought his car might fit the bill. That made him laugh again. He loved the old Torino like a baby and had raised it like one—starting from a decrepit pile of steel found in a barn up in Napa. He'd painstakingly restored it over several years to the showroom-ready collectible it was now.

Would a car work? He didn't think so. Even he knew that was stupid. Poe thought on it more. Nobody and nothing came to mind. He wasn't usually prone to sentimental distress, but he couldn't help thinking now that maybe he had missed some significant milestones in life to not have one, just one, person he could think of who he loved more than his goddamn boss. Ridiculous. Poe scoffed.

Pulling him from his thoughts, the Stream wavered, making the light around him dance. He watched as the shimmy turned into a shake, then a split formed in the middle like a dark fault line. From the gap that appeared, Kid and Linh tumbled through. They fell to the stone dais, and the hole behind them quickly sealed. The two were wrapped in a double fetal position hug as if packed tightly together in a womb.

"Ha!" Poe jumped up and ran to them, surprising himself with how happy he was about their reappearance. He called out, "You fuckers! I knew you'd make it!"

They were unresponsive. Pale and blue-lipped, their entire bodies were covered in a thin layer of melting ice, leaving them shiny and wet. Poe pulled them away from The Stream, checked their pulse, which was steady, then covered them with his jacket. Their chests rose and fell with each breath, and he could see their eyes move under their lids. They just needed some time.

He sat down again, a short distance away. When they woke up, he wanted to be seated with his hands visible and not too close to ensure they didn't feel threatened. The last time he had seen them, it was under slightly more aggressive circumstances. Poe would need a minute to explain things and didn't want to get in another fight next to the giant blue laser beam.

He waited patiently, and finally, they started to murmur and move. Kid rolled over first, onto his back, like someone freshly flopped onto a dock after a long swim. He didn't seem sure of where or who he was just yet—simply staring at the flickering stars in The Dream's low sky.

At last, he noticed Poe and croaked, "Who the hell are you?"

Kid tried to roll over, but his body wasn't listening. He grunted and managed a half turn onto his side, from which position he could look Poe in the face. Linh also woke during the commotion and was similarly immobile.

Poe stayed seated, cross-legged, showing the palms of his hands facing out in a hopefully universal symbol of peace, and said, "Easy guys. I don't want any trouble. At least not with you. Can we talk a minute? Linh, I know you recognize me, even if I was just a pimple-faced teen the last time we met. But Kid, last you saw me, we fought in an alley, and I looked like a Chinese high schooler."

Kid tested his body, struggled to rise, and collapsed again. He whispered, "...Bastard."

"Yeah... I'm a bastard alright, both in the literal and figurative, I guess. But, being the bastard that I am, I got a proposition for you." Kid and Linh couldn't put much effort into a response yet, so Poe continued, "You got problems. So do I. We can help each other out. I might be a bastard, but I'm also a slave. You know how it is, Linh. Mara's got me on a leash, making me do all kinds of heinous shit. I don't have a choice. But I'd like to have a choice goin' forward. You understand?"

Poe pointed to the two, still inert but watchful on the stone. "You're in trouble as well, more than you even realize. See, Linh, when you check out of here, you won't wake up with your nightguard in a safe house. You're under Mara's lock and key now. While you were out, she captured your vessel. It's in the medical ward at The Young School, which you know might as well be a prison. And I'm afraid to say, that old perv Dagan's been watching it like an icie-pop in summer."

Linh's face darkened, but she said nothing.

He turned his head slightly to address Kid, the shadows formed by the flickering blue light shifting on his face. "Kid Thames." Poe emphasized the last name theatrically and added, "Michael's boy. Goddamn, if that's not cool."

He admired Kid like a proud coach watching his star up-and-comer with all the potential in the world. "You're not the zero I thought you were. Not at all. Props, bro." Poe threw Kid an air-dap and winked. "But still, no way you're getting in The School on your own. There's security out the wazoo and all kinds of baddies. Hell—even with my help, we're probably all going to die horrific, tortured deaths." Poe wagged his finger. "But you have a big birthday surprise." He scrunched his face. "Dunno why I said that. Is it your birthday? Kinda seems like it, right? What with the universal portal birth and all? You probably don't even know anyway, huh? Well, I say we call it. Set a reminder 'cause today's the day. Happy birthday."

Poe waved his hand to dismiss the tangential thought. "Anyway, see, nobody thought you had a snowball's chance of escaping hell. Plenty of folks avoid it altogether, but no one, and I mean no one, has gone and come back. Not from the black. No way. So why would anyone think you would? They didn't. Thought you were a goner, for sure. Even Alice—who looked pretty bummed about it, by the way." He glanced to

The Stream, then back to Kid and Linh, and puffed his chest proudly.

"Except one. I was your holdout, bro. I knew you'd make it back. I believed in you." He grinned, "Okay, maybe more hope than belief, but still. I knew if you could make it back, you might be able to help me out." Poe's smirk disappeared and turned serious. "See, I need you to cut this chain around my neck. You can't see it, but it's there, I promise you. Mara's got a hold on me just like everyone else. Linh's Tiger said love or some such nonsense would do it."

Poe scoffed, "But, sadly, I got nothing like that. I need a god-level chain chopper. I figure if you can survive a bane, shadow-blast my crazy sister a new asshole, and slice a getaway outa The Void, well then, you can probably cut me free too." He closed his hands as if in prayer.

Kid thought the guy moved and emoted a lot when he talked. If he wasn't such a jerk, it might be entertaining.

"If you can cut me free," Poe pleaded, "I'll owe you. Huge. Life debt shit. And if I can get out of these goddamn shackles, I'll give you the keys to the castle and help you storm the bitch myself."

He took a much-needed breath after his monologue and slapped his knees. "So?" Poe asked with a movie-star smile. "What'll it be? Can we team up? Pretty please?"

Kid put the clues together and asked, already knowing the answer, muscles tensing like compressed springs, "If Mara's got Linh's body, and you talked to Tom last, then who took her vessel? What happened to Tom? And Alice? Where's that chick with one eye?"

"Alice is fine. Mother won't punish her too bad for

skipping school, especially since she brought back that magic knife." Poe glanced at The Stream and added vaguely, "And don't worry about my sister... she's gone."

"So that was her."

"Yeah, was."

Kid raised his eyebrow at his use of past tense but said nothing.

"Now, the other part..." Poe grimaced and did his best to show that he cared—which he had to admit to himself that he surprisingly did. "Like I said, as you know, I'm a slave, man. For realsies. I had no choice, okay? I tried to bug out a whole bunch of times. But it didn't work. It never does. Despite my trying to back out of the deal, it was these hands that took them both. Tom's last breath, and Linh's body."

Filled with a sudden black rage, Kid snarled, "I knew it!"

He launched toward Poe like an attacking animal. Poe didn't try to defend himself, taking the assault in full force, allowing himself to collapse under Kid's weight. He absorbed blow after blow raining down on his face from Kid's clenched fists and, before long, started choking on the blood that ran down his throat. His eyes swam as he lapsed in and out of consciousness while the hits kept coming.

Linh, still immobile, called over, not with fear but resignation, "Kid. Stop. You're going to kill him."

Kid replied, "I know," and kept pummeling.

The violence was sweet, just as it had been before. He felt the pleasure of the act rippling through him, running from his arm, through his heart, and echoing through his body. He wanted to kill Poe. Like nothing he had ever wanted before. The thought of the thing tasted sweeter than pure honey. The real deal, not the half measure of The Sand or the merciful culling in The Void. Killing a man would be ecstasy. Euphoric joy. He raised his left hand into the air, and the markings glowed white hot. Kid readied to drop the shining executioner's axe in a deathblow.

Poe laid still, not attempting to protect himself. He watched Kid and the glowing weapon as if he wanted the end just as badly.

In his moment of frenzy, the iris of Kid's left eye morphed entirely black, and with the black came vision, the ability to see things just as Delilah had. There really was a shackle around Poe's neck. It was invisible before, but now it glowed in translucent shadow light. A tightly wrapped spirit chain. Kid released his anguish in a guttural yell and brought his hand down. Poe watched it descend with little reaction beyond a halting intake of breath.

55
PACT

At the last millisecond, Kid turned his fist into an open blade and, rather than smashing downward, swiped at Poe's shackle in a sideways chop, changing trajectory like a plane pulling up from a nosedive.

SHhhINK!

An explosion of light erupted with high-frequency sound like two razors scraping against each other at astounding speeds. The shackle split cleanly in two, halves falling to the sides. Much like the heart's bane, the two halves melted into the stone, leaving behind a dark stain framing Poe's head in an oily silhouette.

The darkness in Kid's eye contracted but stopped halfway, leaving the remainder inky black. He had wanted Poe's death. To eat it. Something in him begged for it. At his refusal, that something let out a silent scream only he could hear and then went dormant. He let his hands drop to his sides and shuddered as if an icy wind had come and left him chilled.

Poe gradually regained consciousness and sat up with a

435

grunt. He stretched his neck side to side, hocked up a great bloody loogie, spitting it over his shoulder, then rubbed his throat where the spirit collar had been. "Thank you, Kid. I owe you, and I will pay. On my honor."

Kid asked, "You have honor?"

"Anymore, that's all I got." Rubbing his jaw, Poe added, "Think you busted my chops, bro."

"Good." Kid seethed, the darkness again growing inside him, pulsing, still just below the surface, dampened momentarily, but not far away. It wanted to come back. "If you screw us... I'll end you. On my honor."

"That'd be fair." Poe flashed his movie-star smile again, teeth now red with blood. "Help me up, will you? You got a mean swing, and I'm a little woozy." He reached out, and Kid took his hand reluctantly, pulling him to standing. The big guy wobbled. "Whoooh... Yeah... little concussed there..." He shifted his jaw from left to right, releasing a loud pop. "Fuckin' ouch, man. So, this means a team-up, right?"

"For now," Kid replied.

From the side, Linh let out the telltale groan of moving a sore, aging body. Finally able to stand, she stretched her back and turned to Poe. Eyeing him with hope and suspicion like a returned delinquent nephew.

She glanced at Kid, then back to Poe. "You'll carry your weight, just like I carry mine." Linh sighed and continued, "Tom was my friend. More. He was a brother to me. Perhaps when this is all done, I can sit with this grief." She winced from both emotional and physical pain, the sting of shifting that weight to later. "You'd think I would be angry with you, Poe. And I am. But I think you understand loss. Loss of self.

Loss of love. Loss of life. Regret. And I understand doing things I wish I hadn't."

She stepped close and put her hands on either side of Poe's face. She looked like she might scream or shake him, but she let her hands fall. "You were a good boy once. I believe you can be again."

He didn't say anything, just kept eye contact. There was authentic warmth in Linh's eyes. Something to which he was wholly unaccustomed. He blinked back a tear.

She turned to address them both, "We can't save Tom... But maybe, just maybe, we can help Bian and make his departure worth something."

Poe screwed up his face and asked, "Bian?"

"My daughter. She knows herself as Alice. I thought she was lost, but it was Mara, hiding her all this time."

Poe whistled. "Noooo shit? Well, it looks like we've all got some debts to clear. A double rescue mission then."

"More than that," Kid said. "We don't leave until we end Mara. We have to shut this thing down. Everyone will die if we don't, and I mean everyone, in The Real and The Dream.

"I never thought I'd go back there," Linh said, followed by a somber nod. "You're right, of course. This is bigger than us now."

Poe clapped his hands, "Alright then, so we get the hell out of Middlemost and rendezvous back at The School. After that, we need a plan. What are we thinking?" Poe looked to Kid for an answer.

His scowl deepened. "Why are you looking at me?"

Linh answered, "Whether you knew of this path or not, here you are, Kid. This is yours."

He sighed and relaxed his shoulders as he turned to watch the flickering blue light. How did he end up here? The universe is a strange place, Alice had said. And Hari philosophized something similar on a Tenderloin sidewalk of forever ago. The unpredictable yet synchronous chaos force of the cosmos, man. Real magic. It's a wild world, indeed, Kid thought with a stifled chuckle.

Finally, he answered, "We got an inside man. And now, an inside woman too. If we can get Alice to see reason, we'll already have most of our crew in the castle, thanks to Mara's ego. That means we can surprise her. I say we bumrush the motherfuckers. Sharp and quick, straight for the queen."

"Front door guy, eh?"

"Today, yeah."

"Crude. But they won't expect that. I like it."

"How do I get in and find you?" Kid asked.

Poe asked, "Depends. Where'd you leave your body?"

"Leave my body? I didn't. This is it."

Linh gawped at that, "You mean to say you gated in?"

Kid shrugged, "If that's what you want to call it. Horacio brought me to Middlemost in the back of a box truck."

"Well, that complicates things a bit," Poe said. "Normally, I'd tell a guy they're shit outa luck, but with you and that," he glanced at Kid's arm, "whatever it is—you're no normie. You should be able to gate back out with that power. Same way you got out of The Void. But I got no idea where you're gonna pop up."

"Right," Linh added. "You'll need to focus and try to fall somewhere familiar, somewhere you know intimately. A special place."

Poe continued, "Somewhere unique to you and your memories, a place nobody can see. Gotta tell you, though, topside's gotten pretty hairy since you been gone. It sounds like you've guessed it, but you don't know how bad it is. Total shitshow, bro."

"Are we talking Children of Men bad or 28 Days Later?"

"More like The Omega Man. Not so much dangerous as empty and quiet. At least for now. We're still awake for some reason, guess because we're travelers. Hope we stay that way. But it's desolate. Spooky as hell. I hear the National Guard's involved now. Bridges are both blocked as well as all along the boundary to South Bay. If you accidentally gate out in Oakland or Sausalito or somewhere, you're not gonna get back into the city. It's locked up."

Linh asked, "Do you have a safe place? It needs to be something others can't see. If it's observed, it can't be altered and won't work as a gate. It needs to be hidden, like the inside of that box truck." She thought nervously about Kid's open-air living situation and did her best to ask gently, "Do you have a place like that?"

Kid thought fondly of his nest, realizing that he was beyond homesick for it, and thought about the falcons, his books, and the panoramic view of gleaming city windows. His sanctuary. His heart panged as he thought about going back there.

He replied, "Yeah. I got a spot. So, I just think of it and cut out? Click the heels of my ruby slippers?"

Poe replied, "You got it, Dorothy—no place like home. Now, you need to focus and hold it tight—if you screw up, who knows where you'll pop in. It could be a dumpster in

Fremont, a locked trunk, or a fuckin' sewer, I don't know. So focus. We need you." He looked at Kid's hand, "Along with surprise and a full team blitz, you're our secret weapon."

Kid studied his hand, flexing it in front of him. "If I can cut The Void and your chain, maybe I can cut Mara. And not just her frame."

"Here's hoping. And to top it, Mara wants you. Bad."

"Want means weakness." Kid nodded.

"Exactly," Poe confirmed. "And that, we can work with. I don't know how we'll kill her, though. She'll just hop to another vessel. She does that shit for fun. It's like a fetish for her."

"Maybe the rivener?" Linh asked.

Poe replied, "Maybe, but it's gone. Alice has it. So, I don't know."

"We'll cross that bridge when we get to it," Kid said. "Besides, we got some high cards, more than we could have hoped for. We play them and see what we see."

Poe took a breath, like the kind a person takes before jumping from a diving board, then let it out just as quickly. "Alright, boss. Timing's gonna be tight. We've got a couple hours max, even with the big sleep distracting everyone. The good news is most everyone is passed the fuck out, even at The School, so they're half-manned, at best. But they won't leave the front gate unguarded. You'll need a diversion."

Kid grinned, "I can handle that."

"I bet. You know where the Western Knell building is?"

"Yeah, that old one in the financial district with the gargoyles. Used to be a phone company or something back in the old days, right?"

"Yeah, that's the one. It's all startup bullshit now, except for Mara's penthouse in the top three floors and an area deep underground. In the subbasement of the parking garage, there's a freight elevator drop-off bay. That's the entrance to The Young School and where you're heading. So, you get past those guards, and then I'll meet you at the elevator entrance. I have a keycard, and hopefully, it'll still work."

"Okay," Kid said. "Punk the guard, sneak to the secret elevator. High five, then ride down to the hidden school for psychic spies. Kick everyone's asses and save the world. Then, see if we can still snag some Papalote's burritos and go home to chill. Sound about right?"

"Sounds nice when you say it that way," Linh said.

Poe rolled his eyes. "Yeah, simple as a screwdriver. Now, if we don't meet you there? Well, we're probably tits up at that point, and all gonna die, so don't stress."

Kid nodded. "We'll make it. Somehow. No matter what it takes. Mara is done stealing everything from everyone. She's taken enough. We end this. Now."

They watched Kid with awe that continued to blossom. Poe felt better and more on track than at any other point in his life, finally, on the right side of things. Linh, too, felt hope. A small glimmer of it. She stepped forward and took Kid into her arms. Somehow, even in this place made of dream stuff, she still smelled like her kitchen—onion, lime, bone broth, and garlic.

The scent brought his heart to what he now knew was home. For him, home was only an idea, but it was one he must save, as well as his friends and, now, family. But darkness bubbled up in him too, not far from the surface, barely hidden, controlled only slightly. Mara had taken everything from him —his childhood, his father, and his mother. Twice. And she didn't stop there, no. She wanted to take his friends, his new family, and his dreams, along with those of everyone in the city, likely even the world.

He still had never even met the woman, yet she had the hubris to believe herself righteous, above reproach, and allowed to make decisions and take actions that brought so much harm. Kid knew at that moment that he had it in him to end her, permanently and with great vengeance. Something inside him fed on the grief, the anger, and the rage, growing darker and more bold.

As Linh stepped away from their embrace, she noticed Kid's half-black iris.

She asked, "What happened to your eye?"

"What is it?" He rubbed it with the back of his hand, feeling no pain from the movement. "It's nothing. Taken some big hits on this ride. Got a couple cracked ribs too, if you wanna check those out."

"It doesn't look good." Linh moved to hold his face and examine him.

"Linh, it's fine." Kid pushed her hand and turned away.

Before more could be said about it, Poe broke in, "Alright, candles burning. Kid, you hop out first. I wanna make sure you can get outa here before we go. Cause if not, we'll need a plan B."

"Why can't I just pop into The School? Why go through all this trouble?"

Poe opened his mouth, but Linh replied, "The Young School is guarded against things like that. Firewalled, you could say. It's impossible without a traversal totem and Mara's permission."

"Yeah, well, nothing worth doing is easy, right?" Kid puffed air into his chest to psych himself up and rubbed his hands together. "Okay, then. Just cut out. Same as before. No big deal." He held his hand out like he did in The Void, but it didn't glow. It didn't do anything. Kid stared and pushed, making a vein protrude from his forehead. He looked constipated.

Poe laughed.

Kid blushed. "What's the deal?"

"Just focus," Linh said with an encouraging motherly tone. "Try to remember how it felt before, touching the veil. This time should be easier. We're not so far away now. Close your eyes and hold that texture in your mind. Hold the memory of that energy, what Saría gave you. You still have it, at least a little. Things like that don't just go away. Think about how all that felt. Really capture it in your head. When you have it, you'll feel it click like picking the last tumbler on a lock. Once it does, focus that click into a single point at the tip of your finger."

Kid tried. And failed again.

Poe and Linh started to give him more positive enforcement, but he silenced them with a hand and closed his eyes for another attempt.

He went back in, layer by layer, like gliding into a 3D painting. He thought about his mother's voice. Soothing, filled with love, and that surprising Southern accent. If he hadn't known she was an animi from Middlemost, he would have guessed Atlanta or maybe Charlotte. How'd that work out?

Guess it'd stay a mystery. Funny the things you don't know about your parents. Kid's mind wandered as he entered that diaphanous space between thoughts, daydreams, and memories.

Just before his focus was in danger of breaking again, he began to feel the familiar painless white heat collecting at the leading edge of his hand. Kid felt the texture of a boundary, the astral membrane between this world and the next. Even behind his closed eyelids, he started to see the edges of things glowing like fluorescent marker in blacklight.

Kid reached forward and touched the veil, dragging his finger down from head height to the floor, opening it up again just like he had not so long ago. Once he got it going, there was far less resistance than when they were trapped inside The Void. Rather than feeling like they were separated by light years as they had then, now it felt like the real world and The Dream were merely separate rooms in a hotel. Adjoining ones, with that inner connecting door between them, easy enough to open and walk from one double-queen bedroom with free HBO to the next, assuming you had the key.

He opened his eyes and saw the familiar passageway. It was filled with black just like before, but somehow this time, it was less deep, less cold. He turned to Linh and Poe, doing his best to be calm and not show that he was scared shitless.

Linh wasn't fooled and saw his fear. She said, "You got this, Kid. Think of your special place. Hold that thought good and tight, and that's where you'll go."

Poe nodded in encouragement as well. Kid swallowed a hardening lump in his throat, then stepped through, holding the image of the rooftop nest in his mind's eye.

An oscillating cascade of rainbow light surrounded him—what one might imagine the inside of a fiber optic cable looks like to a careening photon. All the previous sounds and sensory input evaporated—the sound of their feet on the stone as they shuffled about, the flickering light from The Stream, the distant murmur of commerce from Middlemost, and the slight arid wind tugging at their clothes. It all disappeared, replaced with a rushing static electric storm.

———

Then, he was somewhere new.

Wherever it was, it was dark. But not like before, not like outer space. More like early morning in a room with blackout curtains. And musty enough to gag. Mothballs, old wood, old paper. Something like fur pushed against his face, accompanied by a jangle of steel wire. Dust tickled his nasal passage, making him sneeze. The sound was strangely comforting in the small space. Then he heard a high-pitched scratching, like needles on wood.

56
LOCKED

Thanks to their vessels being near one another, Poe and Linh could share the traversal coin and jump back out of The Dream like the old pros they were, quickly and without interstitial incident. His animus landed in a dimly lit transference room, and Linh's returned to her vessel in a medical ward bed.

Poe sat up, pulled the IV out of his arm, and checked the bag's contents. It was completely gone, and the trash didn't have any empties. The telltale sign of how long he'd been down was the fact that he had to piss like a racehorse but had not already wet himself—which put it at eight or so hours. Fun fact, the human bladder can hold about a liter, depending, and it felt like he had all of that. He didn't feel like he could wait another millisecond, but Linh's situation was dire—he needed to get to her fast before Dagan could do his worst. So what if he pissed his pants? He'd rather that be the funny story they told over drinks later rather than not having the drinks at all.

He willed his bladder to hang on another few minutes and trotted to the door portal window, craning his neck to see as far as possible down each end of the corridor. It looked empty enough. He tried the handle, found it unlocked, and counted his luck. Poe stepped out like it was his business to do so, into the hallway and down the direction toward Linh's room. Not a soul in sight. As he passed other door windows, he glanced into the rooms. The beds were filled with sleeping students, many holding two, and several nurses were passed out on the floor. Things were falling apart very quickly now.

With the bright lights, institution-style hallway, and a complete absence of other humans, the vibe was sinister. The ward was never loud, but now the quiet felt deep and final.

Poe came to a doorway connecting the two hallways of the different wings and used his keycard to open it. It worked, a good sign. Either he was still trusted enough that his card hadn't been blocked or, the more likely scenario, anyone who would deactivate it was distracted or in a coma. For the short term, he was cool with either situation. They might actually pull off this suicide mission.

He came to Linh's room and tried the door. Locked.

Poe tried his keycard, and the terminal *Neee-Naah'd* while flashing a red light. The viewport curtain was closed, but the way the fabric ruffled, he could see a good measure of the floor. Haphazard shadows moved across it.

He knocked. No response.

He knocked again, louder.

"Come back later!" Someone growled.

No, not just someone. It was Dagan.

Poe heard Linh shout, followed by the clatter of falling

GARRETT GODSEY

equipment and shattering glass. He stepped back and gave the door a hard kick, but it was reinforced steel with a sturdy electronic deadbolt, and his boot barely caused a quiver.

Linh shouted again, in pain or surprise or attack; Poe couldn't tell which. He stepped back, exasperated, looking up and down the hallway, hoping for some guardian angel of a solution to present itself.

Nothing appeared, and he knew nothing would.

57
FEAST

Light shining from a gap under the door guided Kid's way as he pushed himself through the jumble of coats in what he'd gathered was a dark walk-in closet.

Poe had said that if Kid didn't focus well enough he might end up far away from his intended landing spot. He was shooting for his rooftop nest, but this was obviously not it. Kid hoped that, wherever this closet was, it was reasonably close to downtown San Francisco. Time would tell.

He grabbed an octagonal glass door knob and snuck out. The scratching thing turned out to be a cat, which immediately rubbed itself against his ankles. Other than the mewling animal, the room was silent and seemed empty. But then, before he saw it, he smelled it—stale urine and body odor. Someone was in bed and they'd been there a long time.

Protruding from the blanket-covered mound were the remains of a naked brown foot. It was almost half gone, covered in layers of dry and fresh blood, surrounded by red stains. He had no time to waste, but he couldn't shake the fact that this person needed help. If they weren't dead yet, they would be soon. He couldn't leave them. Whoever it was, he noted that they oddly had the blanket pulled up over their head.

"Hey," He called out.

His voice sounded odd now that he was back in what he assumed and hoped was the real world. It was as if the air had a different density, causing his voice to carry farther. It was like the difference after popping your ears by plugging your nose and blowing.

pOp

"Hey," Kid said again as he moved closer. "You all right or what?" A sense of déjà vu hit him, remembering the old man's body in Chinatown. Cities were stacks of brick and wood shoeboxes. How many lay quiet as this?

They didn't respond, so he pulled the blanket down from the head. She was an older black woman, maybe sixty, with puffy white hair sticking out from under a silk net to keep it in good shape while she slept. Kid imagined she had a name like Shirley or Edna. She looked terrible but not dead. He placed his fingers against her throat to register a pulse. After a long time, he felt one, but it was very faint. Just like Linh's had been. Another sleeper whose animus fell to The Void. Another confused and angry ghost joined the storm.

The cat meowed again. Kid looked down at the animal and, with horror, put the clues together. The rust-red stains around its mouth, the missing half foot, the blood on the sheets and blankets. The cat was eating its owner—toe by toe.

"Ah gross, man," Kid said, stumbling back. He wasn't sure

how this was so much more disgusting than the other stuff he'd seen, but it was. He spotted a charging cell phone on the woman's nightstand. Figuring it would be a waste of time but wanting to try anyway, he picked it up and called 911.

You've reached San Francisco 9-1-1 Emergency Services. All lines are currently busy. Please hold, and we will be with you shortly.

"Yeah, right." Kid put the phone down and noticed the lightning bolt icon blinking. It was charging. Which meant the city still had power. That wouldn't last much longer.

He looked at the sleeping woman and the cat again. Time was running fast, and he knew it, but he did what he could. He rushed to leave a glass of water by her bed and did his best to bandage her foot with some alcohol and gauze he found in the bathroom. He shut the door as he left to protect her sleeping body from other scavengers. There were a couple cans of Fancy Feast in a cupboard, and he opened them up. The cat dove in like a fiend and finally stopped harassing him.

After a final glance inside, he left the apartment with the door ajar so the cat could get out. Feeling the lack of time press in on him from all sides, Kid sprinted down three flights of stairs, using the stair railing to whip around each landing. He popped out from the heavy front door and stopped short in a skid. Despite Poe's warning and his own deduction, the intensity of the crisis was dumbfounding.

Judging by the light, it was daytime, moving toward dusk, maybe four or five. It should have been busy. Rush hour, people returning from work, buying groceries at the corner stores, and hitting local dive bars for happy hour.

Instead, dozens of cars and one Muni bus were strewn

about, none moving—no severe damage or fires, as if they simply drifted away from the thoroughfare. Drivers slumped over steering wheels and against headrests. Sidewalks strewn with scattered sleeping bodies.

Pigeons and rats dined on the street side buffet.

A block down, he saw a survivor wandering around, zigging this way and that. Kid called to them, but they didn't respond, just stared at him shellshocked before stumbling away.

Mass comas and impending infrastructure collapse. Over the years, Kid had wandered into a few survivalist-prepper internet rabbit holes obsessed with Shit Hits The Fan scenarios. He never thought he'd witness one first-hand.

This could be The End. Capital letters. The Big One.

Kid ran his hand over his hair, spun around, and sighed, then took stock of his surroundings, working to figure out exactly where he was. He had been aiming for his rooftop nest to grab some supplies. The angle of the streets, style of buildings, and the sidewalk condition let him know he was close—in the Tenderloin, not far from Market Street. He ran to a corner and spotted La Jefecita laundromat, where the cabbie Jamaal had picked him and Alice up before heading to The Sand. He knew exactly where he was now and started running.

58

GOUGE

Linh's eyes fluttered open to find Dagan stroking himself, watching from the long shadows cast by the single dim table lamp. Next to the light lay his shirt, belt, and gun.

He saw her wake, and before she had a chance to move her aching body, he was on top of her—pinning her down, working to shuffle the bedsheet away and expose her naked body. The thin fabric was the only thing defending her, but it wasn't stopping him from working toward entry, linen and all. Linh bucked her hips to push him up, gaining a small gap to work with.

She kneed Dagan with all she had.

Right in his flopping sack.

It didn't do a thing.

He renewed his grip on her wrists as his face turned red from the absorbed pain. Dagan's grimace turned into a rarely seen smile, the one with a dead grey tooth. Spittle hung from the corner of his mouth like egg white as he said,

"Do it again, you fucking bitch. I like it. And by the way, your hair was better before, more youthful." He licked his lips with a darting tongue. "I hope you didn't change it on my account."

Somebody knocked on the door and jiggled the handle.

Dagan turned to scream at the door, "Come back later!"

In the moment his face was turned away, Linh worked her legs up between his, positioning her feet under his abdomen. Before he could move them out of the way again, she kicked with all her might, launching him backward into medical equipment with a crash. A porcelain coffee mug fell to the tile floor, shattering into gleaming fragments.

She had her moment. It would be short, and she knew she would not find another.

Despite its decades of rust, her martial training kicked in, and without wasting a millisecond, she leaped up, stark naked, taking the bed sheet with her. She flew through the air and twisted the sheet into a thick cord. After landing on Dagan's back, Linh wrapped the makeshift garrote around his neck.

As she pulled the sheet tighter and worked her legs around his waist to keep him on the ground, she heard heavy kicks against the door.

It was Poe.

She felt him there, just like she had sensed things in the old days during her time as navigator of The Dream. All the action was waking things up in her.

Unfortunately, Poe's kicks did nothing, and she was alone.

Linh tightened the bedsheet and her legs with as much strength as she could muster. If Dagan were allowed to stand, nothing would stop him from smashing her around like a rag doll, and she would be finished.

Dagan choked out a *GHURK!* as he struggled without air and slung punches behind his head. Most glanced off the sides of Linh's skull as she hid it behind his, but a few connected, exploding stars in her vision.

She held fast.

As he drifted closer to unconsciousness, his exploring hands found the handle of the broken coffee mug.

Dagan stabbed wildly with the makeshift weapon. The jagged glass cut hectic gouges in the flesh of her thighs, and they bled profusely. She shouted in pain and held on. But the blood was making the hold of her legs around his waist slippery. She needed to end this now, or he would escape.

Linh had one more trick up her sleeve, a technique she had never used, having always been unwilling to harm another living creature so wholly. It was a dark art Mara had taught her long ago. But now, at this moment, she burdened herself with no guilt. To continue, to find Bian, she would utterly destroy Dagan.

The sheet dropped around his chest as Linh let go. He wasn't expecting that, and for a few puzzled seconds, he stopped stabbing. Dagan dropped the weapon and worked to position his feet so he could stand. But at that moment, Linh placed her hands on his head directly over his temples. She focused everything she had into a diamond point, an animus explosion aimed at the center of the monster's skull. It would cost her decades of life, but expended animus could be cast to form a psionic dagger.

Linh snarled, "Your turn," as she penetrated his mind.

They screamed in unison, creating an eerie harmony, then Dagan collapsed. His neck and throat turned a bruised crimson as the hemorrhage expanded down his spinal cord, and a mixture of blood and liquified grey matter oozed from his nostrils, tear ducts, mouth, and ears.

Linh struggled out from under his weight and stood. She shook with adrenaline, pain, surprise, elation, and a million other sensations with no names—emotions that can only be understood by those who have survived. The things veterans of chaos share with each other, and only each other, in the basements of churches and YMCAs around the world.

With hands clenched in fists and naked body shining with the war paint of her blood, she shouted, long and loud, cleansing herself via primal vocal projection.

She was the Silver Doe. And she was fierce.

59
TRIPWIRE

From his rooftop stash spots, Kid collected gear for the fight ahead. He stuffed it all into a single-strap dry bag, which he slung cross-ways over his chest. It had a sturdy buckle like a car seatbelt that latched with a *SNICK*. Remembering one last thing, Kid dug into a cubby hole and pulled out an old spark plug. Rather than re-opening the dry bag, he shoved the bit of porcelain into his front pocket.

For what would likely be the last time, Kid surveyed the trappings of his rooftop sanctuary. A treasure trove of books, music, gear, and vintage concert t-shirts he had spent way too much money on. Foggy and cold as shit sometimes, but undeniably beautiful. Especially now as the sun set, bouncing its halcyon light off the glass mosaic of a dying city.

Something on his hammock glimmered.

A strand of platinum hair.

It was Alice's.

Did she make it back? Had she found her so-called freedom? Or was she still lost in Mara's psychic prison, convincing herself that inherited loyalty was more powerful than the need for true liberty? He held the hair up, letting it dance in the breeze. With a sad smile, he let it go and watched it float away in the wind. His heart stung with a now familiar heat like a transplanted cinder.

Following the sting was the voice of a dark interloper.

You could leave, Kid. Cut out and hit the road. With your new abilities, you can do anything, be anything, anywhere you want. Colorado? That's some pubescent bullshit, and you know it. You're bigger than that now. Bigger than Mara, bigger than Linh, Alice, or Poe. Finally, you could have control. Safety. Power.

The thoughts tasted dark and sweet.

The idea of leaving was enticing, as it always had been.

Escape and survival. His first skills and oldest friends, comforting him since he could walk. Would he disregard his first allies now, in the final hour? Those who never neglected him? The attributes which had protected him in his darkest moments? He knew that the answer was yes. He would leave them behind because they were not allies.

After recently gaining some mastery over that part of himself, he understood. The tools of Kid's early deliverance had mutated into the engines of his disrepair. It was long past time to abandon old wounds. The path is forward, not away—even if it means leaping bare-ass naked into the dark.

"Final dance of the midnight hour."

Kid spun around so fast that his legs tangled up, and he nearly fell. Horacio.

"It is always such a tough call isn't it?" Asked the golden-eyed guardian of wanderers. "I believe The Clash said it best. Should I stay, or should I go?" He swung in Kid's hammock, one leg dangling. Even in the form of a man, he seemed feline. He wore golden eye shadow, faded jeans, black cowboy boots, and a loose floral patterned button-up shirt. "Lovely spot you've got."

Kid couldn't decide if he was happy or irritated to see him again. "Where the hell have you been?"

Horacio clasped his hands behind his head as he watched the dusking cityscape. "I've been busy. And it appears you have also been."

"We could have used your help. The beach alone almost killed us."

"Almost," Horacio replied. "Could have used and needed to become are two entirely different things."

"Needed to become?" Kid grew frustrated, eyes suddenly shining with held-back tears. "Why didn't you tell me? About Linh and my mom? About Mara?"

Horacio replied, "Anger without context, without knowledge, is worthless and dangerous. There were things you first needed to see. Now your rage has shape. Hot steel becomes blade, and now you're ready. Before, you were not. You know this, yes?"

As usual, Horacio was infuriating and cryptic but correct.

"Yeah," Kid replied, reluctantly stifling his temper.

"Thus, we have it. Our gambit. Where skill, strategy, and a lavish helping of luck intersect."

"Glad you showed up then," Kid said. "It sounds like you have a plan."

"Don't be shy. As do you. Let's hear yours first."

"Poe and Linh are inside already. So is Alice, I guess, but I'm not sure whose side she's on, but we're hoping to get her back. I'm going to sneak in and join them, and together, we'll kill Mara."

"Not lacking in bravery, at least. It's a good plan."

"It is?" Kid raised a skeptical brow. "Not gonna lie, thought it seemed desperate."

"It is that. But it's a good plan. Despairing times often call for foolhardy measures." Horacio sat up in the hammock to address Kid directly. "You see, Old Inanna has only two weaknesses. One is her ego, as with most heads of empire. You could as well walk in the front door. But that may raise suspicion. Better to act like you think you may succeed. She will find that amusing. Ultimately, Mara is curious about you and will bring you close. She knows what you are and how to harness your animus to bring the end of The Dream as recklessly as possible. But what she does not know is who you have become."

"What, this dark power?"

"Indeed. Your animus has bonded with the core of The Void. Unprecedented. Powerful. Just the right size and shape of blade to slide between Mara's armor plate. It's said a rivener is a shard of the First Dreamer's crystallized blood. She who fell after birthing our universe. The Void is her womb."

"But, Mara has the knife..."

"The same material that made the blade flows inside you, now, Mister Thames. You gained some skill with it during your time in the abyss, but you must master this ancient ken further, or it will devour you."

"What would happen... if it did?"

"It would leave in its wake a creature far worse than any you've encountered thus far. Even I venture forth no assumption of what you are capable. You feel it, don't you? Gnawing, growing, suggesting selfish things."

"Yes..." Kid twitched at the admission but avoided staying on that topic. "You said Mara had two weaknesses. What's her second?"

"Her second weakness is that which she has created and that which she seeks to destroy—The Dream itself, as well as its wound. There is more, but... First, do you trust me?"

He nodded.

"And do you trust yourself?"

Kid was slower to respond to that question, but eventually, he replied the same with a more subtle tilt of his chin.

Horacio studied Kid's half-black eye.

"Good. And have you the sight now? Can you see the rift?" Horacio glanced toward downtown; his face pinched into a scowl.

Kid followed his gaze but saw nothing strange aside from a gathering storm and shook his head to the negative.

"No, not yet," Horacio said. "But you will." His irises rippled like a wind-blown pond as he considered his next words.

"I am no key. I am no sword. But you are. And because Mara knows this, her ambitions have grown to a universal scale. Before, she was satisfied with the ending of man. Now she wants to bring a close to reality itself. She seeks to rip the First One's womb."

Kid replied, "If that's true, why would we risk it? Why would we still go?"

"Into the maw of the storm? Because what she does *not* know, or is too arrogant to accept, is that you are the key to *both* sides of the door: her success or her downfall. You always have been a child of The Dream. Now you are more. Your power and that of the rivener are all that can stop her and seal the rift for good.

But they are also exactly what she needs to succeed quickly and decisively. We play a dangerous end-game maneuver. If we run away, we will simply continue this path of long-form degradation. It is slower, but the result is the same. You've seen it in The Animus Mundi. The decay of The Dream. The slow death. And it won't stop there. It cannot. You see it here already with the comatose.

The Materia and the Animus are the same. One feeds the other. They are linked and must be rebalanced, or it all falls down. Our path is righteous—laid by the sacrifices of your mother, your father, and many others. You must finish it."

Despite the dark wanderings of his void-touched heart, it was true. Kid knew he had to try. He had come too far and lost too much. For Linh—the warmth and the home she shared with him. For his mother—everything she sacrificed, the last threads of her soul. He would do it for his father—for everything he gave him, despite never having known him. He would do it for Alice and Poe as well. He knew they deserved it. They were worthy of life, choice, and a chance at redemption.

Kid replied, eyes shining, mouth set, "I'll do my best."

"You must. Now, let's talk tactics."

"That will be our moment," Horacio finished. "You will see it, the doorway no one else could—not an ancient nor Dream Dreaming."

Tin cans jingled, and Kid turned to check it out.

"You'll want to make a quick exit now," Horacio said. "Stage left, as it were. That'll be Old Ten Head's men come-a-knocking, searching for their lost loot. We nearly forgot about them amidst the fuss! Goodbye for now, Mister Thames. I hope to see you soon. If not, perhaps our paths will cross again in another universe."

Kid glanced back to say goodbye to Horacio, but the man was already gone. The hammock swung gently in his absence.

The makeshift property alarm did its job. Someone cursed at their accidental noise-making and discarded any further attempt at stealth. Boots crunched across asphalt. Who was it this time? Old Ten Head? Who the hell was that?

"Kid! We know you're in there! Come on out, and there won't be trouble! We got you surrounded. No need for mayhem."

His breath quickened, and his heart raced, but he stayed silent.

"Come on now, it's your old pal Ben. You didn't forget about me, did you?"

Kid *had* forgotten about the man. Almost completely. With the compressed time spent in The Void, it had been a good while since he'd thought of the Lotus men hunting him.

Fuck.

Ben continued, "You did, didn't you? Ah shucks, well, my feelings are hurt, but that's alright. I got thick skin. We can go back to how it was, scout's honor! You liked that, didn't you? How it was before?"

The offer would have been tempting in the past, before the failed job and the adventure into The Dream. But this was a new life, however brief it might turn out to be, and a new Kid. But even with his abilities, he couldn't handle armed men. To save his friends, Kid needed to escape.

He stayed quiet, not wanting to give away his exact position. The plywood walls blocked the wind and the view of him, but they would not stop a hail of machine gun fire.

"Come on," Ben continued, "I already took it up the chain. We think it's time for you to move up in the world. No more street running. We're talking real work! How's that sound? You ready to level up? The boss even heard of you. I don't know how you managed to get on his radar, but there you are. You got the makings of a lieutenant. Get yourself a real apartment and stop sleeping up here like a pigeon. Get you something nice. Chicks, money, threads—the whole shebang!"

The crunch of footsteps fanned out around his position, closing in.

60

WHITE

Whatever bullshit story Ben was trying to sell was off the table now. He and his men were silent. Kid considered the backup second "exit." Through the side door fifteen feet away, he had tied off, coiled, and hidden a rope for this type of desperate occasion. He had imagined using it to escape the police on his ass for some civic infraction, not a swat team of organized criminals. Either way, that's what it was there for, same with the trip wire. Both were doing their job today. He could repel down if he could make it to the building's edge without getting shot.

There was no time to consider.

Kid set his back foot, tensed his body, and sprinted.

As soon as his leading boot hit the roof gravel, automatic gunfire erupted. It punched holes in the plywood wall and shattered the atrium around him in large crashing shards.

He reached the door and shouldered it open at a run. At this speed, his only workable plan was to slide, grab the rope, then jump. Right over the edge. Seven stories. Without enough time for safety, he'd have to wrap the rope around his forearm during free fall. It'd likely yank his arm out of the socket, but if he could hang on, he might live. If that failed, there were bushes, grass, and mounds of dirt in the overgrown courtyard below. Unlikely he would survive the fall. But it wasn't concrete... So, maybe.

CRACK!

Assault rifle across the head.

Ben was waiting, the reckless plan destined to fail. Lights out.

"Where is it?" Ben asked with his trademark lazy-eyelid, no-eyebrow stare.

"Don't got it, man." Warm blood ran down Kid's neck from a pulsing wound.

"Bullshit," Ben spat. "You know you got it. Where's it at?"

Kid's dry bag hung slack in Ben's hand, its contents dumped onto the sagging rooftop—another crowbar, lock-picks, and a bunch of Fourth-of-July smoke bombs. He planned on sneaking into The School by creating a diversion of car alarms and smoke. So much for that.

There were three men, all armed. Ben, a guy with a patchy desperado mustache, and another with sunken eyes. They stood around Kid in a loose circle.

"That's a lotta iron for a little guy," Kid said.

Ben ignored him and turned to the desperado. "Lando, go find it. Turn the place over. Steeze, give him a hand."

"Yeah, boss," Lando said as the two men jogged to the atrium.

Ben turned back to Kid and studied him, lazy-lidded eye taking it all in. "Yeah. Better too much heat than not enough, right?" He sighed theatrically. "We coulda been great, Kid. You had potential. You know that? But you threw it away. What'd you do that for?"

Kid's head rang, and he winced as a piercing headache thumped behind his eyeballs. "Guess I'm an entrepreneur at heart."

"What, on your own? You're a dinghy, and we're a rocket ship. You wanna be on the rocket, Kid. Don't you know that?"

"I like my little boat." Kid spat out some of the blood collecting in his mouth and shrugged his shoulders to shift the plastic zip-ties holding his hands together behind his back.

"Not too comfy, right? It don't gotta be like this, you know. You could be comfy. I can make that happen. Just tell me where it's at."

An idea occurred to Kid. Enemy of my enemy. If he could pit Ben and his crew against Mara, it might be just the distraction he needed. Better than smoke bombs, at least. But he needed to resist long enough to make it believable. He also needed to make it out alive.

"If I tell you, you'll kill me."

Ben screamed, "I'LL KILL YOU IF YOU DON'T!" He stuffed the rage and replaced it with a whisper, "Kid..." He breathed deeply and let it out slowly. "Where's the fucking box?"

Not having to bluff fear, Kid replied, "Okay, okay, shit. Take it easy, alright? Ben, see, it's gone, man. Stolen. Some freaky teens with black eyes. I'm talking demonic-looking shit. They took it."

The grunts returned, and Ben glanced at their empty hands and shaking heads. Lando said, "Dumped the place, couple hidey-holes, some cash, and a bunch of bullshit. Nothing special. No box. Zilch."

Ben was the type of guy whose calm was more threatening than his rage. Like a coiled snake, it meant impending action. He said, in a near-whisper, "Tell me about 'em—the black-eyed fucks."

Kid sensed if he didn't give him something now, he'd be dead.

"I don't know, man. At first, I thought they might be crackheads or something. But they didn't move like bobbleheads. They were too fast. Trained like little soldiers. I barely got out with my ass intact. Guess they're the ones who got your other runner, right? Makes sense. They killed the drop man too. I had to jump off a roof to get away. Almost died. Like several times. I tried. I really did."

Ben leaned in, "Almost died?"

Kid nodded.

"Tell a guy who gives a fuck." Then, with evident curiosity, "What'd they say?"

"Not much, just wanted the box."

"Nothing?"

Kid pretended to think. "Wait, yeah. I remember because it was like a religious cult or something. Said they were going home to Mother."

"I knew it!" Lando scoffed.

Steeze added, "That tricky bitch always startin' shit.

What'd I say, Ben? Had to be Mara. Had to be. Think all this crazy sleep-shit going down is her too?" He fidgeted with a silver ring on his pinky finger. They all had one. "These keepsakes better keep working man. All I'm saying."

Ben's shrugged but didn't say anything more.

Kid filled the silence, "Alright? That's all I got. I swear. I was just trying to stay alive. We can go our separate ways. You'll never see me again."

He glanced him over. "Yeah, okay. Sure, Kid."

The look gave Kid goosebumps. He felt like a piece of meat on a grill. The craving in Ben's eyes was clear as day. A pit in Kid's stomach knew what was next, even if his forebrain hadn't completely acknowledged it.

"No hard feelings." Ben lifted his assault rifle; something about how he held it lazily, like a TV remote. He pointed it at Kid and asked, "Head or gut?"

"What?" Kid asked stupidly.

A guy always wishes he'll have something better to say in a crucial moment, but what comes out is often simple and dumb. Something like, what? Huh? His heart raced, wrists struggling against the thick plastic ties.

"We're friends, aren't we? Friends get to pick. So what'll it be? Head or gut?"

Lando said, "Head's quick, but that's the bitch-way. Gut's got honor, but it ain't no fun. Which're you? Bitch-made or not?"

Kid struggled and managed to get to his knees.

No, not yet. I can't go yet, he thought.

They're waiting for me. They need me.

I need them.

I can't go! Not yet!

Steeze chuckled, "Look at him. He's scared."

Kid growled, "Motherfucker, I'm not scared. It's just—I'm not done, man. I got things to do. I got people."

"You?" Ben asked. "What the hell you got to do? What people you got? You got nothing, you fuckin' gutter punk. Here, lemme pick for you." Ben leveled the rifle barrel at the middle of Kid's forehead. "Bitch-made."

If this was the moment, so be it. Kid had been under the boot of a great many assholes in his life, and he wasn't about to act like the punk they were calling him out to be now. There would be no shaking, no begging, no crying, or pissing.

He sat still and let the steel barrel rest against his head— still warm from firing.

At first, Kid held his eyes open, which felt like the brave thing to do. But he quickly realized that he didn't want the last thing he saw in this world to be Ben's lopsided face. He closed them and was surprised by the first image that came to him.

Afternoon light coming in from a storefront window.
Lush and full of color.
White shell-top Adidas with blue stripes.
A wall painted bubblegum pink.
Alice.
Dancing in the La Jefecita laundromat.
The light shone through her hair, dyed platinum-blonde.
It flowed like long strands of Christmas tinsel.
She moved gracefully to music he couldn't hear.
She was mercury.

She was melting ice.
She was beautiful.
So, this is life flashing.
All right then.
That'll do.

Ben chuckled. "Good. Go out grinnin. That's how men do it."

The rifle fired, and the sound echoed strangely—the fact of an echo, rather than instant death, stranger still. A high-pitched ringing filled the air.

Light, bright white, exploding in all directions, shining from the epicenter that was Kid. Stutter. Squeeze. Stretch.

Tsch tsch tsch tsch.

That's the sound time makes when it breaks.

Tsch tsch tsch tsch.

In the span of a breath, everything was gone—most of the roof, bricks, plywood, glass, weathervane bent by old lightning, calcified pigeon guano, gravel, books, blood, and bone, and a swinging mobile made of stained glass memories, along with Ben, Lando, and Steeze. All were reduced to dust, flying outward from the focal point of a young man. One golden eye and one liquid black.

An embryo, awakened.

Without a roof to hold him any longer, Kid broke through. The wind whipped and tugged his clothes as he watched the obliterated rooftop shrink from the size of the sky to a room and finally to a pinhole.

PART SEVEN
STARBALAST

"Either this is madness or it is Hell." "It is neither," calmly
replied the voice of the Sphere, "it is Knowledge; it is Three
Dimensions: open your eye once again and try to look
steadily."

— EDWIN A. ABBOTT, FLATLAND: A
ROMANCE OF MANY DIMENSIONS

61

FOOL

"Where the hell is he?" Poe paced back and forth across the concrete loading bay, his voice and boots echoing off the cavernous space. The old Ford Torino was still parked nearby, its dark blue paint shining purplish under the artificial light. "He should have been here by now. Do you think he ran?"

"No," Linh replied. "I do not." She had reclaimed her clothes and cleaned up.

There were still splatters of blood along her hairline, which Poe was afraid to tell her about. He found the combination of super-long silver hair and crimson droplets disturbing, intimidating, and unexpectedly attractive. Like some sort of magical, albino lioness after a kill. He no longer thought "Doe" was an accurate code name. Poe's eyes darted back and forth from the car to the elevator doors and then to the direction of the parking garage from which Kid should have already arrived.

"Your car is looking pretty good right now, isn't it?" Linh asked. There was no sarcasm or judgment in her voice.

"Big time. Full tank and fresh rubber. We could get out of here, you know. Make a run for it. Bonnie and Clyde, we ain't, but still could do."

"I ran once. And that was too much." Linh said as she studied his worrying face. "But you could leave if you want. You're free now. Free as it gets anyway. No baggage, no chain. I wouldn't hold it against you. I understand."

"Forget it," Poe sighed. "I'm not going anywhere."

"No?"

"No. And maybe I'll live long enough to regret it."

<hr />

They waited another thirty excruciating minutes. One kept nervous eyes on the elevator, ready to bolt if they heard the telltale sound of the lift coming up the well. The other watched the loading bay entrance, hoping against hope for Kid's arrival.

When they were coming close to giving up, footsteps approached, echoing in the underground parking lot.

Their hearts swelled.

But it wasn't Kid.

It was Alice.

She still wore the vintage David Bowie t-shirt with bright red Japanese characters emblazoned across it. With eyes wide, Linh recognized Kid's shirt and, despite the span of years, her lost daughter.

"Bian..." she said breathlessly.

But something was off. Alice's face was slightly slack and devoid of emotion. She tilted her head in surprise. But it was the wrong kind. More, *Oh, you know?* Rather than, *Oh, it's you.* With a corner-curve smile, she said, "That is not *my* name, Doe."

Half a dozen men filed in behind her, making a V-wing formation. They were clad in black tactical gear, faces covered in full masks like chiseled onyx skulls. Poe and Linh knew them well. The vassal-guardian class didn't talk or think; they just did—impervious to empathy pushes and fully trained to deal with travelers. From the necks of a few, silver necklaces peeked out—small totems protecting them from the void sleep. But it was overkill. Their animi were already shelled to create fortified soldiers. Poe and the rest of the students always called them 'dims.' As if The Young School's education caste was above them in some way, something other than slaves themselves.

The elevator dinged and slid open, revealing another six of the black-skull soldiers. They piled out and fanned around with drawn pistols.

Linh and Poe were trapped.

Fool's errand, Poe thought as he spat on the ground and prepared for his last battle. Linh was less ready to fight, caught off guard by the sight of her daughter. The lack of familial recognition, the seeming absence of even a desire for it, was like a punch to her gut. She grimaced and fought back tears.

Alice turned to Poe. "You've had your playtime. Come along now."

Poe's eyes widened, and he cursed under his breath. It

wasn't Alice they were talking to. It was Mara. It was no surprise the woman inspired so many myths of gods over the millennia. Tiamat, the agent of chaos. Isis, the goddess of children and the dead. And, of course, her favorite: Inanna, the ancient Sumerian goddess of war, sex, fertility, and power.

She was the only known human who could take a vessel without emptying her own. Using a technique called dissension, Mara could leave shards of herself in uncountable vessels, ready to take over at her command.

Perhaps she really was a god.

Poe knew then that he should have jumped in the Torino when he had the chance. He didn't know if the old Ford would outrun an angry deity, but he could have at least tried. That chance was long gone now. What did Tom say in his final minutes? *If you manage to break the chain, stay the hell away. For good. Because if you go back, you're done all over again. She's got gravity. Bitch is a black hole.*

No matter, Poe thought. *I've always been a fool.*

He raised his pistol and said, "Come on, then."

———

They fought hard and managed to take out four dims, but they were severely outmanned, outgunned, and eventually subdued. Six remaining soldiers took their weapons and pushed them toward the elevator.

Mara's-shard-as-Alice stayed behind and gave Linh a knowing wink as she passed by. Watching the ancient woman use her daughter's vessel added a new white hot layer to Linh's purpose—yet she remained calm, boiling rather than exploding. She would wait for the opportune moment and hoped it would come soon.

After the elevator shut, Mara left the body of her protégé with a few final words.

The boy will be here soon.

Bring him to me.

It's time.

62

DUST

Kid tried to move and winced as his vision swam like a 3am drunk. His back screamed at the effort —but with the pain came gratitude. It proved that he was somehow, against all odds, still alive. Not dead. Not broken. Not yet.

But how?

How did I survive that fall? And the bullet?

I heard it fire.

I thought I exploded.

Staggering up, Kid stretched to his full height, his spine crackling. He grunted and gritted his teeth through the discomfort. Dusk filtered through a Kid-sized hole in the ceiling about twenty feet above him. Through that, he could see another fifteen feet through a similar puncture, then past that all the way up to a dimming splinter-framed sky.

Broken boards, concrete, and plaster surrounded him in a loose ring. It appeared his fall was miraculously broken by two floors of rotted-out framing lumber. Surviving a fall from that height? Hard to believe. Improbable. But not impossible. The big question, though—how was he alive after a point-blank bullet to the head?

Judging by the light, he'd been unconscious for a while. An hour. Maybe more. Added to the time spent on the roof and running over from the cat lady's apartment, Kid knew he was tragically late.

He found his way out of the dilapidated building, carefully avoiding rusty nails, treacherous holes, and collapsing ceiling, kicked through a blocked door, and emerged onto a quiet street. Feasting crows and seagulls scattered from a nearby body. The corpses didn't stink yet, but they would. A drone flew high above, its lonely buzz echoing in the silent city.

Quick as he could with his banged-up body, he climbed the fire escape. He needed to find his dry bag and gear. But before he reached the edge, he knew something was wrong. The way the wind whistled was different. He had made this climb so many times that he could pick up the subtle change.

The air sounded unblocked, empty, and wrong.

Worry gnawed his gut.

As his head popped above the perimeter facade, he took a raking breath. The roof was barren, like a table swept clean. Nothing remained but dust, which also blew away in the evening breeze. Careful to avoid the edge of the gaping hole through which he'd fallen, he trotted to the space where the atrium once stood to inspect the blasted area.

Nothing. Just nothing.

Fuck.

About to walk away, something occurred to him. In cold fear, he swiveled to where the Peregrines roosted, Cloud, his mate Zoe, and their two eggs. The pilgrims. Travelers. Those of a wandering sort. His friends.

He scrabbled over on his injured leg, wishing away the worst.

No no no no-nononono. Please, no.

When he arrived, he fell to his knees.

Clinging to the cornice—a single feather, grey with white markings like blotted stripes. It shivered in the wind.

He took it with great care, afraid to lose it to an errant gust, and held it gently between his thumb and pointer finger. Everything else was replaceable. His gear, money, books, at the end of the day, bullshit all of it. But not the birds. The realization of finality washed over him like a polluted tidal wave.

I did this. I don't know how, but I did this.

Revisiting his torturous foster. Destroying a man's face—perhaps not killing him outright, but damn well close enough. Slicing through a giant malformed toddler. Losing his mother. Twice.

Somehow, none compared, and none hit him like this moment.

The birds.

By his hand.

Kid cried.

Deep hitching breaths and hot streaming tears. They ran rivulets through the plaster dust caked on his face, tears pent up from a lifetime, finally released. Never had it been more true that there was no going back, not now, not ever.

How could he continue?

Everything was gone.

He was so, so late.

Poe and Linh must've given up on him already or been captured.

Or worse.

His dreams. His parents. His friends. His nest.

The world itself.

And somehow, worst of the worst, the final soul-splitting loss of it all...

The birds.

God... the birds.

The beautiful, wild things and their babies. Reduced to dust memories.

Kid continued to cry as he held the feather. It felt like it pinned him to the world, like a tack holding a ribbon. Without it, he would simply tumble off the roof. His tired, brittle bones would shatter on the dirty sidewalk below like a man made of porcelain.

Time is hard to measure in moments like that, but finally, his haggard cries slowed and stopped. His heart felt black, filled with nothing but anguish. What was the point? How could this, any of this, possibly succeed?

The remains of his tears formed liquid lenses. Through them, the light and shapes around him bent into oblong versions of themselves. Through the distortion, he noticed something reddish-brown. He wiped the tears away with the back of his hand, and what he saw filled his heart with sudden joy.

Red mottled brown. Like a river stone. Blood agate.

It was the unmistakable shell of a Peregrine falcon's egg.

Somehow, it survived the blast, rolling behind the remnants of the cornice. But it rested dangerously on the edge. As carefully as disarming a bomb, Kid crawled over and scooped up the egg. Then resting back on his knees, he held it reverently in his palms as if it were his own child.

Perhaps, in some way, it was.

Against all odds—like himself, like Linh and Alice, like the world itself—it was still alive. Precariously, probably temporarily, but stubbornly alive.

Kid clutched the egg closer to share the warmth of his body.

Then, on a whim, he tucked the grey and white feather into his jeans pocket. As he did, he rediscovered the spark plug. It was now the only tool he had left following the obliteration of his hideout. But it was something. He turned his face to the sky and squeezed out several new tears accompanied by the careful laughter of gratitude.

If this tiny, fragile thing could survive, it was a sign that The Dream still dreamed, which meant there was hope.

Kid knew the location of the local pet store well, and luckily it was on the way to The Young School. It was where he used to pick up mice to give to Cloud and Zoe on special occasions— the same place he scouted for incubators in what felt like a previous and distant reincarnation of his life.

He wanted to sprint but jogged instead, worried about the

egg. Kid held it under his shirt and busted into the shop with his shoulder, the entry bell jingling. The only employee slept behind a wooden counter, slumped over his folded arms, shaggy hair askew.

Two incubators were running to show how they worked, radiating warm yellow light. Kid placed the egg into the automatic Kebonnix machine. The device ensured correct humidity and temperature and auto-rotated the eggs inside to simulate what the parents did in the wild. He didn't know precisely why it was so important, but he knew he needed to keep the egg safe. For what might come after. Strange but true, as his father had written, the essence of The Dream.

After a final glance behind, he hurried from the store.

As he ran, he went over the plan. It felt good, even though it was probably suicide. He knew in his gut this was what he had trained for his entire life. Kid knew bullies, and that's what Mara was. You do what you have to to get in past their guard. Then you punch them in the mouth. And as Horacio said, her pride would get him close. But what would come after that? He had no clue.

You will see it, the doorway no one else could.

Kid would give himself to fate and the sacrificial wisdom of those who'd brought him this far. And he knew deep in his heart he would give his own life if necessary. If he needed to lean into his dark power, so be it. He figured he had one or two good shots before the thing inside ate his soul.

Slowing to a trot and catching his breath, Kid arrived at the corner across from the Western Knell building at New Montgomery Street and Minna. Surrounded by tall downtown commercial buildings, he stood under the green fabric eve of an Ultra Burger franchise, surrounded by several people sleeping in their plates of food. Two weren't just comatose. Judging by the pall of their skin, they were dead—suffocated in chili fries. Ants and pigeons ate the mess surrounding their faces.

From his corner position, he studied the old Art Deco building in full. It was one of the oldest skyscrapers in San Francisco, originally the headquarters of a robber-baron telecom monopoly founded in the dawn of the 1900s. Now it looked like any typical downtown office space, probably hosting nightly tech meetups.

Kid craned his neck to take in the full height of it, an imposing construction at any time, but especially so with the context of these apparent end-times. It was an ominous grey fortress, filled with baroque 1920s details, sculptures of muscled envoys carrying the world, and massive stone eagles peering down like demonic gargoyles. High above, clouds surrounded the top of the building in a dark swirling halo, a black bruise in what remained of the purple twilight.

Have you the sight now? Can you see the rift?

No, not yet. But you will.

The clouds worked to hide the otherworldly breach within their folds, but Horacio had been correct. Kid could see it now, through the supernatural sight of his stained left eye. It was a jagged rip in the heavens. As he studied it, he noticed glowing ionic streamers feeding into the rupture from all directions, near, far, and beyond the horizon. It required no great leap in logic to realize it was feeding on all the remaining animi in the surrounding area. Even without the sight, he would have felt it, a thing any creature could sense, the electrostatic barometric drop of a supercell storm. The temperature plummeted, and he shivered. It smelled like winter without pine. Barren, cold, deadly.

It was the ruined septic womb of The Void.

Erupting through The Dream to devour the world.

63

DARK

The grey feather touched Kid's lips as if in a quick prayer, and then he tucked it back in his pocket. Next, he pulled out the old spark plug and threw it against the sidewalk to shatter. He picked out the biggest shards and clasped them carefully in his hand before crossing the street to the parking garage, which led to The Young School, deep underground.

From the side of the garage entrance, he could see the guard—just one. Poe had been correct. The security was light thanks to the chaos, but not abandoned. The guard didn't seem special, paunchy gut under a white button-up shirt and long sleeve fleece with a logo of a gold shield embroidered on his chest. Despite the dad bod, he was alert and agitated—pacing back and forth, periodically checking his pistol and a silver necklace hanging from his neck.

Kid psyched himself up and pitched a broken porcelain shard at the booth's security glass. It landed on a dull side and bounced off harmlessly. As the guard noticed the sound and turned, Kid cursed under his breath and ducked back around the corner. After counting to sixty Mississippi, he peaked back around. The guard turned away again, and Kid pitched another shard of porcelain at the window. This one hit home. There was a reason they were called ninja rocks on the street —the super-hard shard of porcelain pierced the surface tension of the comparatively softer glass, shattering an area the size of a manhole cover.

The glass didn't come down entirely since it was interwoven with steel wire, but it didn't need to. As hoped, the guard shouted and ran out to inspect the damage. Kid threw another ninja rock at a car parked on the side street. Its driver's side window shattered like it'd been hit with a brick. The guard yelled and sprinted toward it, brandishing his gun and yelling obscenities in a string of colliding syllables.

With the guard distracted and turned away, Kid snuck underneath the black and yellow striped gate arm, then slid around the back of the booth, moving deeper into the garage, ducking and running behind vehicles. He made his way to the third sub-level and saw the commercial elevator loading bay that Poe had described to him, along with the old Ford Torino. Crouching next to the entrance, he peeked inside but couldn't see anyone. Kid snuck in, hunched low, calling out in a stage whisper.

"Poe! Linh! Where you at?"

Alice stepped into the loading bay entryway behind Kid, cutting off his exit. She'd been waiting to trap him. Her and two serious-looking sidekicks. He thought the two soldiers' black skull masks made them look like samurai of the dark arts, clearly those of the not-to-be-fucked-with type.

"Hey, Kid," Alice said.

Kid held his hands up, palms out, in a sign of surrender. "Nice shirt," he replied.

Alice looked down at the David Bowie t-shirt, seeming to notice it for the first time in a long while. Its bright colors contrasted surreally against her grim and pale face. She glanced back up at Kid, pausing with a thought. As quick as it was there, it was gone. Whatever it had been, she swallowed it. "Come on. You're right on time."

"You don't have to do this, Alice."

She didn't respond and turned toward the elevator and motioned the soldiers to bring Kid along. After they stepped into the elevator, she pushed brushed aluminum buttons in a long winding pattern, clearly a code to reach a typically unavailable floor. Kid's stomach lurched as the elevator raced upward rather than down.

We're going to the rift, he realized.

He watched Alice, hoping for returned eye contact, but there was none. She stood straight-backed with her face forward. The elevator was large enough that the soldiers could stand along the periphery, giving them room.

"Is this what you had in mind?" Kid asked. She didn't respond, but he saw a lump move down her throat as she swallowed. He continued, "Is this the freedom you were looking for? Or was it power you really wanted? It's all going to shit out there, Alice. Have you seen it? The fucking world is ending." He shook his head in frustration. "What's the point of power in a graveyard?"

One of the soldiers moved to subdue him, but Alice raised a hand to stay any interruptions. The whir and swoosh of floors passing by and creaking boot leather were the only sounds until Kid spoke again.

"It's not too late. We can change things."

Kid searched her face for a sign, a clue, of the old Alice, the one who kissed and danced. The girl who'd called him Quasimodo and made him like it. But she wasn't there, or she was hidden. She had the same hair, the same clothes, the same vessel. But it was window dressing over a sad store—malnourished cheeks and hollowed eyes like a youth come back from war.

"Alice... We could do something different."

The elevator stopped, and the doors slid open, revealing a long hallway walled in beautiful stained glass and grey stone, high ceilings of gothic arches, and dark hardwood support beams fit for an ancient church. Perhaps, in a way, that's exactly what it was.

Alice stepped out of the elevator and turned to face Kid. Her skin flushed as if fighting a fever, her irises dull. "We *are* doing something different. It's a second chance, don't you see? The world isn't ending. Just us, just people. This is the rebirth." The corners of her mouth turned up in a tepid smile —as if following the spoken memories of a friend too soon gone.

Kid's mouth opened to respond, but Alice turned and strode away, motioning the soldiers to bring him along, cutting off further conversation. They walked down the great hall, boots and sneakers echoing, then exited through grand double doors onto a stone catwalk.

From the roof of the Western Knell building, Kid immediately recognized the violent sky surrounding them. It was the storm from The Dream. The same typhoon from his near-death experience in The Void. Now they were in the eye of it, here in the real world, in the heart of San Francisco.

The ravenous vortex hung directly above the building like an infected wound, slashing jaggedly through the distended belly of the swollen atmosphere. Now Kid was close enough to feel it, to smell it, and with his dark left eye, to see the truth beyond a guess. Lost souls swarmed and swam from the gangrenous fissure like pale maggots.

Every hair on his body stood on end. Every cell in his body begged him to run, not away, but to the edge of the building, to leap into the air and end this cosmic horror with a speeding juncture of concrete.

It was burnt flesh and ozone.

The soul of the world turned inside out.

Pulsing electric death.

And then there was Mara.

Kid recognized her without ever having met her. The formality was unnecessary. He somehow knew her at an instinctual level. She stood at the center of an octagonal platform of grey stone. Under normal circumstances, it probably served as a helicopter landing pad. She directed black-clad soldiers to close the lids on what appeared to be large black stone coffins.

Four of the dozen containers remained open. As Kid watched a soldier close one of them, he caught sight of the inside. It held a pale, sleeping boy with messy blonde hair. In his cold dream, he looked peaceful and angelic.

Through *the sight*, Kid could see each coffin connected to the vortex above by a ribbon of squirming light. They were the strands he saw from the ground. The design was unmistakable now—Mara was attaching comatose children like daisy-chained batteries. Somehow, she was using the power of their animi to force the rift open, further and further apart, like a ratcheting rib spreader. The sky howled as it fed and grew on their stolen light.

They arrived at the platform, and the soldiers pushed Kid toward the center. Alice and the soldiers remained close by. Mara didn't turn to acknowledge them, and they did not announce their presence, instead waiting patiently and quietly for her attention. Kid took the opportunity to observe his surroundings in closer detail, his eyes widening as he caught sight of Linh and Poe, previously hidden behind their respective sarcophagi. They were beaten and kneeling, bleeding faces dropped to their chests, eyes closed. He noticed they didn't have handcuffs or any other bonding. It was like they were half asleep. The way their hands rested lax in their laps with fingers pointed up reminded him of someone nodding out after a fix.

At last, Mara turned to him.

Her long hair and silk dress fluttered like a dark flag of war.

Though he knew it was a sham, her apparent youth still surprised him. Her vessel was younger than him by at least a year or two. But her eyes betrayed her true age. How they glinted in the light of the storm revealed their ancient knowledge and primitive violence.

Mara stepped close, her nostrils flaring as she took his scent.

A smile played at the corner of her lips.

Like a sommelier naming a spice note in a glass of wine, she said with a lusty sigh, "Spiritborne..." She savored the word as she traced the shape of his skull with her eyes. "I have waited such a long time for you." Her voice infiltrated his mind unobstructed, coated in the opiate honey of a supernaturally persuasive demigod.

Alice and her soldiers stood obediently, along with the others guarding Linh and Poe. Kid counted eight of the black-clad soldiers. His friends didn't move from their head-hung positions, their wardens as motionless as statues.

Electricity of domination infiltrated his mind, muscle, and bone. He was newly certain that this was the worst of ideas and that he should've run when he had the chance, fast and far, years ago. Perhaps some distant outpost of humanity would survive, even after Mara was done with the world. Kid was surer by the second that he would never know. Here, in this place, on top of the oppressive stone skyscraper, crouched under the purple howl of the tempest, Mara was God.

She turned to Alice and said softly, "My love, it's time."

Alice reached under Kid's arm to lift him to walk. It was about ten yards to a black stone container at the center of the platform, aligned with the catwalk, and more massive than the rest. The surface reflected the light of the storm into a rainbow of morphing colors, like a pool of spilled oil. He tried to drag his feet and slow things down. With great effort, he willed himself to speak, surprised to find that he could. Despite Mara's cloud of subjugation, he had a voice.

"Mara... How could you? These children? Everyone? You're a monster. You can hide behind the youth you stole, but I can smell you. The death. Like flowers on top of roadkill. I can see your truth. You're not doing this because you're strong. You're doing it because you're afraid. And weak. And hurt. It's not too late to stop this."

Mara's mouth twitched in irritation, but she couldn't stop a genuine smile from appearing. She found herself pleasantly surprised by Kid's ability to defy her control if only to speak a few naive insults.

She replied, "I wish I were a monster. Perhaps then, I would not have hesitated as long as I have. I am merely a failed parent."

Alice moved to push Kid, but with a subtle tilt of her chin, Mara directed her to allow the moment to play out.

"No doubt I appear evil. Every mother seems the devil to a spoiled brat. Little ones don't have the foresight to understand what their parent is working toward." Mara sighed with what seemed like genuine sadness. "When you've been around as long as I have, you realize that humans are perpetual infants. They simply don't live long enough to mature." She opened her arms. "I worked to solve that too. Over millennia I helped the leaders of the world live long enough to make an attempt at gaining wisdom. Still, they did not. These children do not learn. They refuse. That which is truly invincible—the ignorance and blindness of man."

Mara walked past Kid and Alice to the sarcophagus and slid the lid to the side with surprising ease. It looked like it weighed several hundred pounds. As she worked, she continued, "Look at the state of our home. Chaos, poverty, pollution, war, slavery, gluttony, and the extinction of nearly every other species. These children run amok."

She motioned to Alice to bring Kid to the open casket.

"Truly, calling you children is too kind. I have watched humanity's insufferable nature and penchant for destruction since long before there were even words to describe such things." Kid now close, she took his face in her hand. She was close enough to smell her breath. It smelled of honeysuckle and wet earth. Decay. But also rebirth. Through the scent of sweet, wet earth, she spoke.

"Nothing has ever changed save the efficacy of his weapons. To grow, devour, and destroy, respecting no equilibrium, bounds, or even the host's health. By definition, you are not even a parasite. You are a virus. Now that I have the rivener and you, spiritborne, the world may be cleansed and allowed to heal. Without the sin and baggage of the human disease."

Kid tried to reply, to speak, to utter something, anything, but his flash of autonomy was gone. From a sheath hidden within the folds of her dress, Mara pulled out the rivener, its black blade swallowing all the light around it. Despite the difference in reflectivity of it and the sarcophagus, it was clear they were carved from a similar material.

The crystalized birth blood of the First Dreamer.

Is that where he was going now? Back to the womb of origin?

From behind Kid, Alice slid her hands under his arms. For a fleeting instant, it felt intimate, big spoon and little spoon. Then she pulled his arms apart, exposing his chest. He told his body to struggle, but it refused.

Alice whispered in his ear, "Part of me loved you, Kid. I'm sorry."

Before he could consider what he'd heard, Mara stepped forward.

Smiling as serenely as always, she kissed him on the forehead—laying her claim to his soul. Then she slid the rivener directly into his heart.

The void shard cut like a shadow into fog, without resistance, without friction. His eyes widened, but not from pain, from cold. It was worse than biting, worse than freezing. It was the absolute zero of the vacuum of deep space. As his animus separated from his vessel, what followed the cold was emptiness. He felt himself detach from the part of him that loved and hoped, hated and feared. His spirit was separating and untethering—its strand severed.

I don't like the dark. I don't wanna be down there no more.

64
STORM

Mara grasped Alice's shoulder and guided her to a mirrored version of Kid's coffin, one among a dozen, arranged like the petals of a black daisy. Three remained open. One each—for her, Linh, and Poe. Had Mara planned the event to this level of detail? Or could any student of The Young School have filled the animus batteries? Impossible to say. But as the minutes ticked by, it was clear the situation was going badly. After they shut Kid in, vibrations began. A harmonic rumble emanated from the sarcophagi, shaking the air and stone hard enough to numb feet.

Alice's shoes scuffed the stone platform as she walked. The sound seemed strangely loud. It seemed to say that, perhaps, a flicker of resistance still survived within her. Mara noticed but didn't react, simply moving her hand to the small of Alice's back to continue pushing her ahead, like a stubborn child to bed after a bathroom visit late at night.

With much effort, Alice squeezed out a whisper,

"Mother... I'm scared. I don't think..." She swallowed and pushed, forcing another few words to escape her mouth, "This isn't what I wanted." From some small place in her heart, her soul struggled to break free. Alice felt for a fleeting moment that she made progress. Blinking, focusing, inch by hard-fought inch.

But Mara shoved back, entering Alice's psyche through her dream like smoke through an open window—suffocating, all-encompassing. "What you want? I know something more important. I know what you *need*. Remember, this is everything we've worked toward for a thousand of your tiny lives. We must finish what we start. It'll be over soon, and we will *all* be free."

Alice's face greyed as she lost the battle of wills and mumbled, "Free..."

Mara commanded two dims to take Linh and Poe to their containers. Neither fought back—near catatonic under Mara's dominion, kept only high enough above the threshold of comatose to remain malleable. At this close distance to Mara, whatever psychic chains had been cut made no difference. They were thralls again, walking like life-sentence inmates, accustomed to the weight of their chains. Their faces cast down, thoughts far off, lost in the past of the distant dark.

The rift widened by the second, the potent energy of Kid's spiritborne animus providing the ancient motor a massive power surge. Translucent ribbons of light poured from the uppermost point of Kid's tomb to join the weave from the other sarcophagi and the many other millions in the extended Bay Area. The final sleep reached well past the peninsula, beyond the Bay and Golden Gate bridges, reaching as far as

San Rafael, Walnut Creek, and San Mateo. The expansion would reach Nevada in less than an hour at this rate. Beyond there, it would continue growing exponentially to swallow the world.

The storm wall surrounding the Western Knell building touched down and spun with enough force to pick up anything smaller than a motorcycle. Trash and trashcans, bikes, an old car tire, shopping carts, a wooden dining chair, and nondescript broken pieces of a thousand other things. And, of course, people. Their bodies swung through the air like broken dolls.

65

STARBALAST

S o this is what it means to die.

Kid's severed animus floated high above what appeared to be a glowing network of wires and nodes. His old body remained empty, now far away in the incalculable distance, beyond this nether place in which his essence now existed. His body was somewhere called *the world*. What a strange sound. *Whûrl-dah*

He was angry. This wasn't how it was supposed to go. The good guy bucks up the courage to confront the big bad. From there, the stories all say the good guy wins. *That's* how it's supposed to go.

Not like this.

No, not like this at all.

Despite himself, his thoughts gradually transitioned from anger to wonder. The place felt like many copies of reality layered on each other, only partially aligned. It was like looking at one of those 3D images with the overlapping red, black, and blue, but without the special glasses to help it make sense. Things that started long became suddenly short or turned off into impossible angles. It was a place made of many more dimensions than three.

Kid moved around the infinite gossamer landscape through the force of his will. Forward, back, up, and down—and after some practice, found that he could move in directions that don't have dictionary names.

Diagonoward, frontimes, sidenow, whenwise, portnor, starbalast.

It made no sense at all, at least not in the classical in-body-on-earth meaning of things. But somehow, Kid's animus, severed from his body, understood the place intuitively. He had become nothing more than thought and energy.

What is time? And space? Tricks in perception to prevent the things that live and die from losing their minds.

There is no time, there is no place, not here.

Or rather... ALL *the time is here.*

ALL *the space too.*

ALL *at once.*

This is the Allscape.

If my mind were still contained in a physical brain, it would shatter. We are not meant to see this. We're not built for it. Perhaps this was what some traditional forms of mental illness were—a person, before they were ready, simply seeing the Allscape. Without the proper frame of reference and the appropriate vocabulary, it would seem nothing more than insanity, or if not seem it, would indeed cause it.

But, then he felt that line of thought was incorrect. He realized that, indeed, we *are* built for it. It is our most ancient gift and our oldest evolutionary talent. The ability to feel and travel the connections. Those between animi, through the worlds of The Dream and The Real, and the countless spheres of understanding he had not witnessed yet but was now sure existed. It did not stop there. Not even close.

We're not built to *see* it, at least not without going mad. We are, however, built to *know*. To walk upon the tenuous filagree of existence. And somewhere along the way, sometime in the distant past, we forgot.

But Kid's spirit, as ancient and never-ending as all animi are, was now severed and, thus: free. It remembered. It remembered *everything*. A thousand lives lived and a thousand more. From existing as space-faring neutrinos flying outward from an exploding star, then a smattering of amino acids, proteins, and RNA swimming in a nutrient-rich soup. Eventually, and many times over, his essence became a son, a father, then a mother, a daughter, and back again.

One could get lost in the remembering, the knowing.

But, he found his most recent self, the one called Kid Thames.

It was his all-mother that brought him there.

Her beauty rivaled the star that bore the notes of his melody.

Jewels of stained glass swaying in a cool Pacific wind.

The waypoint of her voice reverberated through the water of her womb. In the Allscape, in which all time existed at once, she was still alive. Her animus whole. Kid was surrounded by the liquid woosh and patterned beats of their neighboring hearts, his fast and hers slow. Then he found a doorway nobody else could see. A blinding light as he entered the world, screaming and confused by the sensory overload of his new infant brain. It was the moment of his most recent birth. His eyesight was blurry, and he couldn't control his body or tongue. But he could make out their faces. Saría Landros and Michael Thames. They looked down on his tiny body in wonder and delight, fear and love.

In feeling that love, *knowing* it—he forgave them for anything and everything. But most of all, he forgave himself. As he did so, as if a switch had been flipped, his many selves merged into one. The one as ancient as the stuff that made stars and the one as new as baby's breath. A shy child, a lost teen, and an apathetic young man. Even the part that had become malformed by the wasting touch of The Void. That which had learned to kill. That which enjoyed it. They stopped fighting each other, they stopped blaming and attempting to control. He, it, she, they, the many, the lost, the dawn, and the dusk, and finally, the one called Kid. They coalesced and were overtaken in a moment of piercing understanding.

I am.
I always have been and always will be.
That is all.
No more, no less.

With that understanding—and with the powers of The Void woven through his animus—came a universal ken. More than perceiving—it was knowing and absorbing the information of the vast fibrous network in all directions and non-directions before him. Kid understood where he could find the gateway to the animus of Linh, Alice, Poe, and of ALL things. Like a newborn discovering their hands for the first time. They're just *there*, right where they are.

Just so.

Kid synced to the spirit fabric of The Dream, The Void, and the Allscape. He found where and how Mara controlled the students, his friends, and his *family*. He uncovered the pathways along which she could create such chains—the doorways and windows through which her black smoke moved.

He found them and, one by one, he destroyed them all.

From there, it was just a hop, skip, and jump back to his vessel in The Real. Mara meant to use him as an amplifier. Instead, he and his friends were now that which she feared most. Free.

Don't put me down there. I don't like the dark.

No, not that fear, not anymore.

Now, and always,

I am *the dark.*

Just as I am *the light.*

As we all are, have been, and will be.

How do you escape a black hole?

You don't. You can't.

You come out the other side. Changed.

66

REDOUBT

Linh returned to the world of the conscious all at once, self-controlled and fully aware. Before she could dwell on the *how* of it, she watched the massive lid of Kid's sarcophagus shoot into the sky like a bottle rocket. It came down a dozen feet away and shattered on the platform into several large hunks, some of which crashed into nearby guards, taking them out at the knees. Two dims would not be getting back up. That left six—four standing by Mara and Alice and one each for Poe and Linh.

Poor odds still, but this was the moment they needed, the one they had hoped for.

It was a window—a small one. But windows can be doorways too.

"Now!" Linh yelled. She and Poe whipped around, launching aggressive attacks against the two black-clad dims guarding them. With the element of surprise, they managed to disarm both. But that was their only freebie; the guards were formidable opponents. Intense hand-to-hand combat ensued, flurries of punches and kicks, each blow and block landing with hard cracks and thwacks, each an attempted kill shot.

Poe knocked the helmet and mask off his opponent, revealing a pale, angry, grey-eyed face. It was somehow young and wasted away at the same time like someone lost in a dark cave for years. Poe realized he recognized him. He was a student some years back. *Basketball.* He had loved basketball. Was he simply a puppet now? Entirely driven by one of Mara's animus shards, or did the shell still contain some vestige of a person? It was impossible to tell. Despite their dead faces, they moved incredibly fast, well-trained, and instinctual. Poe took several hard gloved hits to the head and body, knocking him back. He ducked under the next strike and drove forward, pulling the dim's legs out from under him and taking him to the ground. Poe wrangled for a choke hold, found it, then twisted hard and broke the sad man's neck.

Linh was taking heavy hits as well but making progress. Her opponent was stronger, but she was fast. She rolled to the side under a swinging kick, managed to recover the dim's Beretta from the ground, then fired three quick rounds into the unprotected area under his arm. The bullets hit home, and he collapsed in a pool of blood. She scrabbled around to gain a view of the rest of the platform.

Mara stood watching, no longer calm, her chest heaving in big breaths. The four remaining guards fanned out in front of her in a defensive wedge formation. Linh was closer to Alice, to *Bian.* Her daughter looked around the platform with wide, confused eyes. She had been under Mara's mental dominion for so long that the sudden release from it was disorienting.

Linh sprinted to her and held her.

"Bian, baby, it's me," she said.

"Bian?" Alice asked with shaking breath.

"That's your name, the one I gave you. I'm your mother. Your *real* mother. I'm so sorry I lost you. I'm so so sorry." Linh cried and laid tear-streamed kisses on her daughter's confused face.

Alice mumbled, "I don't understand..."

Mara growled and shot forward in a surprise shadowstep. One moment she was many strides away, behind her guarding dims. The next second, the air seemed to glitch as she passed briefly into the space between the real world and The Dream. She appeared between Linh and Alice, slashing at Linh's belly with the rivener. Mara shadowstepped back to safety, taking Alice with her behind the dims and held the rivener against Alice's throat.

Cursing and falling to the ground, Linh worked desperately to hold in her vital parts as dark blood pooled around her. She held her bleeding gut in one hand and the pistol in the other, trying to find a way to aim at Mara. It would be an impossible shot to take without risking hitting her daughter. She was bleeding out fast, hands shaking, her face going deathly pale, quickly matching the shade of her newly white hair.

Everyone turned their heads as Kid vaulted out of the sarcophagus and landed on unsteady feet. He stumbled left, then right, then pulled to standing as if his shoulders were attached to strings. His eyes opened wide, like a baby's when they're first learning to see. His left iris and pupil were still merged into a pool of black, and his right iris looked as if the gold flecks melted to fill it with molten yellow metal. He was unstable, and not only in the physical sense. Kid looked wild.

His gaze panned around the area as if, for the first time, taking in the sky, the platform, and the people—his facial expression working towards recognition.

Mara said, voice shaking, "How? How did you—"

Her speaking jogged Kid's attention, and he suddenly focused on her. Poe, Linh, and Alice watched, amazed. The remaining guards awaited orders.

In a voice that echoed from several directions at once, creating a strange otherworldly harmony, he said, "Ol' Inanna..." He closed his mouth as if identifying the next words by taste. "Mara Tiamazadeh..." He smiled as he said, "The Black Rose of Babylon. Your epoch is over."

"How do you know my names? How do you—"

Kid ignored her questions and stared at Alice. She was nearly as wild-eyed as he—bewildered from her new psychic freedom and the insanity of the news that the bleeding woman across from her was her birth mother.

As if someone else was talking through him, Kid called out, "Alice. *Not* Unknown. She speaks true. You *are* Bian Phuong. The woman before you is your true mother. Through blood, yes, but more importantly, *agape.* Unconditional love. That which is infinite and without time." He glanced at Linh, who was star-struck by the situation despite her paling face, then back to Alice. "She has searched for you through *all* her lives, long before either of you were born, long before you had names and voices to speak them. *Now* you are free. Rightly so. You feel this truth."

She knew Kid, or whatever entity spoke through him, was

correct—she had sensed it the first time touching Linh back at the Tenderloin apartment. Alice didn't realize what exactly she was sensing back then. The connection was there, even though it was obscured by something Mara had done. And the eyes they shared. Brown like coffee when the sun shines through it. Alice's pupils dilated, and she was no longer alone. She sucked in a breath and took in the situation with sudden awareness.

With Mara still touching her, she felt dirty and used. Smelling the woman's rotting honeysuckle breath and feeling the warmth of the vessel she'd stolen made Alice want to vomit, and she nearly did.

But she focused on Linh, her *real* mother. Through DNA, yes, but we all share that. In the end, the genome is not particularly special. A higher percentage of genetic similarity is not a guarantee or prerequisite for motherhood. What Linh shared with Alice was far more critical. Love. Her All-Mother was here—*for her*. They both sensed it. Unconditional. Timeless. Somehow both painfully deep and as effortless to hold as a feather. Agape.

Despite the pain and deluge of her lifeblood, Linh smiled.

For a brief moment, she was happy.

And then she died.

———

"No!" Alice and Kid screamed.

Mara cried out to her guards, "Enough! You two, take him!"

Two dims moved toward Kid, the other four staying

behind. But before they could get close, Kid moved faster than thought, shadowstepping as deftly as Mara had. After merging within the Allspace, he was in touch with a thousand past selves—many of whom were well-trained travelers and spirit beings of The Dream.

Space-time halted and doubled, and then he was past the guards. In the frozen moment, Mara scowled, and Alice cried. Kid took the false god's wrist in one hand to move the blade of the rivener away from Alice's throat. Though Mara's body did not respond as quickly, her eyes, darkly shadowed with the soot of war, tracked Kid's movement. Once the black knife was away from Alice's neck, he pushed her behind him to relative safety.

The shadowstep ended, and with a stutter, time returned.

Mara growled and bared perfect, white teeth.

As Alice stumbled away, she glanced back in disgust at the woman who had stolen her youth, her mother, her innocence, and her animus. But the last, at least, was returned, and she felt her true power coursing freely through her veins. Trusting Kid to battle the demigod, she turned to address the dims. Holding her hands in front of her, fingers splayed, she extended her dream into what was left of their minds.

She forced her will into them, past Mara's now shattered hold.

Tree roots flash-growing through cracked concrete.

She found damp, fertile soil.

"We are not the enemy," Alice said.

The dims hesitated as their puppet strings were jerked by an unfamiliar hand.

"End your dream!" Alice screamed. "Now!"

As if jolted by electricity, four of the six black-clad soldiers abruptly turned to face one another, forming a messy ring. Each pointed his gun at the temple of the man to his right. All at once, four bullets fired in synchronized mercy. They fell to the ground in pools of blood. Their onyx skull masks shattered, pale faces punctured by lead. The remaining two seemed unaffected by Alice's empathy push, shaking it off like so many cobwebs, and ran toward her and Poe. They fought like a whirlwind as Mara and Kid likewise circled one another, searching for an opening.

Mara held the rivener to the side, waiting. Linh's blood dripped from its tip. Her black dress fluttered like a battle banner as she kicked off her high heels. Her toes splayed as she tested the stone.

Kid focused his power and extended a blade of light from his left hand, then risked a glance at Linh's dead body. He shook his head, growled, and dashed to meet the source of his pain. Their blades collided in a flash of light and sound like a smith's hammer beating the anvil of the world.

The fight tumbled and spun across the stone platform— each shadowstepping left and right, forward and back, attempting to maneuver into a position of opportunity. They unleashed a continuous barrage of punches, kicks, and blade swipes in a hyper-speed blur. Every time the rivener and Kid's hand met, energy and light released into the night sky. Several times the leaping shadow chess match took them to the side of the building, to the edge of oblivion. Neither seemed concerned with the four hundred-and-thirty-foot drop.

After yet another clash and following separation, they

paused to study each other, strafing in a circle. Mara laughed, and Kid lunged.

She smirked and said, "This is fun, but let's see how you fare at the center of things." Like a bullfighter, she used Kid's forward momentum to bring them both through a hole she sliced open with the rivener. Just as Kid had used his hand to escape The Dream, she used the rivener to do the reverse. They tumbled through a vortex of light to land on the familiar stone plaza surrounding The Stream at the lofty peak of Middlemost. The heart of The Dream.

However, the familiarity ended there. Where The Stream was once bright blue, now it shone a deadly red. Where it once gently flickered, like beetles behind paper, now it spasmed as if its light could be spilled into the sky like lifeblood.

Baffled, Kid glanced back through the tear between worlds and could still see Linh on the ground and his friends fighting on the rooftop. He turned around to face Mara, both of them huffing with exertion.

"I *am* Ol' Inanna. Ishtar. Tiamat. I am The First Star," Mara howled into the freezing dream air. "Witness my essence, spiritborne."

She grew like an explosion, taking in the spewing energy of The Stream as fuel. As she did so, an oppressive force erupted from her center, throwing Kid backward, tumbling head over heel into the far stone wall with a bone-colliding crash.

Mara continued to expand and mutate until The Stream was blotted out behind her new form like an eclipsed moon. What manifested was ancient, strange, and terrifying. A creature bred from the stock of giant scorpions, centipedes, and deep sea angler fish. All teeth, legs, and a shining black chitinous exoskeleton.

The gargantuan thing was thirty feet tall, sixty feet long, and covered in long spines that sliced through the air like deadly searching antennae. Where there had once been a woman's face, there were now only teeth—long and impossibly sharp, packed together by the hundreds like a dump truck full of rusted spears. The thing's eyes were pure, desolate white.

It roared like a car crash—charging forward on a thousand centipede legs, tearing the ancient stone into a cloud of dust. If its claws could do that to granite, what would they do to flesh? Kid would soon find out. She was fast, covering the distance like a rocket.

For a fraction of a second, just before shadowstepping away, he could see the reflections of a thousand grasping hands and screaming faces in the reflective surface of her dark armor. Like a congregation of souls trapped behind a black mirror, with silent torn slashes for mouths.

Then they were gone in a charcoal blur, and she charged into the stone wall, sending a boulder the size of a semi-trailer careening through the air to crash into a nearby building in the upper reaches of Middlemost. Screams could be heard as people ran for cover and safety.

After the shadowstep, Kid phased in fifty yards away and felt warmth covering his side. Grimacing, he looked down at deep gashes releasing channels of blood. Even with his new powers, he wasn't fast enough. His brief illusion of invincibility was over.

The titan creature turned, screamed more metal death, and charged again. As before, he shadowstepped to dodge a death blow. But his legs and face bled with new slashes. Pools of crimson collected at his feet.

Vision swimming, heartbeat thrumming in his ears, he dropped weakly to one knee. Kid knew then he did not have the energy to shadowstep again.

It seemed that his time was up; her next attack would be his last. He forced himself to stand on shaking legs, then planted his feet and readied his hand, no longer shining but flickering. Kid was unsure how it could damage the gigantic monster, but it was his last option. If nothing else, he would go down swinging.

The creature bellowed and charged, its massive frame blotting out the light and covering Kid in shadow as it overtook him, ready to rain eviscerating hell from hundreds of impossibly sharp insect claws and teeth.

Then, as death loomed inches away, a light beam roared by, taking the black screaming creature with it. They crashed into the far wall, sending dust and hunks of rock in all directions. The glow bounced away and retracted to reveal Horacio.

He stood, uncurling to his full height, golden eyes shining. "Hello, Inanna. I hoped you might come to dance in my world."

Something like speech emanated from the creature as it slithered and crunched back to a coiled posture. "YellowWwwwww... bAaaSStaRd." The words were distorted almost beyond hearing by the rumblings of its gut and clicking teeth.

Horacio spoke, voice strong and loud, reverberating with power like when he sang back at The Sand. "You may be stronger here. But so are we."

The being that was Horacio vibrated in light. He shone, multiplicative, like The Cognosa, as if a thousand slightly varied copies of him all vied to take up the same space.

He called out, "We are *all* The Dream Dreaming. And you are not welcome here."

As Mara had grown, so did Horacio.

He expanded to a size half that of Mara's—his shape spreading into an avian beak, gold talons, and wings the color of storm clouds. He was a giant falcon, peregrine, shining with halcyon light. The pilgrim and wanderer. Protector of travelers and thieves.

The beast that was Mara watched cautiously, unwilling to make the first move. Before the two giants fought, Horacio took the opportunity to speak directly through the fiber of The Dream—from his consciousness to Kid's.

We are here now. The beginning and the end. Now, it is my turn to sacrifice. Here in The Dream, I have some power. I will try to remove her guise and her armor. But she cannot be stopped here. Not completely. You must destroy her at the rift. Be ready!

Then falcon god and eldritch thing clashed.

Their careening violence shook both worlds, real and dream. Time seemed to slow. Whether they fought for seconds or hours was impossible to tell. It was similarly impractical to determine who was winning through the blur of wings and legs, pincers and eyes, talons and teeth.

Horacio's falcon grasped her like a great snake and flew into the sky on expansive wings. He dropped her, breaking many legs and plates of armor, shaking the platform, and causing massive stones to fall and crumble. Then eldritch centipede coiled and struck out, wrestling him with her many claws.

The air filled with ear-piercing shrieks, gut-turning roars, and a cascading spate of black and aurous blood.

At last, the battle ended.

Mara's black thing limped on its few remaining limbs.

Horacio's falcon form lay dying in a pool of gold.

Into Kid's head like a thunderbolt, he yelled, *GO!*

Kid turned and ran through the torn veil back to the rooftop.

———

Bleeding and broken, both giants shrunk and dissolved down to their humanoid forms. Mara was left in a crouch, anger painted on her face, rivener still clutched tightly in her hand. Horacio lay on his back, deadly gashes covering his body. Directly behind him, The Stream pulsed with unstable red oscillations.

Mara stepped over him and spoke with venom in her voice, "What is it you hoped to accomplish, Horus? All this time? All your careful maneuvers. Your fishing lines, cast to the sea."

Horacio coughed blood. "An old name, that. I haven't heard it in some time." Then he smiled his gap-toothed smile and replied, "Not I, but *we*. Our accomplishment is this moment. This alone."

"If you thought to explore death, I could have shown you a

more pleasurable time," Mara cooed. "But I suppose this, too, has been entertaining. What was it... Did you think a dream could not die? Farewell, jester."

As she swung for a killing blow, Horacio used the last of his energy to roll backward into a suicidal leap, straight for the burning column of The Stream. As the shine turned him to fire dust, his smile seemed to hang in the air for a fraction of a second, then dissipated, a trick of light.

Horacio was gone.

The Dream Dreaming, back to its source.

Mara scoffed, disgusted and confused by his self-destruction, then shook her head and turned to walk back through the hole toward the roof to finish the job on the other side.

Just as she was about to step through, The Stream incorporated Horacio's energy, releasing a massive shockwave. It scorched Mara and flung her through the slice between worlds to land on the San Francisco rooftop in a smoking heap. Third-degree burns covered her body, leaving her gown in tatters.

She struggled to her knees and shouted at the sky, refusing to die. She pulled in energy from the many ribbons of light, using the animus of others to heal her body. As Mara absorbed the power of the lost, her burns started to vanish. In only moments, she would be back on her feet.

Kid and his friends stood around the defeated dims. All bent with fatigue and injuries. Poe held a compress of a ripped t-shirt to a bullet wound in his shoulder. Alice limped on a twisted ankle. Linh's body lay nearby. Kid's shoulders sagged, and he bled from deep gashes.

He whispered, "Guys, I'm sorry, I got nothing left."

Where Kid's left side once glowed furiously, now it barely flickered. Though the gold and black hadn't left his eyes, he looked ready to pass out on the spot.

Alice said, "You're not done yet. You have us." She and Poc made eye contact, nodded, then stepped forward to envelop their friend from both sides. Alice whispered, "Hang on, Kid. We're going to perform an energy graft. Trust us, okay?"

"You don't mind retiring early?" Poe asked Alice. "This'll shave half our lives, easy." He smiled. It was a rhetorical question, and they both knew it.

"Only the good die young," She replied.

As they clasped hands, Alice called out, "*Storge*! Our love to you, Michael Kid Thames. Spiritborne. The one who chose to stay. We give our animus freely."

Through the combination of her unrestricted empathy push and their animus reserves, they transferred a massive surge of their life power to Kid. His eyes shot open, and he shouted in pain. It felt like grabbing a live electric wire. Instinctually, he tried to jerk away, but they held tight and pulled him closer. A bright light erupted from their centers to be absorbed into him. When it was over, Alice and Poe collapsed.

Kid's entire body glowed as his hand once did. It shone with the combination of his own power and that of their gifts. In contrast, Mara's eyes glowed purple, matched by veins of bright energy crisscrossing her body like electric scars. The ultra-black knife, the severer of souls, pulsed in her hand with the rhythmic beat of a dark star.

He faced her and spoke over his shoulder to his friends, "Thank you. Now, get back. I don't want to hurt you."

Weakened by their injuries, Alice and Poe limped away together, stopping at the open door of the catwalk that led to the elevator.

Fully healed and without further warning, Mara flew through the air like an ultraviolet missile. Rather than shadowstep, Kid dashed forward. Their collision exploded in an intertwining maelstrom of amethyst and starlight. Above, the rift glittered like a dark galaxy. It was Xibalba, the old scar. It tasted their wrath and grew ever more hungry.

"I am Michael, and I am Saría. I thank them." Kid called out as he blocked Mara's thrust of the rivener with his right hand, following it with a glowing white-hot strike of his left. It seared her neck and cheek as she narrowly dodged its flame.

She snarled in frustration and attacked his ribs with a spinning kick.

He blocked it neatly while continuing his mantra, "I am child, and I am tree."

Again, she slashed and, again, he deflected and said, "I am light, and I am dark."

Mara performed another desperate shadowstep, appearing several feet above him. She dropped down in a powerful arcing stab. The weight of her attack pushed past Kid's attempted block, and the rivener sunk deep into his left shoulder, driving him to his knees.

The blade was long enough to pierce his heart from that angle. It should be a killing blow.

Mara smiled triumphantly, but only briefly, as Kid looked

up, undaunted. The knife didn't seem to hurt him at all. She held onto it anyway; mouth stretched into a grimace of confusion. Kid rose in an uppercut, driving his shining hand toward her like a white javelin.

It pierced her chest, and she gasped, "How? You're *nothing*..."

Their eyes locked, and he replied, "It's true."

He focused, pulled in the energy of the ages, all the light and all the dark, but The Void hunger most of all, giving it sustenance and purpose. Shining and sharp. He pushed his hand deeper, fully opening Mara's chest, her vessel, her animus all, with a sword of blinding starlight.

It was Ascalon, it was Chrysaor, it was the *first* Michael's burning blade.

Kid pulled her close and spoke with the haunting echo of a thousand voices.

"I am nothing and everything. Now, *I* am the rivener."

The rift, The Void, ol' Inanna, and every lost soul wailed in unison. The sound seemed to find its way through the spaces between atoms and felt as though it would cleave the world in two.

———

As her vessel fell apart and her spirit detached, Mara said, shaking, "I was the one who made you! I gave it to you all! Everything!" Her body seized with the turbulence of what was occurring inside her. "You need me! What will you do? Without your mother?"

A new voice spoke, "You're no mother. I know what you did."

It was Delilah.

Poe's red-haired twin had walked up behind them during the commotion, coming from the elevator and catwalk doorway. Mara didn't bother to acknowledge the accusation, which deepened Delilah's scowl. Her face was drawn and pale, forearm and hand burned away, eye missing. How she still stood was a mystery.

Alice and Poe hobbled away, too severely hurt to defend against an enemy who had their flank. Delilah dismissed their worry with an irritated eye roll.

"Chill, nerds." She said, and they relaxed slightly.

Mara coughed, then said with an arrogant smile, "I'll see you all again. I always come back."

"Not this time," Kid replied.

The tempest created by the rift continued to grow. It gorged on the spirits of all who slept, yet it was far from satisfied. But, perhaps, there was one soul which would satiate its hunger—the animus of the woman who had stolen the light of The Stream and bent it so.

Mara saw Kid then, with new eyes, and she knew he was right. This time was different. She would not be returning. True death.

"No!" Mara called out. "You need me!"

Alice responded, with no sympathy in her voice, "No. We do not. Kid, finish it."

He nodded. One last cut.

Kid stepped forward, spread his arms wide, then brought his hands to center—focusing everything into a final onslaught of positive and negative spirit energy. He pulled in all the light of his friends, family, and love. He pulled in the hunger, the pain, and his void infestation.

He pulled in the anger of the vengeful ghosts clawing at the edge of the gaping rift. He channeled them together and prepared to attack Mara at her revealed core, her true center— the place she hid the scared girl who had once died young and alone on a starlit dune. He would send that girl home to be with her family.

"Fools," Mara spat. "Don't you see? In your obsession for animal survival, you doom the world. *I* am rebellion. Not you lot."

She struggled and coughed, energy flickering in her wild eyes. "You think you're special, you think you're new? You're just more of the same. I have also seen this before, and we will arrive here again. Time is a grinding stone wheel, ever turning, each chip and crack in the ring returning." Mara grimaced through her final words, the light of Kid's building energy attack shining in her face. "I almost broke it... Almost... Goddamn, you... Perhaps not this anima I've long out-wore, but the nemesis force inherent within me—*that* will return."

Kid grunted from bearing the force he had collected and said, "We'll see."

His attack landed like a firing pin on a bullet. One could imagine an audible *tink* before the resulting explosion.

A yin-yang detonation blasted Mara across the rooftop, and a ribbon of light emerged from her rent chest. As The Void tasted it, it grew again, a final spasm before the supernova. The strand of light running from its maw to her heart pulled her high into the air. As she approached the rift, it and she folded in on one another—in a way that's not describable with three dimensions, a blazing origami of reality.

With sudden cataclysmic force, all the lost souls of The Void erupted from the gash in the sky. They leaped forth and devoured the ancient woman in black animal rage. Then, just as quickly, they succumbed to their own gravity and turned in on themselves, winking out of the sky. The howl of the storm stopped, followed by a sickening crash as all the debris and bodies fell back to the ground.

The Ouroboros rediscovered its tail.

The hungry ghosts, their meal.

Mara and the rift were gone.

———

Kid collapsed, his body shining with coruscating light. Screaming in torment, his clothes burned away. He shouted through the pain, "*I can't hold it!*" But still, he tried. "You have to run! I don't want to hurt you!" He managed two more words, "Please! *GO!*"

"Kid! No!" Alice cried as she ran to help him. Once by his side, her skin started to steam as the moisture evaporated. She placed her hands on his body, and they immediately began to burn. Alice screamed but did not try to pull away. She left once before but would not leave again. It seemed that at any moment, he would detonate, obliterating the entire rooftop and who knows how much else.

Delilah cursed under her breath and sprinted forward. She broke through the fiery barrier with some combination of momentum and masochism—shouldering Alice and knocking her sliding away from the blistering danger zone. With Kid's increasing heat, her skin immediately began to sizzle like meat thrown in a pan.

Despite the agony, she forced words through gritted teeth, "You still owe me." Then she placed her remaining hand on his back. It immediately blackened, and she growled through the pain. "Give it to me. It's mine. I was made for this."

"Del!" Poe called as he tried to get close but failed. The temperature was increasing by the second, and moving past the broiling heat was now impossible.

Through vaporizing tears, Alice likewise struggled and repeatedly failed to close the infernal gap. Kid and Delilah were now locked inside a death cocoon of swirling flame.

"Stay back, goddamnit!" Delilah shouted as her flesh charred. Then, under her breath, too quiet for anyone else to hear, "Please... Let me do something good." With all her traveler's skill and the unlocked power of her hidden eye, she absorbed the excess energy of Kid's internal storm—a biological heat sink made of blood and bone.

Delilah screamed as the blaze consumed her.

All that was left was pure white ash, which drifted away.

Kid lay in a heap—quiet, naked, and still.

No power, no markings, no rivener, nor shining light.

Their time—done.

67
SEA

Kid blinked and opened his eyes, letting the light in a bit at a time. He lay in a small twin bed with grey and white sheets. Besides being utterly void of decoration, the room looked like the college dorms from the movies. His eyes adjusted, and he noticed Alice sitting at the foot of the mattress. His whole everything hurt, but seeing her still made him smile.

In a dry whisper, he asked, "What happened?"

Alice had been lost in thought and turned at the sound of his voice. "Hey... You're back. Here." With bandaged hands, she gave him a glass of water and saw that his eyes were normal again. No inky black or molten gold, just standard, pretty hazel. "Drink this." She tipped the cool water to Kid's parched lips.

He grunted and drained it. "How long was I out?"

Alice's cheeks and nose were rosy like she'd been sunburned. "About a day."

Kid looked around the room, lost, searching for a mental foothold.

Alice asked, "Do you remember anything?"

He thought hard, face pained in the effort. "Sort of... No, not really. It's like a dream fading out. Ironic, I guess. Is it all... Are we——"

"Is everything still destroyed? And are we living through the apocalypse? Pretty much. You and I are alive, obviously—Poe, along with some of the students and staff too. Even a few dims who were down in the lower levels when everything happened. They seem kind of lost now."

A broken memory resurfaced and cut Kid's heart like glass. "Linh. She's gone."

"She is..." The corner of Alice's mouth twitched in the ghost of a sad smile. "It was brief... but, for a moment, I felt I knew her."

Kid nodded. "You did. I promise, Alice. Before that, too, though. Mara may have done her best to cover it up, but there's no way to hide a connection like yours completely. She had these daisies, yellow ones. Linh watched over them every day and thought of you..." Kid let out a shaking sigh. "The fact that she lost you once killed her fresh each morning. Every day, she'd wake up, get the kitchen ready and then stare at those little yellow flowers, and she would die again. Then, for just a second up on the roof—when she knew that you knew that she loved you? She rarely smiled and never like that. At that moment, in the middle of the storm, she was happy."

"Me too," Alice said.

"So..." Kid stared at the ceiling and asked, "Was it worth it?"

She sighed. "I don't know. We're not made to answer questions like that."

Kid took her hand and squeezed. "You okay?"

She winced in pain but kept her hand in his. "Is anybody?"

Kid noticed her reaction and relaxed his grip. "What happened to your hands and face?"

"You don't remember?"

He shook his head.

"You were going supernova. I was burned trying to help."

"But, how—we're here, so, what happened?"

"Believe it or not, Delilah. Somehow she absorbed it all, and... well, she passed away. It turned her to dust."

Kid glanced down, feeling oddly guilty for the woman who'd tried to kill them so many times. "Shit," was all he could say.

"Honestly, she seemed pretty happy about it."

"A lot was going on in her head we didn't know about..."

"So it would seem."

Kid studied Alice's face as they chatted, taking in the details of her nuanced expressions. He hadn't seen this softened, honest version of her since dancing together at The Sand. Back when they were all lit and loose from Horacio's powerful empathy push. The Dance of The Dream Dreaming.

It was good to see her again. The truth he knew was there.

"Mara's gone, right? I didn't imagine that?"

"*Mother...*" Alice scoffed and squinted as if tasting something bitter. "I'll never be okay with the sound of that word again." She sighed and smiled in a way that was comfortable and pained at the same time. The way a person smiles when they reveal secrets to someone who's earned their trust. "Yeah. She's dead. Along with the rift. They're both gone for good, I hope."

Kid nodded, remembering pieces, but they were vaporous and fading. His mind kept going through all the lost and missing people like a checklist. He thought of the older woman with the giant Maine Coon cat.

"What about everyone else?" He asked.

Alice shook her head to the negative, unwilling to say the words out loud. As far as she could tell, over the last twenty or so hours, the destruction left behind by The Great Rift and its storm had stopped expanding, but what already transpired was permanent. Nobody who slept recovered. Not a single one. The clock hadn't turned back with some wizard's wand.

Kid sighed.

"What?" asked Alice.

"It's just like how it usually happens, you know? The end turned out to be... not The End. Things are pretty fucked up."

"Far less than they would have been without you. We have a chance to see what's next now. That's something." Kid nodded, and Alice continued, "I'm not sure how far the dead sleep expanded because the internet and cell service aren't working. But it must be catastrophic. With just a little napkin math I did, it's going to be bad."

"It's going to be a different world now."

They held hands in somber silence, both doing their best to find interesting patterns in the grey wool blanket. After a minute, Alice looked up and got Kid's attention.

She struggled the words out, "Kid... I wanted to say... I'm sorry. Sorry for—"

He cut her off, "Sorry? No. Don't. There's nothing to

apologize for."

"What do you mean? That's not right."

"Yeah, it is. It's exactly right. Sometimes we don't have a choice. No matter how hard we try, we get all twisted and turned around." Kid sat up and leaned forward in the bed. Alice mirrored his movement until their foreheads touched. He noticed how soft hers was. "So, stop. No sorries. Not between us. I saw you then. I see you now. Everything led us here."

Alice let out a long wavering breath like she had been holding it in her whole life. She thought the words *thank you* but didn't say them out loud. Instead of sorries and thanks, they kissed.

After their lips parted, Kid said, "I need to go."

Her face screwed up. "Go where? Where is there to go? We just got here. It's quiet now, and I thought, maybe we could finally... You know, have some time to just... *be*."

"I know, I know. Believe me, I wanna stay. But I saw something. Or more like I felt it. Whatever seeing is, where I was. When I..." Kid trailed off, not sure how to finish the sentence.

She tried for him. "When you were dead."

"I guess. Yeah. Dead, severed. Whatever. But I wasn't gone. Not really. I was *everywhere*. Every-when. I can't recall much, probably not supposed to. My head would pop, you know? But there is one thing I remember, at least a little. Something to do with the other ancients. Maybe some way to help the people still sleeping. Help those kids out there. Something to do with my father."

Alice watched Kid struggle with the rest of the memory

and waited patiently for him to fish it out. As his eyes darted back and forth behind closed lids, he spoke.

"I think he's alive. I saw a road sign and mountains. If I can get close, I think I can find him." Kid opened his eyes. "I'm sorry, Alice. I need to go. I have to."

She nodded. "You said no sorries."

He lifted his hands to hold her face. "We're connected, right?"

"We always have been," Alice replied. "It's science."

Kid smiled. "Maybe a little magic too?"

"Maybe a little." she smiled back.

"So, when we dream, I'll find you."

"You can meet me by the sea."

Linh's funeral took place in a grove of redwoods within The San Francisco Botanical Garden. It was always a place of peace and solitude, and now much more so due to its stark contrast against a silent city. It was as if they'd been set free—the concrete prison walls locking them into a set grid broken down. Now the trees, vines, and ferns could grow in any which way they preferred, provided they received rain. The sky looked generous that day—its swollen grey clouds hung just outside the bay. They seemed to be awaiting permission to enter, permission that would come once The Silver Doe's tribute was complete.

Skyward stretching bark and scattered shafts of light created an evergreen cathedral, and the only sound was the rustle of leaves and whispers of the few in attendance. Alice,

Kid, Poe, the nurse Seven, three students, and one dim were there. Linh's grave was in the center, and they surrounded her, further surrounded by the giant trees. Three concentric rings meant to mirror the drawing Alice had made for Kid to describe the topography of the universe.

Alice stood next to the mound of dark earth, tears streaming freely down her cheeks. Since breaking free of Mara's hold, her emotions were erratic—unused to being free. The bouts of unbidden crying, anger, and relief over the last day were becoming tiresome—it felt similar to what she'd read being pregnant was like. But she reminded herself to be grateful and that if there was a moment to cry, it was now.

Holding a single yellow daisy, she thought about the fact that other than their brief embrace on the Western Knell rooftop, she would never get to know her real mother's voice. Any other memory of her touch was locked in the recesses of her infant past.

She didn't know what to say, choosing instead to listen as Kid gave Linh's eulogy, which proved to be quite eloquent. He was full of surprises, and she felt she was starting to figure him out.

He talked about how we can't know for sure how long we have here. That we don't get any warning of the challenges and catastrophes that will test us. We don't get to know the plan, if there is one, of the universe. As their departed friend, Horacio (masked as Kid's street-corner pal, Hari) had said, "The unpredictable, yet synchronous chaos-force of the cosmos, man. *Real* magic."

Real magic is dangerous and raw.

And it is also the beauty that binds us together.

With tear-filled eyes and voice catching on every word, Kid talked about the indisputable fact that if there were such a thing as magic, then Linh was undoubtedly made of it. He remembered she told him she'd come and get him, wherever he was. His surrogate mother had kept her promises and many others.

Of course, Kid said, the woman made big mistakes, like we all do. And for them, she paid dearly. We make our mistakes, and we carry them with us. They are our burden as well as our fuel. All we can do is live our lives the best we can, try to find purpose, and work toward it with honor and love despite our unavoidable failings.

He revealed to the group what he'd told Alice on a dorm bed. That Linh never stopped hoping to find her daughter. That being able to see Alice free, if only for a moment, allowed her to die happy. She was someplace good, and she was not afraid. She was Linh Phuong, The Silver Doe. And she was fierce.

———

As they contemplated the pile of cool soil, neither Kid nor Alice tried to hide their broken hearts and rested their heads against one another. Beside them stood Seven and Poe—his bandaged arm hung in a blue cloth sling, and his face looked like he'd been in a car crash, with stitched gashes and bruises blooming all over. Next to Poe were the three students and the soldier. He no longer wore black, and his vacant face was unmasked. The youngest child, nine-year-old James, held his hand.

After Mara's death, the dims seemed lost and strangely innocent. But they were still strong and obedient, and helped dig Linh's grave and carry her casket. James called the lost soldier 'Buddy.' The new nickname stuck, and he was a dim no longer.

The other two students had done their best to help with the proceedings but were in shock from the ordeal. The fact that they were there at all was a lot—doing their best to remain upright as they worked to understand the world in which they now lived. The Young School was where they could find some semblance of normalcy, but even there, the other sleeping students were a painful reminder of the harsh reality in which they now lived.

Seven looked tired, her face lined with exhaustion. She'd been working tirelessly to keep the remaining students healthy and would continue doing so. They had fuel for the generators for two weeks. After that, nobody knew what would happen. Poe hugged her with his good arm. When he'd told her thank you for staying on to help the children without pay, she'd replied, "Where else am I gonna go, you big dummy."

She grew up Catholic and so knew an appropriate prayer. After the last shovelful of dirt found its place, she spoke it out in her oddly comforting, graveled voice. When she was done, Alice stepped forward and placed the daisy on the soil, her tears continuing to fall.

With no bodies to bury, they also said some words for Saría, Horacio, and Delilah. Kid's lost birth mother and the sly man with golden eyes had sacrificed their lives, and more surprisingly, so had Poe's twin sister. Protection and redemption are often found in the most unlikely of places. They were sure that if there was peaceful respite beyond The Void, they had all found it.

The small troupe made their way out of the gardens, surrounded by the peaceful silence of the redwoods. As they walked, Kid thought about the world they now lived in. It was one injured by death and emptiness, as it always had been. But it was also somewhere love and friendship existed. Where those things had power. Visible, tangible, and real. He took a deep breath, grateful for the people by his side, and resolved to keep moving forward, no matter what the future held.

Back at the school, Kid and Alice walked alongside Poe as he followed Seven. She moved from bed to bed, checking each student's IV and vitals. Occasionally, she would bark an order at Poe, telling him to hold one thing or another, usually calling him *handsome,* or *big boy,* in the process. Poe didn't seem to mind the pet names and was more concerned with each sleeping child who he worried over like a mother hen.

They stopped at a young girl, maybe seven years old. She reminded Kid of a youthful version of Nakawé with her tan skin and thick black hair, which haloed her peaceful sleeping face. He considered The Dream and Middlemost, hoping that things were warming up there. It was not likely. There would be a long way to go before anything returned to normal. Like everywhere, he supposed.

Kid was ready to leave with a black duffel bag he'd found

in the student dormitory. It was packed full of basics and slung over his shoulders crossways.

Poe eyed the bag and asked, "Rocky Mountain high, eh?"

"Seems like a good place to start," Kid replied.

Alice turned to him, her eyes shining with tears again. She rubbed them from her cheeks with an annoyed fist. She wanted him to stay, wanted it badly, but couldn't bring herself to say it out loud. Not in front of everyone. "We could use your help here."

"I can't." He watched the sleeping girl Poe and Seven were tending for a moment, then finished, "I have to learn more. A lot more. This isn't over. You know it as well as I do."

Poe finished fluffing the pillow and tucking the little girl's blanket and turned to address Kid head-on. "These children need somebody, and I'm thinking maybe we can turn this place into something good. But Alice? She was never much of a babysitter. Not the nurturing type." He added with a smirk, "You know what I mean?"

Kid and Alice both looked confused, waiting patiently for Poe's punchline. He reached awkwardly across his body to his right front pocket with his uninjured left hand and dug around. Pulling out car keys, Poe held them up with a smile and a jingle.

"Gonna need wheels, brother. No hitchhiking on my watch."

"What?" Kid stammered, "You're giving me your car?"

"Giving?" Poe raised an eyebrow. "Ha! No way, cool-breeze. That's my baby we're talking about. You'll take care of her and bring her back in one beautiful piece. If there's a scratch on her, I'm taking it out of your ass."

Kid hesitated to hold his hand out, feeling overwhelmed by Poe's generosity. But the burly redhead shoved the keys at his chest. After releasing them, Poe put his hand on Kid's shoulder. "Now here's the deal—The Bay's gonna be locked down tighter than a nun's c—uh..." He glanced at Seven with a sheepish look. "I bet the bridges and Bart will be closed because of this mess. National Guard will be rolling in with reinforcements any time, if they're not here already. You'll need to take the long way south. But it'll be plugged up and slow going. You'll need a co-driver so you can shift-run it."

"But can't you drive with your good hand?" Kid still didn't get it.

"For one thing, it's a manual. Toploader Four on the floor. But that's not the point." Poe turned to Alice. "He's dense sometimes, isn't he? Go on, get outa here, girl. Be where you're supposed to be. Someone's gotta keep this dude out of trouble."

Kid finally understood and grinned at her, "You wanna come?"

"You're just now asking?" She rolled her eyes, "Ugh... You *are* stupid."

He laughed, "You know how to drive a stick?"

"Wouldn't be much of a secret agent if I didn't."

"Show me how, and you got a deal."

"You can't drive manual?"

"I can't drive at all."

Alice gave him the same look she had so long ago back at Linh's apartment, that of tried patience one would take with a child—although this time with levity and a smile as she held her hand out for the keys.

68

EAST

The two travelers stopped at a little two-pump gas station in the farmland area just outside of Modesto. The kind of spot the local old-timers would get coffee and smokes in the morning. They hadn't made it far before burning all the fuel in the tank of the old Torino—a speed boat would get better economy. Avoiding all the highways, bridges, and tolls was slow and took more gas, but it was as safe a way as they would find. They'd scoped out the major highways from a distance a couple times, but they were filled with combinations of traffic, wreckage, military convoys, and news crews heading into The Bay Area.

They'd need to stay off the mains until at least past Sacramento, maybe even as far as Nevada. They hoped the dead sleep hadn't gone that far. Depending on the condition of the roads heading northeast, they'd find out in anywhere from four hours to another day. At least it wasn't winter, so the roads would be clear.

Kid walked into the unmanned station and grabbed an

armful of snacks and drinks—sour cream and onion Pringles, a bunch of beef jerky and protein bars, water, and a few energy drinks. And at Alice's behest, he also took some juice and bananas for a healthy, well-rounded road diet.

As he returned to the car, she finished filling it up and closed the gas cap with a turn and a click. They sat in the old Ford and shut the doors with the satisfying steel *kathunk* that can only be heard in the classics. She kept promising to give him a turn driving but also found she loved the old car and wasn't giving up the pilot's seat until she risked falling asleep at the wheel.

Kid turned to the back seat to check on the incubator. It ran smoothly, its power cord attached to an adapter sticking out of the cigarette lighter. The single egg, tan and speckled red like a blood agate river rock, sat silently and patiently. Kid thought of Horacio and wondered what heart might beat inside the shell.

As he turned back toward the front of the car, he glanced at Alice. He could see the echos of Linh in the set of her jaw and peaceful resolution in her eyes. She turned to give him a quick freckled smile, then cranked the stereo, slapped the eight-ball shifter into first, and peeled out onto the road with a squeal of tires and burnt rubber. She seemed to only know how to drive at one speed, hauling ass with the pedal mashed to the floor.

The radio played Gimme Shelter by The Rolling Stones. Poe had a binder of CDs stashed under the seat, and they were having a blast working their way through them. It was warm out, and the windows were down. Kid flew his hand in the passing wind like an airplane, the air cooling the sweat on his arm.

The carbureted V8 roared as Alice shifted down to maneuver around a car stuck in the middle of the highway, one of many. Kid watched the flat brown landscape pass by in the side mirror, then pulled on a pair of cheap gas station sunglasses to hide his eyes as they flickered black and gold.

THANK YOU

First of all, Dear Reader, I appreciate your time. Choosing to spend almost 600 pages with this rag-tag group of traumatized interdimensional adventurers is a big deal. I'm sincerely grateful.

If you made it this far, perhaps you enjoyed this little romp. In that case, leaving a review on Goodreads and Amazon would be fantastic.

Instagram and TikTok are great too. Reviews are the lifeblood of the algorithms that can spell the success or demise of a debut indie author. Taking the time to leave one, even if it's just a simple star rating, will have a considerable impact.

Thank you again. Take care, and bye for now,
G.G.

REVIEW LINK

Scan this QR code or enter the URL to
go to: The Rivener on Good Reads
<u>tinyurl.com/Rivener-goodreads</u>

ACKNOWLEDGMENTS

The Rivener is an indie joint. As such, it has been the result of many kind-souled folks giving their free time to the cause.

A non-exhaustive list includes the eternally patient mother of my little dragons, without whom this endeavor would have been logistically impossible, along with friends, advance readers, unwitting character inspirations, and—most importantly—epically cool readers from around the world.

My biggest supporters helped with early reads of terrible first drafts, rereads of slightly improved drafts, regular motivational speeches, and catching all those final-final-v9.jpg typos and details (like where the safety is on a Glock). Just a few of their names: Karolina, Chris, Sam, Ro, Matt, Mike, Jessica, Ethan, Jennifer, Miranda, Kyle, Gemma, Hazel, Talitha, Felix, Paul, Jamie, and Sarah.

Before I got my hands on it and did my thing, the black ink drawing of a falcon for the cover was done by the amazingly talented Pedro Correa—he was kind enough to donate it to the cause. Phil Bowne assisted an early pass at developmental editing—his recs helped tighten the mid-game plot considerably.

To one and all, I am deeply grateful.

ABOUT THE AUTHOR

Garrett Godsey is an American author currently living near Prague. Thanks to a life of wandering experiences from the middle-of-nowhere USA to Colorado, San Francisco, Mexico, and Europe—his stories often deal with exploring our soul, identity, and world. As a 90s latchkey kid growing up in zero-supervision chaos with a steady diet of fantastic fiction, his tales often include a through-line of the incredible, strange, and catastrophic. In addition to writing, he works as a product designer for biotechnology companies and is fascinated by the human mind—specifically regarding trauma, addiction, cognition, and perception.

FOLLOW ALONG

For news on upcoming releases and work, sign up for the author newsletter at

WWW.GARRETTGODSEYBOOKS.COM/CONTACT

or follow on various social platforms:

WWW.GARRETTGODSEYBOOKS.COM

WWW.INSTAGRAM.COM/GARRETTGODSEYBOOKS

WWW.AMAZON.COM/AUTHOR/GARRETTGODSEY

WWW.GOODREADS.COM/GARRETTGODSEY

BIBLIOGRAPHY

Works Quoted:

Carroll, Lewis. Alice and Wonderland. CC, 1865.

Blackwood, Algernon. The Wendigo. CC, 1910.

Verne, Jules. Journey to the Center of the Earth. CC, 1864.

Macleod, Fiona. Where the Forest Murmurs. CC, 1890.

Dick, Philip K. Flow My Tears, the Policeman Said. CC, 1974.

Hodgson, William Hope. The House on the Borderland. CC, 1908.

Abbott, Edwin A. Flatland: A Romance of Many Dimensions. CC, 1884.

Printed in Great Britain
by Amazon

26922475R00320